A Novel

Brotherly Love

DARRIEN LEE

SBI

STREBOR BOOKS

NEW YORK LONDON TORONTO SYDNEY

Strebor Books
P.O. Box 6505
Largo, MD 20792
http://www.streborbooks.com

Cover design: www.mariondesigns.com

ISBN-13 978-1-59309-061-6
ISBN-10   1-59309-061-7
LCCN 2006924675

First Strebor Books trade paperback edition July 2006

10 9 8 7 6 5 4 3 2 1

Manufactured in the United States of America

For information regarding special discounts for bulk purchases,
please contact Simon & Schuster Special Sales at 1-800-456-6798
or business@simonandschuster.com

Dedication

I would like to dedicate this novel to all my family members from New Orleans who were affected by Hurricane Katrina. May your lives thrive as you step out on faith and begin new lives in new places.

Acknowledgments

First I would like to thank my family and friends for supporting me as I venture out on a new and exciting journey. I want to send a special thank you to Pastor Vincent Windrow and First Lady, Stacy Windrow, for your prayers and words of wisdom when obstacles try to block my path. You inspire me and I feel so blessed to be in your presence every Sunday.

To The Ties That Bind Bookclub in Murfreesboro, TN, and Sistahs Keeping It Read Bookclub in Nashville, TN. I appreciate your continued encouragement and support. Many thanks go out to Terryl Manning and the Circle of Friends Bookclub in Atlanta for your willingness to promote me in my efforts. To the Women of Color Bookclub in LaVergne, TN, words cannot express my gratitude.

I sent a sincere thanks to Melissa Forbes, for her editing services. Melissa, you are a gem and your expertise is invaluable and I'm so glad we were introduced.

To Keith Saunders, I was so excited when I saw my eye-catching book cover. I'm sure the time and effort to create this sensual cover will be very rewarding.

A special thanks goes out to Cory and Heather Buford of Gateway Online Marketing, who designed my flyers and website. Your creative ability and friendship is precious and I thank you.

I would like to send out a heartfelt thanks to Martina Royal of RAWSISTAZ.

Tee, I appreciate the platform and audience that you give authors like myself every day. You have a big sister quality that I love, and I thank you for all that you do. Kiss Joy for me!

To my dear friends and fellow authors, V. Anthony Rivers and JDaniels, we go way back and words can't express how priceless our friendship is. Allison Hobbs, Tina Brooks McKinney, Shelley Halima and Harold Turley II, need I say more? Our inner circle has shared a lot over the years and I know there are even better things on the horizon for all of us. Keep up the great writing. I can't go on without thanking authors, Deirdre Savoy and Gayle Sloan, who I look up to as sisters. To Laurinda Brown, much love goes out to you for motivating me to keep on keeping on.

Many thanks go out to Zane, Charmaine and the entire Strebor Books staff for your hard work and for giving me the opportunity to be recognized in the literary arena.

I have to thank Art Tucker, a dear friend and computer wiz who always comes through when my computer goes on the blink. You've kept me from throwing my laptop out the window on more than one occasion. Thanks for being on call when I need you.

To my special friends, Brenda Thomas, Tracy Dandridge, Tiffany Lee, Sharon Nowlin, Buanita Ray, Robin Ridley and Monica Baker. Thanks for giving me plenty of colorful material to write about. Remember, I'm always listening.

A special thanks goes out to Ms. Judy Sharp and the staff at the Hadley Park Library and Yusef Harris of Alkebu-Lan Images Bookstore in Nashville, TN for your support. You have allowed me to have a standing invitation at your establishments and I will forever be grateful.

Lastly, to my husband, Wayne, and daughters, Alyvia and Marisa, I want to let you know that I love you. You make me proud every second of every day.

Prologue

Cherise turned the key in the lock and slowly pushed the door open. Before she could walk through the doorway, strong hands quickly pulled her inside the room, startling her. With her back against the wall, she was showered with deep, heated kisses as masculine hands and lips ravished her body. Her tall, dark companion towered over her and knocked over a lamp and vase as he basically ripped the clothes from her body. Seconds later, she stood before him, completely naked and out of breath. Cherise had a fabulous body and being inhibited was not part of her personality.

"If I didn't know any better, I'd think you've missed me."

Without responding, he stared at her mischievously before quickly kneeling in front of her. He made her feel things she'd never felt before and she welcomed his unconditional love. When his lips came in contact with her center, she immediately began to hiss and moan. Her legs trembled and became weak, making it difficult for her to continue standing. He was an expert when it came to pleasure—he could please her just with his smile; however, at the moment it was his mouth that had her screaming for mercy.

He stood and without breaking eye contact removed his clothes. Cherise opened her mouth to speak but he put his finger up to her lips to silence her. He leaned down close to her ear and whispered softly into it.

"You know we don't have much time so I want to make every second count."

Cherise melted in his hands as he gripped her hips and slowly joined his body with hers. A gasp escaped her throat as he filled her body. He smiled and began to move methodically, each thrust causing her to moan even louder.

She held onto his broad shoulders as he wrapped her legs around his waist for easier access. Cherise looked up into his warm eyes as he continued to give her his forbidden love. He kissed her firmly on the lips, dipping his tongue into the warmth of her mouth. Within seconds her name tore loudly from his lips. Breathless, they held onto each other and continued to kiss.

"I love you, babe."

"I love you, too."

He released her so she could finally stand on her weakened legs, but understandably, he had to steady her.

She looked down at her watch and went into a slight panic.

"Oh shit! Look at the time! I have to get out of here!"

He stepped back and watched as she quickly gathered her clothes and began to get dressed. Sighing, he gathered his own clothes and began the same ritual.

"I don't know how much longer I can do this, Cherise."

She studied him as she slid into her skirt and quickly zipped it.

"I know, baby, and I'm sorry. I can't help the situation we're in right now. You told me you could handle it. Are you having second thoughts?"

He sat down on the arm of the sofa and folded his arms, still not fully dressed.

"I don't know what I'm feeling."

From his body language, it was obvious he was frustrated with their arrangement. She buttoned her blouse and sighed. "I love you, but this is the way things have to be until I get everything sorted out. Okay?"

He pulled up his pants without responding. Cherise walked over and wrapped her arms around her lover's waist.

"Please don't do this to me. You know I love you."

He tenderly kissed her forehead and took a step back before glancing down at his watch.

"Yeah, but not like you love him, huh? Look, you'd better get going so you won't get in trouble."

Cherise picked her purse up off the floor and walked toward the door as he buckled his belt. She reached for the doorknob and with her voice barely above a whisper, she made a chilling comment.

"You do know that if he ever found out about us he won't hesitate to kill us."

Within seconds he was standing behind her, kissing the back of her neck while caressing her soft, cascading hair. This one, simple task sent shivers up and down her spine.

"Don't worry your pretty little head about that because he won't find out."

She turned to him. "I wish you could guarantee that for me."

He chuckled and then kissed her tenderly on the lips. "When can I see you again?"

Cherise discreetly opened the front door and looked out before stepping outside. She turned and gave him a quick peck on the lips before walking away. "I don't know but I'll call you later."

He stood in the door with a bruised heart and watched her walk out to her car and drive off.

Nine Years Later

Cherise had wanted to be a crime scene investigator for as long as she could remember. As a child she watched every episode of the TV show *Quincy, M.E.* and had never blinked an eye. Her parents were both retired doctors and wanted her to follow in their footsteps, but it was the mysteries of the afterlife that fascinated her more. Her career had blossomed over the years and now at thirty-eight years old, she was the best crime scene investigator in Atlanta. She did her best not to let the long hours of her job affect her life, but sometimes it couldn't be helped. Luckily her parents, Jonathan and Patricia Jernigan, lived nearby to assist her whenever she needed them.

Her husband, Mason McKenzie, did his best to cope with the stresses in their lives as well. His career was just as demanding as hers because he was a police detective on Atlanta's Anti-Crime Task Force. Forty-two–year-old Mason worked undercover and enjoyed it very much. His job kept his adrenaline pumping, but he had decided to reduce the amount of risky assignments he worked.

On this day, Cherise was preparing to fly out to another conference. She was a dynamic speaker and lecturer at some of the top seminars across the country. Mason was buttoning a starched white shirt when he walked out of their closet and eyed her curiously.

"Now, where are you flying out to today?"

"Mason, I told you it was in Miami," she answered while pulling on her nylons. "We talked about this...remember?"

He tucked his shirt inside his jeans. "It seems like you're never here anymore," he mumbled.

"Mason, don't try to pick a fight with me before I leave. I'm not doing anything any different than the average man would in my position. Baby, I love my job, and this is a great opportunity for me," she explained as she walked over to him and lovingly put her arms around his neck.

"You don't have to do this to prove you're a success to me, baby," he said as he rested his hands on her curvy backside. "You're already a success, but I think you should be home more with the kids. It's one thing that you have long hours at the office, but now you're flying all over the country lecturing."

Cherise backed out of his embrace and folded her arms defiantly

"Mason, I have supported you and your career for the past fifteen years. You work longer hours than I do. You've been gone for days at a time when you're undercover, so don't go there with me. It's not easy being alone here with the kids, but we make it work." At the moment, Mason didn't know what to say. He picked up a brush and started brushing his hair. He stood in the mirror and watched her reflection as he put on his watch,, shaking his head in defeat because he knew in his heart that Cherise was right. He had left her alone on more occasions than he could remember to go off and handle his police business. He'd practically made her a single parent without realizing it. He'd just never dreamed that one day Cherise would be absent from their home just as much, and now that the tables had turned, he was having a hard time coping with it. As Cherise sat down on the bed to put on her pumps, her beige skirt rose high up on her thighs, catching Mason's attention. He stopped grooming himself and smiled at the image in the mirror. She smiled back at him before slowly walking over to him. She tenderly straightened his collar.

"Is that what it takes to get your attention, Detective?"

"Of course not, sweetheart, but it doesn't hurt," he answered playfully.

"You know you could go with me. Mase and Janelle would be in good hands with Momma and Daddy. You know they love any time they can spend with their grandchildren."

He turned around to face her and carefully leaned against the dresser. He scanned her body and admired just how naturally sexy she was. He wanted nothing more than to spend some alone time with her, but unfortunately, at this moment it was simply impossible.

"I wish I could, Cherise, but I'm starting a new case today, and more than likely I'll be going undercover for a while."

She frowned. "When were you going to tell me about it?"

He straightened, kissed away the winkles on her forehead, and apologized. "I'm sorry, babe. I wanted to wait until I had more details about it before I said anything."

She handed him her necklace and turned her back to him so he could assist her. She pulled her hair up so he could snap the necklace in place.

"Well? What does it involve?"

He pulled her hips against his body and kissed her softly on the back of the neck. "The same old, same old—drugs, so there might be some days I won't be home. I don't want you and the kids to worry."

Mason could feel his body heating up from the physical contact with Cherise as he wrapped his arms around her waist. It never did take much for her to get him aroused. Most of the time all she had to do was walk into the room.

"I can't help but worry when you're out there hanging around all those horrible people. What if they find out who you are, Mason? You know they won't hesitate to kill you, and where does that leave me and the kids?"

He tightened his grip on her body.

"I've never let that happen in the past, and I won't let it happen now. You guys are too important to me to take any risks, Cherise."

"I thought you were through with undercover work," she whispered breathlessly.

He turned her around to face him and noticed the tears in her eyes. He lowered his mouth to within inches of hers. "I am. This is my last job," he admitted before kissing her lightly.

Cherise cupped his face and deepened the kiss. This was the part of his job she hated because when he went undercover, his personality changed—and it wasn't always in a good way. She wasn't looking forward to the man he would have to become to slum around with drug dealers. This was the man she loved, and she wanted to absorb as much of him as she could before he went through his metamorphosis. After finally coming up for air, Cherise closed her eyes and nuzzled her face against his warm neck.

"It worries me when you go undercover. Do you have to do this assignment, Mason?"

Mason caressed her backside with love and affection. "You know I do, just like you have to travel around the country doing these lectures. People are counting on us."

Cherise wasn't only worried about Mason's safety. She knew he loved her more than life itself, but being on the job and away from home for weeks at a time still affected him. During one particular assignment, he was working undercover with a female partner and one thing led to another. The only way Cherise found out about the affair was because the woman started pressuring Mason to leave Cherise, or she was going to tell all. Mason wasn't a man you could blackmail; so he got Cherise and his partner together and confessed. Unable to hold the secret over his head any longer, the female detective transferred to another division so she wouldn't have any more contact with him. Mason, on the other hand, had risked everything and knew it would take a lot to get Cherise to love and trust him again.

Cherise was devastated and immediately filed for a legal separation in hopes of clearing her thoughts. She had to decide her future with Mason and it wasn't easy. Unfortunately, it was during their legal separation that things between the pair went from bad to worse. It took a lot of praying, but after some time apart, Cherise eventually forgave him for his indiscretion and Mason made sure he never let himself get into that kind of situation again. He was very sorry for hurting Cherise and was adamant that she understood it would never happen again.

Mason had an idea that those thoughts were running through Cherise's mind once again. He hugged her waist and stared directly into her sable eyes.

"Cherise, baby, I promise this is the last time; you don't have anything to worry about."

She sighed and leaned into him.

"I mean it. I'm burnt out and I want to be home more with you guys. Besides, I'm ready to try something else. I'm thinking about working in the cold case division.

She smiled and gave him one last kiss before walking over to get her purse. "Sounds good. Will I be able to get in touch with you if I need you?"

He grabbed his jacket off the back of the chair and slid into it. "Probably not directly, but they'll get a message to me so I can call you back as soon as I can."

She tugged on her purse strap nervously. "I need to talk to Momma and Daddy about helping out with the kids again."

"Don't worry about it, because I've already cleared things with them. The kids will catch the bus over to their house after school like they've done in the past. If you have to work late, they'll take it from there."

She tucked her cell phone inside her purse and took one last glimpse at herself in the mirror before walking toward the door. Then she paused. "What if I get called out in the middle of the night? Then what? I don't want to have to drag the kids out of the house."

He smiled and walked over to her. He placed his hands on her shoulders and looked her directly in her eyes. "We'll work it out, Cherise, so stop stressing. My case should be over by the time you start on call rotation, and if push comes to shove, Mase is old enough to hold things down if you have to leave."

She sighed. "I guess you're right. Our son is a responsible young man, even if he is only thirteen. I just don't want the kids to start feeling abandoned by us."

He picked his keys up off the nightstand and tucked his badge and wallet inside his back pocket.

"They won't, babe. They know what we do and they understand. You know we have some very intelligent children."

"That we do."

She looked at her watch and he picked up her luggage so he could carry it downstairs for her.

"I know I don't say it enough, but I am proud of you, Cherise."

"I'm proud of you, too, Mason."

They smiled at each other momentarily before Mason reminded her of the time. They walked downstairs together so they could begin their long day. Once in the foyer, Mason set her luggage down at the door and gave her one last kiss.

"Have a safe flight, Cherise, and I'll try not to pout too much while you're gone. Now, let me get out of here before I'm late to work. Are you sure you don't want me to drive you to the airport?"

"I'm sure. There's no reason for you to get caught in all that morning traffic. I've got a taxi coming."

"If you insist, Doctor. I love you."

"I love you, too, Detective."

Cherise opened the front door for him and let out a breath. Mason walked out onto the porch and patted his pockets to make sure he had everything. "Make sure you call when you get to your hotel," he reminded her.

Leaning against the door frame, she folded her arms and cleared her throat. "I will and I'm not going to say it, Mason."

He turned to face her because he knew what she was referring to. "I know, I know. Don't try to be hero."

She always warned him when he was about to go undercover. He smiled as he walked down the sidewalk and around to the garage. Cherise closed the door and watched from the window as he backed down the driveway and pulled out onto the street. Once he was out of sight, she walked into the kitchen to make herself a cup of coffee. As she sat at the table, she realized just how quiet the house was when everyone was gone. Mason had taken the kids over to her mom's the night before since they both had to get up and out so early. She was going to miss them even though she was only going to be gone a couple of days.

Mason drove to his office in downtown Atlanta, eager to find out the details of his new assignment. He had finally gotten burnt out of undercover work and was tired of being away from his family. That was why he was determined to make this his last assignment and do something less risky.

As he sat behind the wheel of his car, he reminisced about the times when he went undercover. In the past he had his brother, Vincent, by his side to help take care of his family when he was unavailable. Like him, Vincent had moved up the ranks in law enforcement, but he wanted to go much higher than Mason did. Mason was always appreciative that Vincent never made him feel inferior once he climbed the ladder of success, and it was Vincent who made sure Cherise and Mase were safe while he was away. He cut the grass and did other things around the house when Mason was undercover. Mason missed his brother, who was now a police chief in Texas. After his promotion, Vincent moved away and Cherise hadn't seen him in nearly nine years. However, Mason did find time to visit Vincent when he could, which was rare because of the job's demands.

Vincent's job was the kind that left him little time for himself. They sent e-mails to each other, but those notes lacked the closeness they were accustomed to sharing. Mason still wanted to go on the hunting trip they talked about but never got around to taking. Maybe once this assignment was over, they would make time to come back together as a family. Mason was jarred out of his trance when a car horn blew behind him. He vowed when this assignment was over he was going to take Cherise and the kids to see the Grand Canyon and swing through Texas to visit Vincent. He wanted to put his relationship with Vincent back to where it needed to be, because the children needed to know their uncle. Mase was a lot younger when Vincent moved away, and Janelle wasn't even born. Mason smiled because his mind was made up about visiting Vincent. A good friend is something no one should be without, and he was determined to have his friend and brother back by his side once again.

Mason finally arrived at work and parked his vehicle in the garage. He exited the car and greeted several coworkers as they walked into the building together. Once in the office, he set his belongings down on the desk and picked up his messages. The room was full of activity. Some of the guys in his unit were on the telephone taking tips on suspected drug and other illegal activities. Mason looked over and noticed that no one had made coffee. He put his messages down and took off his jacket.

"I guess you guys expect me to make coffee every damn morning."

"No one makes it like you, Mason," a coworker nicknamed Tank because of his build, announced.

Mason picked up the coffeepots and frowned as he watched Tank stuff a doughnut in his mouth. If you didn't get there when the pastries arrived, you took a chance on not getting any once Tank got to them. Tank was a former NFL linebacker and had been in the unit for seven years. He stood about six feet, six inches tall and weighed close to two hundred-eighty pounds. His size gave a lot of criminals the perception that he wouldn't be able to catch them. They learned real quick that Tank was fast on his feet.

"I'm going to collect money from you guys so we can get a couple of those coffeemakers that you can set on a timer, because I'm not the goddamn maid around here."

"Why are you in such a bad mood this morning?" Rat, nicknamed for his love of cheese, asked as he leaned back in his chair.

"I'm cool, but you guys are trifling when it comes to pitching in around here," Mason mumbled as he filled the coffeepots with water.

Rat walked over to Mason so they could talk in private.

"Is everything okay? I mean, we haven't even started the case and you're already grouchy."

Mason poured the water into the reservoir of the coffeemakers and opened two bags of coffee. He looked over at Rat and sighed. "Nah, man, everything's straight."

Rat picked up a doughnut and bit into it as he watched Mason pour the coffee into the filters. "I hope so, because from what I've heard, this assignment is going to be a mother," Rat commented.

Mason pushed the button and watched as the hot coffee streamed down into the coffee pots. He folded his arms and directed his attention to Rat. "How so?"

"I heard we're going after some heavyweights this time, but that's all I know," Rat said as he picked up another doughnut.

Mason looked across the room and watched as his unit prepared for their upcoming meeting. Some were on the computer pulling up criminal profiles, while others were mapping out the perpetrators' territory. Seconds later, his commanding officer, nicknamed Domino, called him and the other members of his unit into the conference room so they could go over the details of their assignment. Mason had been a part of the Anti-Crime Unit Task Force for several years, and he enjoyed bringing down the bad guys. He knew in his heart this assignment would be no different, and he was ready to get it over with so he could concentrate on his family.

Cherise walked through the house to make sure everything was locked up before her cab arrived. She glanced at Janelle's calendar on the refrigerator to see when her next social event was scheduled. Eight-year-old Janelle was a serious social butterfly. Cherise had to keep a separate calendar for all the birthday parties, baseball games, slumber parties, etc. that she was involved in. Somewhat of a tomboy, Janelle was always challenging her brother to wrestling matches and other physical activities. And though she had her mother's looks and personality, she also loved wearing her thick, wavy brown hair in a pony-tail, mostly because it fit perfectly under her baseball cap that she wore daily.

She was a daddy's girl and sought every opportunity to talk to him about improving her baseball skills. She was already on the All-Star team and recently started talking to Mason about playing basketball. Cherise wanted her to do more girlie things, but she didn't try to hold her daughter back from doing what she really enjoyed, which was sports.

Cherise smiled when she saw Mase's picture on the refrigerator. Mason Jr., an aspiring basketball player, was turning fourteen next month. He was already nearly as tall as his dad, standing around six feet, one inch. Everyone called him Mase, and he was quiet and very protective of the women in the family. He looked like his father with the exception of his thick eyelashes, which he had inherited from Cherise. Mase had already filled out in all the right places, especially since he had started lifting weights. His physique gave him the appearance of a sixteen- or seventeen-year-old, which was beginning to attract older girls. Cherise was having a hard time keeping the older girls at arm's length from her young son. She knew that sooner or later she would lose the battle. She'd already gotten Mason to talk to their son about girls and sex because they weren't ready to risk becoming grandparents. Mason happily took him on a relaxing fishing trip to break it down to him. Most of what Mason told him, Mase already knew; however, this gave Mase the opportunity to ask his father questions he knew he wouldn't get a straight answer on from his friends.

Reminiscing about her family made Cherise lose track of time briefly. She took one last sip of her coffee before rinsing her cup out in the sink. As she did so, she couldn't help but worry about Mason and the dangerous job he had. She was trying not to let it get the best of her, but she could feel her stomach quiver. When she first met Mason, she wasn't sure what she was getting herself into by dating a police officer. It didn't take long for her to find out, but by then, she was madly in love with him. Standing at the sink, looking out over their backyard, Cherise remembered it like it was yesterday.

She was coming out of a boutique when Mason ran right into her, knocking her down on the sidewalk. He and another man were chasing someone who had just committed a crime. When Mason realized he had hurt someone, he immediately stopped but told the other man to keep going after the suspect while he attended to her. After helping her up from the sidewalk, he noticed blood running down the side of her head, staining her pink silk blouse; she had deep scrapes on her arms and legs. He quickly took out his handkerchief and applied it to her head wound.

"I'm so sorry. Are you okay?"

"I'm not sure," she answered, clearly dazed.

He spotted a bench in front of the store she had just exited and helped her over to it. People were starting to stare as they walked by, and the manager of the store rushed out to assist him. "Do I need to call the paramedics?" she asked.

Mason removed his handkerchief to inspect her wound and frowned. "No, ma'am, I don't think she needs the paramedics, but if you have a first-aid kit, that would help."

The young woman thought for a minute. "I think we do. I'll be right back," she said.

Within moments she returned and assisted Mason with the gauze and tape. Cherise was getting embarrassed with all of the attention. Onlookers continued to hang around to watch what was going on. Mason picked up on the fact that she was uncomfortable and he turned to the crowd and flashed his badge.

"There's nothing here to see, folks, so move along. We have everything under control."

Cherise looked up at his handsome face as he took control of the situation. "Thank you," she whispered.

"You're welcome. I can't have them putting us on the evening news." He joked to try to keep Cherise calm. The wound was still bleeding, and Mason realized he had injured her worse than he thought.

"You're bleeding. Let me get you to a hospital."

She looked at the handkerchief and examined the small amount of blood on it. "It's not that much blood. I'll be fine."

"No, it's bleeding through the bandages. It looks like you're going to need a few stitches."

Alarmed, Cherise tried to stand up. When she did she became dizzy. Mason steadied her and helped her sit back down.

"That's it. We're going to the hospital."

"Do you want me to call the paramedics now?" the manager of the boutique asked Mason.

Mason looked at Cherise and noticed the panic in her eyes.

"No, I'll drive her, but I appreciate all your help."

Mason handed the first-aid kit back to the manager and pulled out a radio that was attached to his belt. It as at that time that Mason really looked at Cherise and saw just how beautiful she was. Just as he was about to speak into the radio, he noticed a familiar face walking toward him. The person had a smirk on his face and a young, black male in handcuffs.

Cherise's eyes widened as she also watched the men close the distance between them. She had no idea what was going on, but whatever it was, it was none of her business. Her concern right now was not her wound, but her torn and stained clothing, and her tousled hair. Cherise did her best to knock the dirt and leaves off her clothes, but since she was wearing white linen pants she was unsuccessful.

Mason automatically assisted her by gently plucking the leaves out of her soft, thick mane. He wanted to help her remove the dirt from her legs, but he figured he'd end up in handcuffs if he followed through on his thoughts. Her pants fit her round derrière perfectly, and it was taking Mason the strength of ten horses to keep himself from becoming aroused. So he turned his attention to the other man—his brother, Vincent.

"You caught him!" Mason said.

Vincent smiled and raised his brow. "I've been outrunning you all our lives, big brother. I wasn't letting this young buck get away."

"Whatever, bro.Look, I need to get this young lady to the hospital. I knocked her down and she's hurt."

Vincent turned his attention to Cherise and noticed the blood on her blouse. His heart skipped a beat when their eyes met. Feeling closed in, Cherise took a breath and once again tried to stand up. This time she was successful.

"I don't need to go to the hospital," she insisted. "Once I get home I'll put some peroxide on and wrap it up real tight."

"Nah, miss, I think Mason's right. You need to let a doctor take a look at you," Vincent said as he inspected Cherise's cut. "It is Miss, isn't it?"

Cherise gave him a disgusted glance. She knew a come-on line when she heard one, and she wasn't in the mood. Her head was starting to throb and she just wanted to get home. She started to massage her temples and then remembered her wound.

"What does that have to do with anything?" she asked angrily.

Vincent raised his hands in defeat.

"You're right. I'm sorry if I offended you, but you really should get that looked at."

"Who are you guys, anyway, and why were you two running after this kid?" she asked.

"We caught *this kid* trying to break into our car," Vincent answered as he reached inside his pocket and pulled out a police badge.

"I'm Officer Mason McKenzie, and this is my brother, Vincent. What is your name, if I may ask?"

"Cherise," she answered as she eyed the young man they had in custody. She continued to hold Mason's handkerchief against the bandage as they stood on the sidewalk.

"Do you have a last name?"

She looked over at him curiously and wondered why she was being cross-examined like she was the one in custody.

"Jernigan. My name is Cherise Jernigan."

Mason picked up Cherise's bags from the sidewalk. Vincent smiled at seeing his brother smitten with Cherise. "We'd better get going. I'd hate for that cut to get infected."

"You're right, Vincent. Cherise, where is your car?" Mason asked.

She pointed to the silver Lexus parked a few feet away.

"May I have your keys?" He held out his hand and waited for her to turn them over to him.

"I believe I'm able to drive myself, officer."

Vincent butted in to help Mason. "No way, Miss! You have a head injury, so we can't allow you to drive because that would endanger public safety. You could black out behind the wheel or something. You wouldn't want that to happen, would you?"

Mason's eyes met with hers and it was hard for him to tear himself away. He was praying she would cooperate so he could hopefully get a chance to ask her out once he knew she was okay.

Cherise sighed.

"I guess you're right. Okay, Officer McKenzie, you can drive me to the hospital, but I'm driving myself home."

Mason opened her car door for her and smiled. "We'll see what the doctor says first. It's my fault you got hurt, and I'm not going to rest until I know you're safe."

Before allowing Mason to escort her to her car, Cherise turned to Vincent and smiled.

"Despite the circumstances, it was nice meeting you, Officer."

"Likewise, Ms. Jernigan," he acknowledged before escorting the suspect down the sidewalk.

Mason strolled around to the driver's side of Cherise's car and climbed in beside her. They were silent for a few minutes as Mason maneuvered the luxury vehicle out into the flow of traffic. Cherise looked over at him and finally broke the silence.

"Are you this attentive with everyone?"

He pulled up to a traffic light and turned toward her. Her breath caught in her throat as she realized just how handsome Mason McKenzie was.

"Only the innocent bystanders."

She smiled and looked away. She wasn't able to look into those eyes for more than a second. Cherise decided it was best that she close her eyes and rest her head against the seat for the remainder of the ride. She'd only known Mason for about fifteen minutes and he was already causing her body to feel things that she hadn't felt in a long time. She had to admit to herself that he was sexy and seemed to be a true gentleman, but a policeman was not on her list as a possible soul mate.

It only took minutes for them to arrive at the emergency room. Cherise received a couple of stitches and a tetanus shot to be on the safe side. Mason held her hand throughout the entire ordeal, and once the doctor was finished with her, Cherise felt like Mason was an old friend. From that day forward, they were inseparable. It didn't take long for their relationship to blossom into a full-blown love affair. By the end of the year they were engaged, and they were married three months later. It wasn't like Cherise to take to strangers like she did with Mason, but he was so warm and loving. She wasn't particularly excited about the fact that he was a police officer, because she dealt with a lot of them on a daily basis in her profession; however, she loved him and would support him no matter what.

Snapping out of her trance, Cherise sighed and looked over at the clock, realizing she didn't have much time left before the taxi arrived. She prayed this weekend would not only be informative, but would also open even more doors for her. Within minutes, the taxi pulled up and blew its horn. She closed her eyes and said a short prayer before walking into the foyer to get her bags. She grabbed the handle on her luggage and took one last look around before letting herself out and locking the door. Then she rolled her bag out to the cabdriver, waiting patiently while he put her luggage in the trunk.

"Good morning, ma'am," he said with a smile. "Where to?"

Cherise smiled back at the gentleman, who didn't appear much older than she was. "Good morning. I'm going to the Hartsfield-Jackson International Airport, please."

The gentleman closed the trunk of the taxi and walked around to open the car door for Cherise. "When does your flight leave?"

"Nine o'clock."

"With all the security, I'll have you there in twenty minutes so you'll have plenty of time to go through the checkpoints."

"Thank you."

Just as the taxi pulled away from the curb, a weird feeling overtook Cherise. It was overwhelming and had her feeling that her life was headed for a major change. She had no idea what was in store for her—no idea.

Chapter Two

As Cherise walked through the baggage claim area in Miami International Airport, pulling her suitcase behind her, she saw a gentleman holding a card with her name on it. She veered over to him.

"I'm C. J. McKenzie," she said.

The man in the black suit smiled and shook her hand to greet her properly. "Welcome to Miami."

"Thank you, mister."

"You can call me Walter. Now let's get going. I'm sure you can't wait to get to your hotel."

"You read my mind," she replied.

The driver led the way out. Cherise's blouse immediately stuck to her body in the hot, humid air. Thirty minutes later, the car pulled up in front of a beautiful Miami hotel.

"We're here," Walter announced. "Welcome to the Paradise Resort."

Cherise removed her sunglasses to admire the hotel. "This is a beautiful building."

Walter walked around and opened the door for her to step out.

"Yes, it is. It's one of the newest in Miami, and I must say it lives up to its name."

Cherise waited for Walter to pull her luggage out of the trunk. They walked through the huge glass doors together and he escorted her over to the front desk. He sat her luggage beside her.

"It was a pleasure to serve you today, Mrs. McKenzie."

Cherise thanked him and gave him a nice tip before saying good-bye.

The lobby had huge skylights and was decorated with plenty of greenery and tropical flowers. She quickly checked in and walked across the marble floor to the elevator. Once inside her room, she fell backward on the bed and sighed. She was tired and hot, and she welcomed a steamy shower before the conference began. First she needed to call Mason to let him know she had arrived safe and sound. She pulled out her cell phone and dialed his number.

"Anti-Crime Task Force. McKenzie speaking," he answered like the detective he was.

"Hey, babe, it's me. I'm at my hotel and it's so hot," she moaned.

He laughed at her whining.

"My poor baby. I guess it's not easy suffering around white sandy beaches and blue ocean water, huh?"

She kicked off her shoes, walked over to the window, and looked out at the beautiful scenery.

"I see you have no sympathy for me. Did the kids get off to school okay?"

"Yes. Your mother said everything was fine. I'll pick them up this evening."

Cherise unbuttoned her blouse as she walked across the room.

"Good. I miss you already, Mason. I wish you were here."

Mason tapped his pen on his desk nervously, a habit he'd had since elementary school. "I miss you, too. Behave while you're down there. I know you crime scene investigators can get kind of wild."

She laughed, sending a tingling sensation down Mason's spine. He'd always loved the way she laughed.

"I see you have jokes."

"I'm just teasing you, sweetheart."

Cherise knew Mason had a hard time dealing with her traveling, so joking was his way of handling it.

"Well, I'm not going to hold you any longer, Mason. I know you're busy. I'll call you guys later tonight."

"Okay, Doctor. Be careful down there."

"I will, and you do the same. I love you," she reminded him.

Twirling around in his chair, he picked up the family picture on his desk and stared at it. "I love you, too, Cherise."

He hung up and immediately made eye contact with Rat. "What are you smiling about?"

Rat leaned forward to talk privately with Mason.

"You, and the way your voice changes when you talk to your wife."

Mason sat up in his chair and started thumbing through some paperwork. "Whatever. I'm sure you're no different when you talk to all those hoochies you hang out with."

Rat leaned back in his chair and let out a barreling laugh.

"You're right. Just call me Don Juan."

The telephone rang on Mason's desk and he answered it. While talking to the caller he jotted down a series of notes. After hanging up, he stood and grabbed his jacket.

"Let's go. I just got a tip that's going to help the case."

Rat grabbed his jacket and they hurried out of the building and into the mean streets.

Later that afternoon, Cherise tried to get her thoughts together. She made her way through the massive hallways to the ballroom where the conference was being held. There were several hundred people already enjoying drinks and hors d'oeuvres. Tonight was only a meet and greet, and she was thankful because she didn't have the energy to speak, even if she had to. Cherise entered and smiled at the receptionist seated behind the desk.

"Hello. May I have your name?"

Cherise pointed to her name tag lined up with all the others on the table. "That's me, Cherise McKenzie."

"May I see some identification?"

Cherise pulled her CSI badge out of her purse and presented it to the receptionist. The young woman pulled an envelope out of a box and handed it to Cherise along with the name tag.

"Here you are, Dr. McKenzie. I hope you enjoy the conference."

"I'm sure I will. Thank you," she said, pinning the badge on her blouse.

Before she could turn around, she heard a familiar bass voice that gave her chills. "If I hadn't seen you with my own eyes, I wouldn't have believed it."

Cherise swung around in disbelief. She hadn't seen him in years, but he still looked and sounded heavenly. It was none other than Mason's brother, Vincent.

"Hello, Vincent," she said, surprised.

She tried to hold her composure as he walked over and pulled her into his arms. He leaned down and kissed her lovingly on the lips before hugging her once more.

"C. J., you still look and feel just as beautiful as you did the last time I saw you." She'd always loved the way he called her C. J. He'd tagged her with the nickname when they first met, and it had stuck ever since. She even used it in her business. But to Mason, she would always be Cherise. She swallowed the lump in her throat and slowly stepped out of his embrace. Folding her arms across her chest in a defensive manner, she took a deep breath before speaking.

"You look great, too, Vincent, and I hope you realize just how long it's been. What are you doing here anyway?"

He pointed to his name tag before shoving his hands in pockets. "I'm on the program. What about you?"

"Guilty as charged," she answered as she tried to keep her lips from trembling.

Vincent, about six feet, four inches tall, was dressed in a pair of brown dress pants and a white shirt. His hair was cut close and he still had a body to die for. With his cocoa complexion, alluring personality, and straight white teeth that flashed in his warm smile. Vincent McKenzie had always been a man to be reckoned with—and it was obvious nothing had changed over the years.

He picked up two glasses of champagne as a hostess walked by and handed one to Cherise and winked at her as they stepped away from the reception table. "So, how have you been?"

"I've been fine, Vincent, but don't you think you should ask me about your whole family?"

Cherise frowned, ready for battle. She gulped the champagne down quickly and set the glass down on a nearby table.

He smiled before taking a sip of his champagne. It was obvious that Cherise was upset with him, and she had a right to be. "I see you still have that temper of yours."

"Whatever, Vincent," she replied as she picked up another glass of champagne. This was a nervous habit Vincent was quite familiar with, so he warned her.

"You'd better take it easy with that champagne, C. J. You know what it does to you."

She gave him a look that could kill. *How dare he?* She wasn't drunk or out of control.

Vincent saw the fury building in her eyes and decided to defuse it. "So, how are Mason and the kids?"

She started to walk off without answering, but decided to indulge him since he had asked. "Why haven't you come back to visit us? It's been years, Vincent."

He finished off his drink before answering her. "Damn, C. J! I talk to Mason all the time."

"It's not the same as visiting, Vincent, and you know it. He talks about you all the time."

Her flushed color signaled to him that she was drinking too quickly. He realized she was upset with him, but he couldn't let her lose control. Not tonight in a room full of their colleagues.

"What's wrong, C. J.? Do you miss me?"

She waved him off. "You're the one who decided to disown your family, not me."

"I didn't disown my family. Correct me if I'm wrong, but you were the one who helped me make the decision to stay away."

They stared at each other in silence. Vincent admired her lavender silk blouse and short black skirt that displayed her incredible legs.

"I still miss you," he admitted in a serious tone. "I miss you a lot."

Cherise swallowed the last of her third glass of champagne and put her hand up to him in defiance. "Vincent, don't even go there." He frowned and ran his hand over his head in frustration.

"Do you have any idea what it has been like for me having to stay away?"

"Vincent, you promised you would leave it alone," Cherise said, clearing her throat.

"I know what I said, but seeing you makes it hard for me to keep my promise, C. J."

She put her hands over her face and shook her head. "I love Mason. I've always loved Mason."

Looking at her from head to toe in a sensual manner, he licked his lips seductively.

"I know you love Mason, but that didn't keep you from making love to me with that sensational body of yours, did it?"

She looked up at him with tears in her eyes. "You're right, and it was a huge mistake."

He took a step toward her. "You can't stand here and tell me we didn't mean anything to each other, C. J."

Just standing in close proximity to him caused her stomach to flutter like it used to. The room was becoming hotter by the second; the air was thinning, making it hard to breathe. The champagne had her buzzing and feeling out of control. She looked away.

"You were a good friend to me and you were there when my life wasn't going so good, but it still doesn't excuse what we did," she said.

"Are you saying you don't have that void in your life anymore? I've talked to Mason, I know how busy he is and how often he's away from you and the kids. I also know that you and I were more than friends because friends don't do the things we did," he calmly informed her.

"You are Mason's brother, for God's sake! We committed the ultimate betrayal, Vincent. Don't you understand that?"

He rubbed his neck and shook his head in disagreement. "I understand how I feel about you."

Cherise briefly closed her eyes and bit down on her lip. "All of that is behind us now."

"Is it?" he asked softly. "Nothing has changed for me."

They stared at each other once again in silence. Cherise's heart jumped up in her throat and she began to sweat. He was still able to make her shiver with emotion. Seeing that he could still affect her physically, Vincent smiled with satisfaction. Looking down at her feet, Cherise pleaded with him.

"Vincent, can we please change the subject? I don't want to talk about us anymore. Okay?"

He tilted her chin up before responding. "So everyone's doing okay, huh?"

Cherise cleared her throat to try to regain her thoughts. What she wanted was another glass of champagne to wash the dryness from her mouth.

"Yes, everyone's fine."

She could feel the intensity of his glare even when she wasn't looking directly at him.

"Something's been bothering me, C. J., and I hope you forgive me for asking, but I need to know. Is Janelle my daughter?"

All the air left Cherise's lungs as if she'd been punched in the stomach. She balled up her fists and gritted her teeth. She couldn't believe Vincent would pull something like this on her in public!

"Hell, no! Don't even try it, Vincent. You know she's not your daughter."

A couple nearby heard Cherise's heated reply and started whispering.

Vincent took Cherise by the arm and walked her out into the hallway for more privacy.

"C. J., you can't be one hundred percent sure she's Mason's daughter."

Cherise suddenly felt ill and started fanning herself. She looked around frantically. "I need to sit down. I can't believe you would ask me some shit like that."

Vincent led her over to a nearby sofa and they sat down.

"Don't you realize that if I knew I wouldn't be asking you, C. J.?"

Cherise pulled a tissue from her purse and dabbed her eyes. "This is not the time, nor the place to discuss this."

He was so close she could feel the heat of his body, smell the sensual scent of his cologne. Vincent leaned over close to her ear.

"We might not talk about it right now, sweetheart, but we will talk about it," he whispered.

"Vincent," she pleaded, "I'm begging you not to push this. She's not your daughter."

He crossed his legs and plucked a piece of lint from his pant leg. "Well, I believe she is, and until I know otherwise, I'm not letting it go."

Cherise grabbed her purse and tried to stand up, but Vincent grabbed her by the arm, preventing her from leaving.

"Look, I know you still have feelings for me, C. J. The kind of passion we had between us doesn't just go away. I love my brother, but I can't help the fact that I'm still hot for you, and I know somewhere deep inside you, you're still hot for me."

"We've been over for a long time, Vincent."

"It's not over until I know whether or not Janelle is my daughter."

Tears began to well in her eyes again—this time of anger. "I know you're not threatening me!"

She was loud, so loud that people walking by turned to see what the commotion was all about.

"I'm not threatening you, but I have a right to know."

She yanked her arm free and pointed her finger in his face. "This is not up for discussion, Vincent. She's not yours, so leave it alone!"

"Look at the time line, C. J. I know we took precautions most of the time, but those other times we were reckless."

This was the last thing Cherise wanted to think about, even though she was confident Janelle was not his daughter. She looked up into his warm eyes.

"Vincent," she said slowly, "for the last time, Janelle is Mason's daughter—period."

He studied her expression and knew he had upset her. The fact remained, however, that he had a right to know and wouldn't rest until he knew for sure. Vincent sighed.

"Sit down, C. J. Please?" he said.

She thought for a moment before rejoining him on the sofa. Neither one of them said anything for several minutes.

"Do you have any pictures of the kids?"

"You know I do," she whispered, still shaken.

"May I see them?"

Cherise studied his expression for a moment and realized he was just as upset as she was. "Yes, you can see them."

She pulled out her wallet and removed the pictures of Mase and Janelle. Vincent held the picture of Janelle in his hand and felt a warming sensation overtake his body. Cherise watched him as he stared at the picture, tears in his eyes. She felt sorry for him at that moment because she knew he wanted so badly for Janelle to be his.

"She's not your daughter, Vincent," she repeated, shaking her head.

Vincent studied every line of Janelle's face. He scanned her picture several times and then handed the photo back to Cherise.

"She's so beautiful, C. J. Even though the McKenzie bloodline is strong, she looks like you. I mean, I see McKenzie in her, but not like I do in Mase. He's all McKenzie."

She slid the picture back in place and closed her wallet. "Thank you, and yes, Mase is definitely a McKenzie man."

She trembled as she placed her wallet back into her purse. With emotions still running high, Vincent unexpectedly took her hand into his and stood.

"Look, C. J., I'm sorry if I upset you, but you can't blame me for wanting to know about Janelle. We were making love almost every day back then."

She slowly pulled her hand out of his grasp and ran her hands through her hair.

"Your timing is jacked up, Vincent. You know you shouldn't have fronted me like that in a crowded room."

"You're right. My timing is off, but I still deserve to know the truth. I've already lost one child with you."

Cherise had miscarried Vincent's child several months before Janelle was conceived. Mason never knew about that pregnancy because as usual he was working undercover and wasn't at home much.

"God knew best, Vincent. It wasn't meant to be."

"That don't stop it from hurting. If Janelle is mine, I have a right to be in her life."

"You *are* in her life!" she yelled.

"As her uncle, not her father!"

Cherise's head was beginning to throb and she desperately needed some medication. "Why are you bringing all of this up?"

"Correct me if I'm wrong, but you weren't having much of a life with Mason back then. I'm not surprised we ended up in bed together—and I won't be surprised if Janelle is my daughter either," he stated.

She looked at him and cupped his face lovingly. "I really do care about you, Vincent, but you need to let the past stay in the past. I was vulnerable back then and Mason wasn't the ideal husband or father, thanks to his job. We're beyond all of that now."

Vincent removed her hands and kissed the backs of them. "I can't forget about the past any longer, C. J. I saw firsthand what Mason's undercover work was doing to you and Mase. I tried to talk to him about it, but he was dedicated to his undercover work back then; I'm sure he still is. From the bottom of my heart, I do hope things have gotten better for you guys."

"They have, thank you," she said softly.

He pulled her into his arms and held her there.

"I am happy for you, C. J., but it doesn't take away the fact that I still love you. That will never change. That's the reason—the only reason, that I've stayed away from my family for so long. I didn't want to be a distraction, especially after you told me you wanted to try to work things out with Mason."

They looked deeply into each other's eyes for a moment and then Cherise's tears began to fall.

"I'm sorry, Vincent," she said with a sob. He pulled a handkerchief out of his pocket and gently wiped her tears away. Knowing that he had hurt her feelings saddened him.

"I didn't mean to bring up the baby. I'm so sorry."

She sighed and slowly moved out of his arms. "I'm okay."

"Are you sure?" He boldly ran his finger down the cleavage of her blouse.

"Vincent, please don't," she pleaded as she stood and moved even farther away from him.

Cherise felt the electrical charge as it shot through her body. His hands were large, yet gentle, and they excited her.

"Yes, I'm sure. My life is happier now with Mason."

He looked at her and knew how sensitive she was to his touch.

"That may be true, but you know a part of you will always belong to me. I love my brother, but you're still in my system, and sweetheart, believe me when I say it's not going away anytime soon. I'll catch up with you later."

Before she could respond, he stood and walked into the crowded ballroom. She gasped for air, only now realizing she had been holding her breath. She hadn't thought about the things she had done with Vincent in years. Yes, she'd had a long, illicit affair with him behind Mason's back; and yes, she knew that if Mason ever found out, he wouldn't think twice about killing them both.

Cherise quickly made her way to the elevator. When she reached her floor she practically ran down the hallway to her room and went straight to the bathroom. Soon as she entered, she threw up in the toilet. Seeing Vincent so unexpectedly had been too much for her. She flushed the toilet and made her way over to the sink. As she leaned against it, she prayed for strength. Dousing her face with cold water didn't help the heat her body was feeling. She frantically removed all her clothing and turned on the shower, sobbing as she climbed in and let the cold water cool down her body. Once she began shivering she turned off the shower and climbed out. She grabbed a thick towel off the towel warmer and dried off. After sliding into her terrycloth robe, she climbed into bed and closed her eyes. Her mind rewinded back to the beginning of her affair with Vincent.

Chapter Three

Nine Years Earlier

S he and Mason were legally separated, and Mason was staying in his childhood home while the pair attempted to work through their problems. Vincent and Mason inherited their house after their parents' death and hadn't had the heart to sell it. One night while Mason was working undercover, Vincent showed up on her porch unannounced. It was a cold, rainy, Atlanta night and the weather had taken a turn for the worse. When he arrived, he told Cherise that Mason had called and asked him to come over to make sure they were okay. Four-year-old Mase was very excited to see his uncle. Vincent allowed him to help build a cozy fire in the family room fireplace while Cherise made hot chocolate and then settled down with them in front of the warm blaze.

Vincent was a perfect gentleman, but he could definitely sense Cherise's anxiety about him being there as he sprawled out on the floor, playing a game with Mase. Cherise didn't know what it was that made being alone with Vincent uncomfortable for her. Maybe it was the fact that her problems with Mason were starting to get the best of her. Maybe it was the fact that she'd always found him attractive. The kind of feelings she experienced around him were a no-no. It didn't help matters that he seemed to be perfect in every way, including the way he wore his jeans. She mentally shook herself and returned her attention to her book.

"Do you want to play with us, C. J.?" Vincent asked.

She looked up, sipped her cocoa, and shook her head. "No, you guys go ahead. I want to finish this book."

"What are you reading, anyway?" Vincent asked while Mase played with the game pieces.

Their eyes met.

"It's a Brenda Jackson novel. She's my favorite."

He chuckled. "It must be one of those romance novels."

"It is. You should read it when I'm done. There might be something useful in here for you," she replied.

"Maybe I will, C. J.," he said softly as he tickled Mase. "It might be interesting to see what gets you women hot these days."

Vincent's comments rolled off his tongue like velvet. His tone was sensual, yet caring. They stared at each other for a few seconds and then Cherise continued to read without responding. She smoothed out her fleece skirt and curled her legs under her body to get more comfortable. An hour or so later, Mase was sound asleep on the floor next to Vincent and Cherise was still reading. It was nearing ten o'clock when the power went out.

"Oh my God!" she said loudly as she jumped up.

Vincent stood and calmly placed Mase in her arms.

"Relax, C. J. I was hoping this wouldn't happen, but we'll be okay. Where do you keep your flashlights?"

She nervously pointed toward the kitchen. "They're in the drawer next to the refrigerator."

Cherise watched as Vincent made his way into the dark hallway leading to the kitchen. He returned with two flashlights. He handed one to her and smiled.

"I'll check everything out and get some more blankets. While I'm upstairs I'll close off the other rooms so we can stay warm in here in case the power stays off for a while."

With the fire illuminating the room, Cherise picked Mase up off the floor and held him close to her chest. She pulled a blanket over them and kissed him on the cheek. Sitting there in the dark she could hear Vincent humming some type of tune as he walked throughout the house. She felt sad that Mason had damaged their marriage, sad that his job was preventing him from being there; but since he wasn't, she was glad Vincent was to make her feel safe.

Vincent returned with extra blankets and pillows. He dropped everything on the floor in front of the fire and set the flashlight down. "There's no telling how long the lights will be out, so we're going to have to make the best of the situation. Hopefully they'll be back on real soon, but you never know, especially if the transformers have blown out. I brought some more socks for Mase so his feet won't get cold. Do you need any?"

She wiggled her feet from under the blanket to show him her feet.

"No, I already have some on, but thanks, anyway. I hope the power doesn't stay off long, because it could get cold in here real quick."

Vincent nodded in agreement and threw more logs on fire. "We have the fireplace, so we should be fine."

He proceeded to form a makeshift bed on the floor with the pillows and blankets, close to the sofa. Next, he pushed two plush armchairs together and made a small bed for Mase. Once he was done rearranging the furniture, he turned and gently took Mase out of Cherise's lap. He noticed the worried look on her face.

"Don't worry. I fixed it so he won't fall out."

Cherise stood and gently covered Mase with the extra blanket. Vincent was so thorough with everything he did, a trait Mason clearly missed out on.

Vincent looked around the room to make sure everything was in place. "I'll sleep on the floor and you can stay there on the sofa. Do you need me to get you anything before I settle down?"

She nervously played with her hair as she watched Mase sleep. "No, I'm fine."

He sat down across from her and yawned.

"I'm glad Mason called me. If he hadn't, I would've come over anyway even though we both know that you can handle anything that comes your way, including this power outage."

"I doubt it," she admitted. "I don't do well under pressure."

He unlaced his athletic shoes and kicked them off his feet.

"You don't give yourself enough credit, C. J. You've had some serious obstacles thrown at you, and you still came out unscathed and stronger."

"I'm not unscathed or stronger." She laughed. "In fact, I feel weaker."

"You're wrong," he replied as he stretched out on the floor.

His expression and the tenderness in his voice caused her heart to skip a beat. Cherise looked away and prayed the lights would come back on real soon. Sitting in the dark with Vincent wasn't where she needed to be right now. She pushed the blanket off her lap, turned on her flashlight, and stood.

"Where are you going?" he asked as his eyes followed her toward the door.

She looked over her shoulder at him and smiled. "To the bathroom. Is that okay with you?"

Yawning again, he stretched his arms high over his head. "Sure, just be careful."

After leaving the bathroom, Cherise made her way into the dark kitchen to find something to snack on. She shined her flashlight into the refrigerator and searched as quickly as she could, unable to find anything that piqued her interest. When she closed the door and turned, she came face-to-face with Vincent. Startled, she let out a short scream and swung at him with her flashlight, causing him to duck.

"What are trying to do, give me a heart attack?" He grinned mischievously. "Of course not."

She looked over his shoulder with sudden panic. "Where's Mase? Is he still asleep?"

He opened the refrigerator and leaned into it. "Yeah, he's safe and sound, and don't worry, he can't get close to the fire. So, what were you looking for in here? I'm a little hungry myself. I guess takeout is out of the question, huh?"

She nodded and backed away from him. The house might be cold, but it was definitely getting hot in the kitchen. "I was just looking for something to snack on, but I couldn't find anything that I wanted."

He opened the freezer and his eyes lit up, as he pulled out a small container of ice cream.

"We might as well eat this before it melts."

Before she could answer, he pulled a spoon out of a nearby drawer, scooped up a spoonful, and held it in front of her. She looked up into his eyes, taken back by his forwardness.

"No, you go ahead and eat it. It's too cold in here for ice cream."

He frowned because he knew she was lying.

"Open up, C. J. You know you want some."

His words had a sexual tone to it, which caused goose bumps to appear on her skin.

"I'll just get a little taste," she replied. "I normally don't eat it."

She opened her mouth and allowed him to feed her the ice cream.

Vincent was immediately aroused by the way her lips slowly engulfed the spoon. Standing in the kitchen with only the glow from their flashlights made the whole scene very erotic and he knew he needed to get himself together. He walked away from her and peered out the window into the backyard. Vincent's body was still fighting against itself, and he cursed himself under his breath. He scooped out a spoonful for himself and closed his eyes, as he ate it, hoping to cool things down. He turned and could only see the silhouette of her body. She was spectacular.

"This is some good ice cream. Do you want any more?"

The tension in the room was so thick you could cut it with a knife. Her heart was beating wildly in her chest, causing her to become short of breath. It seemed that everything he said was causing her to lose hold of her senses. She cleared her throat and waved him off.

"I need to go check on Mase. He's in there all by himself."

He slowly walked back over to her. "Mase is fine, C. J. Why are you in such a hurry to get away from me?" Scooping up another spoonful of ice cream for himself, he waited for her answer.

"You know why," she whispered.

"No, I don't. Why don't you tell me so we'll both know?"

He leaned against the cabinet and dipped the spoon once again into the container of ice cream.

"Forget about it, Vincent! If you want to play dumb, then go ahead."

There was only one more spoonful of ice cream left, so he scooped it up and held it out to her. He knew he was walking on dangerous ground, but he couldn't help himself.

"Open."

Cherise couldn't help but be aware of the way his broad chest was filling out the sweatshirt he was wearing, and the jeans hugged his body to perfection.

"You don't have to feed me, Vincent. I can feed myself."

He glanced down at her lips and back up into her eyes.

"But I like feeding you."

She closed her eyes briefly. Suddenly, Vincent set the carton down and pulled her into his arms. He kissed her gently lingering there to nibble on her lower lip. She braced herself against his chest as he slowly pulled open the front of her blouse. He planted kisses on her neck and chest, unsnapping her bra in the process. He dipped his head and feasted on her heavenly body.

Cherise as he savored the softness of her body. Breathlessly, she said, "Vincent, my God! What are you doing?"

He backed her against the wall and gripped her hips. "I'm showing you how I feel about you, C. J."

"We can't do this!"

They slid down the wall to the floor and were feverishly in each other's arms. Vincent slid his hand under her skirt and removed her thong. He'd always been attracted to Cherise, but it wasn't a line he'd ever planned to cross. There was no turning back now. The allure of the darkness, the fireplace, and the ice cream broke down any resistance he'd had. He inched his hand higher up her thigh until he reached her center and caressed her. This sent Cherise into a heated frenzy as he diligently stroked her moistness.

"Damn it, C. J.," he moaned as he unzipped his jeans.

Cherise wrapped her legs around his waist and groaned as he joined his body with hers. It'd been a while since she had been intimate with Mason, and she was starving sexually. Vincent felt her gasp as he pushed deeper into her heat. He held her firmly in his arms and loved her vigorously. Cherise whimpered as he moved methodically and sprinkled her face with sensual kisses. She moved in harmony with Vincent, sending both of them into overdrive. She held onto his broad upper body as he went where no other man, outside of Mason, had ever been. Vincent made love to her as if she was his and only his. He was in no hurry for this heavenly moment to end, so he savored every kiss and caress between them. Cherise sobbed as her body jerked against his solid frame when the waves of satisfaction overtook her. Vincent continued to give himself to her until he exploded with sheer pleasure.

"C. J.!" he whispered.

His spent body fell against hers and he fought to catch his breath. Vincent was still semi erect when his tongue teased her brown, erect nipples. He ground his hips slowly into her until he was ready to love her again. Once their second round of lovemaking had subsided, Cherise lay there in total shock at what had just taken place between them. The experience had been unbelievably hot, overwhelming, and had left her body full of sexual electricity. Vincent rolled off her body and pulled up his pants in silence. He helped Cherise up from the floor and then zipped his pants. Unable to make eye contact with him, she did her best to salvage what was left of her clothes. At that moment her cell phone rang. Not wanting it to wake up Mase, she hurried back into the family room to answer it.

"Hello?"

"Did I wake you?"

It was Mason. She shivered, instantly flooded with guilt.

"No. The power went off a little while ago so we've camped out in the family room around the fireplace."

"Did Vincent make it over there? I asked him to come over just in case. I didn't want you there alone."

Her hand trembled as she held the phone. Vincent walked quietly back into the family room and threw another log on the fire. She watched his movements and stuttered as she answered.

"Yes, Vincent, uh, Vincent is here. He got here a few hours ago. He let Mase help him build a fire so we wouldn't get cold."

"Cool. Where's my son?"

"He's been asleep for about an hour."

Cherise could feel the tears welling up in her eyes. She didn't know how much longer she could continue to talk to Mason without him sensing something was wrong.

"I hate that I can't talk to him. I don't know when I'll get to call back. I miss you guys," Mason admitted softly.

Cherise swallowed hard and walked over to where Mase was sleeping. She gently caressed his face to wake him up because Mase did need to hear his father's voice, especially since he wasn't living with him now.

"Hold on, Mason. I woke him up so you can talk to him."

Cherise held the cell to Mase's ear so he could hear his father's voice. Mase

37

was still sleepy, but he became more alert upon hearing his dad's voice. Cherise sat there and stroked her son's face as he had a brief conversation with his dad. Vincent was across the room staring out the window in silence. Seconds later, Mase smiled and told his father good night. Cherise wiped the tears from her eyes because she knew Mase missed his father very much. She put the cell back up to her ear.

"Mason, you should see the smile on his face."

"You should see the one on my face. Damn, I miss you guys."

She didn't reply as she watched Mase quickly fall back to sleep. She was starting to get angry because Mason was the cause of their separation.

"Mase misses you, too."

"What about you? Do you miss me?" he asked softly.

Cherise closed her eyes. She wished she could forgive Mason, but she couldn't. If it weren't for his infidelity and inability to be home with her and Mase, what had just happened with Vincent…wouldn't have.

"I don't know how I feel, Mason. I just want to have a normal life."

"Tell me what to do to make things better between us, Cherise, and I'll do it. I love you and I don't want to lose you. I know I hurt you and I'm sorry. I promise I'll never hurt you again."

"Don't start making promises to me, Mason," she said solemnly. "You broke the last promise you made to me, and my life is a wreck because of it. Look, I can't talk about this anymore."

Mason cleared his throat and tried to regain his composure. "Okay, Cherise. Look, let me speak to Vincent for a second."

There was silence between them for a few minutes.

"Mason, I don't want you to think that I don't care about you because I do, so please be careful out there," she said finally.

It wasn't much, but it gave him some hope to hold onto.

"I will, Cherise. I love you and I hope to see you guys soon."

With trembling hands she held the phone out to Vincent without responding to Mason.

"Vincent, Mason wants to talk to you," she whispered.

He turned to face her but did not move at first. Instead he stood there staring at her from across the room. Her eyes pleaded with him to take the telephone before she broke down emotionally. Noticing her struggle, he walked over and hugged her affectionately before taking the cell out of her hand to greet Mason.

"Hey, Mason!"

"What's up, bro?" Mason cheerfully greeted his brother. "Nothing up here, but this case I'm on is keeping me busy. I appreciate you looking out for the family tonight."

Vincent stared at Cherise as she got up and walked out of the room. Once she was out of sight he turned his attention back to Mason.

"Well, they were looking out for me until the power went out over here."

Mason chuckled. "In any case, I feel much better with you there. Thanks for doing it."

"Anytime and I know you'd do the same for me if the tables were turned."

"You know it. Well, I guess I'd better get off of here. Let me holler at Cherise one more time before I go."

Vincent looked toward the hallway to see if he could hear her returning. Unfortunately, he had no idea where she went.

"I think she went to the bathroom or something. Do you want me to get her?"

Mason sighed with disappointment. He really did want to hear her voice once more.

"No, you don't have to do that. Is she okay? I mean, we're still trying to work through our issues, but sometimes I can't tell if we're gaining any ground."

Vincent folded his arms defensively. "I don't know, Mason. C. J. is still hurt by everything, and you're going to have to give her time. She's not going to forgive you overnight."

Mason cleared his throat. "I guess you're right. I know I screwed up, but I do love her and I don't want to lose her."

"I know you do, and C. J. loves you too, but her heart is bruised right now. Give it time. Okay, bro?"

"I'll try. Let her know I might be able to come home this weekend so I can spend some time with her and Mase."

Vincent did his best to act normal under the circumstances. "I will. Watch your back out there, bro."

"Oh, without a doubt. Hey, if it gets too cold, get yourselves out of there and find a hotel or something."

"Will do, but I think we'll be fine here with the fireplace; you had plenty of wood stocked up in the garage."

Mason yawned. "All right. Good night, bro. I love you guys."

"Right back at you. Good night, Mason."

As soon as Vincent ended the call, Cherise returned to the room. She was now dressed in some snug-fitting sweatpants and a sweatshirt, which wasn't making it any easier on him not to get aroused once again. She was walking like a zombie, and she still would not make eye contact with him. She lay down on the sofa and covered herself with the blanket. Vincent immediately walked over to her and swallowed the lump in his throat.

"Mason said he might be able to come home this weekend to spend some time with you guys, but there's no guarantee."

She punched her pillow.

"Why am I not surprised?" she replied sarcastically.

Cherise was clearly bitter with Mason's regular absence from their lives. He claimed he was trying to do better, but she hadn't seen much improvement.

"He also told me to tell you that he loved you and Mase."

She looked at him angrily. "I know you're just the messenger, Vincent, but it's hard for me to believe anything Mason says anymore. He might love Mase, but if he really loved me he wouldn't have done what he did."

Vincent remained still as she closed her eyes. "I'm sorry about all that, C. J., and I wish there was something I could do to help, but I can't. What we did tonight was no different than what Mason did—in in fact, it's a lot worse. You're my brother's wife."

She studied him. Surely he hadn't made love to her in order to prove a point.

"Why did you make love to me, Vincent?"

"Because I love you," he replied softly.

"Love me? Where is that coming from? You wouldn't be trying to blackmail me, would you?"

"Why the hell would you say something like that? I would never blackmail you, and you know it!" He was livid.

She put her finger up to her lips so he would lower his voice. She didn't want to wake up Mase.

"What happened between us was a mistake, Vincent, so forget about it."

He snapped back at her quickly. "I felt you deeper than I've ever felt any woman, and it was spectacular. It wasn't a mistake to me."

She didn't move or respond to his heartfelt confession. He studied her body language because he craved to know what she was thinking.

"So are you saying Mason didn't make a mistake when he slept with that woman?" Cherise said finally.

"I can only speak for myself, C. J. But Mason said he's sorry for what he did. Can you see yourself ever forgiving him?"

She didn't answer right away. It was as if she needed to think about her answer before she spoke; when she did, her voice was strained.

"After tonight, do I really have a choice?"

She turned her back to him and he pulled the blanket higher over her body. He lay down on the bed he'd prepared earlier on the floor and stared at the shadows dancing on the ceiling, courtesy of the fireplace.

"Life is full of choices, C. J. We just have to do our best to make the right ones. I'll admit what happened between us tonight wasn't something either one of us planned, but I don't have any regrets."

With her voice barely above a whisper, Cherise responded the best way she knew how. "I agree, Vincent. I'll admit that you made me feel sexy and alive. But it was still wrong, and you and I both know that two wrongs don't make a right."

"All I know is how I feel about you, C. J."

"Please! You're with a different woman every week."

He shook his head and grunted. "Obviously you don't know me like I thought you did. What happened between us tonight was incredible, and if it never happens again, I would die a happy man. Oh, and just for the record, those women are not half the woman you are."

Cherise lay there with her back to him, listening to him pour his heart out to her. The closeness they were sharing at that moment was tender and warm, but she couldn't allow herself to give in to her desires. Tears rolled out of her eyes as she turned to face him.

"I can't do this, Vincent," she pleaded. "You know I haven't been myself for some time now."

He sat up and wiped the tears from her face. "You'll be okay. You just want to feel loved just like everyone else."

"I gave Mason plenty of love and attention and he still cheated on me. Explain that!"

Vincent didn't have the answers. So instead he ended the night by kissing her tenderly on the cheek before closing his eyes to hopefully get some sleep.

Against Cherise's better judgment, that night was the beginning of many sultry rendezvous between the two. Mostly because Mason was never around and Vincent gave her the love and attention she craved so much. As time went on, Cherise was pulled deeper and deeper into a forbidden and illicit relationship with Vincent. He was giving her the unbridled passion she missed with Mason. It left her unsure if her marriage could survive—especially after she became pregnant. Unfortunately, she lost the baby and Mason never knew about the pregnancy.

After realizing that her heart would always belong to Mason, Cherise realized she'd been spinning her wheels with Vincent. From her standpoint, their relationship was strictly physical; however for Vincent it was the total opposite. This made ending her affair with him difficult but necessary.

Chapter Four

Seeing Vincent again was not something Cherise was emotionally prepared for, and it unexpectedly affected her both emotionally and physically. She needed to hear Mason's voice and those of her children before she fell apart. Sitting up in bed, she grabbed her cell phone and called home. A lump formed in her throat as she spoke to Janelle in particular. Mason's voice was soothing and loving, and was medicine to her ill state of mind. They talked for nearly thirty minutes before hanging up.

Cherise sat there in the solitude of her room going over the events of the day. She was angry with herself for letting Vincent get under her skin. She had actually believed that when the day came they were face-to-face again that she would be able to handle it, but she'd been wrong. The ringing of the telephone startled her, and she quickly picked up, expecting Mason to be on the other end.

Instead, Vincent's sensual voice came through the telephone.

"C. J., I hope I'm not disturbing you. I wanted to call and let you know I'm sorry about today. I was wrong for bringing up all that stuff out of our past, but I couldn't help it. You still look stunning and all the feelings I have for you came flooding back all at once."

She sat there unable to speak. He was making her fall apart all over again.

"C. J.?" he said.

"I'm here, Vincent," she answered softly.

"Look, let me make it up to you. I'm sure it was just the shock of seeing you after all these years that made me so crazy today. It brought back a lot of memories. Do you have any dinner plans?"

She nervously teased her hair and shook her leg.

"No."

"Good. Let me take you out to dinner so I can apologize properly for acting like such an asshole."

"You got that right."

His baritone laugh made her quiver.

"Oh really?" His playful tone caused her to giggle.

"Seriously, C. J., let me take you to dinner. I promise I'll be on my best behavior."

She thought about the invitation for a moment and decided to accept his offer.

"Okay, Vincent. I'll join you for dinner because you apologized with sincerity."

"Perfect!" he replied with a smile in his voice. "Are you able to meet me in the lobby in fifteen minutes?"

"I'll be there. I'll see you shortly." She hung up the telephone and hoped she was doing the right thing.

When Cherise met Vincent, he smiled and kissed her on the cheek.

"Thanks for going to dinner with me. You look great!"

She blushed and fidgeted nervously. Cherise had chosen a sleeveless, peach pantsuit. The sandals on her manicured feet matched perfectly. Her curls fell loosely around her face and her makeup was flawless and natural.

"Thank you. You don't look so bad yourself."

"Thank you, C. J."

Vincent had changed into a pair of casual khaki pants and a white starched shirt. Cherise hadn't complimented a man other than Mason in years. Standing there talking to Vincent out in the open was beginning to make her body tingle.

He smiled and put his hand at the small of her back as he escorted her across the lobby.

"I hope you're hungry."

"Starving!"

"In that case, let's get our eat on. You're going to love the food."

"I'm sure I will."

The pair walked in sync out of the building and into the heat of the Florida air.

Minutes later, Cherise was in awe when Vincent pulled up to the Tudor-style building. She gazed out the window curiously at patrons entering the restaurant and the valets running about.

"What type of cuisine do they serve here?"

His eyes gleamed as they met hers. Her heart skipped a beat as she shyly looked away. Vincent McKenzie was once again making his presence known.

"Patience, my dear. You'll see," he assured her as he patted her hand tenderly.

Vincent gave the valet his car keys, and then walked around to open the door for Cherise. Once again, they made eye contact. She could feel the heat rising on her face.

What the hell is wrong with me?

Vincent took her hand into his, helping her from the vehicle. The warmth of her hand sent an electrical charge through his body, causing his manhood to come alive. He released her slowly and stepped aside for Cherise to lead the way through the entrance. As soon as they walked inside, a Hispanic gentleman greeted them with a huge smile.

"Good evening and welcome! How many are in your party, sir?"

"Two, nonsmoking," Vincent instructed.

The host grabbed a couple of menus and turned to them.

"Right this way."

Vincent and Cherise followed the host across the restaurant to a secluded table illuminated by soft candlelight. The room was beautifully decorated with flowers and candles throughout, giving it a romantic aura. Vincent held out Cherise's chair as she sat down. She continued to look around the restaurant, admiring it.

"Vincent, this is very nice. You always did have good taste," she complimented him.

"I'm so glad you approve."

The waiter came over with his notepad and waited to take their order. Cherise's eyes lit up as she scanned the many delicious entrees. Vincent discreetly watched her as she studied the menu diligently.

Damn, she's gorgeous!

He tried to shake the erotic thoughts out of his head by scanning his own menu, but he was unsuccessful. His body was already defying him, but he wasn't about to mess up after regaining ground with her. Vincent had to do what he could to get his body under control before Cherise saw the evidence of his desire.

As they enjoyed their meal, Cherise couldn't help but look at Vincent with amazement. "This food is delicious!"

He grinned and picked up his glass of wine.

"I knew you would enjoy it."

Cherise was eating some mouthwatering shrimp. Vincent was enjoying a Porterhouse steak and steamed vegetables.

She eyed his plate and licked her lips. "That steak looks so tender."

He cut a piece and held it out to her on his fork. "Do you want a taste?"

Embarrassed, she lowered her eyes. This scene was starting to become eerily similar to that eventful night in her kitchen, years ago, when he offered her a taste of ice cream.

"No, thank you. I was just admiring it."

"Come on, C. J. It's so tender it just melts in your mouth."

She had to admit, the steak did look appetizing. Vincent pushed the fork closer, unable to understand what had come over him.

"That's okay. I believe you."

He laughed and set the fork down on his plate.

"Okay, but don't ever say I don't like to share."

Taking a bite of her food, she thought about his response and knew very well that Vincent would do anything for her.

"Don't worry, I won't."

Vincent picked up his napkin, wiped his mouth, and locked eyes with her.

"C. J., I didn't mean to upset you. You mean a lot to me and I would never intentionally hurt you."

"I know that, Vincent."

There was silence between them as they looked into each other's hearts.

"I'm glad you know that, C. J., because I'm not sure if I should bring this up."

She looked at him curiously. She had no idea what he was struggling with. He looked away from her briefly and then covered his eyes with his hands.

"What is it, Vincent?"

He cleared his throat and squirmed in his seat. "Did you remember that our son's birthday would've been tomorrow?"

Cherise felt terrible. A lump formed in her throat as she closed her eyes and leaned back in her chair. "I'm so sorry, Vincent. I totally forgot."

He looked up at her suspiciously—he knew Cherise would never forget her son's birthday. Vincent pushed his vegetables around on his plate. He had become very somber as he spoke about the loss of their child.

"He would've been nine years old."

"I know," Cherise whispered as she put her hand over her heart.

"Do you ever wonder what he would've looked like?"

Her heart started beating rapidly in her chest. They were discussing a painful part of their lives, and the pain was getting stronger by the second.

"Sometimes, but if I had to guess, I'm sure he would've looked like you."

"You're probably right."

She quickly drained her wine glass as Vincent let out a loud sigh. As she studied him, she noticed his eyes were filled with tears, so she reached out to him and held his hand.

"I'm so sorry, Vincent."

He caressed her hand and stared at her. She was beautiful and he was still in love with her.

"So am I, C. J. They say everything happens for a reason, but I'll never get over losing Jamal or you."

She gave Vincent's hand a gentle squeeze and remembered the day like it was yesterday.

She was four months' pregnant when she decided to break off her affair with Vincent. She realized she had become too emotionally involved and knew once Mason found out she was pregnant, there was no telling what he might do. But Vincent was against ending the relationship, especially since they had a child on the way.

They yelled at each other for nearly an hour, and then she went into premature labor. Vincent quickly rushed her to the hospital; however, doctors were unable to save the baby. They were devastated over the loss and Cherise fell into a deep depression that lasted for several weeks. She honestly believed that God had punished her for her infidelity, so she prayed for strength to make much needed changes in her life.

Cherise continued to daydream and recalled how she was unable to pull herself out of her depression and in clinging to Vincent for support, their affair was rekindled and continued for a couple more months.

It wasn't until Mason was involved in a shooting and was slightly injured that she snapped back to reality. Mason's near-death experience gave her the strength she needed to finally forgive him and give her marriage another try. She broke things off with Vincent permanently, and just like before, he became very upset. He begged her not to end their relationship so abruptly, but this time Cherise was adamant about her decision. She did want to save her marriage regardless of the problems that existed between them leaving Mason ecstatic that Cherise wanted to give their marriage another try. He couldn't wait to move back home and he did so immediately.

Once Vincent saw that Mason and Cherise was getting their marriage back on track, he still felt hurt and despondent. To help relieve his pain, he decided he needed to make a change in his life. Unbeknownst to anyone, he interviewed for and accepted the position of police chief in Houston, and left Cherise in Atlanta for good. Mason was sad to see his brother go, and Cherise was going to miss Vincent, too, but she knew his departure was for the best.

She and Mason did reconcile and approximately nine months later, Cherise gave birth to Janelle. Vincent was faced with the reality that Mason and Cherise's marriage had been mended. This left him no choice but to go on without her, bringing their lives to where they were today.

The waiter walked back to the table to attend to the couple, snapping Cherise out of her daydream, causing her to quickly release Vincent's hand.

"I know what you were thinking about, C. J. You haven't been able to forget about the baby either."

"At some point we're going to have to let it go, Vincent, and let the past stay in the past."

He motioned for the waiter and ordered another bottle of wine. "I can't, C. J., and I don't know if I'll ever be able to."

Cherise had basically drunk the first all by herself. Once the waiter was gone, Vincent put the glass up to his mouth and paused.

"You know it was my fault. If I hadn't been yelling at you." She wiped her mouth and shook her head in disagreement, holding up her hand to interrupt him.

"No and I told you to stop saying that, because it was nobody's fault! If anything it was God's way of punishing me."

"I totally disagree with you, but I digress," he admitted before taking a bite of his food. "Let's change the subject. How are things down at the office? Are they keeping you busy?"

Welcoming the change in their conversation, she rolled her eyes playfully at him.

"More than I would like to be." He looked around at mostly couples having dinner before continuing their conversation. "Do you ever get tired of it? I mean, being around all the death?"

She thought for a second. "I love my job, but there have been a few times that it has gotten to me. Especially when children are involved."

"That's understandable," he said as he took a sip of his wine. When was the last time you guys took a vacation?"

She giggled. "What's that? You know that's not in our vocabulary."

Cherise studied his handsome features, admiring just how much he and Mason looked alike.

"You know you have to step away from the madness sometimes, C. J., or it'll make you crazy."

"I know, Vincent, but I'm a little shorthanded right now, and it's taking all I have to keep up. Anyway, you need to take your own advice in regards to taking time off, Mr. Police Chief."

He scooped the last of his meal up on his fork. Before putting it in his mouth he winked at her.

"Maybe you're right."

"I know I am," she replied.

"What about Mason? Has he taken any time off?"

She rubbed her full stomach and leaned back in her seat. "He's still working a lot, but not the long weeks like he used to, thank God. I can't go back to that life again."

"Good for you."

She tilted her head slightly and smiled shyly. "Good for us."

After finishing dinner, Vincent paid their bill and drove back to their hotel. He escorted Cherise back to her hotel room and before saying good night gave her an innocent kiss on the forehead. She thanked him for dinner and wished him good luck on his upcoming speech. He wished her the same before walking down the hallway to the elevator. Cherise was glad the day was over. Being in close quarters with Vincent wasn't something she planned on, or wanted to do; it had taken her too long to get him out of her system the first time, and she couldn't allow herself to get caught up with him again.

Chapter Five

Mason missed Cherise so he did his best to stay occupied and keep his mind off of her. The following day the kids wanted to go to the mall and to the movies. He didn't particularly care to spend the day in the mall, but if it kept the kids happy, he would do it. Since his job kept him on edge most of the time, the opportunity to unwind didn't come around every day, so he wanted to make the most of it as often as possible.

Janelle spotted a hat she wanted as she skipped alongside Mason and Mase. "Daddy, can I get a Red Sox hat?"

Mason rubbed her head lovingly. "Yes, Janelle, you can get a new hat. By the way, how many do you have now?"

Janelle thought for a moment. "I think I have about twenty, Daddy."

Janelle's baseball hats had become part of her daily attire, along with several pairs of athletic shoes. Mason smiled and then looked over at Mase.

"Is there anything you're looking for in particular, son?"

Mase didn't hear his father talking to him. He was too busy watching some teenage girls as they walked past him, and they were admiring him as well.

Mason smiled. He put his hand on his son's shoulder. "Slow your roll, Mase. You have plenty of time for that."

"Ah, Dad, I was just looking," Mase said, embarrassed that his dad had caught him flirting.

"I know, but you don't have to turn completely around, do you?"

"I can't help it, Dad, they're all so fine," Mase explained.

Mason laughed at his hormonal firstborn. "True, but remember, just because it looks good, doesn't mean it is good. These little girls can get a young man like you in a lot of trouble if you don't use your head. Sometimes it's better when you don't pay them any attention."

Mason made sure he pointed to Mase's forehead as he warned him.

They continued to walk through the mall and finally went into an athletic store and casually looked over the merchandise. Janelle went straight for the hats.

"It's hard not to pay them any attention when they're hugging on you and stuff."

Mason turned Mase toward him. "I know it's hard, Mase, but you're going to have to learn how to have some self-control when dealing with females. It's better for you to learn it early, because you'll be struggling with it for the rest of your life. Women are mysterious creatures; you can't help but love them."

"Is that how it was with you and Momma?"

Mason laughed and shoved his hands inside his pockets. "Your mother was special. It was love at first sight after I nearly killed her."

"What did you do, Dad?" Mase asked. "Did you shoot her or something?"

Janelle walked over, interrupting their conversation. "How does this look, Daddy?"

Mason looked down at his daughter, who was sporting a Red Sox hat and matching jersey.

"You look great," he said as he knelt down to speak to her. "But I could've sworn you only asked for a hat."

"I know, Daddy, but this jersey goes so good with it."

"You're a brat, Janelle," Mase said.

"Shut up, Mase!"

Mason put his hands up in the air. "Chill, guys!" He turned back to Janelle. "Janelle, make a decision. It's the hat or the jersey, but not both."

"Ah, man!" Janelle walked off in disgust. Mason looked over at Mase.

"Now, where were we? Oh yeah! I nearly killed your mother because I was chasing a suspect and I knocked her down on the sidewalk. I had to take her to the hospital to get some stitches. It was love at first sight, so I chased her around like a sick puppy until she married me."

"You're kidding, aren't you, Daddy?"

Mason pulled a throwback jersey off the rack. "No, it's the truth. If you don't believe me, ask her when she comes home."

"That's funny," Mase teased.

Janelle walked back over wearing the hat.

"Okay, Daddy, I choose the hat because I can't wear the jersey without a matching hat."

He pulled her ponytail playfully. "Good girl. Let's go pay the cashier."

Mason and Janelle walked toward the front to pay for the hat, and Mase walked over to price some athletic shoes before they all continued on their shopping spree.

Cherise had attended seminars all day, though she wasn't on the schedule to speak until tomorrow, but Vincent was supposed to give his speech in about an hour. She hoped to get a chance to hear him because he was a man of power and conviction. Vincent was an excellent speaker, and a thorough police officer. He and Mason had come out of the academy together, but they chose different departments once they reached detective status. While Mason joined the Anti-Crime Task Force, Vincent went on to make lieutenant in the homicide department. He'd run a very tight and successful squad before moving further up the ranks.

Snapping back to reality, Cherise felt flushed. She looked at her watch and noticed that Vincent's speech would be starting shortly. She needed something cool to drink and some fresh air so she stood and quietly exited the room. After stepping outside she went into the lounge and ordered a tall glass of lemonade. Then she found a seat near the back of the ballroom and waited for Vincent's speech to begin.

The seminars were running on time so as soon as the room filled up, Vincent was introduced to the audience. After a thunderous applause, he began his speech. What Cherise witnessed was a more refined Vincent. He was chief of police now, and his power was clearly visible in the way he spoke. She sat there in awe as he continued to woo the crowd with statistics and other facts about law enforcement. He looked so debonair in his suit, and he seemed very comfortable speaking in front of a large crowd.

When it appeared he was nearing the end of his speech, she eased out of her seat. Her morning had started early, and before turning in for the night, she wanted to go over her speech once more. She walked into the elevator and punched the button for her floor. As she entered her room, she stepped out of her shoes and lay across the bed. She rolled over and picked up the phone to leave Vincent a "job well done" message on his hotel voice mail. After hanging up, she dialed Mason at home. As the phone rang on the other end, she waited with anticipation. After several rings, she looked at her watch.

"Come on, Mason, pick up the phone," she mumbled.

Moments later the answering machine picked up, so she left a message for him to call her when he got in. Wanting to relax, she undressed and ran a hot bubble bath. As she prepared to step into the sudsy water, the telephone rang.

"Hello?" she answered.

"C. J., I hope I didn't disturb you."

It was Vincent. Cherise smiled.

"I was just getting ready for a nap. I heard your speech, and as expected, you were fabulous."

"You're biased, but thank you anyway, and thanks for the message," he said with appreciation.

She laughed.

"Well, I'm not going to hold you, C. J., but do you have any dinner plans for tonight?"

"Not really. I was going to order room service and go over my speech."

"I really would like it if you would have dinner with me again. We haven't seen each other in a long time, and I'd like to catch up on what's been going on in the family."

She played with her hair nervously. "Well, since you put it that way, why not? What time do you want to meet?"

Vincent checked his watch.

"Can you meet me in the lobby at six o'clock?"

"Sounds great."

He paused for a second before speaking.

"C. J., does Mason know I'm down here?"

"No. Why?"

Vincent paced the floor of his hotel room as he spoke. "Are you going to tell him?"

Now it was her time to question him. "Do you want me to?"

"I'll leave that up to you. Just let me know what you decide so we'll be on the same page."

"I will," she replied. "I'll see you shortly."

"Will do."

Vincent hung up the telephone and removed his jacket. He felt a familiar ache in his heart. He cleared his throat, mumbling to himself. "Come on, Vincent. She doesn't belong to you. Let it go, brotha."

He sighed as he sat down in his chair. Out of all the women he'd dated in his lifetime, he had to fall in love with his brother's wife.

"Shit!" he yelled as he jumped up and raided the minibar.

After Cherise hung up the telephone, she got a little nervous. She didn't know why she was so worried about Mason knowing Vincent was at the conference. It wasn't like he suspected anything, but if she didn't tell him and he found out later, he'd wonder why she'd hidden it from him. She put her hands over her face.

"Damn it!! What are you going to do, Cherise?" She headed into the bathroom, hoping to find the answer in her bubble bath.

Mason entered his bedroom and immediately noticed the blinking light on the answering machine. He played Cherise's messages and looked at his watch. He dialed her number and waited.

"Hello?"

"Hey, babe," he said with a smile.

"What are you guys up to?"

"Oh, I was hanging out with the kids. We went to the mall and to the movies. How is the conference going?"

"It's okay."

"Have you seen any familiar faces?"

She hesitated briefly. "A few. Where are the kids?"

"They're in their rooms. Hold on so you can talk to them. They're going over to your mom's house in a few because I have to work tonight. This case I'm working on is really heating up."

She frowned. "You're not out there doing anything crazy, are you?"

He scolded himself for revealing that his job was heating up. "Cherise, I'm careful, so don't worry."

She ran her hand through her hair frantically. "I can't help it, Mason. You know I worry about you when you're out there."

He sighed. "I know, babe, but I promise—this is the last assignment."

Cherise closed her eyes and said a short prayer. "I hope so. I miss you guys."

"Well, we miss you, too," he admitted. "What are your plans for tomorrow?"

"I have a few seminars, my speech, and then I'm flying home. Are you still picking me up?"

"Yes, dear, I'm picking you up. Call me tomorrow after your speech, and if I don't get a chance to talk to you later, I love you and have a safe flight."

"Definitely, and tell Momma and Daddy I said hello."

"I will. Now hold on so I can get the kids."

Mason called the kids to the telephone so they could talk to Cherise. They talked for several minutes and then she told them she loved them and asked for them to put Mason back on the line.

"I'm here, Cherise."

"I'm not going to hold you any longer. I love you."

"I love you, too. I'll give your mom a kiss for you."

"Thanks. I'll talk to you later, Mason."

Mason hung up the telephone and sighed. It was becoming harder for him to hide the unpleasantness of his job from Cherise. And if she ever found out the details of his current assignment, she would never forgive him.

Chapter Six

Cherise met Vincent in the hotel for dinner. As usual, he looked very sexy. Tonight she had chosen to wear a pair of gray pants and a teal blouse. Her makeup seemed to make her skin and eyes glow. They chose a table out on the veranda so they could enjoy the scenery and the ocean breeze.

Vincent raised a spoonful of fruit to his mouth.

"How old did you say Mase was now?"

"He's almost fourteen, but he looks like he's much older," she answered proudly.

"It seems like only yesterday that he was three or four years old."

"Tell me about it."

Vincent stared at Cherise and tried to keep his body under control. "I'm sure the girls are all over him."

Cherise rolled her eyes and shook her head. "Yes, they are, and it's driving us crazy. Mason had a talk with him, so hopefully he won't end up a teenage father."

Vincent sipped his wine and set it back down on the table just as the waiter arrived with their entrees. Cherise couldn't wait to taste her smoked salmon over rice with steamed vegetables. Vincent's Cornish hen, mashed potatoes, and salad looked just as appealing.

"I'm sure he'll listen to his dad. Mase is a smart kid."

Picking up a warm roll, Cherise reached for the butter and began to question him. "So, Vincent, is there anyone special in your life?"

He smiled, showing her his dimples. "No one special yet. Maybe one day, though."

Cherise eyed him carefully. "Vincent, all work and no play will make you dull."

He looked up at her with his eyes gleaming, and leaned forward. "Cherise, you know for a fact that I'm anything but boring."

Cherise blushed and lowered her eyes. His comment had an intimate tone to it, and he was right. He was the king of excitement. She took a sip of her wine and looked off into the distance in silence.

"Are you okay, C. J.?"

"I'm fine. It's just this heat."

She wiped moisture from her brow and shook her blouse to try to get some cool air to her body. The weather was pleasant, but Vincent was causing her temperature to rise a few degrees.

"If you like, I could rub some ice over your neck to help you cool off."

Cherise squirmed in her seat and picked up her fork in embarrassment. "That won't be necessary, Vincent. I'll manage."

Vincent smiled and continued to eat his meal. He knew he had struck a nerve with Cherise, and he was enjoying every minute of it.

"Have you been back to Atlanta since you skipped town?"

"A few times," he answered. "I never stayed more than a day, though."

She frowned. "You could've found time to come by the house."

His thick lashes blinked slowly. "If you must know, C. J., I thought about it a couple of times, but I decided it was best if I didn't."

"Mason talks about you all the time."

Vincent scooted his salad around on his plate. "What does he say?"

"He just doesn't understand why you never visit us."

With raised eyebrows, he studied her. "Really?"

She took a bite of her food and nodded. "I told him you probably got arrogant after your promotion, thought you were better than everyone else, and didn't have time to visit us little people."

He let out a loud baritone laugh. "Are you serious?"

"What do you think, Vincent?"

He saw the fire in her eyes when she spoke.

"I thought you never wanted to see me again," he reminded her.

"That wasn't my intention. He's your brother, Vincent!"

He wiped his mouth with the napkin. "Yeah, and I slept with his wife every chance I could, didn't I?"

Cherise felt a migraine coming on. She rubbed her temples in despair because it wasn't a subject she wanted to discuss.

"Have you talked to him today?"

"Of course I did," she replied, aggravated.

He folded his arms and leaned back in his seat. "Did you tell him I was here?"

"I couldn't do it," she whispered, shaking her head.

"Why not?"

"I wasn't sure how he would react. He would start asking me a lot of questions about you and would want to talk to you. I wasn't ready for all of that."

"You do know if he finds out he'll wonder why you hid it from him," he warned her. "It will make us look suspicious."

"He won't find out," she snapped at him before drinking the rest of her wine. "I'm not going to tell him, and neither are you."

"Are you sure about that?"

"Yes, I'm sure because if you do I will hunt you down and beat you senseless."

He laughed. "Be careful, C. J., I might like that."

"You're so silly, Vincent," she said with a huge smile. "I am serious, though."

"I'm glad you still approve of me," he said. "Damn, C. J.! I can't believe you can still arouse me by just smiling."

Her body shivered, then she quickly changed the subject.

"This food is delicious, isn't it?"

With the same admiration, he flirted openly with her. "Yes, you are."

"Vincent," she pleaded with him. "Please stop."

He put his hands up in surrender and smiled. "You can't hate a guy for trying, and just so you know, I'm coming to hear you speak tomorrow. Are you nervous?"

She tilted her head with surprise. "I wasn't, but I am now, thanks to you."

"I'm sorry. I thought you were a pro at this by now," he said.

"To tell you the truth, I really don't care for standing up in front of a lot of people, but I manage."

He motioned for the waitress.

"I guess I'll see for myself tomorrow, huh? Do you want some dessert?"

"No, do you?"

"I'm looking at what I want for dessert," he whispered. "God! I love the way you taste."

"If you don't stop talking like that, I'm going to get up and walk out of here," she demanded as she shifted in her seat.

"I can't help it, C. J.," he revealed as he licked his lips seductively. "You are a hell of a woman."

"I'm sure you say that to all your women."

He laughed. "I don't have women, C. J., and if I did, they couldn't hold a candle to you."

She sat there and stared at him in amazement. The waitress walked over and put the check down on the table. They both reached for it at the same time, but Vincent snatched it out of her hand.

"Don't even think about it, C. J.! You know I'm not going to let you pay!"

"I'm not going to argue with you."

Vincent paid the check and stood. "Let's get out of here."

Cherise stood and pulled her purse onto her shoulder. They walked out into the hotel lobby together. "Are you going to the mixer they're having for us tonight?"

She shyly looked down at her feet and fidgeted. "I really need to go work on my speech."

"Bull! You and I both know you already have it fine-tuned."

"No, seriously. I need to work on my speech. Are you going?"

"I might check it out for a minute, but it would be more fun if you're there."

They walked toward the elevator and got on together.

"I really need to work on my speech, Vincent, but if I decide to go down there it'll only be for a moment."

He smiled down at her. "Well, it's too beautiful down here to stay in your room all night."

"I know, Vincent, and I want to thank you for dinner," she answered.

"You're welcome," he replied as the doors to the elevator closed.

They walked down the hallway in silence. When they reached her door, Cherise turned to him and he immediately pulled her into his arms and hugged her tightly.

"It's so good seeing you again, C. J. I'm sorry I stayed away so long."

She backed out of his embrace and straightened her blouse.

"Same here. Good night, Vincent. I'll see you tomorrow if I don't see you later—so don't get into any trouble tonight."

"I'm not going to make any promises," he responded before brushing his lips lightly against hers.

She watched him as he strolled down the hallway to the elevator. Once inside, Cherise breathed a sigh of relief because she was finally away from Vincent. She crossed to the bed, sat down, and kicked off her shoes. She did want to work on her speech a little longer, so she opened her notebook and began the tedious task of practicing. Maybe going to the mixer was not a bad idea after all. A lot of her colleagues would be there, and it wouldn't hurt to spend a little time with them before turning in for the night.

Chapter Seven

M ason pulled into the abandoned warehouse and waited. He was using the alias Mirage, and he hoped his nemesis wouldn't be late. He hated this part of town. Unfortunately, it was infested with the drug activity he was trying to stop. As he sat there listening to Tupac, he decided to do a radio check with his unit.

"Holler if you hear me, players."

Headlights flickered in the distance to let him know they had their eyes and ears on him. He also knew there were others close by in case things went bad. Ten minutes passed before he noticed the headlights of a Suburban truck approaching the location. He let out a breath of relief as well as his signature phrase.

"Let's get this party started."

He exited his vehicle, stood in a defensive stance, and waited. He knew they would try to search his body for wires, so his unit was using a long-range listening device to record the conversation. As the truck came to a stop next to his car, he noticed five silhouettes sitting inside. The doors came open and out stepped T-bone, the leader of one of the local gangs. Beside him was his right-hand man, Menace. In the backseat were Kilo and Tiny, and last was Vada. Vada was T-bone's sister and Mason's main contact in getting to T-bone. He had to play his cards right to get close to her, but being charming with women was one quality Mason had, so it wasn't hard to get Vada to fall for him. In the process, Mason had to make sure he kept his personal life and feelings out of the situation. He knew this assignment was going to be tough on him emotionally, because it involved a woman and might lead to him cheating on Cherise, again.

"Hey, babe, you're looking fine as ever."

He looked her up and down, appreciating the tight jeans covering her round derriere. The blouse she wore showed off her voluptuous breasts and smooth skin. He held her close to his side, occasionally caressing her hips, playing the part of the boyfriend like an expert. Vada smiled and gave Mason a sultry kiss on the lips.

T-bone folded his arms arrogantly. "So this is the dude you've been going on and on about, Vada?"

"Yes, and he's smarter than any of these knuckleheads. Mirage, this is my brother, T-bone. T-bone, this is my boo, Mirage."

Mason stepped forward and offered his hand. T-bone stared at it for a moment before reluctantly taking Mason's hand. T-bone nodded at Menace, who walked over and instructed Mason to put his hands on his head.

"Put your hands up and turn around."

Vada frowned and started yelling. "Menace! What the hell are you doing? T-bone, you need to get your boy!"

"Shut up, Vada! My man is doing his job!"

T-bone watched as Menace frisked Mason.

"What kind of name is Mirage?" T-bone asked.

Gritting his teeth, Mason looked over at T-bone with fire in his eyes. "I guess it's the same kind of name as T-bone."

Menace continued to frisk Mason's legs and found a nine-millimeter in an ankle holster. Menace sat the gun on top of the truck and checked Mason's other leg. T-bone looked over at the gun and then back at Mason.

"That's a nice piece of steel, Mirage. Do you always come to meetings strapped?" Aggravated from being frisked, Mason finally had had enough. He pushed Menace away from him. "I earned it! Now, are we here to play name games or do business?"

Menace looked at T-bone and nodded. "He's clean."

Vada was clearly upset that T-bone had disrespected her man, but she knew she couldn't fuss too much about it. Mason looked at T-bone and squinted at him. "I don't have time to waste out here with you fools! Why did you want to see me?"

T-bone chuckled. "Vada said I should hire you because you know the business, you're connected, and you could help me make my organization more profitable. If that's the case, you might be what I'm looking for. I'm anxious to expand and I don't have a lot of time to spare."

Mason looked at Vada curiously, and then walked closer to T-bone.

"Oh…really? Well, Vada's not my agent or publicist, and for the record. I decide who I do business with. Not Vada, and definitely not you. If I decide to work with you, I do all the negotiations and I want a fifty-fifty cut in the profits."

T-bone realized right away that Mason wasn't a man to let a woman lead him around by the nose or take any crap from anyone. With his chin up in the air, T-bone picked Mason's gun up off the hood of the truck, and held it out to him.

"I hear you, Mirage. I'm glad we had this little conversation. I'll be in touch."

Mason frowned. "Yeah, whatever, and just for the record, my offer is not negotiable."

Mason put his gun back into his ankle holster and pulled his pants leg down. T-bone and his crew climbed back inside the huge truck and closed their doors. T-bone leaned out the window.

"I hope you're worth it, Mirage."

Vada snuggled up to Mason like a feline and smiled with appreciation. "Oh, don't worry, T-bone, he is. I can personally vouch for that."

T-bone stared at the pair from inside the vehicle. "Vada, are you coming or what?"

She wrapped her arms around Mason's waist and kissed his neck. "Am I hanging with you tonight, baby?"

He opened his car door for her and looked over his shoulder at T-bone. "Vada's with me, so ya'll can bounce."

T-bone nodded. "Take care of my sister, man."

Mason nodded back to him without speaking. Once T-bone and his crew drove off, Mason climbed into the car next to her. She ran her hand up his thigh, caressing him.

"Don't pay my brother any attention. He's just cautious, but you can't blame him. He doesn't let outsiders in that often."

Mason started his vehicle and pulled off.

"Why? It's hard for an organization to grow without expanding."

She turned to him. "Without telling you all his business, I can say he is a major player around here. He controls most of the streets."

Mason laughed. "So what you're saying is he's a kingpin or something?"

Vada leaned over and stuck her tongue into his ear. Mason became aroused and tried his best to maintain control of his vehicle.

"Let's just say my brother is not one you would want to cross," she whispered. "He can be ruthless at times."

"I see," Mason said.

"So what do you think? I could tell T-bone was impressed with you. You stood up to him and you weren't nervous at all. Most people that meet him for the first time can't even talk because they're so scared. So are you going to join up? If you do, you'll make a lot of money."

Stopping at a traffic light, he turned and looked at her. "What makes you think I need money?"

She laughed out loud and fingered her hair. "Everybody needs money, Mirage."

"No, you and all the other women on this earth need money to support your shoe fetish."

They laughed together as they hit the expressway. Mason knew playing this type of character could threaten his marriage again. Vada was putting some serious pressure on him to have sex with her, even though they'd only known each other for a hot minute. He hated to be in this position, but he knew if he had to, he would. Getting a major player like T-bone off the street was worth it. He just prayed God—and Cherise—would forgive him of his sins in the name of justice.

They arrived at the condo his unit had set up for Mason thirty minutes later. Mason pulled into the driveway and put the car in park. Vada quickly unbuckled her seat belt.

"Is this your place?"

"Something like that," he said, smiling. "Are you hungry?"

"Now that you mention it, I am a little hungry. Don't tell me you cooked?"

He looked at his watch. "I know my way around the kitchen a little bit."

They walked up to the front door together and he unlocked it, letting her go in ahead of him. He flipped on the light and watched as she inspected everything.

"This is nice, Mirage. You have some pretty good taste."

He set his keys down on the table and slid his hands inside his pockets.

"I appreciate the finer things in life."

"I'm impressed," she responded as she walked over to him. "Really impressed."

She cupped his face and pressed her lips against his. Her perfume caressed his nostrils and the heat from her body once again aroused him. Her denim jeans looked like they were painted onto her shapely body. The red silk blouse she wore accented her melon-shaped breasts and small waist. Vada slid her hand down between their bodies so she could touch him. Her intimate touch caused him to let out a soft moan.

He looked into her eyes. "Are you ready to find out what I cooked for dinner?"

"As long as I can be your dessert," she said flirtatiously.

He laughed and stepped away from her. "We'll just have to see, won't we?"

"Sounds good to me."

Mason took her by the hand. "Come on into the kitchen. I guarantee you'll love what I cooked up."

"I'm sure I will," she said as she walked arm in arm with him into the kitchen.

Mason's commanding officer, Domino, selected Vada as the logical choice to get inside T-bone's organization. Surveillance allowed the Task Force to pinpoint Vada's movements around Regal, Georgia, as well as those of her brother for a long time before Mason was allowed to make his move. They had to find a way for him to get close to Vada and get her to trust him. This, in turn, would hopefully get him inside T-bone's organization. They found out that Vada had expensive taste in clothes and was a shopaholic. It wasn't uncommon for her to drop a grand a week on clothes, shoes, and jewelry. They also learned that she was T-bone's bookkeeper, so getting to any files she possessed would be pertinent.

Mason made contact with Vada during one of her shopping sprees. He discreetly observed her as she picked up a pair of shoes two or three times. After trying them on, she stood in the mirror for several minutes, posing in different positions. She already had several bags, and when she saw the price of the shoes, she sighed. After putting the shoes back on the shelf, she moved on to the food court to get a bite to eat.

Mason saw his opportunity and moved in.

"Excuse me. I couldn't help but notice you were eating alone. Do you mind if I join you?" he asked politely.

Vada looked up from her Chinese food into the most handsome eyes she'd seen in a long time. She took her foot and scooted the chair across from her outward so he could sit down.

"Sure. It's a free country."

"Thank you," Mason said as he sat across from her.

Vada looked down at his food curiously. "What are you eating?"

He smiled. "A gyro. It's Greek cuisine."

"Oh I see."

"What's your name?" Mason took a bite of his gyro.

"Excuse me?" she asked defensively.

"What's your name? There's no reason to get all defensive when you've already let me share a table with you."

She laughed. "I guess you have me on that. My name is Vada. What's yours?"

He looked around at the people mingling in the food court and then took a sip of soda. "Mirage," he revealed.

"Mirage?"

He locked eyes with her again. "Yes, Mirage. Do you have a problem with it?"

"No, it's cool," she answered.

"You sure do have a lot of bags," he pointed out. "Are you shopping for your man or your kids?"

She pointed her fork at him defensively. "Who said I had a man and kids?"

He looked at her with a sly grin. "I'm just asking."

She took another bite of her shrimp fried rice.

"You sure are nosy. Where's your wife and six kids?"

He laughed so hard the people at the table next to them looked over. Mason leaned forward and whispered to her, "I don't have a wife and kids, at least not yet."

"Good for you," she answered sarcastically.

"Look, I'm just trying to get to know you, sweetheart. Why are you being so mean?"

"I'm not being mean, and who said I want you to get to know me?"

"You will. That I guarantee."

For the next few minutes they ate in silence. Mason noticed Vada sneaking glances at him. He had made sure he was dressed neatly in jeans, a white shirt, and a black leather jacket.

Vada had already picked up on the Hugo Boss cologne he was wearing. It was her favorite, and it aroused her, but she didn't want him to know it.

Mason finished off his gyro and swallowed down the rest of his soda. He wiped his mouth and stood.

"Well, it was nice meeting you, Vada, and thanks for letting me eat lunch with you."

She smiled and stood up also. "No harm done, Mirage," she announced, blushing slightly.

"Good," Mason said as he reached for her tray to dump her plate into the trash. When he returned, he picked up his shopping bags. "Well, I guess I'll let you get on your way. But before I go, here's a little token of my appreciation for letting me eat lunch with you."

Vada looked at him in confusion as he handed her the bag. She recognized the logo immediately. Taking it out of his hand, she asked, "What is this?"

He winked as he backed away from her.

"It's just a little something I picked up just for you. Good-bye, Vada, and it was so nice to meet you."

"Good-bye, Mirage."

She watched him as he walked out of the food court. Vada sat down and opened the bag. Inside was the pair of shoes she had tried on earlier, but didn't purchase. She smiled and quickly closed the bag. She wanted to find Mirage, thank him for the shoes and apologize for being so unkind. Mirage was definitely mysterious. She didn't want to admit her heart thumped in her chest the moment he spoke to her. Vada walked as fast as she could out into the mall to look for him. She eventually found him, and they had been hot and heavy ever since.

But their love affair was all a lie, at least for Mason. He had to be very careful, because if anyone from his real life ever saw him with Vada, it could be disastrous.

Chapter Eight

C herise had dozed off more than once while she was still going over her speech. She looked at her watch, set her notebook aside, and climbed off the bed. After a long yawn she decided to throw on some clothes and go down to the mixer after all. Maybe Vincent was right and she really did need to have a little fun. Her speech was fine-tuned; she couldn't perfect it any more than it already was.

The conference room was decorated with colorful balloons and party favors. Cherise was dressed comfortably in a navy pantsuit with a powder-blue blouse. The room was full and almost immediately someone she'd met at a conference in Los Angeles earlier in the year ran over to greet her.

"Cherise, it's great seeing you again! You look great!"

"Hello, Charles, it's good seeing you, too."

He shook Cherise's hand and tried his best to talk over the loud music. "I have an empty seat at my table so follow me. There are some people I want you to meet."

She followed him through the crowd until they came to a table with three other people. Charles pulled Cherise's chair out for her and then introduced her to the two men and the woman already seated there. Cherise shook their hands and greeted them. Charles asked her what she would like to drink and immediately hurried off across the room to get her a glass of wine. While he was gone Cherise found out the woman worked in the medical examiner's office in Baltimore; the gentleman sitting next to her was a cold case file detective from Chicago. The other gentleman was a fingerprint analyst from Washington, D.C.

Charles made his way back over to the table with two drinks in his hands. After sitting down, he made sure everyone was comfortable before asking Cherise to dance. She accepted. After dancing to a couple of songs they returned to the table to catch their breath.

"That was fun, Charles. I'm glad I changed my mind and decided to come down here."

He took a sip of his drink and winked at her. "I'm glad you came, too."

The fingerprint analyst looked at the other young woman and asked her if she would like to dance as well. Soon they were out on the dance floor enjoying each other's company. As Cherise sipped on her wine, she occasionally looked around to see if she could spot Vincent somewhere in the crowd. Unfortunately she didn't.

Unbeknownst to Cherise, Vincent was across the room and he was keeping a close eye on her and her companions. She seemed to be having fun with her friends, so he decided not to interfere. Instead, he mingled with some police detectives he'd met in the hotel bar before coming to the mixer.

Cherise continued to have a wonderful time at the mixer. As she sat there talking to Charles and the others, she nibbled on chilled shrimp, stuffed mushrooms, and other delicious hors d'oeuvres and was finishing off her third glass of wine. She closed her eyes briefly and put her hand up to her chest, because her heart felt like it was racing. Charles looked at her curiously.

"Are you okay, Cherise?"

"I don't know. I feel a little weird." Her body was hot and tingling.

Charles stood and helped Cherise out of her chair. "Maybe some fresh air will help you. Let's get out of here." He took Cherise by the arm and led her across the room. When they got to the door, Vincent stepped out of the shadows and blocked their path.

"What's going on here? C. J., are you okay?"

Vincent pulled Cherise out of Charles's clutches and tilted her chin upward so he could look into her eyes. Cherise appeared to be intoxicated and slightly disoriented.

"Vincent, I didn't know you was here. I don't feel so well."

Vincent frowned at Charles. "What happened to her?"

Charles immediately began to stutter. "I—I don't know. She was fine one minute, the next she said she didn't feel well. I was just helping her to her room. Who are you, if you don't mind me asking?"

Vincent gave Charles a deadly glare. "I'm her brother-in-law. How much did she drink?"

Charles took a step back and shoved his hands inside his pockets. "She only had about three glasses of wine and a few items off the buffet table. Cherise, is this man really your brother-in-law?"

Cherise wrapped her arms around Vincent's waist and laid her head against his chest as she spoke softly to Charles. "Yes, he's my brother-in-law."

Vincent stared at the man suspiciously. "I'll take care of Cherise from here. What's your name and room number in case I have more questions for you?"

"Charles, uh, Charles Ridley. I'm in room 726."

Vincent continued to stare at Charles. He didn't know what this man had up his sleeve, but he wasn't about to let Cherise go off with a strange man in her condition.

"I'll definitely be in touch with you, Charles Ridley."

Vincent took Cherise by the arm and slowly led her over to the elevator. By the time they got inside she was clinging to him. He opened her purse and pulled out her room key.

"I feel terrible, Vincent."

He put his arm around her waist and stroked her cheek lovingly. "I know you do. You just drank a little too much. Don't worry, I'll take care of you, C. J."

By the time the elevator doors opened, Cherise had basically passed out. Vincent had to carry her down the hallway to her room. He laid her on the bed and removed his jacket, hanging it on the back of the chair. He rolled up his sleeves so he could attend to Cherise. It was clear that she had been drinking, but three glasses of wine shouldn't have made her pass out. He removed her shoes, slacks, and blouse before pulling the comforter back so he could tuck her in. Once she was securely in bed he took a cool cloth and gently placed it on her forehead. Concerned, he pulled the chair over next to the bed and watched over her as she slept. Minutes later, he also dozed off into a deep sleep.

Vincent didn't know when he fell asleep, but he woke up to a familiar and heavenly sensation. Once his vision cleared he looked down and found Cherise on her knees in front of him, pleasuring him orally. Startled, he quickly sat up and yelled at her.

"What are you doing?"

She stopped what she was doing, looked up at him and smiled mischievously. Vincent found it hard to resist the waves of passion that were consuming his body. Cherise was completely naked and she straddled his lap and feverishly started giving him a lap dance. Vincent was in a state of shock. He gritted his teeth and tried to pull away from Cherise.

"C. J., what's going on with you?"

She leaned down close to his ear and whispered, "I know you want me, Vincent. Come on, baby, make me feel good."

She was right about one thing; he did want her, but he never thought anything like this would ever happen between them again. Cherise was very aggressive and her moans were loud and constant as she gyrated her body over him. Vincent was trying to understand what had come over Cherise but his morals was being drowned out by the things she was doing to him.

He brushed his lips gently against hers. She was out of control and it turned Vincent on even more. This was the Cherise he knew and remembered.

"Come on, Vincent! Love me!" she yelled.

Kissing her more feverishly, he caressed her soft skin as he stood and carried her over to the bed. Cherise shivered as his large hands covered her breasts. Right before his eyes, C. J. melted in his hand as he stroked her sensitive area. They locked gazes as his fingers continued to work her like magic. Cherise moaned and wiggled beneath him. He felt her body respond to him like clockwork. He stopped touching her and stared directly into her eyes. Chills ran all over her body as she squirmed and begged him to make love to her.

"C. J., you're driving me crazy, so crazy that I can't think straight."

Everything Vincent said was true. He was precise and thorough in everything he did. Giving her what she wanted was no different than in the past as he held her hips securely. Cherise's entire body trembled as he towered over her and buried his face against her warm neck. He kissed her quivering lips and whispered her name. Vincent noticed the changes in her breathing as he dipped his head and ran his tongue over her firm breasts. Cherise's body arched upward against him as he nibbled on her voluptuous body. Skin to skin, he positioned himself above her, covering her body with his. He wanted Cherise to remember just how well their bodies were in sync with each other. She held onto his strong frame for dear life because the force of his body moving against hers caused her to become even more excited. He whispered proclamations of love continuously as he loved her. Cherise's body shivered and she moaned his name over and over again. Electricity shot through her body, causing her to scream. Vincent followed as his body stiffened and then relaxed.

"Just like old times, huh? You make me feel so damn good. I don't think I'll ever get enough of you."

Still inside her, he hit her spot once again, and Cherise moaned. He smiled, knowing he was giving her just as much pleasure as she was giving him.

"I want more, baby. Please, give me more."

Vincent couldn't believe his ears. Earlier in the day, Cherise was adamant that her marriage and love for Mason were sound. What they were doing now was telling him a different story. Suddenly, she started trembling uncontrollably. Vincent moved away from her in a panic.

"C. J., what's going on? Are you okay?"

Her teeth were chattering and her body continued to tremble violently. Vincent studied her and noticed the glazed look in her eyes. Then, as if a light bulb went off, it hit him. He jumped up off the bed.

"Shit! That son of a bitch!"

Cherise had been drugged! Her behavior indicated it could be the powerful drug, Ecstasy. He'd read about it and attended seminars on it but had never seen it in action. She was sweating profusely and was out of breath. Vincent frantically grabbed his cell phone and called a friend, a physician back in Texas, for advice. He wanted to take her to the hospital, but he didn't want Cherise to have to answer a lot of embarrassing questions—especially after he'd just had sex with her. An incident like this wouldn't be good for either of them.

Vincent nervously sat on the side of the bed with his head bowed and listened as his friend gave him instructions on how to treat Cherise's condition. Snapping the cell closed, he quickly climbed back into the bed and pulled

Cherise into his arms as instructed. He needed to use his body heat to get her temperature under control and keep her hydrated. The drug was raging through her bloodstream and it would be at least four hours before it was out of her system. Vincent just prayed Cherise would sleep the rest of night and be back to herself by morning.

Cherise woke up with a excruciating headache. Vincent heard her moan just as he stepped out of the bathroom.

"Hey, C. J., how are you feeling?"

She could barely open her eyes. "What are you doing here? What time is it?"

Vincent walked over to her and sat down on the side of the bed. He lowered his head with guilt and tried his best to explain to her what happened.

"C. J., someone drugged you at the mixer."

"What? Drugged me? Why?"

Vincent walked over to the window and rubbed the back of his tense neck. "I'm not sure, but I think that guy Charles might've put Ecstasy in your drinks."

"Ecstasy! That stuff makes you crazy! No wonder my head feels like someone's hitting it with a sledgehammer! I can't believe Charles would do something like that to me! Are you sure?"

Vincent was very sympathetic as he answered.

"The reason I think it was him is because he was the one trying to help you out of the room. Don't you remember that?"

"I don't remember much of last night at all, but I'm glad you were there. I'm going to call Charles and give him a piece of my mind!"

He sat down in the chair and fumbled with the buttons on his shirt. "I can't prove it was him, but I'm pretty sure it was. Don't call him, C. J. I'll take care of Charles Ridley."

Cherise sighed, sat up in bed and froze. "Vincent, where are my clothes?"

He walked over to the closet, pulled her robe off the hanger, and handed it to her before sitting back down.

"C. J., I need to talk to you about something."

She slid into her robe and tied the belt. When she tried to stand, her legs were weak. Vincent jumped up out of the chair and steadied her. "Let me help you to the bathroom."

Cherise smiled as she allowed Vincent to assist her. "I think I can make it from here."

Vincent stepped back and proceeded to pour Cherise a cup of the coffee he'd made before she woke up. Cherise opened the bathroom door, happily accepting the cup, quickly drinking it.

"Vincent, I can't believe I let something like this happen to me. I feel terrible. I don't know if I'm going to be able to give my speech today," she said as he helped her back to the bed. As he watched Cherise sip her coffee, he decided to be truthful with her.

"C. J., there's something I need to tell you. Something happened between us last night."

She looked up at him with concern. "What do you mean?"

He cleared his throat and took a sip of his coffee. "You were out of control last night and when I say out of control, I mean it. Before I realized what was really going on with you, it was too late."

Cherise sat her cup on the nightstand. "I don't understand, Vincent. What are you trying to tell me?"

Cherise could see Vincent clearly struggling with his words.

"C. J., you seduced me in a way I've never been seduced in my life, and I honestly thought it was real."

"I seduced you? What did I do?"

Vincent took her hand into his and caressed it.

"Sweetheart, I had dozed off and you woke me up on your knees. You did everything and then some. It wasn't until after we made love the second time that I realized something was really wrong. You scared the hell out of me. That's when I called a friend in Texas, a doctor to get help. I was afraid to take you to the hospital because they probably would've done a rape kit on you and possibly contacted Mason. I didn't want to put you through that."

Cherise sat there stunned. She knew that being oversexed was one of the drug's possible side effects. She swallowed hard before speaking.

"I don't remember any of it, Vincent."

He kissed her forehead and hugged her lovingly.

"I know you don't. I guess it was too good to be true to think that you actually wanted me like that again. I love you but I would never take advantage of you."

She leaned against his shoulder and closed her eyes.

"I know you wouldn't, Vincent. Look, don't beat yourself up about what happened between us. You saved me and that's what important. You're special to me and I'll always love you, but I can't go back to that life again, okay?"

He looked into her beautiful eyes. He loved her and would've never forgiven himself if he hadn't been able to save her from the likes of Charles Ridley.

"I love you, too, C. J., but what happened last night brought everything back for me."

She cupped his face and kissed his cheek. "Vincent, I'll always cherish you, but please, let the past stay in the past. I'm going to have to try and get through my speech some kind of way and I'm going to need your support."

Vincent stood and grabbed his jacket. He was in love with her; he never was able to dismiss their relationship as easily as she could.

"It's about eight o'clock, C. J. I'll get out of your way so you can get yourself together. I'm sorry about everything. Make sure you call me if you need anything."

"I will."

Vincent walked over to the door and let himself out. Before going to his room, he made his way to room 726 to pay Charles Ridley a visit.

Charles Ridley was just about to go to breakfast when he heard a knock on his door. He opened it and before he could utter a word, Vincent burst through and quickly grabbed him by the throat. He slammed the door shut and pinned Charles against the wall.

"I should break your goddamn neck for drugging my sister-in-law! You don't know who the hell you messed with when you chose her. If anything had happened to her, your family would be making your funeral arrangements as we speak, you son of a bitch!"

Charles struggled for air as Vincent tightened his grip on his throat.

"If I see you anywhere near Cherise again, I will kill you. Do you understand where I'm coming from?"

Charles gave somewhat of a nod before Vincent released his grip. He fell to the floor, gasping and coughing, as Vincent made his way out of the room.

About three hours later, Vincent sat in the audience mesmerized by Cherise's presentation. She wasn't showing any adverse effects from the drug, and her gift as a crime scene investigator showed clearly in her speech. She was informative and the slide presentation she used to accompany her speech was spectacular. Vincent stared at her as she seemed to glide across the stage. Just the sight of her caused his body to harden. She was the type of woman he would kill to have by his side. What was it about Cherise that got his blood boiling any time he was near her? It was everything. While the night they shared might not have been real, it did stir up a lot of emotions for him. Maybe it was time for him to visit his dear brother after all, because it would give him an opportunity to finally put to rest the one question that had plagued him for years.

Chapter Nine

Cherise was thankful the conference was over and she was on her way home. Before leaving, she thanked Vincent again for saving her and wished him a safe trip home. Vincent wished her a safe trip as well and gave her a tender kiss before they went their separate ways.

As the plane landed and taxied over to the terminal, Cherise whispered a short prayer and a sigh of relief. She was anxious to see her family and was glad to be home. Once the plane came to a complete stop, she quickly jumped up out of her seat and gathered her bag out of the overhead compartment. She was glowing and looked fabulous in her gray suit. The skirt displayed her shapely legs and accentuated her girlish figure. She couldn't wait to see Mason.

Her heart thumped hard in her chest and a huge smile graced her face as soon as she spotted him. He was a sight for sore eyes and she practically jumped into his arms, kissing him deeply. She was breathless when she finally came up for air.

"Did you miss me, Detective McKenzie?"

He held onto her securely as he hugged her waist tightly.

"You bet I did! I'm so glad you're home, and I want you to know we have the house to ourselves tonight. I plan to pamper you beyond your wildest dreams. Are you up for it?"

She caressed his face and noticed he was getting a five o'clock shadow. "Are you sure you don't have to work tonight?"

He smiled and hugged her again.

"I'm sort of on call, but I'm not expecting anything, so I'm all yours."

Mason didn't like talking about the cases he was working on, especially this one because it involved a woman, so he changed the subject as they walked off arm in arm.

"So how did you do on your presentation?"

"Oh, it was okay. The weather was nice and the food was excellent."

"That's good," he answered right before he spotted Cherise's suitcase circling the turnstile. He grabbed her luggage and her carry-on bag.

"Is that it?"

She straightened his collar and nodded.

"Good, then let's get out of here."

Holding his hand, they walked out of the airport together.

The next morning, Cherise couldn't help but sleep in—because she was exhausted, not only from her trip, but also from Mason properly welcoming her home. Mason had left earlier to pick the kids up from her parents' house. As she lay there she couldn't help but think about what could've happened to her in Florida and what did happen. She realized one thing; a part of her heart would always belong to Vincent and that he still loved her very much.

A few miles away Mason picked up the kids from his in-laws' house. Grocery shopping was next. It was a perfect day to throw some food on the grill and hopefully get a repeat performance with Cherise tonight. His interlude with her had been very romantic and more intense than usual. If he didn't know any better, he would think something was wrong, but things had been going perfect for a long time now. Being able to make love to her without any interruptions or distractions was like striking gold, especially since both of them had been so busy lately with their jobs.

"Where's Mommy?" Janelle asked as they pulled into the garage.

"She's asleep, so when we go into the house, I don't want you two to make a lot of noise. Okay?"

Mase looked at Janelle and they nodded.

"I can't hear nods."

"Okay, Daddy," the pair replied in unison.

Mason climbed out of the car first, grabbed two bags out of the trunk, and handed them to Mase.

"Be careful with those." Mase usually carried the bags loosely.

"I got it, Daddy."

Mason watched his son carry the bags into the house with ease. He was growing up.

Turning to make sure Janelle had unbuckled her seat belt, he called out to her. "Baby girl, grab my cell phone."

"Okay, Daddy."

Janelle climbed over the seat and retrieved Mason's cell phone before getting out of the car. Mason pulled the rest of the bags out of the truck and entered the kitchen, with Janelle following close behind. Once inside, he noticed Mase had his head stuck inside the refrigerator.

"Mase, put the food away while I start the grill. Janelle, go check on your mom, but if she's asleep, don't wake her."

Mase closed the refrigerator and did as he was told. Janelle grabbed an apple off the table and ran from the room singing. She couldn't wait to see her momma and tell her everything they did while she was away in Florida.

Upstairs, Janelle took a bite of her apple and slowly pushed open her parents' bedroom door. Cherise's back was to her so she tiptoed around to the other side of the bed to face her. Careful not to wake her, Janelle leaned down and kissed her on the cheek. Cherise stirred, and then slowly opened her eyes to a beautiful and familiar smile.

"Hi, Momma. I'm so glad you're home. I missed you."

They hugged each other tightly. Cherise pulled her daughter up on the bed next to her and kissed her forehead.

"I missed you, too, Janelle. Where are your dad and brother?"

Leaning against her, Janelle took another bite of the apple. "Daddy told me to come check on you, but not to wake you. I'm sorry I woke you up, Momma. Don't tell Daddy. Okay?"

Cherise held Janelle close. She realized her daughter was growing up very fast, and wouldn't be her baby much longer. Her legs were very long and she was getting too heavy to pick up for a hug.

"I'm glad you came to check on me, and I'm glad you woke me up."

Janelle looked at her curiously. "Momma, where are your clothes?"

Cherise had forgotten that she was nude, thanks to Mason. Having her daughter confused startled her. She tried to think of something quick to say. "Uh, Momma was a little hot so I took them off. Isn't it hot in here to you?"

Janelle climbed out of the bed and shook her shirt. "Just a little bit. I was sweating when we were at the store."

Cherise covered her body and wiggled her finger for Janelle to come closer. "Sweetheart, come here for a second. I want to tell you something in your ear."

Janelle giggled because her mother was acting playful, and she loved it when they played games. She hopped up on the bed and put her ear close to her mother's mouth.

"Go back downstairs and tell your daddy that I'm still hot, and I would appreciate it if he could help me cool off."

Not knowing she was a pawn in an adult-only game, Janelle hopped off the bed and skipped toward the hallway.

"Okay, Momma."

Cherise lay back on the bed laughing as Janelle hurried downstairs to deliver her seductive message.

Mason washed off the last of the chicken and seasoned it for the grill. Janelle walked in and sat down at the kitchen table. She finished off the last of her apple and threw the core in the trash. Mason looked over at her and frowned.

"Did you check on your momma?"

"Yes, Daddy. Momma's awake and told me to tell you that she's still hot and needed you to help her cool down."

Mason dropped the bowl he was holding for the salad. Thirteen-year-old Mase burst out laughing. Janelle was startled by the sound of the metal bowl hitting the tile floor. She curiously looked at Mason, then back over at Mase.

"What's so funny?"

Mason knelt down to pick up the bowl. Mase was laughing so hard he almost fell out of his chair. Mason gave his son an irritated glare. His son was getting too grown for his pants.

"Mase? Daddy? What's so funny?" Janelle repeated, upset that they wouldn't let her in on the joke. Mason walked over to the table, set the bowl in front of Mase, and gave him some instructions.

"Mase, stop acting asinine and watch the grill. Once you get the meat on the grill come back in here and wash off the lettuce so I can make the salad."

Mase rose from his chair, still laughing. "Way to go, Daddy!"

Frowning, Mason turned to his son and handed him the tray of chicken. "Mase! I asked you to put the food on the grill!"

"Aight, Dad. I'm going, I'm going."

Mase walked out on the patio, still laughing. Janelle stood up and put her hands on her hips.

"Will somebody tell me what's so funny?"

Mason walked out of the room without answering her. He could still hear his son laughing as he climbed the stairs. When he entered the bedroom, Cherise was lying in the bed. He walked over and sat on the side of the bed, causing her to open her eyes. He reached over and caressed her cheek.

"Janelle gave me your nasty little message, and Mase is downstairs laughing his head off."

Cherise sat up, allowing the sheet to fall away from her upper body. Mason's eyes immediately scanned her body. She pulled him closer and cupped his face.

"Mason, don't worry about Janelle. She didn't know what I was talking about, and as far as Mase is concerned, he's at the age where he's going to think that everything said or done in his presence relates to sex. The poor boy's hormones are raging."

Mason couldn't help but stare at her beautiful body, which in turn caused his lower body to come alive. He swallowed hard and tried to concentrate on their conversation.

"Well, he needs to calm his little adolescent ass down."

Cherise kissed Mason's lips gently. "He's a teenager, sweetheart. Now can I please have a real kiss?"

Mason kissed her the way she loved to be kissed. Cherise wrapped her arms around his neck and melted in his arms. Mason could feel his body heat up even more, but knew he had to put things on pause since he'd left Mase downstairs with the grill. He reluctantly pulled away from her and stood.

"I'll take care of your little heating problem a little later. Right now I need to get back downstairs because I left your son watching the food on the grill, and I would never live it down if the fire department had to come save our house."

Cherise climbed out of bed and giggled. "I'll be down to help out after I take a shower."

He turned on his heels and mischievously teased her.

"Would you like me to join you?" he teased her mischievously.

"I wish," she answered. "If the kids weren't home, it would be on."

He leaned against the door frame and stared at her from across the room. "Hold that thought. Once the kids are in bed, you and I have a date."

Cherise padded across the floor in all her glory. Before entering the bathroom, she turned to face him.

"After the kids go to bed tonight, I'm all yours."

"You have yourself a date. Now, let me get back downstairs before we're eating scorched chicken for dinner."

"I'll be right down."

Mason closed the door behind him as he left. Before Cherise could step into the shower, her cell phone rang. She clutched the towel around her body and ran over to answer it without looking at the ID.

"Hello?"

"Hey, C. J. Can you talk?"

The baritone voice belonged to Vincent, and it made her extremely nervous.

"Now is not a good time, Vincent."

He sighed. "Where's Mason?"

She looked toward the bedroom door and whispered. "He's downstairs, but he could walk in at any minute. What's up?"

He sounded wounded. "I need to talk to you."

Cherise paced the floor. "Call me at my office tomorrow. I can't talk to you right now."

He held the telephone in silence for a moment before answering.

"Okay, I'll call you tomorrow."

Cherise closed her eyes briefly and then hung up without saying good-bye. She reentered the bathroom and tried to keep her body from trembling. Her past was coming back to haunt her and she was going to have to let Vincent know he couldn't call her any time he felt like it. Especially since he'd been basically non-existent in their lives for several years.

The next morning, it was Mason who was physically unable to get out of bed. The pair had shared another night in each other's arms. It was about six a.m.

when Cherise slipped away to go to work. When she walked into her office, she went straight to the stack of cases on her desk. As she thumbed through the folders, the ringing of the telephone interrupted her thoughts.

"Dr. C. J. McKenzie."

"I hope you're not angry with me about calling you at home yesterday."

"I'm not angry, Vincent, but it was risky. "

He let out a breath. "I know and I'm sorry, C. J., but seeing you this weekend did something to me. I've tried to forget about you, but I can't. I also need to know about Janelle."

She leaned back in her leather chair, tossed the folder on top of her desk, and sighed. "Vincent, you're going to have to get a hold of yourself. What happened between us wasn't real as far as I'm concerned. Hell! I don't even remember it! As far as Janelle, leave that alone!"

Vincent cleared his throat and solemnly replied. "I'm trying, C. J., I really am, but it's not so easy. You said and did things to me that blew my mind. It was just like old times."

She was silent on her end of the telephone as she listened to him.

"I haven't been able to think about anything else but you and Janelle."

"Please don't do this to me, Vincent," she pleaded.

"It can't be helped, babe," he whispered. "I can still feel your hands and mouth all over me. Look, I'll try my best to be cool, but I can't make any promises."

Cherise hung up without saying good-bye. Her heart thumped in her chest—it was obvious Vincent was going to continue to press the issue on Janelle and that he was having a hard time dealing with what happened between them in Florida. She just wished she could remember what had happened. Rising from her desk, she headed down the hall to her lab.

Chapter Ten

Weeks later, Cherise was relieved that Vincent hadn't called anymore; however, she had received numerous e-mails from him. She was back in the swing of her routine, and so was Mason. His hours had gotten longer since he was working undercover again, and some nights he was unable to come home at all. She always worried about him and prayed God would protect him from all the bad people he was fighting against. She never knew the specifics of his cases, and she didn't want to know because it would cause her to worry even more. Having him home safe and sound was her main focus.

At lunch one day, she received a call regarding a homicide that had taken place across town. She gathered her belongings and got in her car to join her team at the scene. When she arrived, there were policemen swarming everywhere. She put her badge around her neck and grabbed her clipboard off the car seat. She exited the vehicle and was greeted by a familiar face.

"Hey, Mallory. I haven't seen you in a while. What have you been up to?"

The detective raised the crime scene tape and laughed. "You don't want to know, C. J."

"How old is she?"

"I plead the fifth."

"You are so sad, Mallory. You'd better leave those young girls alone."

He couldn't help but laugh. The pair walked into the house and Cherise immediately noticed the house in disarray. Mallory turned to Cherise briefly as he led her through the house.

"The vic is back here."

Cherise followed the police officer into a back bedroom to join the Coroner. Members of her team were already taking pictures and collecting evidence. The victim appeared to be a young black male, in his mid to late twenties, with a gunshot wound to his chest. He was lying halfway off the bed and was fully clothed. A handgun was on the floor not far from the victim. Cherise put on a pair of rubber gloves and turned to the Coroner.

"Hello, Thalia."

"Hello, C. J."

Cherise pointed toward the victim and asked, "May I?"

"Go right ahead," Thalia replied.

Cherise leaned over the victim and started examining him. "Thalia, did you notice any other injuries besides the obvious gunshot wound?"

Thalia stopped writing on her clipboard. "Not that I saw right away. I have the tentative cause of death down as a GSW. I'll know more once I get him on the table."

As the two women spoke, Mallory took notes.

"Talk to me ladies," Mallory said. "Does this look self-inflicted to you?"

Cherise inspected the vic's hands and the wound more closely.

"Not at all. Whoever did this caught him off guard." Thalia looked over at Mallory and said, " I agree with C. J."

Mallory's partner, Pamela Ray, walked up. "The victim's mother is at the neighbor's house. She said she left about two hours ago, and when she returned she found her son dead."

Cherise and the Coroner rolled the victim over and found several hundred-dollar bills lying under him.

"What is this kid doing with all this money?" Mallory asked.

"He's probably a drug dealer," Ray said.

Cherise stood and eyed Detective Ray. "Don't assume anything just because you see a black guy with a large sum of money in his possession. If you don't know, let me educate you: Not all black men sell drugs."

The detective, stunned at Cherise's outburst, turned and walked out of the room without responding. Detective Mallory and Thalia laughed together.

"Where did you get her from, Mallory?" Cherise turned her attention back to the victim.

"We've only been together for about three weeks. I'm working on her. She's still green."

She stood and looked around. "Has anyone found any drugs or drug paraphernalia in the room?"

"No, he looks clean," Detective Mallory said.

She folded her arms and thought. "Whoever killed him could've taken the drugs if the vic was into that. I'll have the team go over the house with a fine-tooth comb. If drugs have been in this house, we'll find residue. I'll also order a tox screen on him and get the results back to you as soon as possible."

"Give me something to work with, C. J.," he begged.

"Talk to his mother and his friends. Other than that, he looks clean."

"How soon will you know something?" Mallory asked.

"Check with me later this evening. This is such a waste."

Thalia said, "Unfortunately, we're seeing more and more cases like this, C. J. I'll see you guys a little later. I should be finished with the autopsy by five ."

She watched as Thalia and her assistant put the victim in a body bag. Gathering her belongings, she turned to Cherise and Mallory. "Don't work too hard."

Mallory said, "I wish."

Cherise followed Thalia out of the house and watched as she loaded the body into the van. Thalia closed the doors to the van.

"I'll be by the lab a little later, Thalia."

Thalia opened the door to the van and climbed inside. "Okay. If I find anything before you get there, I'll give you a call."

Before returning to the house, she looked around and noticed that a large crowd had gathered to see what was going on. Hopefully she could come up with some evidence so Mallory could solve the case.

Mason was getting more involved with T-bone and his organization. He had spent the past few days hanging out with T-bone and his crew. So far, Mason had given his task force plenty of information on how the crew operated with the help of the wire he was discreetly wearing. His unit was always nearby in case his cover was blown. However, Mason was so good at his job that that was never really anticipated, but they still needed to stay on their toes. T-bone was impressed with his initial meeting with Mason; at the urging of Vada, he decided to let Mason become a part of his entourage—but on a probationary basis.

On this day, they sat around in the small wooden house smoking, drinking, and playing video games. Mason was amazed at the firepower T-bone and his crew possessed. They had everything they needed to fight a small war: nine-millimeters, assault rifles, and Uzis. T-bone was puffing on a blunt as he played the video game. He looked over at Mason and held it out to him.

"Hey, Mirage, you want to hit this?"

Mason took it out of his hand and hit it once before handing it back. He knew he had to play the part to get closer to his target. He leaned back on the sofa and closed his eyes, the smoke already starting to take effect. Vada walked through the door like a fashion model and smiled as soon as she saw Mason. She gave T-bone a folder full of paperwork and then sat down on Mason's lap. She planted a wet kiss on his lips.

"Hey, baby! Hmmm, I've missed you."

He rubbed her thigh seductively. "Hey, babe."

T-bone put the video game down and started looking through the papers. Seconds later he cursed and threw the folder over on a nearby chair. Vada turned to him and frowned.

"What's wrong with you?"

T-bone looked over at Vada angrily. "Is that shit right?"

She jumped up and put her hands on her hips in defense.

"You didn't leave anything out, did you?" he asked.

She walked closer to T-bone and leaned down until they were eye to eye. "How long have I been doing this? Huh? You know I don't make mistakes, and it pisses me off that you would even question me."

He started playing the video game again and mumbled. "I guess that accounting degree you got is good for something. My bad."

Vada put her hand up to her ear and chastised him. "I can't hear you!"

"I said my bad, now leave it alone, Vada."

Mason sat silently as the brother and sister battled with each other. He was curious to know what was in the folder, and why T-bone was upset about it. Vada crawled back into Mason's lap and hugged his neck.

"Is everything okay with you guys?" Mason asked.

T-bone slowly turned his head toward Mason. "Yeah, man, everything's cool."

Vada watched her brother's mood change quickly. She leaned down and whispered into Mason's ear. "Don't mind him, Mirage. He's just a little upset with the books."

"Shut your damn mouth, Vada!" T-bone snapped angrily.

"You can't tell me what to do, T-bone! I say what I want, when I want."

T-bone stood up and lunged toward Vada. Mason quickly pushed Vada out of his lap and got in T-bone's face.

"Chill out, T-bone! I know Vada's your sister, but I'm not going to stand here and let you put your hands on her."

T-bone was breathing hard as he stood there clenching his fists. Mason stared T-bone down.

"Vada, you need to learn how to keep your damn mouth shut. I decide what I want Mirage to know. Not you!"

Without addressing Mason, T-bone sat back down and continued to play the video game. Vada stood and grabbed her purse. "Let's get out of here, babe. We don't have to stay where we're not wanted."

Mason pulled her back down on the sofa and put his finger in her face.

"Look, Vada, T-bone's right! There's a time and place to discuss business, and tonight was not that time! I haven't earned T-bone's trust yet, so please don't piss him off and mess this up for me. Okay?"

She looked at him in shock—she hadn't expected him to turn on her. He was her man, and it was because of her that he had been allowed into the organization in the first place. Now she felt like everyone was turning on her. Tears formed in her eyes as Mason reprimanded her.

"I didn't mean to get everybody's blood pressure up tonight. I'm sorry, Mirage! Damn!"

T-bone lit another joint and shook his head with disgust. "You're damn right you should be sorry!"

Mason turned slowly toward T-bone. "Look, man, Vada's cool. Now if you don't feel like you can trust me, just say the word and I'll step. But if I step, so do all my connections."

T-bone stared at him in silence as he continued to smoke the joint. Mason stared back at him and picked up his car keys.

"I could give a damn about your books. I was already in business for myself when Vada brought me in. Cutting you in on my shit doesn't affect my profits. I'm trying to educate your dumb ass!"

Hearing Mason disrespect him in front of his boys pissed T-bone off. Mason saw him twitch and he knew what T-bone was about to do. He pulled his gun at the same time T-bone pulled his nine-millimeter from his waistband. They aimed their guns at each other's heads in silence. Vada screamed and went into a panic.

"What the hell are you doing? Mirage, please don't shoot my brother. T-bone, put your gun down before someone gets killed!"

Mason held his cool as he kept his gun pointed at T-bone. Vada watched the two men in her life square off in a deadly stance. His crew sat across the room and anxiously awaited the outcome of the draw. T-bone lowered his gun first. He put the joint back in his mouth and sat back down in his chair. Mason was thankful he wasn't shot, but he knew if T-bone had pulled the trigger, his backup would've been inside the house in seconds. Mason's adrenaline was still pumping when he finally lowered his gun. T-bone looked over at him once again.

"You got a lot of balls pulling a gun on me up in my crib, Mirage."

"Whatever." Mason frowned as he put his gun back in his pocket and walked over toward the door. "Look, when you decide to let me in on the game, give me a call. I'm out!"

Vada glared over at her brother and then trailed Mason out the door. Before he could get into his car, she hugged his waist and pressed his body against the side of the car.

He looked down at her. "What the hell are you smiling at?"

"You," she teased.

He tried to push her away so he could get into his car.

"I don't have time for this. I have things to do."

She held onto him tightly.

"Mirage, you're not pissed off about what happened in there, are you?"

Mason removed her hands and opened his car door.

"I don't play, Vada. I could've blown his ass away."

"Then you would be dead, too, because his boys would've taken you out, and where would that leave me?"

He turned and sighed.

"You need to ask your crazy-ass brother that, not me. I don't have time for his shit."

"He likes you, Mirage. No one has ever stood up to him like you did. You're as good as in. You'll see."

Mason stared at her. She stood on her tiptoes and put her arms around his neck. Her lips were within inches of his when she whispered. "Why don't you take me home so I can show you just how much I really care about you?"

Mason saw this as another opportunity to possibly get a peek at T-bone's books. He knew sleeping with Vada was something he wouldn't be able to avoid much longer because she would get suspicious of him. Working under-cover wasn't all it was made out to be, especially for a married man, because it required him to do some unthinkable things.

"Come on, baby. The night is young. Can't whatever you have to do, wait?"

"Get in."

She kissed him on the lips and caressed his groin before sliding into the car next to him.

Before Mason could get through the door, Vada practically attacked him. She ripped open the front of his shirt and started kissing him greedily. Mason's body responded to the aggressive contact with Vada instantly. She giggled and hurriedly pulled him into her bedroom. They tumbled onto her bed and Vada immediately straddled him. He stared up at her as she pulled her blouse over her head and removed her bra.

"You like?"

He reached up and palmed her breasts. "Nice, very nice."

"I have something even better to show you."

Mason caressed her thighs. "Damn, girl! What are you trying to do to me?"

She leaned down and whispered to him, "You haven't seen anything yet, Mirage."

Vada hurriedly removed the rest of her clothing. Mason smiled as he watched Vada unzip his pants and devour him. He lay back and closed his eyes as Vada worked her magic. Mason couldn't help but enjoy the pleasure she was giving him. Once she finished giving him one of the best blows he'd ever had, she performed a seductive dance as she removed the rest of her clothing. Mason looked across the room at Vada's computer and hoped he would get a chance to take a look at her files. He pulled her down on the bed and rolled her over onto her back. He kissed her neck and breasts tenderly, causing her to moan. She arched her body upward as his tongue sampled her soft body. She cupped his face and pulled him down to her.

"I'm ready for you, baby."

He said a prayer to himself and pulled a condom out of his pocket. She stared at him in anticipation as he applied it and hovered over her. He pulled her hips closer to him, allowing her to wrap her legs around his waist. Mason groaned as he pushed his body into hers. Vada closed her eyes and whimpered as he moved his hips against hers. It was hard for Mason not to enjoy the sensations rippling through his body as he moved in and out of her. If Cherise ever found out about this, it could ruin their lives forever.

After several heavenly minutes, Vada rolled over until she was on top of him. Her eyes gleamed as she looked down at him.

"Damn, Mirage! I can barely handle you!"

Mason lay back and savored Vada's rhythmic ride. Then he rolled her back over onto her back and took complete control. Vada screamed and moaned as Mason rode her petite frame until she was nearly delirious. Waves of pleasure rocked her body hard. She yelled out his name and lay under him, completely exhausted. He kissed her neck and followed closely with his own release. Taking shallow breaths, Mason rolled off of her. Guilt flooded his body. He lay there gathering his thoughts for a moment and realized he couldn't let his thoughts of Cherise and his marriage mess with his head. At least not now, even though it was taking every ounce of strength for him to keep from falling apart. Vada looked over at him and purred.

"I hope you don't think I'm easy, Mirage."

He nibbled on her earlobe and caressed her bottom.

"I think you're beautiful, tough, sexy, and incredibly smart, Vada."

She kissed him with appreciation. "Well, you're not so bad yourself. You make me feel out of control, Mirage, and I like that."

He gave her a peck on the lips and excused himself to the bathroom. Upon returning, he sat on the side of the bed, staring at her laptop. She scooted over and hugged his neck lovingly.

"Nice laptop."

She hugged a pillow and let out a breath. "Yeah, T-bone got it for me. He said it's one of the best on the market."

Mason stood and slipped into his briefs.

"I'm in the market for a better computer myself. Do you mind if I try it out?"

Vada lay back on the bed seductively. "I'd rather you try me out again," she announced.

"We have the rest of the night for that. Besides, I'm starving. What do you have to eat around here?"

She posed even more seductively and Mason laughed out loud because he knew what she wanted. "Vada, I'm sure you are delicious, and I know I'll find out for myself in due time."

She giggled loudly and hugged his neck. "You're different from all the other guys T-bone hangs out with. You're sexy, educated, and tough as hell. My brother would be a fool not to let you in the business."

He looked into her eyes and played in her hair. "Sweetheart, I'm sure he's just being cautious. Now go before I starve to death."

"Okay, Mirage. I'll go fix us something to eat."

He patted her on her bare bottom as she stood to slip into her clothes.

"Can I play around with your laptop for a while to get a feel for this model?"

She walked over, turned on the laptop, and logged on. "Sure, baby. I have some good games on there. I like playing poker."

"Thanks, Vada," he said as he watched the computer upload.

She walked out of the room and toward the kitchen. Mason did what he could to get a look at T-bone's files. He knew if he wasn't successful, he might have to repeat today's performance with Vada to get her to allow him more time on her computer. The sooner he could get evidence against T-bone, the sooner he could get home to Cherise and the kids.

Chapter Eleven

Back in Texas, Vincent sat behind his desk and looked over his itinerary for the week. He had a couple meetings and a few conference calls coming up, but after that his schedule was very light for a couple of weeks. There was an e-mail memo from the mayor's office, reminding him that it was mandatory that he use some of his accumulated vacation time. How lucky he was at the timing, because his experience with Cherise was still heavy on his mind, as were a few other important matters. He especially wanted to see Janelle. He logged on to the computer and went to a Web site advertising DNA kits. If he ordered one, all he would have to do was convince Cherise to get a sample from Janelle. As he stared at the computer screen, he knew he wouldn't be able to rest until he knew the truth for himself. He typed in the necessary information and hit the submit button just as his telephone rang.

"Chief McKenzie."

A silky feminine voice came through the telephone line. "Vincent, this is Rachel. Where have you been? I haven't heard from you in a couple of weeks."

Vincent leaned back in his chair and sighed. "I've been around. What's up?"

He had met Rachel during a state dinner a year or so ago, introduced to him by a fellow police officer. She worked in the governor's office and wanted more from him than he was willing to give her.

"I've missed you and was wondering when we were going to get together again."

He punched a button on his computer, opened an e-mail response from Cherise, and smiled.

"I don't know, Rachel. I'm been really busy and I don't see things slowing down anytime soon. I had to go out of town this past weekend to a conference, so I really can't say when I'm going to be free."

"I was hoping you would invite me along on one of your trips. Wouldn't you like the company?"

He looked out the window of his office and tried to figure out how to avoid having this conversation. "I don't know, Rachel. Look, I don't want any confusion about where our relationship stands."

"Where does our relationship stand, Vincent? I mean we've been intimate on more occasions than I can count. According to public opinion, we are a couple."

"First of all, my private life is no one's business—I won't let the media or anyone else decide who I should be in a relationship with," he said angrily.

"I didn't call you to make you angry, Vincent. I miss being with you, and I would like to spend some time with you tonight if possible. I'm not going to beg, but it has been a couple of weeks since we had dinner or anything."

"Why don't you just say you want to have sex, Rachel?"

"That's not fair, Vincent," she said in embarrassment.

He laughed. "Am I lying?"

"You don't have to be so vulgar," she whispered. "I'm not a street whore and I won't let you treat me like one."

"I didn't say you were, but if you want something, just ask for it instead of beating around the bush."

"Vincent, you are an eligible, handsome bachelor in a prestigious position. Is it a crime that I want to spend some time with you?"

He leaned closer to his computer to begin reading Cherise's e-mail. "If my memory serves me correctly, you seemed to like it when I talked dirty to you, and no, it's not a crime."

"Listen, Vincent, I'm inviting you over to my house for dinner tonight at seven. All I ask is that if you're not coming, please have the courtesy to call and let me know."

"I'll let you know, and thanks for the invite, Rachel, seriously. I'm sorry. I haven't been myself lately. I've been pretty preoccupied."

"You're welcome," she said with a smile in her voice before hanging up.

Vincent replaced the phone in the receiver and read Cherise's e-mail.

Hey Vincent,
I'm doing well. I'm still overwhelmed with work, but I'll get through it. I always do. I hope all is well with you. Mason and the kids are fine. He's still working hard and I'm sure he would love to see you. Be safe and stay in touch.
With Love
C. J.

Vincent began to type a response:

C. J.,
I'm glad to hear that you, Mason, and the kids are all doing well. Don't let the job get the best of you. Just pace yourself. As far as Mason is concerned, don't worry about him. He knows how to stay safe when he's on the job. I can't wait to see you again. I love you and I miss you.
Love always,
Vincent

He turned his computer off, grabbed his jacket, and headed out the door to his meeting.

Later that evening, Vincent arrived at Rachel's house for dinner. He had decided to take her up on her offer because he really did feel bad about the way he'd talked to her earlier. When she opened the door he was met with a huge smile. Vincent kissed her on the cheek and handed her a bottle of wine before walking inside her home.

"Good evening, Rachel. Something smells good in here."

Closing the door, she turned and smiled.

"I'm so glad you decided to come over."

She had a short black dress that was cut low in the front and the back. She took him by the hand and pulled him toward the dining room where the table was beautifully set with candles and flowers. Vincent took off his jacket and got comfortable in his seat.

"This is nice, Rachel. Can I help you with anything?"

She massaged his shoulders and kissed him on the cheek.

"No, I can manage. You sit right here and I'll get some glasses so we can sample this delicious wine."

He watched as Rachel disappeared into the kitchen. She was statuesque and very attractive. Any man would be a fool not to want to be with her, but for him she was just a companion and no more. That little black dress she was wearing provided him with a great view of her shapely legs. Vincent stood as she returned to the room with two wineglasses and a corkscrew. He opened the bottle and poured the wine. Rachel held her glass up to his and grinned.

"What should we toast to?"

"How about to a delicious meal, great wine, and a very beautiful dinner date."

She blushed. "Thank you, Vincent. I would like to toast you for being the only man to inspire me to do things I never thought I could. I mean that professionally and intimately."

He winked at her and took a sip of wine. "I'll drink to that."

They sipped their wine, and then Rachel jumped up when she heard a timer go off in the kitchen.

"Dinner is served. I'll be right back. I hope you're hungry, Chief McKenzie."

"As a matter of fact, I'm starving."

Rachel returned to the room with a couple of platters. She hurried back into the kitchen and brought out a few more items for the table. Vincent sat up in his chair and rubbed his hands together. He couldn't wait to tear into the Cornish hens, corn bread dressing, and steamed asparagus.

"Rachel, when did you have the time to cook all of this?"

She put her napkin in her lap and proudly lowered her head to say grace. Vincent also lowered his head, but he was able to study her during the prayer. She was nearly perfect in every way, but there was still something missing that kept him from giving himself to her totally.

"It wasn't as hard as it looks. I hope you like everything," she replied once she finished her prayer.

"I have no doubt about that. I'm glad I came."

She picked up her fork and said softly, "So am I."

The pair savored Rachel's delicious meal as they talked about work, the changing weather, and other current events. After dinner they sat around listening to music while Rachel opened another bottle of wine. Before Vincent realized it, the clock was nearing eleven o'clock. It was time for him to head home.

"Rachel, time really got away from me. I need to get home if I plan to go to work in the morning. Dinner was great and your company was very nice."

She snuggled up to him and purred.

"Do you really have to go? You've had a lot to drink and I would hate for the chief of police to get pulled over for a DUI."

Vincent stared at her for a moment, and then leaned over, kissing her tenderly, first on the neck and then on the lips. Rachel let out a very slow breath. Vincent looked into her eyes and knew her body was beginning to heat up.

"Hmmm, that feels heavenly, Vincent."

Rachel was right. He did have a slight buzz from all the wine they had drunk; he really wasn't in any condition to be driving. The last thing he needed was to get pulled over by one of his own officers. Rachel kissed his neck and made a bold suggestion.

"Why don't we just call it a night? You can leave early in the morning in plenty of time to change and get to the office."

He looked at the clock on the wall. "I don't know about all night, but I could hang around long enough for some of this wine to get out of my system."

It was clear to Vincent that Rachel was happy that he was staying. At this point she would accept whatever extra time she could get with him. Rachel blew out the candles and led him upstairs. Once upstairs, Vincent didn't hesitate to unzip her dress. He watched her as she let it fall to the floor. She blushed as she stood there in nothing but a black lace thong. Vincent sat down on the bed. Rachel knelt before him, unbuckled his belt, and unzipped his pants. His breathing increased as he felt her warm, moist lips surround him. She knew exactly what his weakness was, and she was very good at helping him to unwind.

He threw his head back and closed his eyes as he felt her consume him with ease. His heart was beating loudly in his chest and he felt his body began to sizzle and shiver. Rachel increased her actions, especially when she heard Vincent moan with pleasure. He grabbed a fistful of her hair and guided her over his shaft. He hissed and cursed as he stared down at her.

Rachel looked up and gave him a perfect view of the magic she was performing on him. She retrieved a condom out of the nightstand. She quickly opened it and fitted it perfectly over his body. Vincent was happy to allow Rachel to have her way with him, because it had been a while since they'd been together. She straddled his lap and moaned as their bodies became one. Vincent clutched her hips and gave her exactly what she wanted. At times he could tell he was going deeper than she could withstand, but it didn't stop him from continuing. Rachel held on as best she could as she begged for mercy. He gripped her even tighter and worked her into hysterics as she moaned with each thrust. Rachel screamed at the top of her lungs as she reached her peak. Vincent continued to invade her body until he felt his own body spasm as orgasm overtook him. He closed his eyes and fell onto the bed. Rachel laid her head against his neck, totally spent. She wrapped her arms around his neck and kissed him with sincere affection.

"I love you, Vincent," Rachel said breathlessly.

He cupped her face and kissed her deeply. "I love you, too, C. J."

"C. J.! Who the hell is C. J.?" Rachel yelled.

Vincent cursed himself under his breath for that little slip of the tongue. He hadn't made this kind of mistake since high school. His eyes gave away the guilt and embarrassment in his heart, and he knew he needed to get in control of the situation quickly.

"I'm sorry, Rachel. I didn't mean to call you out of your name."

She angrily grabbed her robe and covered up her body.

"I want to know who the hell this C. J. is! Are you sleeping with her, too?"

Vincent got up off the bed and pulled on his briefs, then zipped his pants. Rachel was almost in tears.

"Rachel, it's none of your business who I sleep with. I made that very clear to you when we started hanging out. It was an innocent mistake, and I said I was sorry."

She pointed her finger at him and yelled even louder. "I don't believe that for one minute. You must think I'm a fool to stand here and let you call me another woman's name while you're making love to me."

He walked over to her and gently grabbed her by the shoulders to calm her.

"Rachel! You need to calm down! We're not married, engaged, or even seriously dating. I like your company, and I enjoy spending time with you. I never told you I was seeing you exclusively."

She folded her arms and pouted before responding. "This is not working for me. I need someone who's going to pay attention to me and me only, Vincent, and it's obvious your mind is on someone else. I feel like I'm wasting my time with you."

Vincent buckled his belt without responding. She was right about one thing— his mind was on someone else. But why? It wasn't like he had a chance in hell with C. J., because she belonged to his brother.

"I'm sorry, Rachel, but I thought you had a clear understanding of where our relationship stood. Look, if I'm not paying you enough attention, then we need to end things now, because I can't give you any more time than what you're getting from me right now."

Tears dropped from Rachel's eyes. She knew whoever C. J. was, she had all of Vincent's attention. It was that woman who was in Vincent's head when he and Rachel had made love, not her.

Vincent tucked in his shirt and looked over at Rachel with concern. "Are you cool?"

She wiped the tears from her cheek. "Whatever."

He sighed.

"Look, I really am sorry about what I said. It's best that I get out here, but I don't want to leave with any hard feelings between us."

She cleared her throat, pulled a tissue from a nearby box, and wiped her eyes. With her voice barely above a whisper, she answered him.

"I'll be all right."

He walked over to her and tilted her chin so he could see her eyes up close. She was a beautiful woman, but he couldn't see himself with her forever.

"Are you sure? I'm not heartless, Rachel. I really do care about you."

"You're still welcome to stay if you want."

Vincent hugged her and gave her a kiss on the forehead before walking toward the hallway.

"Thanks, but my head is a lot clearer than it was before, I'll be fine."

She took his hand and walked him downstairs to the door. Before walking out the door, he leaned down and kissed her tenderly on the lips.

"Good night, Rachel. I'll call you."

"Okay," she answered with a smile.

She watched as he walked out to his car and drove away. She closed the door and slowly made her way back upstairs. Her heart was still wounded from being called another woman's name. Whoever C. J. was, she was the real reason Vincent couldn't love her like she needed to be loved. Ending things between them now seemed like the logical thing to do.

Rachel turned out the light in the foyer and climbed the stairs to her bedroom, hurt, but comfortable with her decision.

Chapter Twelve

Mason arrived home just as Cherise and Janelle were headed out to Mase's basketball game. Cherise could tell by his eyes that he was exhausted and hadn't had much sleep. He hugged and kissed both of his favorite women.

"Where are you ladies headed?"

Excited to see her daddy, Janelle hugged his waist tightly.

"Mase has a ball game, Daddy! Come on!"

He looked at his watch. "Damn! Let me jump in the shower and change real quick so I can ride with you."

Cherise and Janelle followed him back inside the house.

"Okay, Mason, but you'd better hurry. You know Mase likes us to be there at tip-off."

He sprinted up the stairs. Cherise was happy that Mason made it home in time to see Mase play his first game of the season. She sat at the kitchen table with Janelle to wait. Within fifteen minutes, Mason was back and ready to go. Before going out into the garage, Cherise turned his collar down for him.

"Do you want me to drive?" he asked with gleaming eyes. She smiled.

"No, I'll drive," she said. "You just sit back and relax."

They arrived at the gym just in time to take their seats before tip-off. Mase's face lit up as soon as he saw his family in the bleachers, especially his dad. He played an exceptional game, but his team still lost in the end. As they waited for Mase to change, Cherise and Mason talked to other parents they were friendly with. When Mase solemnly joined them, Cherise pulled him into her arms.

"You played a great game, baby. I'm sorry you lost."

"Thanks, Momma. Hey, Daddy." He greeted Mason with a hug.

Mason put his arm around his shoulder and whispered to him. "Hold your chin up, son. You did great, and I'm so proud of you. It's hard to win every game, but as long as you do your best, it doesn't matter whether you win or lose. Understand?"

"I understand, Daddy," he answered.

Mason clapped his hands together. "Now! Are you guys ready for some dinner? I hope you are, because I'm starving!"

Cherise knew Mason was exhausted, so as they walked to the car she made a logical suggestion. "Why don't we get some carryout and eat at home tonight? We can go out tomorrow night for dinner."

"It don't matter to me," Mase said sullenly. He was still suffering from their loss.

Cherise and Mason looked at each other, knowing their son was hurt from losing the game. Janelle danced as she walked across the parking lot and made another suggestion.

"Can we go to that place where the waiters wear the big hats?"

Mason picked her up and placed her on his shoulders. "Are you talking about that Mexican restaurant?"

"Yeah, Daddy, that's it. I like their nachos and cheese."

He put his arm around Cherise's waist. "Is Mexican okay with you, babe?"

"Whatever you guys want is fine with me, but I know you're tired, baby. You haven't slept in your bed in two weeks, and I've missed you."

"I missed you, too. Let's get out of here."

Mason was fully aware that he hadn't slept in his bed, because he'd been bumping and grinding with Vada. He tried his best not to let guilt ease into his heart, but it was difficult.

Back at home they sat around the table enjoying the Mexican food they'd picked up on the way home. Mase's spirits had lifted somewhat; he was laughing at all of Mason's jokes. Cherise stood behind Mason and massaged his shoulders tenderly. He leaned his head back against her chest and closed his eyes.

"Baby, that feels so good. Thank you."

"Mommy, massage me next," Janelle said as she looked up at Cherise.

She laughed at her daughter. "I don't think so. Your daddy's been working very hard and I'm just trying to relax his tired muscles."

Mase finished his food and stood up.

"Momma, Daddy, can I go over to Quincy's house? We're going to play video games for a while."

"Not tonight, Mase. Your father just got home and you haven't seen him in two weeks. You can see Quincy tomorrow."

Mase sighed with disappointment. "Yes, ma'am."

Cherise turned to her daughter. "Janelle, it's getting late and you need to get ready for bed."

"Can I watch a movie before I go to bed, Momma?"

"Only for a little while," Cherise responded.

Mason got up out of his chair and put his paper plate into the trash. "Mase, if you feel like a challenge, I'll play videos with you."

A huge smile graced Mase's face. "Cool, Daddy! I'll go set it up."

After Mase left the room, Mason kissed Janelle on the cheek. "I'll be up to tuck you in shortly, sweetheart."

"Okay, Daddy!" she yelled with excitement as she sprinted toward the stairs.

Cherise walked over to Mason and put her arms around his neck. He pulled her close and buried his face against her warm neck.

"You just made both of your children very, very happy."

He kissed her lips and caressed her backside lovingly.

"I know, and I plan to take care of you just as soon as I get the kids settled down for the night."

"I'm counting on it, Mason."

Janelle made her way back downstairs.

"Momma, are you going to watch the movie with me?"

Cherise smiled. She held Janelle's hand and walked toward the stairs.

"I might watch a little of it with you. I've missed your daddy, so I want to hang out with him a little while tonight. Okay?"

"Okay, Momma," she happily answered.

"Mason, you go ahead and play the videos with Mase. I'll take care of Janelle."

He poured himself a glass of water and drank it down in one swallow.

"Okay, babe. Janelle, I'll be up to tuck you in shortly."

"Okay, Daddy!"

Cherise and Janelle made their way upstairs while Mason and Mase settled down in the family room for a game of *Madden 2006* football.

Upstairs Cherise helped Janelle settle into her bed. She asked to watch *Shrek 2*, so Cherise pulled it off the shelf and popped it into the DVD player.

"Thank you, Momma."

Cherise kissed Janelle on the forehead. "You're welcome. Now, you're all set so I'm going to take a shower, but I'll be back to check on you shortly."

Janelle grabbed her stuffed teddy bear and got comfortable in her bed.

"Okay, Momma."

Cherise walked down to her bedroom and found Mason stretched out asleep across their bed. She smiled and sat down next to him. She ran her hand across his cheek and whispered into his ear.

"I thought you were going to play videos with Mase?"

He rolled over and pulled her down on the bed next to him and caressed her face. "So did I but he forgot he loaned the game to a friend."

"You're tired, anyway."

He sat up on the side of the bed and ran his hands over his face. "You're right. Mase is tired, too, but he didn't want to admit it."

Cherise removed some of the pillows and pulled back the comforter on the bed.

"I knew he was. I'm getting ready to shower. I think Janelle is waiting on you to tuck her in."

"Okay," Mason replied.

Cherise took a long, hot shower. Once she finished, she found Mason sitting on the bed watching ESPN.

"Is Janelle still up?"

"No, she's asleep now," he answered as he stood and began to remove his clothing.

Cherise climbed into bed and watched as Mason walked toward the bathroom.

"I'll be out in a second. You can go ahead and turn the TV off if you want to."

"Okay. Take your time, baby."

Cherise heard the shower turn on. While she waited for him to return, she said a quick prayer of thanks that he had made his way safely back home this time. Soon, Mason exited the bathroom with a towel wrapped around his waist. He removed the towel, climbed into bed, and immediately pulled Cherise over to him so he could look into her beautiful eyes.

"Damn! You don't know how bad I've missed you."

"I have an idea. It's hard for me to sleep in this bed when you're not here."

He hugged her tighter. "Why do you put up with me?"

"Because I love you, Mason. That's why. I worry about you so much when you're away. You are being careful out there, aren't you?"

He nibbled seductively on her earlobe.

"You don't have to worry about me, baby. I'm taking every precaution necessary to make sure I come home to you and the children."

Tears welled up in her eyes as she hugged his neck. "But I do worry about you, Mason. When are you going to be through with this case?"

"As soon as I can, sweetheart. I hate being away from you and the kids."

"I know," she whispered. "Can I ask you something?"

"Uh-huh," he replied.

"Where do you stay when you're away from us?"

Mason was silent for a moment.

"They got a place for me to stay, so don't worry. I'm not sleeping in my car or anything."

She let out a sigh of relief.

"Mason, I hope you can end this case quickly."

He patted her on the bottom and grinned.

"I'm working on it, and soon I'll be all yours, sweetheart."

For some reason, Cherise had a feeling Mason wasn't being completely honest with her. But right now all she could do was go by what he was telling her.

"I love you, Mason," she whispered.

He kissed her lips gently.

"I love you, too, sweetheart. Good night."

"Good night, Mason. Get some sleep."

He held her securely in his arms and was asleep within minutes. The following morning, Cherise welcomed Mason home properly.

Chapter Thirteen

C herise was back in her lab trying to get through the many cases she had outstanding on her log. In only three days, the CSI office had logged three more homicides. She and her team were trying to catch up on the tasks homicide detectives needed done in order to investigate their cases. Cherise had gotten an early start so she could complete tests on at least two cases by lunch.

Sitting at her desk, she punched in data to update her caseload. Her neck and eyes were strained, and her stomach was growling from hunger. She received a call from one of her assistants just as she was about to leave for lunch.

"C. J. McKenzie," she answered.

"Dr. McKenzie, this is Ellen. We just received a call involving a possible carbon monoxide poisoning."

Cherise sighed. "I'm on my way."

Cherise grabbed her jacket and badge and headed out. She and her assistant were met by police and paramedics at the scene. Cherise's heart jumped into her throat: She knew it was bad by the look on the detectives' faces. They escorted Cherise and her assistant into the house.

"What do we have?"

"Back here, C. J. This one's pretty bad, too. There're children involved in this one."

Cherise and her assistant, Paul, followed the detective into a back bedroom where three little girls were tucked soundly in their beds. She noticed all the windows were up and she could hear a man sobbing in another room. Cherise and Paul began to examine the children and take pictures. It broke her heart; the children's ages ranged from approximately six to ten.

"Who found them?" she asked the lead detective.

He wiped away a tear before answering.

"The father came home from his night job and found them. When he couldn't wake them, he called the paramedics."

Cherise shook her head sadly.

"Where's the mother?"

The detective pointed down the hallway to the next room. Cherise asked her assistant to continue with the children while she went to examine the mother. Just like the children, the mother was in bed like she was sleeping, except that the husband had obviously grabbed her up.

"What time did the call come in?" she asked the detective.

He looked at his notes. "At approximately ten-thirty. The father and some coworkers stopped off for breakfast when they got off at seven-thirty. He said he last talked to his wife around nine last night."

Cherise shook her head again.

"This was so avoidable, Larry."

"I know," he replied.

"Who opened the windows?"

Larry looked down at his notes once again. "The husband did. "

"Does he have family he can stay with until we process the scene?"

"Yeah, we're going to take him over there after he packs some belongings. When will you have the official results for us, C. J.?"

"I'll try and have it for you by six but it looks like a clear case of carbon mon-oxide poisoning. I don't see any evidence of foul play. Show me the suspected source of the carbon monoxide. Once we get pictures of the source and the mother, we can transport the bodies back to the lab," she informed him.

He nodded and took down a few more notes before leading Cherise to the basement. After a preliminary inspection of the gas water heater and the gas furnace, she made her way back to the children's room so she could help her assistant load the bodies into their van. Dealing with children always tugged at her heart, but she knew it was part of the job.

Cherise never did make it to lunch. Instead, her team ordered takeout so they could get a jump on the tests involving the carbon monoxide poisoning case. It was a difficult but necessary task. They needed to rule out foul play and log the official report that the family did in fact die from carbon monoxide leaking from a gas water heater. They had plenty of smoke detectors in the house, but no carbon monoxide detectors, which had caused fatal results.

By the time Cherise pulled into the garage, it was almost seven-thirty and the images of the deceased children were still in her head. She was exhausted both mentally and physically, especially since she had been at the lab since six a.m. When she walked into kitchen, she yawned. She couldn't wait to kiss Mason and her children and go to bed. As she walked down the hallway toward the family room, she heard male voices. When she turned the corner to go into the room, she froze.

Mason stood up proudly.

"Hey, baby! I didn't hear you come in. Can you believe it? After all this time, look who's here!"

Cherise nearly passed out when she came face-to-face with Vincent. Without missing a beat, he walked over and pulled her into his arms.

"C. J.! It's so good to see you! It's been a long time!"

Vincent had always been good at lying. Tonight was no different. She hugged him and did her best not to appear shaken.

"Vincent, I'm surprised to see you. You look great."

"How do you think I felt when I opened the door? Mason said. "Vincent, I should whip your ass for staying away from the family for so long."

Vincent laughed and looked directly at Cherise.

"I missed you guys, so thought I would take some time off to come visit my family. I've been gone too long, and I needed to get back here to see what kind of trouble Mason was getting himself into."

Mason smiled and playfully threw a punch at Vincent. "You're full of it, Vincent."

Cherise was still in shock, and a little angry that Vincent hadn't let her know he was coming. Him showing up like this made her feel very uncomfortable, but she couldn't show it.

"Baby, are you okay?" Mason asked as he studied her expression. "Why don't you come in and have a seat?"

"No, you guys go ahead. It's been a long day. I had to do some children today and it kind of got to me. I'll catch up with you tomorrow. I'm exhausted."

Vincent hugged her again and this time kissed her on the cheek.

"It's never easy dealing with children, especially when you have kids of your own. It's okay, C. J. Go ahead and get some rest. We'll have plenty of time to hang out."

She nodded in agreement, but before stepping into the hallway, she turned to Mason and spoke tenderly. "Sweetheart, are the kids here?"

Mason picked up the remote control and proceeded to surf the channels.

"They're with your dad. I think they went to the movies. They should be back soon."

"Okay. Vincent, are you staying with us while you're in town?"

Vincent sat down in the recliner and raised the footrest.

"Mason offered, but you know me. I like my privacy. I'm staying at the Marriott downtown so I can be in the center of things."

"I understand. Have you guys had anything to eat?"

Mason was tuned in to a boxing match on the TV screen.

"Yeah, Mason took me out for dinner earlier. Thanks for asking, anyway," Vincent replied.

Cherise sighed and pulled her purse onto her shoulder. "Okay, guys, I'm going to call it a night."

Vincent winked at her. "Sweet dreams, C. J."

Cherise saw the way Vincent looked at her. She was glad Mason was into the boxing match and didn't notice.

"I'll talk to you tomorrow, Vincent. Mason, tell the kids to come say good night when they get home, and don't let them stay up too late."

"Will do, babe," he answered.

Vincent and Mason watched as Cherise disappeared down the hallway. Mason had no idea it was the shock of seeing Vincent that had her shaken more than her chaotic day. She just hoped Vincent wasn't in town to turn her life upside-down.

The next morning, Mason yawned as he walked into the kitchen. Staying up late talking to Vincent had taken a toll on him. Vincent hadn't left until around two a.m. It was now six-thirty and time to get the kids off to school. Cherise had already left to try to get a head start on her day. Mason sipped on his coffee and realized Cherise was leaving earlier in the mornings and coming home later at night. He would be happy when Cherise could get home at a decent hour. He worried about her just as much as she worried about him. Her job required her to go into undesirable neighborhoods at ungodly hours. If anything ever happened to her, he wouldn't be able to go on.

"Mase! Janelle! Let's go before you're late for school!"

"We're coming, Daddy!" they yelled in unison.

Janelle came running downstairs with her book bag in tow. Her hair, as usual, was pulled back in a ponytail. She was sporting her new baseball cap. Mason watched her grab a fruit roll-up and tear off the wrapping.

"Janelle, you're not wearing your cap to school. You know it's against school policy,"

"I know, Daddy. I only wear it during recess. I want to show it to Regis," she begged as she blinked her eyes at him.

Regis was Janelle's teammate and best friend. Mason and Cherise weren't surprised that she had a boy as her best friend. Their daughter was one of only two girls on the baseball team, so they knew it was only a matter of time before it happened.

"Take the hat off, Janelle, and don't try to take it to school again. Where's your brother?"

"Maaaaaaase!" she screamed.

"Janelle, sweetheart, Daddy could've done that," he said as he rinsed out his coffee mug.

"I know, Daddy. Where's Momma?"

He zipped up her jacket and put a strand of her hair back in place. "She had to go into work early again."

Janelle sighed.

"I miss Momma taking me to school."

"I know, but she's working, and hopefully she won't be busy much longer.

That goes for me, too. Once I'm done with this case, I'll be around a lot more with you guys."

Mase walked into the kitchen looking every bit of sixteen, even though he'd recently turned fourteen. He had on a pair of G-Units with a matching shirt. Mason watched him grab an apple out of the fruit bowl.

"Boy, I don't know what I'm going to do with you," Mason said as he looked at his son in amazement. "You are growing up too fast for me."

"What you talking about, Daddy?" he asked with a smile.

"Never mind, son. When you guys get out of school, ride the bus over to your grandparents' house and I'll pick you up from there."

"Daddy, I have to stay after school for weight training," Mase informed him.

"What time is that over?"

"Five o'clock," Mase replied.

"Just call me when you're done. One of us will pick you up. If not, your grandparents can. We'll work it out. Let's roll."

The kids piled into Mason's car so he could take them to school. After dropping them off he decided to check on Cherise. He dialed her number and waited.

"Dr. C. J. McKenzie," she answered.

"Hey, baby. How's your morning so far?" he asked.

"Hectic as usual. Are you on your way to work?"

"Yes, but only for a second. I'm going to hang out with Vincent today," he answered.

Cherise tapped her pen nervously on her desk. "What are you guys going to do?"

"I don't know. I'm sure we'll come up with something. It's good to see him, isn't it?"

She was silent for a moment. "Yeah, it's good to see him. I can't believe he just waltzed back into town like he's never been gone."

"Aren't you happy to see him, babe?"

If you only knew, Mason. "Yeah, it's good to see him, Mason, but he's wrong for staying away from you for so long."

Mason smiled proudly.

"I love it when my baby defends me. Don't worry, Cherise. I'm a big boy and

Vincent and I have talked about that. We're going to be seeing more of each other from here on out."

She bit down on her lower lip nervously upon hearing that news. She had no idea what Mason meant, but she would definitely find out the next time she spoke with Vincent.

"I see. Well, I need to get back to work. Are you going to be able to pick up the kids today?" she asked.

"I can if you have to work late," he responded.

"No, it's okay, I'll pick them up. Go on out and have fun with your brother. Just be safe," she instructed him.

"Will do, and don't work too hard. I love you and I'll see you later tonight. Oh! Mase won't get out of school until five. He has weight training and Janelle will be with your dad."

"Well, remind Daddy it's a school night and not to let Janelle con him into going out. You know he don't know how to tell her no."

Mason laughed because he had the same weakness with his daughter.

"Don't worry, I'm sure if he takes her anywhere, your mom will make sure he brings her home at a decent time."

Cherise thought for a second and agreed. There was no way her mother would let her father keep Janelle out on a school night.

"You're right, Mason. I'll call when we get home. Have fun."

"Will do. Good-bye, Cherise."

She hung up the telephone and hoped Vincent would behave himself while he was in town. The last thing she needed was for him to do something stupid to make Mason suspicious of them.

Chapter Fourteen

As Mason pulled into his parking space at Task Force headquarters, his phone rang—the special cell set up just for his assignment.

"Hey, sexy! I know you're an important man and all, but you promised we would spend some time together tonight. So when are we meeting? You know I'll make it worth your while."

He leaned back against the headrest of his car and sighed. "I'll see what I can do, Vada. I'm busy today, so I might have to cancel."

"You promised, Mirage," she whined.

He laughed. "Dang, girl! I just saw you the other day."

"I know, baby, but I can't help it if you have me addicted to you already," she purred like a cat. "T-bone asked about you."

"Why? The last time I saw him he wanted to kill me."

Vada giggled like a schoolgirl. "I told you he didn't mean it, baby. He wants you to come by tonight."

With a wrinkled brow, Mason quizzed her carefully. "What does he want?"

"I'm not sure, but I told him I wouldn't blame you if you didn't show up since he treated you so foul."

Mason contemplated meeting T-bone. He didn't want the man to think he could tell him to jump anytime he wanted. He had made his decision.

"Tell T-bone I already have plans and I'll call him when I get good and damn ready. Let his ass simmer in that for a while. I'm nobody's punk."

Vada became quiet on her end of the telephone. No one ever blew T-bone off, and when they did, there were consequences.

"Are you sure about this, babe?"

Mason opened the door of his car and climbed out. "Yeah, I'm sure."

Vada was worried about taking Mason's message back to her brother—worried that he might blame her, but she knew how to handle him. "What about me? Will I see you tonight?"

"I'll see what I can work out, Vada. I'll call you later."

"Okay, Mirage."

He clicked off and immediately made a call to his commanding officer. As the telephone rang, he exited the car and entered the building, wondering why T-bone wanted to see him. Finally his commanding officer answered.

"Domino, it's me. I'm on my way up to your office, but Vada just called and said T-bone wanted to see me tonight."

"I'm not in today. Did Vada say what he wanted?" Domino queried.

Mason walked into the elevator and pushed the button for his floor.

"Nah, she didn't say. I told her to tell him I was busy."

"Do you think that was a good idea? I mean things are getting hotter and there's a lot at stake."

The elevator door opened and Mason greeted people as he walked down the hallway toward his office.

"I'm in a good position. I have to let T-bone know I'm not a pushover."

"Maybe so, but you're not in yet, so don't be too hard."

Mason chuckled, walked over to his desk, and picked up his messages.

"I'll try."

Domino quizzed Mason a little more about Vada. "What else did she say?"

"Nothing much except she's trying to hook up with me tonight."

Domino became serious—because he knew the risks Mason was taking. "I'm not going to tell you to watch your back, because I know that you know that we can't risk your cover getting blown. T-bone is a ruthless character and he doesn't care who gets hurt."

"I know," Mason answered as he sat down at his desk. "That's the main reason I want to hurry up and finish this case. I can't put my family in harm's way."

"I understand, but you know we have a job to do, and unfortunately we have to do some things we otherwise wouldn't do."

Mason sat silently at his desk as he thought about what Domino had said.

"Look, Mason, do what you have to do, but if you decide to meet up with Vada, let the unit know. If you need me, give me a call."

"Cool. I'll holler at you later."

Mason sat there for a moment, then dialed Vincent to postpone their plans. An hour or so later, he was headed for his meeting with Vada, mostly because he didn't want her to start tracking him down. It didn't take long for her to pull up next to him in the parking lot of the Regal, Georgia, mall. He climbed out of the car and she threw her arms around his neck and greeted him with a big kiss.

"Hey, baby. Why did we have to meet here? I thought we were going to spend some time together."

"I told you I had something to do today, so this is all I have for you, Vada. Don't start tripping."

She put her hands on her hips in defiance. "So you're just going to leave me?"

Mason took her by the hands and pulled her closer. "Listen, Vada, I don't stay in one place too long. You're a wonderful woman, but I have some business I want to look into out West. If I decide to pass through this way later, I'll look you up, okay?"

Tears formed in her eyes, catching Mason off guard. She wiped away her tears and looked over at the patrons headed into the mall.

"I thought you was going to work with my brother."

Mason smiled, hoping to make her feel better. He never could stand to see a woman cry. "I haven't made any decision yet, Vada."

Vada cuddled closer to Mason, kissing his neck.

"He really does want you to work with him. They have some big shipments coming in, and I heard him say he could really use your connections."

Mason was excited to get that bit of information, but he didn't want to show it. He hugged her waist and kissed her lightly on her rose-colored lips.

"I don't know, Vada. I really do want to get out West and get my own thing going."

Vada hugged him tightly, pressing her hips into his. "There's a lot of money involved, and I know you love money, Mirage. Whatever you have waiting out

West would be more profitable with your pockets lined with a lot of money."

Mason pulled away and walked toward his car.

"I don't know, Vada. I'm supposed to be out on the West Coast by Thursday."

"Do it for me, Mirage? Maybe I could even go out West with you."

He laughed as he reached down to open his car door. "You're good, Vada, I have to give you that. Look, sweetheart, T-bone has a short fuse and I only deal with people who are smart and cool. Your brother is a ticking time bomb, and I can't afford to have him mess up what I'm trying to do."

"Come on, baby. Do this for me."

Mason dropped his head in thought and then looked over at her. "When is the shipment coming in?"

Vada eased over to Mason and slowly ran her hand down his thigh. Mason looked around to see if they were drawing any attention.

"I'm not sure, Mirage, but I think it's next weekend. T-bone said it was big, just like what I'm feeling right now."

He closed his eyes and groaned as Vada caressed him intimately. Breathless, he spoke with a stutter.

"Tell him I'll…damn! Tell him I'll think about it and get back with him."

Vada ran her tongue across his neck. "Come on, Mirage. Let's go back to my place so I can give you a real massage."

He took his keys out of his pocket and leaned against his vehicle.

"Vada, if we go back to your place I'm sure a massage is at the bottom of your list."

She giggled, knowing he saw right through her invitation. "You can't hate a girl for trying."

He ran his hand over his head and looked Vada up and down. The skirt she had on displayed her shapely legs and round derriere. He leaned over and kissed her on the cheek.

"I hate turning you down, Vada, no matter how tempting you look in that skirt, but I have to take care of business before pleasure."

Disappointment showed in her face as she took a step back from him. "I see. Well, I hope you at least do this upcoming job with T-bone. It will really help him out and keep this smile on my face. I still have to do a few bookkeeping transactions for him, then I'm turning it back over to him. I want to open my own business, and I can't do that fooling around with him."

He caressed her back and then hugged her. "I know, sweetheart. Just count your blessings you have that nice computer to help you."

She smiled and then kissed him long and hard. She released him reluctantly. "I hope you stay in town, because you're the only man that can light my fire. Call me."

He opened her car door so she could get inside. When she sat down the short skirt rose even higher up her thighs.

"I will. Drive safely."

When Vada drove off, Mason climbed into his vehicle and leaned against the steering wheel.

"Goddamn it!"

His unit was nearby watching and listening to everything. One of the members of his team decided to break radio silence only because Vada had already driven off.

"You cool?"

Mason's car was wired discreetly so not even T-bone would be able to find the devices. It would take an engineer to find out where the microphones were hidden. Mason turned the key in the ignition to start up his car.

"Yeah, I'm cool."

After Vada drove away, she placed a call to her brother.

"Yo!"

"Hey, bro, I just left Mirage and he's talking about leaving town. I don't know if I was able to convince him to stay. You'd better call him and talk to him. Maybe you can persuade him to stick around."

"Chill, sis. I'll give your little boyfriend a call," he said, laughing.

"Whatever! Let me know what he says," Vada requested before disconnecting.

T-bone immediately dialed Mason's number, who answered on the second ring.

"What's up, man? Vada told me you were leaving a brotha hanging."

Mason sighed. "Yeah, T-bone. I have some business ventures out West that I want to get into. I told Vada I don't stay in one place too long, and I don't think I want to put down roots here."

"Damn! I thought you were going to stay and let me make you a rich man. You have skills, and I like that in my partners."

Mason laughed because he had T-bone at the point of almost begging. "I appreciate the offer, but I think I'll pass on the partnership."

"Okay, then just help me close out this thing I have coming up next weekend. I'll make it worth your while, and all you have to do is help me through the final negotiations. Once the exchange is made, I'll give you your cut and you can go do your thing on the West Coast."

Mason was silent a moment. He had enough information to bust T-bone, but this deal sounded like he could quit working undercover in style. Against his better judgment, he played along.

"When are things jumping off?"

"I'll give you a call later and let you know. So are you down or what, Mirage?"

Mason paused. "Let me think about it overnight, and I'll get back with you tomorrow. I have to make sure I'm not walking into anything foul. Cool?"

"That's a bet," T-bone said before hanging up. T-bone leaned back in his chair and thought heavily about the upcoming shipment of merchandise. This was going to be much more profitable than what he'd been selling before. He'd never let anyone get close to him or his business except his homeboys or family, until Vada introduced him to Mirage. There was something that he liked about him the moment their eyes met. It was his tough-as-nails personality, and his knowledge of the streets. It was obvious he was business-savvy, which made him profitable to T-bone's organization. T-bone hoped he could convince Mirage to stay in town and in business with him. If not, he just might have to make the man an offer he couldn't refuse.

Chapter Fifteen

Cherise sat behind her computer going over some information. There was a knock on her door. Without looking up, she said, "Come in."

When she did look up, Vincent was standing there dressed handsomely in a black suit, accented by an elegant and decorative tie. Cherise was shocked that he had showed up at her office unannounced. Chills ran down her arms as she stood to greet him.

"Hey, Vincent. What brings you down here? I though you and Mason were hanging out today."

He walked into her office and smiled. "We were, but he called and said he got tied up with work so I thought I would drop by to see you, since I was in the area."

Cherise greeted him with a hug. "I see."

"You look stunning, C. J.," he said as he wrapped his arms around her waist and returned the hug.

"In these scrubs? Come on, Vincent."

He gave her waist an extra squeeze and looked down into her warm eyes. "You look great in anything, C. J."

She lowered her head, blushed, and then stepped away from him. "Don't even go there, Vincent. Why are you so dressed up, anyway?"

Vincent watched her as she slowly moved back behind her desk to take her seat. He unbuttoned his jacket and sat down in the chair in front of her desk. He crossed his legs and gave her a look that made her shiver.

"Oh, I figured I'd make a few goodwill visits downtown while I was in town."

She studied him closely and realized he was still pursuing her, just in a more subtle way.

"I see. Am I one of your goodwill visits?"

He laughed and smoothed down his tie. "As a matter of fact, you are. I came to take you to lunch, sweetheart, that's all."

She shook her head. "I don't think that would be a good idea. Besides, I'm mad at you for not telling me you were coming to Atlanta. Do you know how that made me feel when I walked into the house and saw you and Mason hanging out?"

"I thought you would be happy to see me, C. J."

"Vincent, we have a history and it's a history that could get us both in a lot of trouble. Plus I don't like surprises."

With his voice barely above a whisper, he questioned her reluctance. "Are you afraid of being alone with me, C. J.?" His voice was seductive, yet soothing.

"Yes, and I don't have to explain why, either. You have an advantage over me, since I don't remember what happened between us in Florida—you know all my weaknesses."

He sat up in the chair and cleared his throat. "C. J., I can't help the way I feel about you. That erotic encounter with you in Florida was unbelievable—the best sex I've ever had. I just hate it was drug induced. So are you going to lunch with me or not?"

"I don't think so. Besides, I have too much work to do."

Vincent frowned. He wasn't getting anywhere with her. So, since she was playing hard he'd have to play hardball. He pulled out his cell phone. Cherise ignored him as he did so—until she realized whom he had called. Her heart jumped up in her throat.

"Mason, it's Vincent. I was calling to see if you could talk some sense into C. J. I stopped by to take her to lunch and she's tripping, talking about she can't go to lunch with me."

He was silent for a moment as he listened to Mason's reply. He looked up at Cherise and winked.

"Okay, I'll put her on."

He held his cell out to her and she froze.

"Here you go, C. J. Mason wants to talk to you."

The smirk on his face made her want to choke him. She held her fist up at him and slowly took the telephone out of his hand. Gathering her thoughts, she finally put the phone up to her ear and cheerfully answered.

"Hey, baby."

"Cherise, is Vincent for real? Why won't you go to lunch with him? Come on, babe, you know I don't mind you two having lunch together, especially since I had to postpone our plans for a few hours. You're starting to get a little weird on me. What's going on with you?"

"I—I just didn't want any misunderstandings."

"Now why would I misunderstand? Look, go to lunch, have fun. You guys haven't had a chance to talk since he's been back, anyway. Tell Vincent I'll pick him up at his hotel around two o'clock."

"He's right here. You can tell him and I'll see you tonight. I love you."

"I love you, too, Cherise, but you need to get some rest because I don't like it when you're weird like this."

Without responding, she gave the cell back to Vincent. Vincent stared at her as he spoke to Mason. He was so relaxed and confident, which made her feel even more vulnerable in his presence.

"Hey, bro, C. J. is cracking up down here. You'd better hurry up and take her on vacation or something before she flips out," he joked.

Cherise sat there listening to his conversation with Mason. She couldn't hear what Mason was saying, but she knew she couldn't afford to make him suspicious of them. Seconds later she saw Vincent look at his watch and then back at her.

"Okay, Mason. I'll see you then. Later."

When he hung up, Cherise shook her head in disbelief. "I can't believe you did that, Vincent."

"What did I do?" he asked innocently.

"You just handled me, and I don't like being handled."

He stood up and slid his hands inside his pockets.

"You were worried about Mason not knowing we were hanging out, so I called him. Come on, C. J., stop acting so guilty and let's go to lunch."

She grabbed her purse out of her desk. "You're a trip, Vincent."

"No, you're the one that's a trip. All I want to do is take you to lunch," he assured her.

When they got to her door, she turned and looked up into his loving eyes.

"You still didn't have to embarrass me by calling Mason. I'm not a child."

"You wouldn't be going to lunch with me right now if I hadn't called him," he responded firmly. "Anyway, it's over and I just want to sit down and have a nice lunch with you."

As they walked out of the building together, Cherise wanted to believe he was being sincere, but she'd known him too long. Vincent was a man who always had a Plan B in the back of his mind.

Vincent's call freed Mason up to see what T-bone had up his sleeve. He pulled into the parking lot of a fast-food restaurant to call T-bone back. He dialed the number and waited for him to answer. T-bone arrogantly answered on the second ring.

"I knew you'd call back, Mirage."

"Whatever! Go ahead and fill me in on the details before I accept being a part of this thing."

"Meet me over at Vada's in five minutes, and I'll tell you everything."

"Are you sure? After all, you did pull a gun on me."

"Look, can't we drop that shit? I'm ready to make some money, and I need to know if you're game. I could really use you on this deal," T-bone stressed.

"Why do you want to include me?" Mason asked sarcastically.

T-bone sighed with frustration. "Let's just say I like how you handle your-self in tense situations. Look, just meet me at Vada's house."

"Okay, I'll see you shortly."

Mason hung up the telephone and then met with his unit so they could hook him up with a wire. The tape recordings were going to be critical to the case to bring down T-bone and his crew once and for all.

Mason pulled up to Vada's house and exited his vehicle. He walked up to the front door and rang her doorbell. When T-bone opened the door to let Mason in, he nervously looked up and down the street before closing the door. T-bone turned and clapped his hands together.

"Whassup, Mirage? You're right on time!"

"Yeah, I believe in being punctual. Where's Vada?"

T-bone picked up a bottle of beer and turned it up, swallowing the amber liquid.

"She's running some errands right now. Are you ready to get down to business?"

"The sooner the better," Mason said as he sat down opposite T-bone. "Fill me in."

A couple of the guys in T-bone's crew were also present. They nodded in Mason's direction before making their way toward the kitchen. Mason nodded back and waited on T-bone to tell him what his role consisted of on the upcoming deal.

T-bone leaned forward and whispered. "Mirage, I know these dudes who have some prime blow, and they're willing to do business with us if the price is right. Once the deal is set, we can cut it down and sell it so we can get the funds to purchase the firepower we need out here on the streets. I plan to own this city, and I can't do it with these toy guns we have now. So what do you think?"

Mason sat there staring at T-bone while he absorbed what he had just heard. There was no way the police could let T-bone, and those like him, destroy lives and communities. Mason cleared this throat.

"Who are you getting the blow from?"

T-bone leaned back in his chair and opened another beer.

"This dude I know gets it from some cats in South America. It's prime product."

"What guarantees do you have that these guys won't double-cross you?" Mason asked.

"That's where you come in. I know dude, but I don't trust him," T-bone admitted.

Mason frowned. "So where do I fit into this? I don't deal with drugs," he stated.

T-bone put his gun on top of the table. "Why not?"

Mason crossed his leg casually, never breaking eye contact. "Because drug dealers are the lowest. The people I deal with are into bonds, diamonds, and priceless artwork, things on that level."

T-bone started nodding his head to the beat of a song booming from the stereo. "That's cool, but that kind of crap is hard to move."

Mason picked up T-bone's gun and inspected it. "That's why you have to be connected. If you're not connected, you won't be able to move items like that," he informed T-bone. Mason's eyes followed T-bone's crew as they reentered the room. "What are those guys going to be doing while you're completing your deal?"

"They'll be there to cover us, as well as the perimeter. I need you up front with me so they'll know I'm all about business. So are you in or not?" T-bone asked him.

"I told you I don't deal with drugs. Besides, I've seen you in action and I can't jeopardize my plans for the sake of a kilo or two." Mason set T-bone's gun back down on the table. T-bone picked it up and started twirling it on his finger like a Western gunslinger. "It's your loss, Mirage."

Mason knew he couldn't appear too anxious to participate in the deal. He studied T-bone and thought about the luck he was having. He was going to have so much evidence against him there would be no way he would ever see the light of day again. If T-bone was going to purchase the quantity of drugs he said he was, he would be in jail for a long time.

"When and where is this meeting taking place?" Mason asked.

T-bone grinned, showing off a couple of gold teeth. "I knew you would change your mind. We're meeting down on the riverfront Friday night at midnight. You meet me here at ten so we can make sure everyone understands their assignments. I'm going out on a limb with this investment, Mirage. Failure is not an option," T-bone stressed.

Mason stood and walked over to the window. "Who are these guys? I'm not down unless I know what type of characters I'm dealing with. I don't like surprises."

Mason needed as much information as possible before walking into an unsafe situation. This would also allow his unit to be able to back him up properly.

T-bone stuck a toothpick in his mouth and put his feet up on the coffee table. "Damn Mirage! If you just have to know, his name is Pootie. Aight?"

Mason turned and folded his arms. "Cool. Now, that didn't hurt one bit, did it?"

"Whatever, man."

Mason pulled his keys out of his pocket.

"Look, I have somewhere to be. I'll see you later."

T-bone stood and gave Mason a brotherly handshake. "So does this mean you're down?"

"Yeah, I'm down, but just this once."

Mason opened the front door and walked out onto the porch. T-bone followed him out to his car. When Mason opened up his car door, T-bone put his hand on Mason, preventing him from getting inside.

"Yo, Mirage, my sister really is into you. I'll be pissed off if you break her heart."

Mason leaned closer to T-bone and said in a low voice, "Vada knows where our relationship stands, so I don't need your advice on how to deal with her. So in other words, stay out of my damn business."

T-bone burst out laughing. "Damn, Mirage! You need to loosen up a little. You're too serious. I was just messing with you. I already know my sister can hold her own, so don't think she's as soft as she acts. Vada is no joke."

"Thanks for the heads-up. Now, if you don't mind, I have somewhere to be."

T-bone backed away so Mason could get inside his car. He stood in the driveway and watched as Mason backed out onto the road and pulled back.

As Mason drove back to Atlanta he played back the events of his conversation with T-bone. After hearing everything said through the wire, he knew the unit already would be investigating "Pootie." Hopefully, by the time he got back to his office they would have the information he needed before his meeting the next night. Walking into an ambush with some low-life drug dealers was not an option.

It didn't take long for Mason to make it back to Atlanta. He pulled up in front of the Marriott and called Vincent on his cell phone. "Hey, man, I'm downstairs. Are you ready to roll?"

Minutes later Vincent hopped inside the car and greeted his brother. "Hey, man. What do you want to do today?"

"It doesn't matter to me. How was lunch with Cherise?"

Vincent nodded. "It was good. We went over to that seafood buffet on Peachtree Street."

"That place has some good food, and Cherise loves crab legs."

As Mason pulled off into traffic, Vincent laughed. "Yeah, you should've seen how many crab legs your wife put away."

"Why didn't she want to go to lunch with you?" Mason asked curiously.

Vincent looked at Mason seriously and sighed. "C. J. is still mad at me for not visiting you like I should've. She's very protective of you, Mason.; if I didn't know any better, I'd think she wanted to take a swing at me."

Mason laughed and pulled through the traffic light.

"That's my baby! I'm surprised she didn't hit you for real. Cherise can get very intense sometimes, but I think it's because of her job. She has to let off some steam somehow."

"I guess you're right. So, where are we going?"

"Well, are you up for a round of golf? I want to run some things by you regarding this case I'm working on."

"Sounds good to me. I haven't had a chance to play in a while."

"Me neither, to tell you the truth."

Vincent pulled out a stick of gum and put it in his mouth. "So, what's going on with this case? Things are going okay, aren't they?"

Mason sighed. "Sort of, but I have a serious problem."

He had Vincent's full attention now.

"What's wrong?" Vincent asked with genuine concern.

"There's a woman involved," Mason reluctantly admitted. "And she's all over me, bro."

"Is she the mark?"

Mason pulled into the parking lot of the country club and put the car in park.

"No, her brother is the target, but she's the key to getting my hands on all his financial records. I've had to lie to her to break her down, plus do some things I'm not proud of."

"Well, you've always known it's part of the job to do some bad things to get the bad guys off the street," Vincent reminded him.

"I know, but this is the first time I've had to sleep with a woman as part of the job."

Vincent's eyes widened at hearing that bit of information. It was obvious that Mason was having trouble dealing with it, especially after his and Cherise's rocky past.

"Mason, you can't think about C. J. when you're on the job. You have to become that imaginary person in order to make the streets safe for Mase and Janelle. That's what you need to think about. Do you understand what I'm saying?"

Mason popped the trunk before they got out of the car, then pulled out his duffle bag and a set of golf clubs.

"I guess you're right, but I feel so guilty when I go home and look Cherise in the eyes."

Vincent put his hand on Mason's shoulder to reassure him. "Look, bro, we've all done some things in our lives we're not proud of, but that doesn't mean we're bad people. You have a job to do, so do it!"

Walking toward the doors of the country club, Mason thought about what Vincent had said. "I guess you're right. I have to psych myself up when I have to meet up with her, though. So far she thinks she's the only woman in my life, but I told her I never stay in one place too long. I told her I was headed out West to start my own business."

"It's good you're letting her know there are no strings attached. Keep it that way, and everything will be just fine. Now come on so I can whip your ass," Vincent teased Mason.

Mason stopped in his tracks and smiled.

"Would you care to put a little wager down on that, little brother?"

Vincent laughed, reached inside his pocket, and pulled out a crisp one-hundred-dollar bill. He kissed it and waved in front of Mason's face.

"I love taking your money," Mason said.

"You wish!"

Mason then noticed a solemn look on Vincent's face as he stuck the money back into his pocket. "What's the somber look for?"

He exhaled loudly. "I'm thinking about resigning as chief."

Mason sat the golf bag down in disbelief. "What? You're not serious, are you?"

"Yeah. I've been giving it a lot of thought. I'm not happy being a pencil pusher, Mason. I really miss the action."

Mason couldn't believe his ears. "Wait a minute. Let me get this right. You want to give up the prestige and financial security of police chief to climb back down in the trenches?"

"Crazy, huh?" Vincent asked.

"Not really. While though I'm burnt out on undercover work, I understand where you're coming from—I could never work at a desk job. I'm proud of your accomplishments, little brother. At forty one years old you're one of the youngest black police chiefs in the country. You're a walking black history fact, Vincent."

"I guess. All I know is I miss the action and I miss my family. I want to move back to Atlanta," Vincent admitted.

Mason hugged his brother lovingly. "Well, I support whatever you decide to do, and just for the record, we would love it if you moved back, but we also love the fact that you're a police chief."

"Thanks, Mason. I really appreciate that. Well, come on, so I can take your money from you," Vincent said.

Mason gathered their belongings and headed out onto the golf course.

"Now you're really talking crazy."

Chapter Sixteen

Cherise left work early for a change and drove to the high school to pick up Mase before heading to her parents' house for Janelle. As she headed down the expressway she wondered why Vincent was being so nice to her. Was it the calm before the storm, or had he finally realized she could never be his? Whatever it was, she was glad he wasn't trying to put the full-court press on her at lunch. They'd actually had a very nice time, and didn't mention their past relationship at all. Instead, they discussed jobs, the family, and current events. It was like old times, and this was the Vincent she loved the most.

When Cherise pulled into the parking lot of Mase's school, she called Mason's cell phone. He answered cheerfully.

"Hello?"

"Hey, babe. I was calling to let you know I got off work early and I'm picking up Mase. What do you want for dinner?"

"From what I hear, you shouldn't be hungry for about three days," he teased.

"You tell Vincent he talks too much!" She could hear her brother-in-law laughing in the background. "Where are you guys, anyway?" she asked.

"Out on the golf course. I'm taking Vincent's money."

"I should've known," she responded. "So, what about dinner, babe?"

"I'm sure whatever you fix will be delicious, sweetheart," he assured her.

"What time should I expect you guys?"

"We'll be there in a couple of hours. I'm sure Vincent will want to change after I finish whipping up on him," he joked.

"Okay. Drive safely and I'll see you soon."

"Good-bye, sweetheart."

"Good-bye, baby." She hung up and waited for Mase to exit the gym.

Mase walked out with a young girl attached to his body. Cherise sat up in her seat and watched them as they unknowingly walked directly toward her truck. The girl was hugging Mase tightly around his waist and he was happily returning the favor. It was obvious that her son was enjoying the attention he was receiving from the girl who continued to be very physical with him, even kissing. Mase was laughing, until he finally he looked up and noticed his mom sitting in the truck watching them. He discreetly whispered something to the girl and removed her arms from around his waist. The girl waved good-bye to him, walked over to a car, and drove away. Mase opened the door of the truck and climbed inside. He leaned over and kissed Cherise on the cheek.

"Hey, Momma."

"Hello, son. I see you've had a nice day."

He blushed and looked away from her briefly. "I guess it was okay."

She started up the truck and put it in drive. "Just okay?"

Her very handsome son was growing like a weed. Cherise realized she was going to have to get used to an entourage of young girls flocking after him, but he was still her baby.

"Yes, ma'am," he replied.

Cherise smiled, sensing she was making him uncomfortable. "So, who was the girl attached to your hip?"

"Just some girl I know," he said, sliding down in his seat.

She looked over at him and realized she was torturing him, but she needed to know. "She has a nice car. How old is she?"

He blushed again.

"She's sixteen, Momma."

"I see," she responded casually. "Is she your girlfriend?"

"No, Momma, she's not my girlfriend. No, Momma, I haven't had sex with her. She's only a friend, so you don't have to get all freaked out. Okay?"

Cherise waited until she'd stopped at a traffic light before turning to her son. It seemed she had struck a nerve because he had never talked to her that way before.

"I love you, Mase, and all I want to do is protect you. I have a right to ask you about any girl I see hanging all over you. So you'd better watch your tone with me, young man."

"I know, Momma, but you're going to have to chill out. Daddy talked to me about all that girl stuff. I'm not going to bring home any babies, if that's what you're worried about. I know not to do anything stupid."

She leaned over and kissed him on the cheek. "I know, son, and I'm so proud of you. I guess it just caught me off guard."

"Thanks, Momma."

During the rest of the drive to her parents' house, they talked about school, summer vacation, and much more. When they pulled up into the driveway, Cherise and Mase climbed out and were greeted at the door by her father. Mase hugged his grandfather and quickly disappeared into the house.

"Hi, Daddy. Is Janelle ready to go? I need to get home so I can start dinner," Cherise said.

Jonathan Jernigan hugged and kissed her. "Why don't you guys just eat here?" She straightened her father's collar and smiled.

"I would, Daddy, but Vincent is in town visiting."

He folded his arms and leaned against the door frame.

"Really? That's nice. He hasn't been home in a long time, has he?"

"No, so they've been catching up on things with each other. They're out playing golf now."

Janelle ran to the door with her book bag in tow.

"Hey, Mommy!"

Cherise leaned down and kissed her cheeks. "Hey, precious! Did you have a good day at school?"

"Yes, ma'am," Janelle said as she reached up for her grandfather. "Bye, Grand-daddy!"

"See you tomorrow, sweetie pie."

They kissed each other good-bye before she ran out to the truck. Patricia Jernigan came to the door and hugged Cherise.

"Hey, baby. You look tired. Are you getting enough rest?"

Her mom seemed to have X-ray vision most of the time; it was hard for Cherise to hide anything from her.

"Yes, Momma, I'm getting enough rest. Thanks for looking after Janelle for me."

She put her hands on her hips and frowned. "Cherise Jernigan McKenzie! You know you don't have to thank us for looking after our own grandchildren."

"I still appreciate it, Momma," she replied before giving her mother a hug and kiss. "Well, I'd better get these two home. Where is Mase?"

"He's probably in the kitchen eating," her father replied. "I'll go get him. Drive safely, and tell Mason and Vincent I said hello."

"I will, Daddy."

Jonathan returned seconds later with Mase, who was eating a ham sandwich. They all said their good-byes and walked down the sidewalk toward the truck.

Mason and Vincent finally finished their round of golf. Once they got back to the car, Mason rubbed his hands together and laughed.

"Pay up, little brother. I told you I was going to kick your butt."

Vincent pulled out his wallet; with a smirk on his face he slapped the hundred-dollar bill into Mason's hand.

"You were lucky today, my brotha. Don't spend all of this in one place."

Mason took the bill and held it up to the sun to inspect it. "Luck has nothing to do with it. I'm better than you are, and you know it."

Vincent laughed as he put his wallet back into his pocket. "Don't worry, Mason, I will redeem myself next time."

Laughing, Mason continued to tease Vincent. "Wishful thinking, little brother."

"Whatever!" Vincent said, opening the car door. "Enjoy your victory while it lasts."

Mason climbed into the driver's seat. "Do you want to go back to your hotel before coming over for dinner?"

"Yeah, I need to take a shower and change. Did C. J. say what she was cooking tonight?"

"I have no idea, so be warned. We're at her mercy," Mason joked as he pulled out into traffic. Vincent laughed.

"You're full of it. You know C. J. is an excellent cook."

"You're right about that."

Before returning Vincent to his hotel, Mason drove him through their old neighborhood. Vincent was amazed at how much Atlanta had changed, and all of it wasn't for the best. About a half-hour later, Mason pulled up in front of the Marriott. Vincent opened the car door and climbed out.

"I'll see you guys in about an hour," he said before closing the door.

"Will do," Mason said before pulling away from the curb.

Chapter Seventeen

Back at the house, Cherise was putting together some spicy Cajun dishes. One of Mason's favorites was Etouffée. Cherise heard the garage door going up, alerting her that Mason was home. She opened the kitchen door, which led to the garage, so she could greet him. Their eyes met and they smiled back at each other. He shut off the car as the garage door lowered. He climbed out and greeted her with a huge hug, lifting her off the floor.

"I missed you today, Dr. McKenzie."

She held onto his neck and kissed him greedily on the lips.

"Hmmm, that was very nice," he acknowledged.

He carried her into the kitchen and Cherise nuzzled his neck.

"I just wanted to show you that I missed you too, Detective McKenzie. How was your golf game?"

He sat down in a nearby chair with Cherise in his lap and happily pulled the one-hundred-dollar bill out of his pocket and proudly displayed it.

"Where did you get that money from?"

"I won it off of that playboy brother of mine. I told him he couldn't beat me at golf."

Cherise laughed and eased out Mason's lap to walk over to the stove so she could stir her dish. "You guys are always competing."

Mason followed her and turned her around to face him. He seductively tucked the money down into Cherise's blouse and kissed her neck. He whispered so no one could hear him but her.

"This is for you, sweetheart. Buy yourself something hot and sexy that will drive me wild."

She moaned as he continued to sprinkle her neck with butterfly kisses. "You're about to start something, Mason."

He patted her playfully on the backside and looked into her wanting eyes. "I can take care of that a little later."

"I'm counting on it, babe."

He smiled. "I'll be back down to help you with dinner after I take a shower."

Turning back to her dish, she blew him a kiss. "Okay, sweetheart."

Mason disappeared up the stairs while Cherise set the table.

It didn't take him long to return to the kitchen to help Cherise finish up dinner. He was a pretty good cook, considering he didn't get many opportunities to showcase his talents. He removed the top to a nearby skillet, closed his eyes, and inhaled the aroma of the Etouffée. As expected, it was mouthwatering.

"Do you want me to put this in a casserole dish?"

She turned to him and pointed to a cabinet door. "Yes, use the blue one on the top shelf."

Mason took the dish out of the cabinet and started spooning the food into it. "It's great having Vincent home, isn't it?"

Cherise, with her back to him, spoke softly.

"Yes, it is. It's just like old times. I cook, and you and Vincent eat. Plus, you guys always find something to compete against each other in. Basketball, video games, pool, darts; you name it, you guys challenged each other. I would hate to know how much money you lost as teenagers between the two of you."

Mason laughed. She was right. She would be surprised, because they always made huge wagers with each other. He placed the dish into the oven and set the timer.

"Come on, Cherise, it's in our blood to compete. I just wish he'd settle down. He's not getting any younger; he needs a good woman by his side."

She opened the refrigerator and took out the iced tea. "Maybe Vincent doesn't want to get married. It's not for everyone, you know."

Mason got the utensils out of the drawer. "That's a possibility, but something tells me he does."

"Why do you say that?" she asked.

He shrugged. "I don't know. He's so suave with the ladies. It just seems like a waste if he doesn't. I want him to have a wife and children to grow old with like I do. He's my brother and I want more for him."

Cherise walked over to him and put her arm around his shoulders.

"Vincent is a grown man, Mason. When he finds the woman of his dreams, I'm sure he'll make her his own."

"I hope you're right," he said as he kissed her forehead.

Vincent arrived about forty-five minutes later. At dinner, he fascinated Mase and Janelle with stories about him and Mason growing up, and their time at the police academy. They asked a thousand questions about Texas and wanted to know when they could come for a visit.

"Uncle Vincent, is it true that it gets hot enough in Texas that you can fry an egg on the sidewalk?"

Vincent wiped his mouth. "Yes it does, Mase."

"So I guess that means the girls don't wear a lot of clothes when it's that hot?"

Cherise's head snapped around.

"Mase! You don't need to worry about what girls are wearing. You should be asking your uncle if there are any good universities out there."

"Ah, Mom, I was just asking. Dang!"

Vincent smiled, and Mason laughed at his son's question and the way his wife reacted to it. Vincent winked at Mase to put him at ease. "I'm sure by the time you graduate from college, your question will be answered, Mase."

Cherise put her fork up to her mouth in silence and eyed Mase. Janelle picked up a piece of garlic bread and waved it in the air.

"I'm going to be the first woman to play in the major leagues, Uncle Vincent."

Impressed, Vincent said, "Really? You're that good?"

She jumped out of her chair. "I'm better than good, Uncle Vincent. I've won the Most Valuable Player award every season. You wanna see my trophies?"

Mason put his hands up to slow Janelle down.

"Janelle, I'm sure your uncle would love to see all your trophies, but it'll have to wait until after dinner."

Vincent gave her a high-five.

"Your dad is right. I'll get a chance to see you play while I'm here."

Cherise stood up and began to remove the empty dishes from the table.

"Janelle, come help your mom get dessert for everyone."

"Okay, Momma," she answered.

Vincent leaned back and patted his stomach. "No dessert for me. I can't eat another bite."

Mason stood and agreed with Vincent. "Me neither, sweetheart."

"Are you sure?"

"Yeah. Vincent, come on into the family room. I have something you might be interested in."

Vincent followed Mason into the family room. Cherise smiled and stacked up their plates. "I'll bring you guys some coffee in a second."

She handed Janelle the stack of plates. "Janelle, take these into the kitchen for me, baby, but be careful."

"I will, Mommy."

Janelle followed her mom's instructions and exited the room with the dishes. Cherise then turned to Mase just as he was about to sneak out of the room.

"Hold it right there, young man. I think it's your night to do the dishes, so don't even think about disappearing."

"Ah, Mom!" he whined.

"Mase! You know the rules," she reminded him.

She hugged him and kissed his cheek. Grabbing his chin, she looked into eyes that were just like Mason's. Eyes she loved very much.

"Mase, no arguing."

"Well, I guess I'd better go bust those suds, huh?"

"Knock yourself out."

They laughed as they walked into the kitchen together, where they found Janelle helping herself to Cherise's homemade apple pie.

"Janelle! What are you doing?"

"I'm having my dessert, Momma. Want some?"

"First of all, young lady, you know that piece of pie is too big for you. Secondly, you were supposed to be helping me clear the table. Now, go take your bath so you can get to bed."

"Momma!" She pouted.

Cherise folded her arms. "Janelle!"

"Janelle, you'd better go on before Momma snaps on you, too," Mase warned. "She might make you sit out of one of your games."

Janelle walked over and gave Cherise an apologetic hug. "I'm sorry, Momma. Can I go tell Uncle Vincent and Daddy good night?"

"Of course you can. Look, Janelle, I know you're my baby and we're guilty of spoiling you, but don't you ever try to talk back to me again. Okay?"

"Okay, Mommy." Janelle walked over to Mase and hugged his waist. "Good night, Mase."

"Good night, Angelica. I'll be up to read you a story a little later."

Angelica was a mischievous character from one of Janelle's favorite TV shows, *Rugrats*. Whenever Janelle acted like a brat, he called her that name to irritate her even more.

"Mase!"

He laughed as she stomped off to her room. After Janelle left the room, Cherise turned to Mase.

"You do know that you are not helping," she said, fighting back a smile.

"She's my little sister, Momma. I'm supposed to bug her."

Cherise arranged the coffeepot and cups on the tray. "Let me get this coffee in there to the men. I'm sure they'll be up for a while talking. Hurry up and finish the dishes."

"Okay, Momma."

Cherise took the coffee into the family room and set it down on the table. "Mason, I'm going up to bed. Mase is in the kitchen doing the dishes."

He stood up and gave her a kiss. "Okay, sweetheart. Get some rest."

Vincent stood and walked over to Cherise. He leaned down and kissed her on the cheek.

"Good night, C. J. Dinner was delicious as always. Thanks for the invitation."

She turned to walk out of the room. "You don't have to thank me, Vincent. You're welcome here anytime. I'm just glad you're home."

"So am I," he admitted. "Hey! Why don't you two come have breakfast with me at the hotel in the morning? They have a great breakfast buffet. My treat!"

Mason lit a cigar. "If you're treating, I'm there."

Cherise frowned.

"Baby, don't smoke up my house. I don't know, Vincent. I have a lot of work waiting on me at the office."

Mason wrapped his arms around her waist. "Come on, baby. He's feeding us for a change. We have to accept."

"Well, if you put it that way," she said as she fanned the smoke away from her face. "I guess I can go into the office a little later."

Vincent clapped his hands together in victory. "Good! I'll see you in the morning around nine."

"Don't you two burn down my house with those cigars!" Cherise yelled as she exited the room.

Neither of them responded to Cherise's warning. While Mason poured their coffee, Vincent lit his cigar and couldn't help but sneak a glance at Cherise's heavenly body as she exited the room. His body immediately hardened when he started having flashbacks of their sexual encounter. He wanted Cherise and he wanted her bad.

"Do you want some coffee, Vincent?"

Mason's voice snapped him out of his erotic trance. "I think I will, Mason, thank you."

Mason handed Vincent the cup and sat down next to him as the boxing match they wanted to watch began. Vincent, on the other hand, was praying he would be able to get his body under control by the twelfth round.

Chapter Eighteen

After dropping the kids off at school the next morning, Cherise and Mason headed to the Marriott to meet Vincent. He greeted them in the lobby and led them toward the dining area. Once they were seated, Vincent said, "Guys, you're going to love the food. I think I've gained ten pounds already."

Mason laughed. "You couldn't gain ten pounds if you wanted to. You work out too much to allow yourself to gain any weight."

Cherise looked around the room at the delicious food on the plates of other patrons. Moments later, the waitress approached their table and took their drink order. The threesome then was told they could help themselves to the buffet table. Cherise was the first to return to the table. She blessed her food and then started eating. Being growing boys, it took Mason and Vincent a few minutes longer to fill their plates. They returned to the table together, discussing what they were going to get on their second trip to the buffet table. Cherise looked at their plates and shook her head in disbelief before sampling the crispy bacon, eggs, and fruit on her own plate. She put the fork in her mouth and closed her eyes. She was enjoying the food so much she didn't hear Vincent call her name.

"C. J.!" he yelled.

She nearly jumped out of her chair. Mason snickered and continued to eat.

"Oh, I'm sorry. I wasn't paying attention."

"That's an understatement. Where were you?"

Embarrassed, she lowered her head. "About a million miles away enjoying this food," she whispered.

Vincent looked over at Mason. "See, that's what I'm talking about. You see how edgy she is? C. J., you'd better start chilling out before they make you go out on personal leave or something."

She fumbled with the napkin in her lap. "I'm fine, Vincent," she said angrily.

"Take it easy, baby," Mason said. "He's just making an observation."

"I'm sorry. I just have a lot on my mind," she said.

Mason lectured her as Vincent looked on. "If work is getting to you, sweetheart, you're going to have to learn to let it go. That's the only way any of us can get through the day. I know it's hard, baby, but you have to fight those demons."

Vincent put his fork up to his mouth and stared at her. Their eyes met and held there for a few seconds. Cherise took a breath before speaking.

"I'm sorry for yelling at you, Vincent, and I appreciate your concern, but I'm okay."

"No harm done. I'm a big boy—so I'm used to women yelling at me."

Mason laughed out loud. "Speaking of women, when are you going to settle down?"

Vincent frowned and waved him off. He sat his fork down and wiped his mouth with the napkin.

"Don't even try it, Mason. Since I've become police chief you should see the women who throw themselves at me. It's ridiculous!"

"Aww, look at the poor baby! What the hell is wrong with you, Vincent? Do you know how many men would love to be in your position? The guys at the station ask about you all the time."

Cherise tried her best not to act interested in the conversation.

"Are some of the women skanks?" Mason asked.

Vincent laughed. "What the hell? Man, you know I don't fool with skanks."

Cherise giggled at Mason's remark, which caused Vincent to look directly at her.

"You know I only deal with the best of the best. They have to be intelligent, physically fit, love sports, and sexy."

"What about beautiful?" Mason asked.

"Don't get me wrong, I love beautiful women, but I appreciate a woman who is naturally attractive and uninhibited. That's sexier to me than anything."

Vincent's comments piqued Cherise's interest, so she decided to get into the conversation.

"So, brother-in-law, do you have any prospects? You know you're not getting any younger."

Vincent buttered a croissant before answering. He'd picked up on Cherise's interest and decided to have a little fun with her.

"I might have a few prospects on the horizon. Who knows, I might be headed to the altar before the year is out."

Mason laughed.

"Yeah, right! I'll believe it when I see it, but I would feel better if you had someone to look after you. I can't think of my life without Cherise and the kids. It brings some normalcy into my life after working that crazy-ass job. You have to have a good woman by your side."

"I can see that," Vincent admitted. "It can get kind of lonely coming home to an empty house every day."

"Then why don't you do something about it?" Cherise asked with a raised brow.

Vincent realized she was definitely challenging him. "Well, C.J., when I can finally get my hands on the right woman, I just might do that. Too bad you're not available."

Cherise almost spat out her juice. She gave him the evil eye.

"You wish!" Mason yelled through laughter. Vincent laughed along with him.

"I was making sure you were paying attention, big brother."

"Don't worry, I was."

Cherise didn't see anything funny about Vincent's comment. It was like he wanted Mason to find out about them.

"Seriously, though, I am sort of dating a woman named Rachel who works in the governor's office. She's cool, but she's a little clingy," Vincent admitted. "She's always in business mode and she doesn't know how to relax."

Cherise held her glass up to him and said with obvious sarcasm. "Well, I'm sure you know how to help her relax."

He winked at her.

"I have my ways."

Mason stood and stretched. "Well, if it's not Rachel, I hope you find some-body soon, little brother.

"Me, too."

Mason then looked over at Cherise. "Sweetheart, do you want anything else from the buffet table?"

She looked up at him with true admiration.

"Yes, honey, I would like an omelet with the works and a little more fruit."

Vincent held his plate out to Mason playfully.

"What about me? Aren't you going to ask me if I want anything else?"

"I'm not your woman, get your own food," Mason grumbled as he walked away.

Vincent laughed and watched Mason walk toward the buffet table. The wait-ress came by their table to refill their drinks. Vincent sat there staring at Cherise without blinking an eye, causing chills to run all over her body. She put her coffee cup up to her mouth and whispered discreetly to him. "Stop staring at me, Vincent."

"I can't help it that I'm in love with you, C. J.," he whispered without showing any emotion.

"Stop it," she replied as she looked up to make sure Mason was still occupied at the buffet table.

"I want to kiss you so bad right now that I'm hard," he informed her. "That's why I'm going to have to wait a few minutes before I can go up to the buffet table."

"You are so nasty, Vincent."

He leaned forward and spoke to her with seriousness. "I'm just telling you the truth. All I can think about is how your skin feels against mine."

Cherise closed her eyes and squirmed in her seat. He was once again stirring up memories that she was trying to forget. While her eyes were closed, Mason walked up unnoticed.

"Why are you guys looking so serious?"

Startled, Vincent sat straight up and cleared his throat.

"C. J. was telling me about that case she was working on involving those children."

Mason sat two plates down on the table and took his seat. With a worried look on his face, he observed Cherise's behavior.

"Is that still bothering you, sweetheart?"

She took a sip of her coffee and hesitated before answering. "Sometimes."

"I'm sorry, sweetheart."

She patted his hand and smiled.

"I'm okay, Mason, but I don't want to talk about it anymore. Okay?"

Vincent was finally able to stand up.

"It's okay, C. J. Sometimes it's good to talk about your cases because it'll eat you up inside if you don't."

She nodded as Vincent headed up to the buffet table. Mason gave her hand a squeeze.

"Are you sure you're okay?" he asked.

She leaned over and kissed him tenderly on the lips. She then wiped the remnants of her lipstick from his lips.

"I'll be fine, baby. Thank you."

His cell went off, interrupting them. He looked down at it and cursed. "Damn!"

"What's wrong?"

He got up from the table. "Hold on a second. It's the office. I'm going outside to call them and see what's up. Tell Vincent I'll be right back."

She nodded. He kissed her and then walked out toward the lobby. Vincent returned to the table with a full plate and sat down.

"Where's Mason?"

"He got a page from the office. He said he would be back in a second."

Vincent dug into his food. "I see."

They ate in silence for several minutes before Vincent spoke again.

"Just for the record, I meant what I said, C. J. It's driving me crazy being this close to you and not being able to touch you."

She banged her fist on the table and gritted her teeth.

"Stop it, Vincent! Don't you realize Mason could've heard our conversation when he walked up?"

Calm, cool, and collected, he just smiled. "But he didn't."

She eyed him angrily. "Well, you're going to have to forget about me because I'm not available anymore. I'm sorry that man drugged me in Florida, causing me to seduce you. I'm sorry the drug-induced sex turned you out. You'll be fine when you get back to Texas to that woman in the governor's office."

He laughed at her comment.

"Baby, contrary to what you think, I was turned out by you the first time I saw you smile. And just for the record, that woman in Texas could never measure up to you."

She rolled her eyes in disbelief.

"Are you jealous, C. J.?"

She jabbed her fork into her fruit. "No, I'm not jealous!"

He knew Cherise didn't like hearing intimate details about him dating another woman, so he decided to push her buttons even more. He took a sip of his coffee. "I think you are jealous because you know how I make you feel. You don't want anyone else to get that feeling from me, do you?"

"What you do with your women is your business, not mine."

"All you have to do is say the word and I won't touch that woman ever again. But in return, you'll have to be available for me whenever and wherever I want you. Something tells me that Mason's not satisfying you like I can."

The way Vincent was sensuously speaking to her made her extremely hot, and it angered her. "Shut up, Vincent," she whispered without looking at him.

"C. J., all you have to do is say the word, baby, and I'll start giving you those multiple orgasms again. It's your call," he said as he sat back in his chair and casually ate his food.

By this time, her lower region was throbbing because Vincent was right. Mason was a great lover, but Vincent was even better. Mason returned to the table and sighed. "Hey guys, I have to jet. Honey, is it okay with you if Vincent takes you back by the house to get your truck, because I won't have time to do it."

Vincent waved him off.

"Why don't we do this? Mason, you go ahead and drop C. J. off at work since her office isn't far from here. I'll pick her up and make sure she gets home safely. It doesn't make sense to go all the way back out to the house right now."

She stood up and grabbed her purse. "It doesn't matter to me. Mason, do you have time to drop me off?"

"Sure, babe, let's go."

She swallowed hard because she could feel Vincent's eyes burning into her skin. He signed the receipt for breakfast and thanked both of them for joining him.

"Let me walk you guys out."

He escorted the pair out into the parking lot. Before they drove off, he looked over at Cherise.

"C. J., call me when you're ready, and I'll pick you up."

"I will, good-bye."

Vincent backed away from their vehicle and watched as they drove off.

When Mason joined the members of the Anti-Crime Task Force for a briefing, Domino handed him the file on Wendell James, aka Pootie. He had a long criminal history; now at the ripe age of thirty, he had become one of the top dealers in the city. As their commanding officer went over the file with them, Mason studied every line of his face, especially his eyes.

"Mason, I want you to have extra backup this meeting, so I'm calling in additional manpower to make sure everything goes smoothly. I don't want you to use the wire this time. We'll use our long-range equipment because Pootie has a reputation of being paranoid. He'll surely frisk you," Domino said.

"I'm down with that," Mason responded. "T-bone is starting to loosen up and trust me a little more, but I haven't been able to get access to his files. His sister doesn't leave the computer up all the time."

"Why don't you try to watch her fingers when she types in her password? Then when she's asleep, you'll get your chance to log on," Rat suggested.

Mason twirled around in his chair.

"That's cool, but what if she wakes up? She'll want to know how I got her password."

"Oh yeah. I didn't think about that one."

The others chuckled.

"Tell her you want to use her computer," Tank said. "Then get her drunk or something."

Mason shook his head and laughed. "You guys are crazy. She's too smart to let something like that happen to her. I'll work it out."

"I've seen Vada," Rat joked, "Just say the word and I'll switch places with you."

They all laughed again. Mason threw a crumpled-up piece of paper at him.

"I know this is all a joke to you guys, but if my wife ever finds out about Vada, I'm history."

Domino put the folder on the desk and looked at Mason and the rest of the unit seriously.

"Mason, we all know you're putting a lot on the line to get creeps like T-bone and Pootie off the streets. As you all know, we have an iron code in this unit that no one, and I mean no one, reveals the things we do for the good of the community. We're a family and we protect our own, so don't ever forget it."

The group agreed loudly, with high-fives and pats on the back. Mason stood up and folded his arms.

"Look, guys, I appreciate all of you for having my back all these years, and it's good to know that you'll do whatever it takes to protect my family. Most of you know my wife works closely with the department, and I just want to reiterate how important it is that nothing leaks out of this unit that could damage my marriage."

"Mason," Domino interrupted, "we'll protect you just like we would want you to protect us if we were in your position. Now, with that said, let's go over the layout of the riverfront and the backup plan."

Mason sat down at his desk and picked up the telephone.

"First, let me call my wife and let her know not to wait up for me."

While he was making his telephone call, the rest of the unit went over photographs, diagrams, and other information they had obtained about the perpetrators. Mason leaned back in his chair and put his feet up on his desk. He was disappointed when he got her voice mail, because he really wanted to talk to her before going back undercover. He was reduced to leaving her a message so she would know he wouldn't be home tonight, and possibly the rest of the week. After leaving the message, he rejoined his group and briefed them on everything T-bone told him about the upcoming meeting.

After Cherise arrived at work, she immediately went to her lab. Her staff was already busy with their duties, and she joined them so they could try to clear the many cases they had on their logs. As she put on her lab coat and goggles, she couldn't help but remember her conversation with Vincent. It angered her that she responded physically to his taunting behavior. It also angered her that she was jealous when he mentioned the woman in Texas. She wasn't looking forward to riding home with him later today.

Vincent arrived to pick Cherise up at her office. He signed in as a guest of Cherise's and received his visitor's pass to enter the building. He waited for her in the lounge area, but within minutes, she sent word for him to wait in her office. It took Cherise longer than expected to finish up. She hurried into the office, took off her lab coat, and hung it up.

"Vincent, I'm so sorry you had to wait so long for me. It took longer than expected to run that last test."

He smiled.

"It's okay, C. J. It's not like I had anywhere to be."

"Well, I still want to apologize. I'll be ready to go as soon as I take care of a few things," she said as she sat behind her desk. She sent a couple of e-mails and checked her voice mail. "There! I'm all done. Are you ready to go?"

"Whenever you are."

Cherise turned off her computer and stood. She glanced over her desk to make sure she had everything she needed, then unlocked her desk drawer and pulled out her purse. As they walked out into the hallway, Vincent asked her if they needed to pick the kids up on the way to the house.

"You don't have to do that. You can just drop me off so I can get my truck and I can go from there."

"It's no problem, C. J.," he volunteered. "We can go ahead and get them now so you won't have to come back out."

"I know, but it's not necessary."

"Suit yourself," he answered as he drove out onto the expressway.

Their ride in rush-hour traffic put them at her house around six-thirty. Vincent pulled into the driveway and shut off the engine. Cherise opened the car door and turned toward Vincent.

"Thanks for the lift home. I really appreciate it."

He opened his car door and climbed out of the car.

"You know I don't mind helping out. Let me see you in safely."

"You don't have to do that, Vincent. I'm just going in for a second, then heading right out to get the kids."

He ignored her and continued to walk down the sidewalk to the front door. When they reached the porch, Cherise nervously fumbled with her keys.

"Relax, C. J., I'm not going to bite you."

Cherise slowly opened the door and walked inside. Vincent walked in behind her and closed the door. She turned around to face him, but she couldn't make direct eye contact with him.

"This really isn't necessary, Vincent. I come home alone all the time."

"I'm sure you do, but today I'm responsible for you, so it's my job to make sure you get inside safely. Besides, I wouldn't be able to live with myself if something happened to you."

The chills were back and they were running all over her body. She turned on the light in the foyer and dropped her keys on the hall table.

"Can I get you anything to drink before you go?"

He walked over closer to her, stopping within inches of touching her. He already knew the answer to the question he was about to ask her, but he decided to ask her anyway.

"Why are you in such a hurry to get me out of here?"

She backed away from him. "I'm not throwing you out, Vincent. I'm just tired and want to get settled, that's all."

He shoved his hands inside his pockets.

"Okay, C. J., I'll back off, but there's something you need to do for me."

She looked at him curiously. "What?"

He pulled the small envelope out of his pocket and handed it to her. She looked at it and frowned, then held the envelope back out to him.

"You're crazy! Get that away from me!"

"C. J., I'm serious about this. I have a right to know if Janelle is mine. I ordered this DNA kit online so our privacy can be protected. No one will ever have to know but us."

She shook her head in disagreement as she leaned against the wall. "I can't do it, Vincent. Why can't we just leave things as they are?"

He cupped her face and kissed her tenderly on the lips. "Because I deserve to know the truth, and deep down you know you want to know also."

She put the envelope inside her purse and lowered her head. "What are you going to do if Janelle is your daughter?" she asked softly.

"Honestly? I don't know. I'll have to cross that bridge when I get to it."

Frustrated, she looked up into his weary eyes. "You're not going to leave it alone, are you?"

"I can't, C. J."

They stood there staring at each other. He looked at his watch, breaking the spell.

"Well, I guess I'd better be going. I have a dinner date and I don't want to be late. I would appreciate it if you could get this done as soon as possible. Do you want to swab me now?"

She threw up her hand in disagreement.

"No, I need time to think about this."

He walked toward the front door without answering. Cherise followed so she could see him out. He put his hand on the doorknob and then turned to her.

"Don't wait too long, C. J., because if you don't do it, I will."

"Okay, Vincent. Thanks for the ride home."

"You're welcome. Well, I guess I better get out of here, huh?"

She nodded in agreement and had to will her body to stop trembling. Vincent walked out onto the porch, but again he turned back around to talk to her. "Do you love me?"

She closed her eyes briefly and then looked up into his dark brown eyes.

"You know I love you, Vincent," she answered.

"No, I mean do you love me?"

Cherise knew exactly which kind of love he was talking about. He was standing so close to her that she could hear his heart beating. She definitely cared deeply for him, but it was Mason whom she loved.

"Vincent, I can't give you what you want, emotionally or physically. Not anymore."

He stood there and stared at her in silence, making her feel very uneasy. The air was becoming thin and the heat from his body was starting to make her simmer. There had always been an explosive and strong sexual chemistry between them, and at the moment, Vincent was playing upon her obvious weakness.

"Shouldn't you be getting ready for your date?"

"Just get the swab, C. J. Good night."

Cherise didn't respond. All she could do was watch him walk to the car and drive off. She closed the door and took a deep breath. She wasn't going to be in any hurry to get a sample from Janelle. Gathering her senses, she grabbed her purse so she could pick up the kids from her parents' house.

After picking up the kids, Cherise ordered pizza for dinner. She wasn't very hungry, mostly because she felt a headache coming on. She knew it was the result of her earlier encounter with Vincent. Mase noticed her quiet demeanor and became concerned.

"Momma, are you feeling okay?"

She looked over at him and smiled. "Yes, baby, I'm fine. I have a headache, that's all," she admitted.

"Do you want me to drive the rest of the way?"

Cherise gave him a surprised look. "Mase, you know you're not old enough to drive."

"I know, Momma, but you have to admit, I can drive."

Pulling off the freeway, she pulled up to a traffic light. "I know you can drive, Mase, but it's against the law unless you have a permit."

"I know, but if you're not feeling well, I could drive the rest of the way. If we get stopped, I'll just tell them you're sick."

She caressed his cheek.

"It's just a headache, sweetheart. I'm okay."

Cherise looked in the rearview mirror and noticed that Janelle had fallen asleep. Mase turned around and looked at his sleeping sister.

"Momma, you don't have to pick us up from Granddad's house every day. I'm old enough to look after Janelle until you get home."

"I don't know about that, Mase. I wouldn't feel right leaving you two at home without adult supervision. I worry about you enough as it is. I wouldn't be able to concentrate at work because I would be afraid of the house catching fire or someone breaking in."

Mase frowned and slumped down in his seat. Once again he had been shot down because of his age. He was trying to be a man, and his mother was trying to keep him as her little boy.

"I know, Momma, but I know I can do this. Even though I just turned fourteen, you have to admit I'm bigger than most eighteen-year-old guys."

Cherise continued to drive in silence. Everything Mase was saying was true. He was very responsible for his age, but he was still too young legally to do the things he wanted to do. She did hate picking them up so late, which caused them to get in bed even later. She wanted nothing more than to be at home with them at a reasonable hour. Maybe her mom and dad could come over and sit with the kids until she got home, or at least check on them. She would have to give it more thought when her head wasn't throbbing.

"Mase, I don't know. That's something I would have to discuss with your dad, and I'm going to tell you now, I'm a little nervous about it. I'd feel better if you were at least sixteen before you guys were home alone. At least then, if anything happened, you could drive over to your grandparents' house."

His eyes lit up, and he grinned.

"Does that mean I'm going to have a car by the time I'm sixteen?"

She laughed. "Don't push it, Mase."

When they pulled into the garage, Mase unbuckled his seat belt and jumped out. "I'll bring Janelle in, Momma."

"Thank you, sweetheart. I'll grab the food," she responded as she unbuckled her seat belt.

They entered the house and Mase sat a sleepy Janelle down at the kitchen table. She was still groggy, but she woke up once Cherise put the pizza box on the table.

"Janelle, are you up to eating a little something before you go to bed?"

"Yes, ma'am," she answered as she laid her head down on the table.

Cherise walked over and kissed her daughter on the cheek. "Janelle, I'm sorry I picked you guys up so late. I know you're tired."

Janelle hugged her momma's neck and assured her they were fine. "I'm okay, Momma. I ate over at Granddad and Grandma's house, but that was when I got in from school. I'm hungry again."

"Go wash your hands and I'll fix your plate for you."

Janelle hopped up and walked slowly toward the bathroom. The telephone rang just as Mase returned to the kitchen. "Hello?" he answered.

"Hey, son! How are you doing?"

"Hi, Daddy. I'm cool. We're just getting home and about to eat."

Cherise looked at her son, who was obviously happy to hear his father's voice. It brought a smile to her face because she could see Mase becoming a man right before her eyes.

"How was school?" Mason quizzed him.

"It was all right. Are you still at work?" Mase questioned his dad.

"Yes, and unfortunately I'm going to be tied up for a few days. Where's your mom and sister?"

"Janelle's in the bathroom, and Momma's right here. Hold on a sec."

Mase looked over at Cherise and held out the telephone. "Momma, Daddy wants to talk to you."

"Thank you, Mase."

"You're welcome," he replied as he sat down at the table to eat.

Cherise put the telephone up to her ear. "Hey, Mason."

"Hey, sweetheart, did you get my message?"

"No. Did you leave it on my cell or here at home?"

"I left it there at the house," he answered.

"No, I haven't had a chance to check messages yet. When Vincent dropped me off I left right out to pick up the kids, and we're just getting back home," she said as she prepared Janelle's plate.

"I see. I'll have to call him and thank him for taking care of you."

If he only knew what had really taken place between us. "You probably won't reach him. He said he had a dinner date tonight."

"Who's the lucky lady?"

"Who knows. So, am I going to see my husband tonight or not?"

"No, baby, and I'm so sorry. There have been some developments in my case so I doubt I'll be home for a couple of days."

Cherise was clearly disappointed. She really needed to feel Mason's arms around her because it'd been a tough day, especially ending it with Vincent. She sighed softly. "I'll be glad when you're done with undercover work."

Mason ran his hand over his head in frustration because he was well aware his job was once again putting a strain on his marriage. Especially this case, because of Vada and the things he was doing with her in order to bring T-bone down. Little did he know that Cherise was struggling with her own demons. She was slowly being pulled back into a world she had fought so hard to get out of.

"Honey, you know I want to be there with you. I miss you, too, and I'm not even going to say how much I miss my children. Please, don't make this any harder on me. I love you, Cherise, and I promise you this is my last case. Domino already has my transfer papers."

She tried to swallow the lump in her throat, but it wouldn't move. "I don't want to make your job harder, Mason and I know you hate being away from us. I just hope you're serious when you say this is your last case," she informed him.

"I promise, babe. Make sure you call the office if you need me, but only if it's an emergency. Otherwise, I'll check in with you when I can."

"Okay, Mason. I'll do my best to be patient and I want you to know that I love you, so be careful out there," she instructed him.

"You bet. If you need anything or have any problems, call Vincent; he can help wherever he can. Let me talk to my daughter before I go."

Cherise turned to Janelle just as she walked into the room.

"Here she is. Be safe, Mason."

"I will," he answered.

Cherise handed Janelle the telephone and she began to give him a full report of her day.

The conversation lasted about fifteen minutes until Mason had to go. After she hung up, they all sat down at the table for conversation and delicious pizza.

Chapter Nineteen

Mason pulled up at T-bone's house a day early and hoped the information he had on Pootie would let T-bone know that Mason was trustworthy enough to involve him in more details of the operation. As he approached, he noticed several cars in the driveway. He didn't see Vada's car, and he was thankful because she would automatically expect him to spend the night with her. He was going to do his best to avoid her, if at all possible. He stepped up on the porch and tapped on the door. Menace opened the door and greeted him.

"Yo, Mirage. What's up?"

Mason stepped inside and turned to the large-framed man. "Nothing much, man. Is T-bone in?"

He nodded and pointed toward the hallway. As usual, T-bone and one of the other guys were playing the PlayStation in the family room. Mason walked in and sat down in a chair, making sure he didn't interrupt the pair. Grown men and their video games were serious business. T-bone looked over at him and smiled.

"What's up, Mirage? I didn't expect to see you until tomorrow."

Mason took off his jacket and placed it across the back of his chair.

"I figured that, but I just wanted to come by to make sure everything was in place for the meeting tomorrow. We can't afford to be caught off guard, or look like we're amateurs."

T-bone stood and motioned for one of the other guys to come take his place on the game.

"If you got something on your mind, Mirage, let's rap."

T-bone led Mason out onto the patio so they could talk in private. He immediately lit up a joint and took a deep puff. Mason leaned over the rail and sighed.

"I asked around about this Pootie character we're going to be dealing with tomorrow."

T-bone took another puff and frowned. "Oh really? Who did you ask?"

Mason leaned against the railings and folded his arms.

"I know people, T-bone. Don't think you're the only one who's connected with the streets."

T-bone laughed. The smell of the drug was strong and Mason could tell it was top-grade product.

"Well, excuse me! So, what did you find out?"

"He's ruthless and he's known for not trusting the people he deals with."

T-bone held the joint out to Mason. Without hesitating, Mason hit it a couple of times before handing it back to T-bone.

"I could've told you that, but we're cool. I've known Pootie since we were kids. We grew up together," T-bone acknowledged.

"When you're dealing with people like him, you always have to be ready for the double cross. I don't care how long you've known him."

T-bone looked over at Mason and studied his body language. "You sound worried, Mirage."

"I'm always worried when I'm dealing with people I don't know."

T-bone continued to puff his joint. "Well, Mirage, since you're so worried, do you think we have enough backup?"

"I don't know, but just in case, I'd feel more comfortable bringing in one of my partners. You know, just in case."

"Wait a minute, Mirage. I don't know about bringing in somebody else. Hell, I barely know you!"

"Fine with me," Mason said. "I just thought I would offer you some extra firepower, and my partner is one of the best. He knows how to hold his own."

T-bone was silent as he finished off the joint. "I'll think about it, Mirage."

"That's cool, but if he's not there, then don't expect to see me, either."

T-bone stared at Mason in disbelief. He could see that Mason wasn't budging.

"Aight, man. Come take a ride with me. I want to check out the spot for the meeting and I have a stop to make."

Mason followed him toward the door. "Where's Vada?" he asked.

"I think she's with one of her girls at the beauty salon. I'm sure she would love to see you."

The last thing Mason wanted was to entice Vada into a roll in the hay. T-bone walked into the house ahead of him. "I don't know what you did to my sister, but she can't stop talking about you."

"Vada's cool people," Mason responded. "I like hanging out with her."

T-bone picked his nine-millimeter up off the table and put it in his back waistband.

"Tiny, let's ride. We need to make a few stops. Mirage is going to ride along with us."

At about three-hundred pounds, and six feet six inches tall, he was anything but tiny. Mason, T-bone, Tiny, and couple of other guys climbed into T-bone's Suburban and headed out into the night. Mason was relaxed in the fact that his backup was close behind and would protect him, no matter what T-bone was about to get him involved in.

Cherise was just getting into a deep slumber when her pager went off. She turned and looked at the clock; It read twelve forty-five a.m. She sighed and turned on her light. She picked up her phone and called into her office. A body had been discovered in Piedmont Park and she had to work the crime scene. She didn't want to drag the kids out in the middle of the cool night, especially since they had to go to school. Instead, she decided to see if Mase could really be responsible enough to get himself and Janelle up and out to school in case she wasn't back home in time. She dressed hurriedly, tiptoed down the hall to Mase's room, and gently woke him.

"Mase, wake up, baby."

He slowly opened his eyes and then sat up quickly in bed. "What's wrong, Momma?"

"I have to go out to work and I don't know if I'll be back in time to get you guys out to school."

He wiped his eyes and lay back on his pillows. Cherise kissed his forehead.

"You wanted me to trust you to take care of Janelle, so this is your chance. I don't feel comfortable leaving you guys in the house alone, but I don't want to drag you out in the middle of the night, either."

"It's okay, Momma," Mase whispered. "I can do it. I have my clock set for six o'clock so I can get Janelle up and out if you're not back."

"Are you sure, Mase? Because I can call Granddaddy to come on over here and stay with you guys," she suggested.

"I can do it, Momma. Okay?"

Cherise stood and gave the situation one more thought.

"I'm nervous about this, Mase, so call me the minute you get up. If you need me for anything before I get back, call me on my cell. I shouldn't be long, but I just never know."

"I got it, Momma, now go," he said as he turned over and pulled his comforter up over his body.

Cherise walked toward the hallway and stopped. Before she could speak, Mase interrupted her.

"Go, Momma! I got this!"

She smiled at him.

"Good night, Mase," she said as she walked out of his room and down the stairs.

It was in the middle of the night so it only took Cherise about twenty minutes to get to the park. When she arrived, there were police lights flashing all through the area. She exited her vehicle and walked under the crime scene tape, making sure her CSI badge was visible. As she approached the scene, a pair of homicide detectives greeted her.

"Hello, Dr. McKenzie. I'm Detective Tucker and this is Detective Coleman." Cherise shook hands with the detectives and then greeted the Coroner.

"What do we have, Thalia?"

Thalia stood and sighed.

"C. J., this was a violent death. Cause of death appears to be strangulation. Outside of that, I'll know more once I get her back to the lab."

"We need whatever you two can come up with as soon as possible," said Detective Tucker. "If I'm not mistaken, Houston detectives have investigated cases with the same M O."

Thalia wrapped the victim's hands in plastic bags to preserve evidence. "I hope we don't have a serial killer on our hands."

"Me, too," Cherise added as she took pictures of the victim.

Cherise knew exactly who she could talk to about a possible link in the killings.

Once all the pictures were taken, she moved in even closer and listened as Thalia recited information for the detectives. "We have a partially nude black female in her mid to late thirties with defensive wounds on her forearms from a sharp object. She has an obvious blow to the head as well as bruising around her neck. It seems that some type of metal wire was used as a ligature, but it wasn't left at the scene."

"The position she's in seems to indicate the perp wanted the victim to be humiliated," Cherise added.

"Do you think she was raped?" Detective Coleman asked Thalia.

"I would say yes, but I won't know until the autopsy is complete. Hopefully we'll be able to get a DNA profile."

"What a waste," Detective Tucker said. "You know, it's odd."

"What's that, Detective?" Cherise asked.

"She sort of looks like you."

Cherise shook her head. "No she doesn't."

Thalia looked at Cherise and chuckled before continuing her examination. "There are no signs of overkill, but I wouldn't cancel it out as being a crime of passion. She hasn't been dead more than two to four hours. My tests will hopefully tell us this young lady's story, and why she ended up dead tonight."

Cherise looked in the area surrounding the victim. "Did anyone find her clothing or undergarments?"

"No, but we're looking for them now," Detective Coleman answered.

"Did she have any identification on her?" Cherise asked Thalia.

"No, officers are canvassing the area and checking all the cars in the area to try to determine if the victim drove here, or if she was just dumped here."

Cherise pointed out various items at the crime scene.

"I don't think she was dumped, and all the evidence points to her being killed here. I need to get the evidence bags out of the truck. I'll be right back."

As C. J. started to walk off, Coleman called out to her.

"Hold on, Doctor. C. J., I'll walk you out."

As soon as Cherise and the detective crossed the crime scene tape, the local media swarmed them. One reporter stuck his microphone in Coleman's face.

"Detective, does Atlanta have a serial killer on its hands?" the reporter asked.

Detective Coleman put his hand up to shield the light of the cameras. "What we have is a homicide. That's all we know until we have the opportunity to do our investigation. That's all we have to say at this time."

The reporter then stuck the microphone in Cherise's face.

"Dr. McKenzie, what's your opinion? Should the residents of Atlanta be concerned that a serial killer may be on the loose?"

Cherise frowned.

"I'm sure you will be briefed by the detectives once they have any information to report. Other than that, I have no comment."

Several reporters tried to get comments from the pair, but they were unsuccessful. Cherise retrieved the items from her truck and returned to the crime scene. She looked at the clock and realized it would take her several hours to get all the information the detectives needed.

Hours later, she and her team had completed the tests and now had a preliminary report for the detectives. It would take a few more days for some of the other test results to come back. The medical examiner had finished the autopsy and Cherise was scheduled to meet her for a briefing in about an hour.

She looked over at the clock; it was almost six o'clock. She wanted to check on the kids, but she decided to wait and see if Mase could handle things by himself first. She sat there staring at the clock. At one minute after six, her cell phone rang. She smiled when she saw which number came up on the ID.

"Good morning, sweetheart."

"Good morning, Momma," a deep, groggy voice replied.

"Did you sleep okay?"

"Yes, ma'am. You sound tired. Have you been up all night?"

She could tell Mase was walking through the house as he spoke.

"Yes, baby, I'm very tired," she answered.

"Hold on, Momma. Janelle, wake up. It's time to get ready for school."

He sounded so mature and she was so proud that he was anxious to help out.

She could hear Janelle wake up, yawning as she said, "Where's Momma?"

Mase handed her the telephone. "Here, Momma's on the phone. She had to go to work last night."

Janelle took the phone and sat up on the side of her bed. "Momma, where are you?" she asked in a timid voice.

"I had to go to work last night while you were asleep, baby. I'm giving Mase a chance to see if you guys can get yourselves ready for school without me. Is that okay with you?"

Janelle yawned. "I guess so. I miss you, Momma."

"I miss you, too, Janelle. I promise I'll be home when you get in from school today, okay?"

"Yes, ma'am," she answered.

"Good, now get up so you can get dressed and do what Mase tells you. Your grandfather will be over to drive you to school."

"Okay, Mommy."

Tears formed in Cherise's eyes because leaving her children alone while she worked wasn't something she had ever planned to do. "Where's Mase?"

"Hold on, Mommy. Mase, telephone!" Janelle yelled.

Mase rushed back into room and took the telephone out of her hand. "Dang, Janelle, you don't have to scream like a crazy person."

He put the telephone up to his ear. "Yes, ma'am?"

"Mase, I'm so proud of you."

"It's no big deal, Momma."

"Yes, it is. Look, son, I'm going to have your grandfather pick you guys up and take you to school. I'll check back with you in about thirty minutes."

"All right, Momma. I have to get going because I have to make sure Janelle gets breakfast before we go."

She chuckled. "No oven, Mase," she said seriously.

"I'm going to microwave some oatmeal, Momma. Gotta go. Love you!"

"I love you, too, Mase."

When Cherise hung up, she immediately dialed her father and explained to him what the situation was. He assured her he'd be on his way over to her house soon. Cherise was now able to relax a little bit, knowing her father would be with the kids. As she sat there, sleep started to take over her body; she couldn't wait to crawl back into her bed to get some rest. Knowing Mase and Janelle were in the good hands of her father, she could now concentrate on work.

An hour later, Cherise put her test results into the detectives' hands and could finally call it a day. When she worked overnight, she was required to take the day off to rest up before coming back into the lab. As she drove home, she thought about the dead woman and what the detective said about Houston having a similar case. Just as she was about to get on the expressway, she decided to stop by Vincent's hotel to see what he knew about the case in Texas.

It was about seven-thirty when she knocked on Vincent's hotel door. She'd tried to call him before arriving at the hotel, but his voice mail came on. She left a message instead. It took Cherise several knocks before Vincent opened the door. When he did, it was clear that she had interrupted his sleep.

"Hey, C. J., what's up?" he asked as he tried to clear his vision.

"I'm sorry for stopping by so early, Vincent. I called you, but I didn't get an answer. Do you have a minute? I need to talk to you."

He was shirtless, displaying his chiseled abs. It was hard for Cherise not to stare.

Vincent rubbed his eyes and sighed. "Couldn't it have waited until later? I'm on vacation, remember?"

Looking back over his shoulder, he ran his hand over his head and leaned against the door. "C. J., right now is not a good time. I guess you forgot I had a dinner date last night."

Cherise was totally embarrassed that she had interrupted Vincent and his female companion. She put her hands over her mouth. "Oh, I'm sorry, Vincent. I wasn't thinking. I'm sorry for interrupting."

She backed away, but Vincent stopped her by grabbing her wrist.

"It's okay. You can come in," he whispered.

She shook her head as she tried to pull away from him.

"Are you crazy? I'm not coming in there with you and your woman."

With a smirk on his face, he easily pulled her into his room. Once inside, she immediately saw that no one else was there. She turned to him and frowned.

"Why do you always have to mess with my head?"

He pulled her into his arms and hugged her. "Your head is the last part of your body I want to mess with. Besides, I love it when you're jealous about me."

She tried not to smile. Deep down, she had to admit, she was a little jealous at the thought of another woman being in his bed. "Vincent, I didn't come here to do anything but talk," she reminded him.

He laughed and then released her. "Okay, now tell me what has you at my door so early in the morning. Have you swabbed Janelle yet?"

She slowly made her way over to the chair and sat down.

"No, Vincent."

He pulled two cups out of the bar and started making coffee. While waiting for it to finish brewing, he sat down across from her and looked at the woman who owned his heart.

"Don't drag your feet on this, C. J. I want to know, and I want to know as soon as possible."

She jumped up out of the chair.

"Okay, Vincent. Look, I'm not here about that. There was a body found in the park late last night, and one of the detectives mentioned that Houston had a case with the same M.O."

"Oh, really? That's interesting. Do you take sugar with your coffee?" He handed Cherise a cup and she began to fill him in on the details of the homicide.

"Yes, please. I'll take a little cream if you have some."

He walked back over to the bar and got the cream. Vincent sat both the sugar and cream on the table in front of her. Cherise added the cream and sugar to her coffee and sipped it. Vincent sat down and drank his coffee black. "Now, fill me in on the details."

She pulled a copy of the file out of her purse and told him everything she had so far on the crime.

"Here are the pictures. Do you notice anything different or similar to the Houston case?"

He picked up the file and scanned through it quietly. Cherise watched him as he studied each line and crime scene photograph very carefully. He glanced up at her and frowned.

"Do you see anything?" she asked eagerly.

"Yes. You look exhausted," he said.

She ran her hands through her tousled curls. "I'm fine."

Vincent sat the file down and took another sip of his coffee. "No, you're not. You look like you're about to pass out. How long did you work last night?"

"I got called around midnight and I just finished right before I came over here. I'll be fine once my head hits my pillow."

"It shows. You need some rest."

She thanked him for his concern. Vincent jumped up out of his chair and walked back over to the bar. As he poured his second cup of coffee, he asked, "Guess what?"

Cherise looked at him curiously. "What?"

He walked back over to his seat and sat down. "I'm thinking about resigning as police chief."

Cherise nearly spat out her coffee. "Why would you do something like that, Vincent?"

He crossed his legs and sighed. "I'm not happy, and I miss doing real police work."

Cherise shook her head in disbelief. "I'm speechless. Have you talked to Mason about this?" she asked after yawning.

"Yeah, I told him. He was just as surprised as you were, but he said he'd support me with whatever decision I make." He took her hand into his, and caressed it.

"Have you really thought about this? I mean, why would you want to put yourself at risk when you have a nice job running the department?"

Cherise closed her eyes momentarily as he kissed the back of her hand.

"I want to move back to here so I can be close to my family. The short time I've been around you guys has brought back a lot of memories—good memories. And I don't have that in Texas."

Cherise slowly pulled her hand away from him and yawned again. "You just can't throw it all away. You've worked so hard to get where you are."

"I'm not throwing my life away, C. J. I just want to be happy, and I'm happiest when I'm here."

They looked deeply into each other's eyes. His were as mesmerizing as they came, and they had a hypnotic effect over her. It took everything in her power to break free of his trance. That claustrophobic feeling was coming back to her again. He had his own way of melting away her defenses, and she was beginning to feel the heat. "So, do you see anything?" she asked.

Vincent licked his lips and continued to stare at her.

"Vincent! Stop staring at me. Now do you see anything in the file or not?"

"I see a few things," he answered as he continued to study her, but not as intensely. "Who's working the case?"

"Detectives Tucker and Coleman," she informed him as she yawned a third time.

He slid the file back over to her.

"Well, I noticed the victim's clothing wasn't found at the scene, and the positioning of the body is similar. I'm sure once I'm fully awake I can look at it more closely. Now, back to you. Why didn't you go home so you could get some sleep? You could've called me about this later."

"I wanted to talk to you while everything was still clear in my head. You are coming over for dinner tonight, aren't you?"

"I wouldn't miss it for the world."

"Good," she replied as she leaned back in the chair and briefly closed her eyes.

He studied her body language and then revealed his findings.

"C. J., you're basically dead on your feet. I can't let you leave here until you've had some sleep."

She froze. "Excuse me?"

"Don't excuse me. You know I'm not kidding, so don't push me, C. J."

He walked over to her and pulled her jacket off her shoulders.

"Vincent, you're not going to make me do something I don't want to do. I have news for you; I'm going home!"

Her tone was forceful and slightly angry. She reached for her jacket, but he held it out of reach.

"Sweetheart, I've never done anything to you that you didn't want me to do, and you know it. If you want to blame someone, you need to look in the mirror," he snapped back at her.

She walked toward the door. When she got it half-open, he slammed it closed.

"C. J., if you want to fight about this, bring it on!" he yelled. "You're not leaving."

Without turning around, she gritted her teeth. "Let me out of here, Vincent."

He turned her around so she was facing him. He needed to calm down because she was really pushing him. He took a breath and caressed her face lovingly, causing her to turn her head away from him. With his lips within inches of hers, he whispered dangerous words to her.

"If you want to challenge me, C. J., go right ahead. I'll call Mason if I have to, but I'm not letting you leave this room in the condition you're in. If you like, I can get you a cab and then bring your truck to you later, but you're not driving yourself home."

She folded her arms defensively. "You always have to be in control, don't you?"

He smiled and brushed his lips against hers. She turned her head away from him again. With her body pressed against the door, he gently kissed her neck.

"I care what happens to you, C. J. That's the only reason I'm bullying you."

They looked into each other's eyes before Vincent kissed her lips again. She was too tired to fight with him anymore, and his kisses were starting to weaken her. Cherise and Vincent enjoyed the taste of each other for several seconds until she unexpectedly allowed a soft moan to escape her lips. Vincent pulled back momentarily to smile down at her, then kissed her more deeply. He felt his body come alive and knew that if he didn't stop now, he wouldn't be able to, but he had to touch her. He slid his hand down inside her pants and gently touched her. She shivered, unable to move as he continued to lightly kiss her neck and lips

"Vincent, why are you torturing me like this?" she whispered. "I'm trying so hard to do right."

He licked her earlobe. "I'm just trying to give you some brotherly love, sweetheart," he whispered. "Don't it feel good to you?"

She couldn't respond because his touch had her in a state of uncertainty. She moaned and shivered in his arms. Bringing Cherise to the brink of orgasm, he removed his hand.

"Goddamnit!"

Cherise swallowed and looked at him with tears in her eyes. He stared back at her, wishing he could make love to her. Giving her pleasure just now wasn't enough; he knew it could be so much more satisfying if he could have his way. Being with her like this was sheer torture, so he gathered what little strength he had left and backed away from her. His voice was strained as he spoke.

"I'm sorry I couldn't take you all the way, baby. I wouldn't be able to control myself if you had moaned one more time."

She couldn't talk; however, her eyes said it all. They were glazed and weak. Vincent had heated her core, and had he finished what he'd started, they would be in bed at that very moment.

"Don't worry, C. J., I'm not going to do anything to you that you don't want me to do, but I will say this. If the opportunity arises again, I'm not going to be able to restrain myself. Take this as your first and only warning."

"Vincent,"

He put his finger up to her lips, stopping her from speaking. "I said this is your only warning."

Cherise took Vincent's advice very seriously because she could tell he didn't have much self-control at the moment. Their past was full of heated lust and flaming passion, but somewhere along the line Vincent had fallen deeply in love with her. Though the scorching, uninhibited sex left her yearning for Vincent on a nearly daily basis, her heart, however, was still with Mason, even though he had been unfaithful to her.

"C. J., I'm going to get dressed and go downtown to talk to those detectives working the case. You have the room to yourself so you can grab a nap before going home, unless you have a better suggestion."

He was challenging her and she knew it, but he wasn't playing fair, especially after he had set her on fire with those fierce kisses.

"Vincent—I really am trying to do right. I appreciate your concern, but I can't stay here. You just warned me what could happen, and I can't let myself get in that position again," she replied.

He moved even farther away from her. "You're safe for now."

"Am I?"

Vincent had a weird look on his face. He walked across the room, picked up the phone, and started dialing. Curious, Cherise walked toward him.

"Get away from me, C. J."

"Who are you calling?"

He ignored her as he put the phone up to his ear. "This is Chief Vincent McKenzie of the Houston police. I'm Mason McKenzie's brother and I need to speak with him, so if you could patch me through to his unit, I would appreciate it."

Cherise's eyes widened with surprise as she listened to Vincent. She rushed across the room and tried to take the telephone out of his hand. He put his hand up to keep her at bay.

"Vincent! Don't!" she begged.

Vincent looked at her. "Are you going to stay?" he whispered.

"Yes!"

"Will you give me your keys?"

"Yes! Just hang up!" she frantically pleaded.

He stared at her and then spoke. "You can cancel that call. I'll see him when he gets off duty. Thank you for your time."

He hung up and looked at Cherise. He knew his brother didn't suspect anything going on between him and Cherise, and Mason would agree that she needed to rest once Vincent described her condition.

"Where are your keys?"

She reached inside her purse and let out a breath as she dropped them in his hands.

"Thank you, C. J. Now that wasn't so hard, was it?"

Cherise knew Vincent meant business, but she hated being held against her will. She was tired, but she honestly felt like she could drive home with no problem. He motioned to the bed. She sat down and removed her shoes in silence. She felt like a child being scolded by a parent, but she had brought it on herself. She never should've stopped by the hotel. Maybe deep down inside she wanted Vincent to seduce her and give her the fiery passion they used to share between them. He sat down next to her and put his arm around her shoulder.

"C. J., I love you, and I don't say that lightly. You mean the world to me, and if anything ever happened to you I don't know what I would do."

She lowered her head. "I know you love me, Vincent, and no matter how hard I try to deny it, I love you. I just can't love you like you need me to. I can't make love to you, even though it gives me indescribable feelings. I need you to help me do the right thing."

He kissed her forehead before standing.

"I can help you with almost anything but that. You're inside me, C. J., and making love to you is something I can't get out of my system. It's killing me now just being here with you like this. I want you so badly, but I'm going to try to respect your wishes."

Cherise was unable to respond. There was no doubt that she loved Mason, but there was something about the way Vincent touched her and spoke to her that made it impossible for her to stay completely emotionally detached.

"You are a wonderful man, Vincent McKenzie."

He smiled.

"I know. Now let me get out of your way so you can get some rest."

Vincent went into the bathroom to take a shower. Defeated once again, she looked at her watch and set the clock on the bedside table. A few hours of sleep would do her some good. But she would make sure she was home before the children got in from school. Vincent exited the bathroom and found Cherise sound asleep. He leaned down and kissed her tenderly on the cheek. He quietly walked over to the table and picked up his wallet and change. His cell phone vibrated and he recognized the number immediately. So he wouldn't wake up Cherise, he hurriedly left the room and answered the phone as he walked down the hallway.

"Talk to me," he answered.

"Hey, bro, what's going on?" asked Mason.

It was Mason.

"C. J.," he answered.

"What's wrong? Is she okay? I saw her talking to reporters on the news this morning about a homicide in the park last night. She's not at work and she's not answering her cell."

Vincent punched the button for the elevator and checked the time on his watch. "Calm down, bro. She's all right. She's just tired."

"Vincent, you had me worried there for a minute."

The elevator doors opened and Vincent stepped inside. "Sorry about that.

C. J. had to work all night on that homicide. We had a similar case in Houston so she stopped by my room early this morning to ask me questions about our case. She was about to pass out from exhaustion, so I made her stay to take a nap because she looked like hell! I was afraid she would fall asleep at the wheel if she tried to drive home. I'm headed downtown to talk to the detectives working the case to see if I can help with the investigation."

"Thanks for looking out for Cherise."

"No problem, bro."

Mason thought for a moment and then remembered the case. "Was this the one you told me about where the victims appeared to have been posed by the killer?"

"That's the one. Our case is still unsolved so maybe I can help solve both cases while I'm here," Vincent said.

"Don't forget you're on vacation, little brother."

Vincent stepped out of the elevator and walked across the lobby. "I won't."

"Look, Vincent, I need a favor," Mason said.

"What's up?" he asked.

"I need you to come with me to a meeting tonight with these thugs I'm dealing with. I told them I had a partner who could add some presence just in case things jumped off. Are you up for a little action? I know it's been a while since you've done some real police work," Mason teased.

Walking outside, Vincent handed the valet his keys.

"Whatever. Yeah, I'm there, but fill me in on the details first. Especially how I'm supposed to dress."

Mason laughed.

"You always have to dress the part, don't you?"

"Of course," Vincent responded. "I can't let you outdress me."

The valet returned with the car. Vincent tipped him and climbed into the vehicle.

"Is this okay with Domino?" Vincent asked.

"He said it was my call. I mean Rat and Tank are cool, but I want somebody beside me who can think fast on their feet. That's why I want you."

Vincent smiled hearing his brother compliment. "What time is this meeting anyway?" Vincent asked as he drove off.

"I have to meet at T-bone's house around midnight. I'll pick you up," Mason informed him.

"Sounds good. I'm looking forward to it, but pick me up at your house. I'm not missing dinner."

"Okay, don't tell her I'm coming; I want to surprise them. Thanks again for looking out for Cherise today. She's been putting in a lot of hours lately. I worry about her all the time."

"I know you do. That's why I wouldn't let her drive home. You guys really need to go somewhere and chill for a week or two."

"You're right. When this case is over, I plan to take her somewhere exotic so we can get our groove back. I've been neglecting Cherise, and I need to make it up to her," Mason admitted.

"I'm sure she would love to go sooner. If you need me to keep the kids, I'm available," Vincent offered. "Cherise is a passionate woman and the best advice I can give you, big brother, is not to let the fire go out."

"You're right, and I just might have to do that," Mason acknowledged. "Hey, Vincent, whatever you do, don't tell Cherise anything about this meeting," Mason urged him.

"I won't," Vincent replied.

Mason hung up the telephone and yawned-the result of a long night of planning with T-bone and his gang. They had surveyed the riverfront site from every angle to make sure there were no surprises when they met with Pootie. He turned over and looked at the clock, then rolled back over and closed his eyes. He hated that Cherise had to work all night, and he wanted to call her so badly. He needed to hear her voice so he would know she was okay, but he knew she was sound asleep at the moment. Tonight was the big meeting with Pootie, and he needed to check in with Domino to let him know Vincent accepted riding along with him.

As he continued to lie there in the condo set up for this assignment, his stomach began grumbling. Minutes later, there was an unexpected knock on his door. Only one person outside his unit knew where he lived, but just in case, he got his gun and cautiously made his way to the front door. He peeped out and found Vada standing outside looking as fresh as the morning sun. He lowered the gun and opened the door.

"Hey, girl," he greeted her with a smile. "What are you doing here?"

"Well, good morning to you, too," she said as she glided through the door.

Mason closed the door behind her. "This is an early wake-up call. What brings you by so unexpectedly?"

She sat down on the sofa and crossed her magnificent legs.

"Since you hung out with my brother all night, I thought I would get to you first thing this morning."

Mason smiled and put his gun down on the table. Vada was dressed in a bright yellow blouse and a short, denim skirt. Mason was a man, and he knew beauty when he saw it. Vada was full of it.

"So where did you guys go last night?" He sat down next to her and yawned.

"Did you ask your brother?"

She put her arm around his neck and pressed her body up against his. "Yes, but he told me to mind my business."

He tilted her chin upward. "Exactly. If T-bone wanted you to know, he would've told you, so don't come over here trying to get me to violate the trust I'm trying to build with him."

"I know, baby, but I wanted to see you so badly last night."

"You do know you can't always get your way, don't you, Vada?"

Rubbing her hand across his chest, she kissed his cheek.

"I guess you're right, but it's your fault. You've spoiled me, Mirage, and I can't get enough of you."

"Well, you're going to have to chill, Vada, because I have some business to take care of with your brother. I can't have you distracting me; though I must admit you are a very beautiful distraction."

She straddled his lap and wrapped her arms around his neck.

"Why, thank you, babe. So, do you have time for me right now?"

He cupped her hips and pulled her closer.

"I might be able to arrange a little something, but next time, make sure you call me before showing up on my doorstep. Understand?"

"I'm sorry, babe."

"Now do we have a clear understanding of the rules?" She pouted again as she gyrated on his lap.

"Mirage, you're making me think there might be another woman in your life. Do I have a reason to be jealous?"

"Don't worry your pretty little head about that. Besides, we're just kicking it, remember?"

Vada kissed Mason seductively on the lips and continued to give him an unbelievable lap dance. Mason laid his head back on the sofa and closed his eyes.

Dressed in sweats and a T-shirt, he didn't appear to be the dark, mysterious man she had fallen in love with. He now had the appearance of a normal man who existed far away from all the violent and illegal activity she was accustomed to being around.

"I'm sorry I came over unannounced, baby. I won't do it again," she apologized.

"That's my girl. Now, are you hungry?" he asked.

She put her hands on her hips and posed seductively for him. She slowly looked him up and down, stopping at his midsection. "Now that you mention it, I think I am."

Mason could feel the heat from her gaze, and he knew exactly what she wanted to do. She slid down to the floor in front of him, causing his heart to beat loudly in his chest. Vada's hand moved slowly down his thighs as she looked deeply into his eyes. Mentally, he tried his best not to enjoy the physical contact with Vada, but his body told him otherwise.

"Hold on, baby. You're going to love this," she whispered.

Mason couldn't respond as she reached inside the waistband of his sweats and touched him. He was in full effect and Vada's eyes widened in delight. As she caressed him amorously, she looked up at him with devilish eyes and licked her lips. Mason swallowed hard when he noticed she had pierced her tongue. She clicked the silver stud against her teeth, then covered him with her lips. Mason closed his eyes and sucked in his breath in total defeat. Vada moved over him slowly and precisely, each time taking him in deeper. The hissing noises coming from him caused her to move faster. He couldn't resist grabbing her hair as she savored him. Mason opened his eyes so he could witness her unbelievable talent. Watching her made his body heat up even more. She stopped momentarily to get his approval.

"Do you like that, Mirage?"

Somehow, he was able to answer her.

"More than you know, baby. Damn!"

Vada winked at him and dipped her head once more. Mason felt his body shiver and knew he was about to detonate. Vada felt the sensation, so she moved over him even faster. Seconds later, Mason grunted as his body released. He was amazed as he watched Vada consume the very essence of him. She crawled back up into his lap and laid her head on his shoulder in silence. Mason struggled to catch his breath.

"Vada, that was incredible. You almost gave me a damn heart attack."

She smiled and then kissed him on the cheek.

"I just want to make sure my man is happy, and I'll do anything to make you feel good," she announced.

"Well, you definitely succeeded."

Vada kissed him seductively on the lips. "Now, what do you have for me?"

Mason had to play the part. He smiled and escorted her into the bedroom where he gave her exactly what she wanted. The only thing he didn't expect was Vada scratching up his back. He knew there was no way he would be able to explain the scratches to Cherise. He would have to make sure she would never see them.

"I'm starving, Vada," he said after what felt like hours later.

She giggled. "Are you still inviting me to breakfast?"

"You bet. You can shower first so we can go grab a bite."

"Why don't we save time and do it together?"

Mason agreed because he wanted to do whatever he could to hurry Vada out of his house.

After breakfast, Mason and Vada went their separate ways. She had definitely put it on him earlier, and the only complaint he had, outside her showing up unannounced, was that she had scratched up his back. He returned to the sofa at the condo and thought about the events of the morning. He worried until he ended up with a migraine.

Chapter Twenty

Down at the police station, Vincent met with Detectives Tucker and Coleman, who were working the Strangler case. They were excited to meet him, especially since he'd had a similar homicide in his jurisdiction. Now they hoped he could add some insight to their investigation so they could solve both cases.

"So do you guys have any suspects?" Vincent asked.

"Well, Chief McKenzie," Tucker started.

Vincent put his hands up. "Before we go any further, it's Vincent. I'm here on vacation, so my visit is not official. I just want to help as much as I can."

"Any help you can give us is appreciated, Vincent. The file said your detectives were real close to catching the perp at one time," Coleman stated.

"Well, officers were patrolling a local park one night and discovered a body that was still warm. They noticed someone close to the scene and gave chase, but the suspect managed to get to his car and get away. They were close enough to get the license plate, but as you know, the vehicle had been reported stolen a few days earlier," Vincent added. "It's only a matter of time before the perp makes a mistake and he gets caught."

"Thank you, Vincent," Tucker replied.

After several hours of comparing notes, Vincent stood to leave. They all exchanged business cards and agreed to contact each other if they had any fresh ideas on the cases. They shook hands and Vincent wished them good luck before leaving.

Back at the condo, Mason was feeling guilty about Vada so he pulled out his cell phone and dialed. The telephone rang several times before it was answered.

"Hello?"

"Cherise? Did I wake you, baby?" he asked.

"Yes," she answered, yawning and looking at her watch. It was nearly ten o'clock. "I had to work all night. I didn't get off until around seven this morning. How are you?"

"I'm sorry I woke you, but I needed to hear your voice. Vincent told me he made you crash in his room this morning because you were so tired. I was worried about you."

Cherise almost swallowed her tongue. Her throat was dry and it was hard for her to speak. "When did you see Vincent?"

"I called him. Baby, I don't want you taking chances when you're tired. Vincent did the right thing by making you stay there," Mason scolded her.

"He threatened me, so I agreed to stay."

Mason chuckled at Cherise's admission.

"Vincent can be overbearing at times, but he means well. Anyway, I'm glad you got some rest. Tell the kids I love them and I'll see you as soon as I can. I love you."

She yawned one more time and stretched. "I love you, too. Be safe and I'll talk to you later. Good-bye."

"Good-bye, Cherise."

After hanging up the telephone, Cherise looked around the room. She could still smell Vincent's cologne on the pillow. She sat up and walked into the bathroom. Just after she entered the bathroom, she heard Vincent return. She splashed some water on her face and then went out to greet him.

"Hey, Vincent. You're back sooner than I thought you would be. How did it go?"

He sat down on the bed. "It went well. What are you doing up?"

"I felt rested, so I decided to get up. Where are my keys?"

"I have them."

"You can give them to me now. I feel much better now that I've gotten a couple hours of sleep," she replied.

"I'm glad."

"Mason called and mentioned that you told him I was here."

His eyes met hers.

"Why did you tell him I was here? Do you want him to find out about us?" He touched her cheek.

"There's nothing to tell. Besides, I didn't want to lie to him because that would make things look even more suspicious. He didn't think anything about it anyway."

She sat down and began to put on her shoes. "What exactly did you tell him?"

"I told him the truth. That you came by to talk about a case and were too tired to drive home, so I made you stay."

Cherise thought long and hard about what Vincent had done. Maybe telling Mason the truth was the best thing. "Whatever. I need to get home."

Vincent stared at her. Their eyes locked for a moment.

"Vincent, I really have to go," Cherise said softly. She held her hand out for her keys.

"Cool." He smiled, reached into his pocket, and then dangled the keys over her open palm before dropping them into her hand.

"Thanks for letting me crash here."

"You're welcome, C. J. Let me walk you to your truck."

They walked out the door together and into the parking lot. It would be a few hours before they were in each other's company again, and Cherise welcomed the distance.

Several hours later, Mason pulled into the driveway of his house and parked the car. He leaned back against the headrest and closed his eyes for a moment of prayer. Tonight was going to be tense, and he hoped everything went as planned. He finally exited the car and slowly walked up to the door. Before he reached it, Janelle opened the door and yelled. "Daddy's home!"

Mason swung her up into his arms. "Hey, baby girl!" He closed the door behind them. "Where is everyone? Mmmm, something smells good."

Mason carried Janelle into the family room where he found Vincent and Mase going at it on the PlayStation.

"Hey, guys," Mason greeted them.

Without looking up, Mase greeted his father. "Hey, Daddy!"

"Hey, bro," Vincent said, not looking Mason's way, either.

Mason left the pair to their game and carried Janelle on his back into the kitchen. Cherise was in the dining room setting the table and hadn't heard Mason come in. He sat Janelle down so he could greet Cherise properly.

"Hey, baby," he said with a huge smile.

Shocked, Cherise ran and embraced him lovingly. "Mason, I didn't think you would be home tonight."

He kissed her hard on the lips. "Well, I'm not supposed to be here, but you sounded so sad on the phone. I had to come see about you."

Tears welled up in Cherise's eyes.

"Thank you," she whispered as he hugged her waist. "Don't thank me too soon. I do have to leave after dinner."

"I'll take what I can get, Mason," she answered.

Janelle stood there watching them kiss. She tugged on her daddy's jacket. "Daddy, I want a kiss, too."

They laughed and he picked her back up, kissing and tickling her playfully.

"Dinner's ready, so go tell Mase and Vincent they can pause that game and come on to the table."

"Wait a couple of minutes. I need to wash up first."

She walked back toward kitchen. "Take your time. By the time you get back down, I'll have everything on the table."

He took off his jacket and walked toward the hallway. "I'm starving. It'll only take me about five minutes," he said as he headed upstairs.

Everyone enjoyed dinner, especially the kids. They'd missed Mason just as much as their mom had. Janelle was especially excited because she was a typical daddy's girl.

After dinner, Cherise took Mason by the hand and led him upstairs for some private time. She knew it could possibly be days before she saw him again, so she decided to take advantage of the situation. Vincent suspected what the pair was up to, so he had no choice but to keep the kids occupied while they were upstairs.

Once inside their bedroom, Cherise locked the door and turned out the lights. Mason became very nervous when Cherise began to rip the clothes from his body.

"Sweetheart, do you think this is a good idea? I mean, Vincent and the kids are right downstairs."

Cherise giggled. "I won't scream if you don't, Mason," she said playfully as she removed her own clothes.

He crawled into bed next to her and embraced her, making sure his back was concealed. Her soft, warm body was soothing and exciting. This was where he really wanted to be, but he knew if she saw the scratches, she would be pissed. Cherise was breathless from his kisses.

"I don't know why I feel nervous. It's like we're sneaking around behind our parents' backs," she said.

He nuzzled her neck. "It's because I've neglected you, sweetheart, but I'm going to make everything up to you and more. I promise."

"Shut up, Mason, and make love to me," she demanded.

He towered over her and in one swift motion he was inside her. The sensation was unexpectedly volatile, taking her by surprise. It was obvious Mason had some catching up to do with her; she just didn't expect for him to put it on her like he was doing tonight. They tried not to make noise as their bodies intertwined with each other, but neither of them could help themselves. Cherise held onto Mason's muscular arms as their bodies melted against each other. Mason could hardly contain himself as he savored the feel of her curvaceous body under him. It didn't help that she was moaning loudly, which caused him to lose control. Their bodies climaxed in unison as they proclaimed their love for each other. Tears spilled out of Cherise's eyes as she lay across Mason's chest. He held her close as he tried to gather his senses and regain a normal breathing rhythm.

"Cherise, no matter what obstacles we've been through or that may come our way, I want you to know that I'll always love you. I'm sorry my job has taken such a toll on you and the kids, but that's about to end so I can be here for you like I should be."

"Mason, it has been hard not having you around, but I know how important your job is to you. I can't have you out there worrying about us while you're trying to work, so we'll deal with it the best way we know how. I'm just glad it's almost over."

He kissed her on the lips. "So am I, sweetheart."

They kissed each other passionately for several minutes.

"Damn! I have to go," Mason said.

"Do you really have to go?" she asked while snuggling closer.

"I don't want to, but I have something I've got to do, and Vincent is going to ride along for company."

Cherise rolled over to turn on the light, but Mason stopped her.

"Wait! That light is too bright. Let me turn on this other one." He cautiously moved across the room and turned on a softer light. "What are you smiling at?" he asked.

"You," she informed him. "I like what I see."

He walked over and tilted her chin upward. "What are you going to do with yourself for the rest of the evening?"

She fell back on the bed and sighed. "Since I'm off for the next couple of days, I'm going to have a couple glasses of wine, climb into the tub, and read a book."

He looked over at her bookshelf. "What are you reading now?"

"Guess," she challenged him.

"It better not be that Brenda Jackson woman again. I don't want you reading her books when I'm not here to reap the benefits," he warned her jokingly.

"Okay, okay. I guess I'll read a murder mystery or something educational."

"Thank you."

He walked over to her bookshelf, selected a novel for her, and returned to the bed.

"Here, try this one. You've been waiting to read it and now is a better time than any."

He handed her a Zora Neale Hurston novel. Cherise took the book out of his hand and looked it over.

"You're right. I need a change of pace anyway. Thank you, baby."

"You're welcome," he said as he winked at her. "I'm getting ready to jump in the shower."

"Would you like some company in there? We could wash each other's backs."

He swallowed nervously. He never turned down a shower with Cherise, so he had to come up with a clever excuse for passing on one now.

"I'm sorry, babe. I'm going to jump in and out because I really need to get back to work. I'm late now. Can I have a rain check?"

She rolled over onto her stomach and sighed. "You have yourself a date, Mason."

He smiled and disappeared into the bathroom. While he was showering, Cherise climbed out of bed and put on her clothes. She heard the water shut off and knew Mason would be out momentarily. She made up the bed and told Mason that she would wait on him downstairs. He called back to let her know he would be down as soon as he got dressed. Cherise walked out of the room, but as she got halfway down the stairs, she remembered that she had left her pager on the nightstand. She made her way back up to the bedroom. Just as she was about to enter, she saw Mason dressing through the half-open door. He had no idea she was standing there, nor did he know that she saw the scratches on his back—scratches that she hadn't put there.

Vincent and the kids were playing video games in the family room. Janelle sat close to her uncle as he battled Mase in football.

She looked up at him.

"Mommy and Daddy have been upstairs a long time, Uncle Vincent. What are they doing?"

Mase snickered as he waited to see what answer Vincent was going to give Janelle. Vincent looked over at Mase and frowned.

"I don't know, Janelle. They might not get to see each other for a few days, so I guess they're catching up on things."

"What things, Uncle Vincent?" she asked inquisitively.

Vincent tried to hold his composure under the watchful eye of this precocious eight-year-old. Mase laughed even louder, causing Vincent to throw a pillow at him. He put the football game on pause and turned to her. She was beautiful, and he could see Cherise in her.

"Janelle, sweetheart, you know how excited you were to see your daddy tonight?"

"Uh-huh," she answered.

"Didn't you want to hug and kiss him?" Vincent asked.

"Yes, Uncle Vincent," she answered with a smile.

"Well, your mother was excited to see him, too, so she wanted to hug and kiss him, too," he explained.

"Is that why they were doing all that kissing in the kitchen?"

"Exactly."

"But why did they have to go upstairs? They kiss in front of us all the time."

Mase rolled over on his back and snickered once more as he watched his uncle be put on the hot seat by Janelle.

"Because they probably want to talk about some grown-up things, too. They needed to go somewhere quiet so they could hear each other. As you can see, it's a little noisy in here."

"Oh. I'm glad my daddy's home."

Vincent kissed her on the cheek.

"Me, too, Janelle."

"Are we going to finish this game or not, Uncle Vincent?" Mase interrupted.

As Vincent took the game off pause and continued to play, Janelle tugged on his sleeve.

"I'm glad you're here, too, Uncle Vincent," she whispered.

He put the game on pause once more and pulled Janelle into his lap for a big hug and kiss. "Thank you, Janelle. I'm glad I'm here, too," he acknowledged.

As he played the game, he was jealous that Mason was upstairs doing the things he craved to do with Cherise. It was killing him, but he knew he had to remain cool.

Cherise walked into the family room in a zombie-like state. Vincent looked over at her and noticed her blank expression.

"You okay, C. J.?"

She picked up the sofa pillow Vincent had thrown at Mase and placed it back on the sofa.

"I'm fine."

About five minutes later, Mason made his way downstairs and let Vincent know it was time for them to leave. They grabbed their jackets and walked out into the foyer. Mason kissed the kids and approached Cherise last before walking outside. When he kissed her good-bye, her response was robotic and unemotional. Vincent stared at her. She wasn't the same person who had gone upstairs with Mason. He didn't know what had caused the change in her personality, but whatever it was, it concerned him. Even Mason noticed the difference. He pulled her into his arms and she reluctantly hugged him back. He took a step back and looked into her empty and weary eyes. He caressed her cheek and kissed her again.

"Cherise, don't cry. I'll be home in a few days. Okay?"

Mason didn't have a clue. She wasn't sad because he was leaving. She was sad because he was walking around with evidence from another woman on his body.

"I'll be fine, Mason. Just go."

He didn't like leaving her in such an emotional state, but he had to get to his meeting with T-bone. Mason walked down the steps.

"I'll call you the first chance I get, Cherise."

She nodded without responding verbally.

"What's wrong with C. J.?" Vincent asked once they were outside.

"I shouldn't have come home," Mason answered. "It makes it harder on them when I show up and leave like this."

Vincent wasn't totally convinced that was the reason behind Cherise's demeanor.

"I see. Are you driving?"

"No. Let's go in your rental, bro. I like it that it has those California plates. That'll make T-bone think you're from out West. I told him I did a lot of business out there and would be headed that way soon."

"Fine with me, Mason. I'm just glad I took out extra insurance on it in case it gets shot up or something," Vincent said, laughing.

"I see you have jokes," Mason replied. "This meeting needs to go smoothly. We can't afford for anything to jump off."

"I know. Now fill me in," Vincent requested.

On the drive to T-bone's house, Mason briefed his brother on T-bone and his crew. Vincent was excited to get back into the game again. And he was looking forward to meeting with the infamous T-bone.

Chapter Twenty-One

Vincent and Mason put on their game faces before getting out of the car at T-bone's house. Mason walked up to the door and knocked. T-bone opened the door and greeted Mason happily.

"What's up, Mirage? Who's this?"

"This is my partner, Samson," Mason replied.

T-bone stared at Vincent, who stared back without saying a word. T-bone stepped aside so Mason and Vincent could enter. Once inside, T-bone stood directly in front of Vincent and looked him up and down. Vincent took his sunglasses off and stared back at T-bone without blinking. In the deepest voice he could produce, he asked, "Do you have a problem, bro?"

T-bone put his toothpick in his mouth. "No problem, man. If you're with Mirage, I guess you're all right. Are you strapped?"

"Chill, T-bone," Mason intervened. "I told you my man knows what to do. He holds his own."

"We'll see," T-bone responded.

"I guess we will," Mason replied.

T-bone looked at his watch. "We'd better roll out," he said. "I don't want to be late. Pootie's not someone you want to keep waiting."

He nodded toward Tiny and the rest of the gang. They pulled out their weapons and checked them one last time before heading out the door to their vehicles.

It was obvious Pootie was already at the warehouse because one of his men was standing guard outside the door.

"Yo, man, Pootie's expecting me," T-bone said.

The man put his hand up, preventing him from walking past. "He's expecting you, not the whole crew."

T-bone laughed and turned around to look at his entourage. He turned back to the muscular man.

"Well, they're with me, and Pootie knows I don't roll alone, so if they're not welcome, this deal is over before it gets started."

T-bone and the guy stared each other down for a few minutes until the guy pulled out his cell and made a call.

"Yeah, it's me. He's here but he's not alone." He listened for a moment, then hung up. "You can go in now," he growled.

T-bone put a toothpick in his mouth. "I know that's right. Get the hell out of my way!"

T-bone, Mason, and Vincent entered the building while Tiny and the rest of the crew secured the perimeter. Pootie and a couple of his gang were shooting dice. Mason looked over at Vincent as they moved in closer.

"What's up, Pootie? Can I get in on that action?" T-bone yelled.

"This game is for high-rollers only," Pootie said without looking up.

T-bone laughed as they walked closer.

"That's cool. I don't think you could handle me taking all your money anyway."

Pootie rolled the dice once more and also laughed.

"Yo, Pootie, why do you have Godzilla out there blocking the door? It's me! I'm your boy!"

Pootie calmly picked up his money.

"You never can be too careful, especially since I see you have some new faces rolling with you."

"They're cool! They're with me!"

"Whatever, T-bone. Let's get this over with because I have somewhere I have to be."

Mason looked around. The headlights of one of Pootie's vehicles illuminated the warehouse's interior. Stacks of old wooden pallets were piled around, as well as some empty metal barrels. Pootie nodded at one of his men who produced a duffel bag. Sitting the bag on top of one of the barrels, Pootie rubbed his hands together.

"Don't you have something for me?"

Mason sat a briefcase on top of another barrel. T-bone stepped forward with a smile on his face. Vincent carefully watched the other men who were standing behind Pootie to make sure no one got any itchy trigger fingers. He was securely strapped for protection. "Why don't we do this at the same time?" T-bone said.

Pootie laughed and slowly reached into the duffel bag, but Vincent quickly stepped forward, stopping him. Pootie's men pulled their weapons, but by that time Vincent already had two guns out, one aimed at Pootie's head.

"Goddamn! Chill, Samson!" T-bone yelled.

Mason's heart jumped into his throat. He knew Vincent would be an asset to bring along because his hands were quick and his temper was short. He laughed out loud, trying to defuse the tense situation.

"My man's just making sure the only thing in that bag is what should be in that bag. I'm sure you all can appreciate that."

T-bone looked at both of them in amazement. Mason walked over and looked inside the duffel bag. He nodded back at T-bone, who smiled at Pootie.

"My boy is right," T-bone said. "A man can never be too careful. I don't care how long I've known someone."

Pootie frowned and pulled out two large bricks of coke.

T-bone opened his briefcase and revealed a cash payment large enough to fund a small army. Pootie pulled a switchblade out of his pocket and opened it.

"You fools are crazy as hell. Do you want to sample the product or not, T-bone?"

T-bone sniffed and stepped forward.

"And you know this, man!"

Mason and Vincent watched as Pootie cut into the merchandise and held a sample on the tip of the knife. T-bone greedily snorted the powder and savored the instant effect of the narcotic. T-bone turned to his crew and gave the merchandise two thumbs-up.

Pootie put his knife back inside his pocket. "So do we have a deal?"

T-bone wiped his nose. "We're straight. All the money's there, but feel free to count it."

Pootie had one of his boys flip through the money. "I'm sure it's all there, because if it's not, you're not going to like the house call I give you."

"I know you're not threatening me."

Pootie closed the briefcase and smiled. "Of course I am. It was nice doing business with you."

As Pootie and his guys walked toward their vehicle, Mason grabbed the duffel bag and zipped it up. Just as Pootie was about to get inside his vehicle, he turned to them.

"Yo, T-bone, tell that fine-ass sister of yours to holler at me. It's been a while since we kicked it together."

Surprised, Mason looked at T-bone who looked away. Apparently T-bone didn't want Mason to know that bit of information. It wasn't that he cared, but it did open the door for him to quiz Vada about Pootie and his secrets. Pillow talk was the best way to get information. Mason and his unit now had the opportunity to bring down not only T-bone's clan, but Pootie's as well.

"I'll give her the message, but I think she's spoken for."

"We'll see about that. Vada's always been available for me. I'll holler," Pootie said as he opened the car door.

T-bone, Mason, and Vincent made their way out of the warehouse and to their ride without incident. Once they hit the main highway, T-bone turned around and looked at Vincent.

"Yo, Mirage, for a minute, I thought your boy Samson was going to set it off up in there."

Mason looked over at Vincent. "Well, he had to be sure it wasn't an ambush because things could've got messy up in there."

"Word," he responded. "Your boy is all right."

"I'm nobody's boy," Vincent angrily replied. "All I did was make sure you didn't get me killed tonight."

T-bone turned back around and put his toothpick in his mouth.

"You and Mirage definitely need to learn how to chill. You guys definitely have too much hostility."

Mason laughed. "Don't worry, T-bone. We're cool like that."

The rest of the ride was quiet as they pulled around to the rear of a house Mason had never been to. Vincent looked at Mason curiously, but neither spoke as they approached the back door. Tiny unlocked it and they went inside, into the kitchen. T-bone sat the duffel bag on the table and pulled out the product.

Tiny disappeared into another room, returning with two scales and some small plastic bags.

T-bone went to the refrigerator and pulled out a forty-ounce.

"We might as well get busy breaking this stuff down. I want to have it on the streets in forty-eight hours. The sooner we can make money, the quicker we can get our business off the ground."

Vincent watched as Kilo, Tiny, and T-bone started working on the first brick. Mason stood and slid his hands inside his jacket.

"Well, if you don't need us anymore, I would appreciate a ride to my car."

"Why are you running off so quickly?" T-bone asked. "I thought you guys would like to stay here and help us break this down."

"No, I have other business I need to take care of; plus I might run by and holler at Vada if that's okay with you," Mason informed him.

"We can do that, and if you see Vada, tell her I'll have some work for her tomorrow."

"Aight. We're out," Mason replied and Vincent followed him out the door. Tiny stood and told T-bone that he would be right back after dropping Mason and Vincent off.

"Yo, Tiny!" T-bone yelled. "Go by Preston's Rib Shack and pick up some ribs."

"Okay," Tiny answered as they walked out the door.

The threesome disappeared out the door.

Once Vincent and Mason were back in the privacy of their car, Mason exhaled.

"I'm glad that's over with. I didn't know what was going to happen when you pulled out your guns."

Vincent patted his brother on the shoulder.

"Big brother, you know I wasn't going to let anything happen to you. I didn't like the way they were looking, so I had to let them know we meant business."

"Well, I think they got the message, especially T-bone."

Mason started the car.

"I guess. Was old boy talking about your girl?" Vincent asked.

"Yeah. I had no idea Vada used to kick it with him. I'm going to see what I can find out from her. Maybe this way we can bring down both Pootie and T-bone."

Vincent looked over at his brother curiously. "Are you serious?"

"Hell yeah, I'm serious! This way, I could really go out with a bang."

"You just make sure you be careful. I haven't been in the game in a long time. Tonight took a lot out of me, but it did feel good. I miss that kind of action," Vincent explained to Mason.

"You're crazy! I can't wait to leave this mess behind me," Mason replied as he drove out onto the expressway.

"Where are we going now?" Vincent asked as he looked out the window.

"You're going to drop me off at Vada's so I can see what she knows, then you can bounce."

"How are you going to get back to your place?" Vincent laughed.

"Don't worry, I'll get back," Mason assured him.

"Are you sure about this? I don't feel right leaving you like this."

"I'll be all right. Do you want to meet Vada?"

"Sure," Vincent finally responded.

About twenty minutes later, Mason pulled into Vada's driveway and pulled out his cell phone. Vincent cleared his throat.

He dialed her number and waited. Seconds later, she answered.

"Hello?"

"Hey, it's me. I'm in your driveway. Come open the door."

"Really?" Vada asked with excitement.

"Yeah, I'm sure, and don't come to the door naked because I have someone with me."

"Okay, I'm on my way to the door, babe," she answered.

He hung up the phone and opened the car door.

"This woman is wild, bro. A man could easily get caught up with a woman like Vada. You'll see."

Mason and Vincent walked up to Vada's porch and Vada opened the door. She had on a short, white nightgown, which revealed her full breasts and shapely hips.

"Hey, baby. Who's your friend?" she asked as she posed seductively against the door frame.

Walking in, he turned and frowned at her.

"I thought I told you not to come to the door naked."

She closed the door after they entered and stared at him seductively.

"I'm not naked, Mirage. Besides, I'm sure your friend has seen a lot more than what I'm showing."

She walked over to Vincent and held out her hand. Vincent politely shook it.

"Hi. I'm Vada, and you are?"

"Samson. It's nice to meet you, Vada."

"Hmmm, I like that. Are you as strong as Mason?" she flirted.

"I might be," he said.

"Show me," she challenged him as she moved closer.

"Vada!" Mason yelled jealously. "Leave the man alone and go put some clothes on!"

She put her hands on her hips and pouted.

"I was just playing with him. You guys sit down and help yourself to a drink. I'll be right back."

Vincent and Mason watched as Vada twisted her hips out of the room and closed the door behind her. Vincent sat down.

"Damn!" he whispered. "Your girl is a trip. You do have your hands full."

Mason sat down across from him.

"I told you."

Vincent was enjoying his undercover role with Mason. Vada returned to the room with a robe over her scantily clad body. She sat down in Mason's lap and kissed him hard on the lips.

"Is this better, baby?"

Mason cleared his throat. "Much better."

She cuddled with him. "What brings you by so late? Not that I mind."

"Don't worry about it. All that should matter is that I'm here."

"You're right." She looked over at Vincent. "Are you going to hang out with us tonight, too? You could help me fulfill my fantasy."

Vincent stood up and shook his head. "I don't think so. Mirage, I'll see you tomorrow. Have fun."

Mason pushed Vada out of his lap. "Hold on. I'll walk you out."

Vada crossed her legs slowly and waved at Vincent provocatively.

"Good-bye, Samson. It was nice to meet you."

"Likewise," Vincent responded as he walked out the door.

Mason followed him out to his car.

"Drive carefully, Samson. I'll call you sometime tomorrow," Mason told him as they gave each other a brotherly handshake.

"I will, but you're the one that needs to be careful in there with that wild woman."

"I'll be all right. Can you go by at the house to get my .38 out of the glove compartment? Since we came in your car, I forgot to get it. I don't want anyone to get ahold of it," Mason said.

"Okay. What do you want me to do with it?"

"Just take it with you and I'll get it from you later. Try not to wake up Cherise and the kids."

"I'll be as quiet as a mouse," Vincent said as he backed out of the driveway.

By the time Vincent made it to Mason's house it was almost three a.m. He pulled into the driveway and turned off the motor. As quietly as he could, he opened Mason's car, pulled the gun out of the glove compartment, and stuck it in his waistband. As he started walking down the driveway, the garage door started going up unexpectedly. He watched the door rise slowly and then noticed Cherise standing in the light of the garage. He walked toward her and she met him halfway. It was cool outside and she didn't have on a jacket.

"Where's Mason?" she asked with her arms folded.

Taking off his jacket, he wrapped it around her shoulders.

"He's at work. What are you doing up so late?"

"I couldn't sleep," she answered as she looked up into his eyes. "I have some things on my mind."

"Well, it's cold and it's late. You should get back inside."

She took his hand and led him toward the house.

"Come on inside. We need to talk."

"C. J., it's really late and I'm really tired."

He'd had fun hanging out with Mason tonight. Now all he wanted to do was get some sleep.

She looked back at him.

"It'll only take a minute. You can have one drink with me, can't you?"

Vincent didn't know what Cherise was up to, but it gave him an uneasy feeling. She closed the garage door as soon as they entered the kitchen. She pulled a bottle of wine and two glasses out of the cabinet. Vincent pulled the gun out of his waistband and set it on the table. He sat down and watched Cherise pour the wine and bring it to the table. She sat down and sipped her wine.

"What are you doing with that gun, and what did you two get into tonight?" Without making eye contact, he put his glass up to his mouth and sipped.

"Nothing much."

"Well, you're dressed like Shaft and you're carrying a gun, so whatever you guys did was probably something crazy, huh?"

He put his glass down and leaned forward.

"What do you really want to know, C. J? You've seen me with a gun before."

She hesitated and then sighed. "Is Mason cheating on me again?"

Vincent almost spat out his wine. He blinked and tried to compose himself. "Now why would you ask me something like that?"

"Because you would know. Now answer the question," she begged.

He shook his head in disbelief. Hopefully Cherise hadn't found out about Vada, because if she had, it could put Mason in danger of having his cover blown.

Attempting to distract her, he tried to change the subject.

"Come on, C. J. I know you and Mason got busy tonight. What happened? Did it make you feel guilty or something?"

She pointed her finger at him angrily.

"All I need you to do is tell me whether or not he's seeing another woman."

Vincent could see the tears building in her eyes, but he knew he couldn't reveal anything. "Mason loves you, C. J."

"I love him, too, but that didn't stop me from sleeping with you, did it?"

Vincent folded his arms in defense. "Why are you asking me this?"

She put her hands over her eyes and mumbled. "I saw scratches on his back, and I didn't put them there."

"What?"

She looked at him and slowly repeated herself. "I said he has scratches on his back. Female scratches, and they're not mine!"

Vincent's heart thumped in his chest. Surely Mason wasn't that careless.

"So what if he does have a few scratches on his back? In our line of work, we get all kinds of scars."

Elevating her voice, she jumped out of her chair.

"I know fingernail scratches when I see them, Vincent! I'm not stupid!"

"I didn't say you were, C. J."

They sat there in silence for a moment.

"I should've asked him about the scratches while he was here. Mason's not a good liar so as soon as I looked into his eyes, I would have known the truth."

"Leave it alone, C. J. The man has enough to worry about while he's out there in the streets. He doesn't need you throwing any unfounded accusations his way. If he's not focused, it could get him killed."

"I knew you would say something like that. I don't want to see anything happen to Mason, but for some reason he can't seem to keep his hands off other women."

Vincent sat there listening to Cherise's anger boil over. He really wanted to get out of there so she would stop quizzing him.

"I know about that lawyer he slept with when we were separated. Is she back in town?"

Vincent just sat there, unable to move. He'd had no idea she knew about that!

"I knew you would play dumb if I ever asked you about her. Don't worry about it, Vincent, because I'm going to let you off the hook."

Vincent still remained quiet. Cherise poured another glass of wine and laughed.

"When I found out about that woman, I knew I had to break things off with you. I also knew I had to let that heifer know she wasn't going to take my husband from me, so I sent her packing. She thought she was doing something by confronting me about her affair with Mason. I told her if she didn't get out of my face and out of town before sunset I would make sure she didn't see the light of another day. I sweetened the deal by showing her my .357 Magnum up close and personal. My life was a mess, and it was in the process of falling apart. I couldn't let that happen."

Vincent almost fell out of his chair after hearing Cherise's confession. Knowing that she threatened the woman's life with a gun was a clear indication that she was serious about being true to Mason.

"Look, C. J., I'm not the one you should be throwing all these questions at. Talk to Mason if you have suspicions."

"This is going nowhere. I'm going to bed."

He drank the last of his wine.

"I'm not the enemy, C. J.," he whispered.

She walked over and put her glass in the sink.

"I didn't say you were, but I know you know something, Vincent. If you really cared about me, you'd tell me the truth."

"The truth is all I'm trying to get to also, C. J. When are you going to get the swabs for the DNA test so they can be sent off? I'm not going to wait much longer."

She banged her fist on the countertop.

"Will you leave it alone, Vincent, please!"

"No, C. J., I want to know!"

She slowly turned and looked at him. It was very clear that Vincent wasn't going to rest until the test results were back.

"I'm going to bed. It don't make any sense for you to be on the road this time of night, so feel free to stay over."

Cherise walked out of the kitchen and up the stairs to bed. She realized Vincent wasn't going to reveal any information regarding Mason, or forget about the DNA test.

Vincent made his way into the family room and camped out on the sofa. He was well aware that Cherise would never understand the circumstances Mason was working under, or that they both needed to know if he was Janelle's father.

Chapter Twenty-Two

At Vada's house, Mason lay in the bed next to a satisfied woman; however, guilt filled his heart. She turned over toward him, caressed his chest, and purred.

"You never cease to amaze me, Mirage."

"Why do you say that?"

"You always seem to know when I need you. Tonight was no different. You try to act like you don't care about me, but I know you do."

He frowned.

"I don't know what to think anymore, Vada, especially after hearing Pootie talking about hooking up with you. What's up with that? Are you playing me?"

She sat up in bed, surprised that he knew about her relationship with Pootie.

"Who told you about Pootie?"

Mason pretended to be jealous. He sat up on the side of the bed and started getting dressed. "I heard it from him. Are you kicking it with him when I'm not around?"

"No! I haven't hung out with Pootie in a long time, and when I did it was over before it got started," she explained.

Mason laced up his shoes and stood. "That's what you say. He seemed real sure that he still had a claim on you."

Vada wrapped the sheet around her body and climbed out of bed.

"Well he doesn't, because you're all I want, Mirage."

Mason still wouldn't look at her. Instead he walked into the living room and slid into his jacket. She followed closely behind him with tears in her eyes.

"You're not leaving, are you?"

He turned to face her. His expression let Vada know he was very upset at the moment.

"Why should I stay?"

She hugged his waist and snuggled up to him.

"I don't give a damn about Pootie. He's nobody to me."

He stared down at her without hugging her back.

"I don't like him. He's arrogant and seems dangerous. What is he into?"

Vada kissed his chin and did her best to soothe him. "Do we have to talk about Pootie tonight? I told you he was nobody to me. Let's go back inside the bedroom and pick up where we left off."

He pushed her away. "Not until you tell me about Pootie, and I mean everything."

She threw the sheet over her shoulder.

"How did you and Pootie end up together anyway?" she asked.

"Business, baby. Don't you worry your pretty little head about that. Just tell me what you know about him," he persuaded her with a heated kiss.

Vada melted against his chest and took him by the hand.

"Come back to bed and I'll tell you anything you want to know about him."

Mason took off his jacket and threw it on the chair before following Vada back into the bedroom. She closed the door, locked it behind them, and then smiled devilishly at him. Next she walked over to the nightstand, switching her hips as she moved. She bent over and turned off the lights before cuddling up to him once again.

"So, Mirage, is that a gun in your pocket or are you just happy to see me?"

He smiled. "What do you think?"

She ran her hand down his thigh and rested it on his midsection. Nibbling on his ear, she whispered to him. "Hmmm, I guess you are happy to see me."

Mason closed his eyes and tried to stay focused. He knew he needed to get his hands on all the files on Vada's computer. He just hoped she would leave it on all night so he could make a copy. Unfortunately, there seemed to be only one way to keep her distracted. He pulled her hair playfully.

"Get in the bed."

She ran her tongue over his lips. "You don't have to tell me but once," she said breathlessly.

Mason's eyes glanced over at the computer screen as they made their way across the room. She walked toward the computer, but Mason grabbed her, pulling her hard against his chest. He kissed her hard.

"That can wait, but I can't."

His aggressive demands excited Vada. She proceeded to undress him, and once they were both completely bare, Mason playfully pushed her down on the bed. She scooted back on the bed and giggled.

"Mirage, you're such a thug."

He crawled into bed next to her.

"You like it," he said.

"You'd better believe it."

Mason held her hands over her head as his head dipped down to her voluptuous body. Vada was a beautiful woman, and she was built almost exactly like Cherise. They shared similar sized breasts, which enabled him to pretend he was with Cherise instead of Vada. This also allowed him to let himself go during lovemaking. Vada squirmed and panted as Mason ran his tongue over her sensitive breasts until he decided to move lower.

"Mirage! Baby, wait!"

He didn't respond to her pleas. Instead, he kissed her inner thighs and ran his tongue over her throbbing flesh. Vada's body jerked as she held onto the headboard. She moaned as Mason seemed to consume her soul. Her legs trembled uncontrollably as Mason sent her into overdrive. She screamed as she felt her body giving into the waves of pleasure Mason was giving her.

"Mirage!"

He pulled up at the last moment and watched as Vada's body jerked uncontrollably. He had her right where he wanted her. Now all he had to do was work her body so good she would sleep sound enough for him to copy the files. Before Vada could catch her breath, Mason was on her again. He kissed her.

"Are you okay?" he asked.

Still panting, she laughed. "Hell no, I'm not okay, thanks to you."

He smiled mischievously. "Good, because I have something even better for you."

"Mirage, you're going to make me have a heart attack."

"If that's the case, I'm really getting ready to take you out."

Her eyes met his as he slowly moved over her body. Vada waited anxiously as he joined his body with hers. Vada groaned and moaned as she gyrated her soft body against his muscular one. He wanted to prolong their session as long as possible so Vada would have no choice but to fall into a coma-like sleep. Just as Vada was about to peak, he would stop and then start all over again. His actions were driving her out of her mind, and she didn't know how much more of it she could take. Mason flipped her over onto her stomach and entered her swiftly from behind. Vada gasped every time his flesh pressed against hers. He felt his own body about to explode once she began to cry out for mercy. Mason's breathing became erratic as he moaned out loud.

"Damn it, Vada!

Seconds later, his body stiffened. He rolled off Vada's body and exhaled loudly.

"Damn, girl!"

Vada whimpered as she tried to get control of her breathing. Mason glanced over at the clock. He had about thirty minutes to spare, and he hoped Vada would fall asleep soon.

It took her twenty minutes to fall into a deep slumber. Mason quietly climbed out of bed, slipped a CD into Vada's computer, and started copying her files. He nervously watched her as she slept soundly in the bed across the room. It only took a few seconds for him to download everything onto the CD. Next, he gathered his clothes and entered the bathroom to take a quick shower. There was no way he could step out of the house with the scent of Vada on him. Once he was completely dressed, he left Vada a note and placed it on the pillow next to her. He looked at his watch before quietly leaving her house and locking the door behind him.

Once outside, he called the members of his unit to pick him up. Once inside the van they made a copy of the CD and immediately made their way to the interstate for the long trip back to Atlanta. Mason felt guilty about the things he'd done with Vada. It violated his marriage vows and everything he believed in. No longer would he jeopardize his life for the sake of others. His family and the life he'd built with Cherise were too important to him to risk any longer. Tonight was the last time he would share a bed with anyone besides Cherise.

The next afternoon, Cherise thought she would treat herself to get her mind off of things. It had been a long time since she went on a shopping spree, but her coworkers had told her about a mall in southern Georgia that was having some great sales. She decided to make the drive to see if it was worth her time. Since Mason had her truck blocked in, she decided to drive his car instead. Besides, it didn't burn as much gas as her larger SUV, and Mason probably wouldn't be home for a few days anyway.

As she pulled into the parking lot and shut off the engine, she leaned down to get her purse off the floor and immediately heard a tapping on the window, which startled her. She sat up and noticed an attractive young woman standing outside the door.

"What the hell?" she mumbled as she opened the car door and stepped out.

The young woman, who was also startled, took a couple of steps back.

"Can I help you?" Cherise asked curiously.

"I'm sorry. I thought you were someone else. He has a car similar to this one. I'm sorry if I frightened you."

Cherise frowned as she thought about the scratches on Mason's back and wondered if by some chance this was the woman who put them there. She folded her arms.

"He?"

"Yes, I thought this was my man's car," the young woman said with a stutter.

With a scowl, Cherise took a step forward. "Well, you're wrong. This is my husband's car."

It took every ounce of self-control in Cherise's body not to jack this woman up, because she had a gut feeling Mason knew her. Cherise looked at her from head to toe and noticed how groomed and well dressed she was. She seemed to be several years younger than Cherise, and could see how Mason, or any man, would be attracted to her. It made her heart ache. Cherise swallowed hard and offered the young woman some valuable advice.

"Well, you need to think twice before you run up to someone's car. You could've gotten shot."

The young woman stared at her and then curiously asked Cherise, "Do you know a guy named Mirage?"

"No, and if I did, I wouldn't tell you," Cherise responded defensively.

Vada pulled her purse up on her shoulder and apologized. "Forget it. I'm sorry I bothered you."

Vada knew in her heart that this vehicle was Mirage's car. She'd been in it and she would know it anywhere. Before hurrying across the parking lot, she jotted down the license plate number just in case. Within minutes, she disappeared inside the mall. Cherise stood in the same spot for several seconds, thinking. As she shopped, she couldn't get her mind off the woman in the parking lot. Her face was now embedded in her memory, and if she ever saw her again, she would remember her.

On the way home Cherise decided to stop by the precinct to see if Mason was there. She had to clear her conscience and she hoped Mason could reassure her she had nothing to worry about. She walked into the building, showed the receptionist her identification, and received a visitor's pass. When she entered his office, he was on the telephone. When he saw her, he smiled and waved her over to his desk. She sat down and waited for him to finish his phone call. He hung up the telephone and kissed her lightly on the lips.

"Hey, baby! What brings you down here?"

"I'm worried about us, Mason. Am I losing you?"

He was surprised by her admission; he didn't know what had come over her. Mason scooted his chair closer to her and took her hands into his.

"What's wrong, baby?" he whispered. "Why would you think you're losing me?"

Cherise sat back in her chair and sighed. "I was approached by a woman in a mall parking lot today and she thought I was her man. Someone named Mirage."

Mason nearly fell out of his chair. His insides crumbled, but he couldn't reveal his panic to Cherise.

"How could someone make that type of mistake? You don't look nothing like a man," Mason said jokingly

"I'm not laughing, Mason. I was in your car," she explained as she stared directly at him.

Mason could hear his heart beating in his chest, and he wondered if Cherise could hear it, too. There was only one woman who knew him by that name, Vada. He'd made a mistake driving his undercover car home, which had allowed

Cherise to get behind the wheel of it. It put her in danger, and that was the last thing he wanted to do.

He leaned forward and kissed her forehead.

"Cherise, you are the only woman for me, and I'm no one's man but yours. I'm sure it was an honest mistake."

She pulled a tissue from the box on his desk and wiped her eyes. He stood and pulled her into his arms, hugging her.

"Cherise, don't get yourself upset over nothing. I'll tell you what, let's get out of here and go home. I was just finishing up here anyway."

She was too upset to speak, so she nodded instead. He caressed her chin.

"Just let me sign out and I'll be right with you, sweetheart."

As Mason walked into Domino's office, she decided she would ask Mason about the scratches, even though he assured her there was no other woman. The scratches hadn't appeared on his back on their own, and she wanted to know who put them there.

Once at home, Mason led Cherise into the family room and they sat down on the sofa.

He embraced her lovingly.

"Mason, I feel like we're drifting apart again. Even when you're with me, it's like your mind is always somewhere else. You job has affected our lives for too long time, and it's caused some problems in our relationship."

He sighed. "I know, baby, and I'm not happy with what I've put you through, either, but it's my job—somebody has to do it to make the streets safer for you and the kids."

Cherise sat up and faced him.

"Mason, I don't think you understand what I'm saying. We need to make some serious changes in our relationship and quickly. I can't deal with the stress of my job, and the stress of my marriage, too. It's too much for me to handle."

Mason looked into her eyes curiously. "What are you saying, Cherise?"

"I love you, Mason, but I need you to tell me the truth."

Mason squirmed in his seat and lowered his eyes. He had an idea where the conversation was headed, and he prayed he could get through it. Tears fell onto Cherise's cheeks as she swallowed hard before finding the strength to continue.

"Mason, are you seeing another woman?"

"Why would you ask me something like that, Cherise? You're my wife and the mother of my children. No woman comes before you."

Cherise didn't believe him. She jumped up out of her seat.

"Who put those scratches on your back?"

Mason's face felt hot. He thought he had been able to hide the scratches from her, but he obviously had not. He covered his face and was trying to figure out how he was going to explain Vada. He always tried to keep work out of his personal life; however, this was the first time a woman was involved. Mason knew he had to find a way to make Cherise understand that his relationship with Vada was strictly business, but something told him it wasn't going to work with her. Mason took a breath.

"Sweetheart, the case I'm working on does involve a woman; however, you have nothing to worry about because everything will be over in a few days. I promise you."

Cherise's eyes widened as she listened to Mason's admission. Mason sprang off the sofa and paced the room nervously.

"Her brother is the person I'm trying to bring down, but I could only get to him through her."

Cherise made fists as she listened to him. She knew what the answer was before she asked.

"Are you sleeping with her?"

"Come on, Cherise!" he pleaded.

She was calm, which worried him.

"It's a simple question, Mason. Either you are or you aren't."

He turned to her and this time it was he who had tears in his eyes. Cherise's heart nearly stopped beating. She cleared her throat, and with apprehension she asked him one more question.

"Have you put me at risk?"

"No, baby! You know I would never do that!"

He was sick to his stomach, and so was she. She glared at him.

"You don't have the right to call me baby anymore. I want you out of here—today."

Mason put his hands over his face and tried to plead his case

"It's not like I'm with her all the time, Cherise. I spend most of my time with her brother and his crew, gathering evidence to have them arrested," he divulged.

She stood up and walked quietly toward the hallway. Mason walked over and grabbed her arm, turning her toward him.

"Cherise, baby, please don't take this the wrong way. That woman means nothing to me. It's just a job!"

She looked at him.

"Don't minimize this, Mason. How would you feel if I told you I was having an affair?"

Mason tilted his head and studied her. She was too calm and relaxed, and he had no idea what she was thinking. It troubled him.

"What do you mean?" he asked.

"Just what I said, Mason. How would feel if you found out I was sleeping with another man?"

Mason realized she was upset, but he didn't expect this. Anger settled in his gut and he could feel his blood pressure elevating.

"I would be pissed and would want to kill someone!" he informed her.

"Exactly!"

She picked up her purse and walked out of the room into the garage. She climbed into her truck and drove away, leaving Mason standing there with his thoughts. He knew Cherise was hurt, and he had to do whatever he could to reassure her that their marriage was not threatened.

Chapter Twenty-Three

Mason couldn't find Cherise anywhere. He'd been back by the house twice and also drove past her parents' house, but he still couldn't find her. He tried to call Vincent to see if he'd seen her, but only got his voice mail. He called Domino and informed him that Cherise had found out about Vada and he was taking some time to straighten things out. He had searched everywhere he could think, but he still was unable to locate her.

Hours later, he gave up and decided to just go home and wait for the kids to come home from school. When he walked into the kitchen, he found Cherise leisurely cooking dinner. He didn't know what to do or say, especially when she didn't look up or even speak when he came through the door. He took off his jacket and laid it over a kitchen chair. He got up enough courage to approach her from behind. He wanted to pull her into his arms, but decided it was best to keep his hands to his sides. With his voice barely above a whisper, he spoke to her.

"Cherise, I've been looking all over for you."

"Well, you found me," she said sarcastically.

"I hope you don't think I'm proud of what I've done."

"Mason, not now, okay?" she answered as she continued to prepare dinner.

He reached up to touch her shoulders.

"Sweetheart, we need to talk about this."

The moment his hands came in contact with her skin, she turned. She was still holding the knife she was using to chop the vegetables; however, her hand was trembling.

"I said I didn't want to talk about it right now."

He backed away because that was a definite sign that she was still very upset. He decided to leave her alone, for now. Picking up his jacket, he left the kitchen and retired to their bedroom. Cherise leaned against the sink and exhaled. Tears started streaming down her face as she thought about her own infidelity with Vincent. How could she judge?

Mase walked through the door singing along to his CD player. Cherise tried to conceal her tears, but it was too late. He took the headphones off his ears and confronted his mother.

"What's wrong, Momma? Why are you crying?"

Without looking directly at him, she responded, "I'm fine, Mase. Go on up and start on your homework. Dinner will be ready soon."

He sat his CD player on the table and walked over to her. Towering several inches above her, he embraced her lovingly. Mase had always been the sensitive one in the family, and he was always in tune with everyone's emotions.

"I did my homework at school. Now tell me why you're crying, Momma."

Wiping her hands on her dish towel, she smiled.

"Oh, I'm just feeling a little down, that's all."

About that time, Mason re-entered the kitchen and looked at his wife and son. Cherise and Mase both turned to look at him. Mason lowered his eyes and went to look in the refrigerator. Mase looked over at his father as he picked up his CD player.

"Daddy, what's wrong with Momma? Did you know she was crying?"

Mason closed the refrigerator door and opened a bottle of water.

"Your momma will be okay. It's nothing for you to worry about."

He glared at Mason. "Any time my momma is hurt, I'm going to worry about her. What happened?" Mase asked angrily.

Mason had to catch himself because Mase had stepped to him so aggressively. He was about to get involved with something beyond his years, and a fight with his son wasn't something he wanted to add to the already volatile situation. What Mason failed to realize was that Mase was old enough to remember the tears, even though he wasn't old enough to understand why.

"Son, I said it doesn't concern you."

Mase didn't fear his father, so he approached him and stood eye to eye.

"Daddy, I am concerned. Did you do something to hurt Momma?"

Mason's nerves were already on edge.

"Mase, I'm not going to tell you again! This doesn't concern you! Go to your room!"

Mase would not move. Cherise went over to her son and grabbed his hand. She knew he was about to get in over his head. He was very protective of her, and this was the first time he had challenged his father like this.

"Honey, I'm okay. Please go on upstairs. I'll call you down for dinner shortly." Her smile was weak, but tender.

Mase would not take his eyes off his dad, who was now putting some fruit in a bowl. He knew that whatever had caused his mother's tears, it involved his dad. He took his eyes off Mason long enough to kiss Cherise on the cheek.

"I'm going down to the park to wait for Janelle to finish practice. I'll bring her home."

Before Cherise could stop him, he was out the door, slamming it behind him. Sighing, she turned to look at Mason, who was staring at her. Without saying anything to him, she walked out of the kitchen and into the dining room. When she returned, Mason was in the family room watching television.

Later at the dinner table, Janelle sensed something was wrong because no one was talking or looking at each other. She ate her food quickly and asked to be excused to her room, leaving Mase at the table. Once Janelle was out of the room, Mason looked over at Mase.

"Son, I want to apologize for the way I talked to you earlier today. The thing is, your mom and I have some things we need to work through, and it's hard on the both of us. I love your mother and I would never do anything to intentionally hurt her. Okay?"

Cherise sat there in silence as she listened to Mason try to explain the reason for her sadness. Mase set his fork down and looked over at his father.

"Daddy, I love Momma, too, and I don't like to see her cry. When you're not here, which is often, I'm the man of the house and it's my job to take care of Momma and Janelle. When one of them is hurt, I want to know why so I can make them feel better."

Mase's words cut Mason like a knife.

"I'm sorry I haven't been around much, son, but I'm going to change all of that real soon. I hate not being here with you guys, but I want you to know that I love you, your sister, and your mother very much. I know it might not seem like I'm here for you guys, but I am, Mase."

Mason stood and took his plate into the kitchen after his speech. He cut a piece of pie and made his way into the family room to watch TV. Mase leaned over and kissed Cherise on the cheek.

"I love you, Momma. You can go on to bed if you want. I'll do the dishes."

She smiled and patted him on the shoulder. "You don't have to, baby. I'll get them."

He stood and took her plate out of her hand. "No, I got it, Mom."

"Thank you, Mase," she replied as she rose from the table and headed upstairs.

Once upstairs, she looked in on Janelle, who had already taken her bath and was lying across the bed watching the Disney Channel. Cherise walked in and lay across the bed with her. Janelle hugged her neck.

"Are you feeling okay, Momma?"

Playing with her daughter's ponytail, Cherise kissed Janelle's cheek.

"I'm just fine, sweetheart. I'm just a little tired. How was school and practice?"

"Everything was great, Mommy," she answered with a yawn.

"I'm glad, baby. Well, I'm going to take a long, hot bubble bath. Don't let your bedtime sneak up on you."

"I won't, Mommy. Good night," she answered.

Cherise smiled and left Janelle's room. She walked into the bathroom and lit some candles before adding fragrant oil to her bathwater. As she was waiting for the tub to fill, she dimmed the lights in the bedroom and turned on some soft music. She needed everything she could to ease her tension. Once the tub was full, she took off her clothes, eased down into the steamy water, and let out a breath. In the silence of the bathroom she closed her eyes and did her best to let the events of the day melt away.

About thirty minutes later, the telephone rang downstairs.

"Hello?" Mason answered.

"Hey, man. I'm sorry I missed your call. What's up?" Vincent asked.

"All hell broke loose," Mason said.

"What happened?"

"Cherise found out about Vada, and it was ugly."

"How?"

"She saw some scratches on my back and Vada approached her in a mall parking lot because Cherise was driving my other car. I tried to hide the scratches, but she saw them anyway. I had no choice but to tell her about Vada," he said.

"Damn! What did she say?"

"She was pissed. She left and stayed gone for hours. Vincent, I was so worried about her. That's why I called you because I thought maybe she was with you."

"No, I haven't seen C. J. since the other night. Dang, man, I'm sorry to hear about this. Is there anything I can do to help?"

Mason lay back against the plush sofa.

"Bro, she asked me how I would feel if I found out she'd slept with another man. I almost passed out."

Vincent was quiet for a moment trying to figure out why Cherise would risk revealing her infidelity. Trying to play off his nervousness, he laughed.

"I'm sure C. J. was just trying to get back at you, Mason. Finding out you were sleeping with another woman is a hard pill for her to swallow, especially since it's not the first time. I'm sure she'll be back to her old self once this case is over and you're out of that department."

"I hope you're right, little brother," Mason said. "I'll holler at you tomorrow. I'm getting ready to go upstairs to check on her."

"Okay, Mason. Holler at me if you need to. I'll probably be heading back to Texas in a couple of days."

"So soon?"

"I need to get back and turn in my resignation," Vincent reminded him.

"So you're really going to do it, huh?"

"Yeah, I'm ready to come home."

"Well, when you come back, you're welcome to stay with us until you find a place. We'd love to have you, and the kids—well, you know how they feel about you," Mason said.

"Thanks, Mason, I'd love that," Vincent replied. "I don't want to leave, though, until you're done with this case with T-bone. Do you think you'll be able to tie things up over the next few days?"

"I'll try. I'll check with Domino tomorrow and see if we have enough evidence to arrest him and Pootie."

"Keep me posted," Vincent said before yawning. "Good night and holler at me tomorrow. Don't worry about C. J. She'll be all right."

"I hope you're right, because I can't lose her over this mess. Good night."

They hung up the telephone at the same time. Mason sat there for a moment and wiped his eyes. He turned off the TV and headed upstairs to their bedroom. When he entered, he noticed the bathroom door was cracked; he could see the light of the candles illuminating the room. He didn't know whether to interrupt her serenity or not. But what he did know was that he didn't want to lose the love of his life. He felt bad that he had to reveal unpleasant things about his job to Cherise, and he was determined to find a way to reassure her of his love. Mason walked over to the bathroom door and slowly pushed it open. He found Cherise asleep, and looking as beautiful as ever, surrounded by the romantic glow of candlelight. Mason knelt down beside their massive tub and laid his head against its edge. He was heartbroken that he had hurt Cherise, not knowing what she had been doing to him behind his back. Cherise opened her eyes.

"How long have you been in here?" she whispered.

He looked up at her with weary eyes. "Not long. Do you want me to leave?"

"No, but you can hand me a towel if you don't mind."

Mason stood and helped Cherise out of the tub. He wrapped a thick towel around her body and held her lovingly. Cherise looked up into his eyes and saw despair. She cupped his face and kissed him softly on the lips.

"Thank you," she said.

He kissed her.

"You're welcome, honey. Now let me get out of your way."

"Mason," she called to him.

"Yes?"

"I believe you when you say that woman doesn't mean anything to you, and I also know you love me. Look, I've done some things in my own life that I'm not proud of, so I'm not in a position to judge you. Just hurry up and finish this case so we can get back to our lives," she pleaded.

He walked back over to her and pulled her into his arms.

"Cherise, I'm sure if you've done anything undesirable, it's the result of the life I've forced on you."

If he only knew.

She lowered her eyes in guilt.

"Could you check on Mase and Janelle and make sure they're settled?"

"Sure. I'll be back shortly."

After Mason left the bathroom, Cherise dried off her body and slid into her lingerie. By the time Mason returned to the bedroom, Cherise was asleep. He showered, climbed into bed next to her, and held on to her until morning.

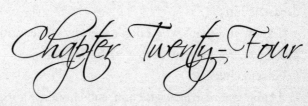

Chapter Twenty-Four

The next morning, Mason got up and took the kids to school so Cherise could sleep in, but she was unable to sleep peacefully after Mason got out of the bed. She had to admit she did feel more secure when he was around.

Her cell phone rang twice before Cherise answered.

"Hello?"

"Hey, C. J. Are you still in the bed? Where's Mason?" Vincent asked.

Cherise looked over at the clock.

"I think he took the kids to school. Why are you calling so early?"

Vincent smiled at the sound of Cherise's voice.

"I talked to Mason last night. He told me what happened. Are you okay?"

She rolled over in the bed and sighed.

"No, I'm not okay. You knew about that woman, didn't you?"

"C. J., I'm not going to get in the middle of this."

"Vincent, whether you want to believe it or not, you are in the middle of this!"

"Not really. Mason told me what you said. Why would you hint to him that you could be having an affair?"

"I don't know. I was pissed and I wanted him to hurt!"

Vincent was angry now.

"How many times do I have to tell you that Mason could get hurt if he's not focused? If he's out there stressing over you, he might make a mistake and it could cost him his life!"

"You know I wouldn't want anything to happen to Mason no matter how angry I am at him. I'm hurt that he would allow himself to get into that position after everything we've been through."

"C. J., don't you think you're being a little hard on Mason? Let me ask you something: How do you think Mason would feel if he found out about us? We're two people in his life that he loves very much, and our betrayal could devastate him."

"I know and that's why I don't see why you continue to try and seduce me. I love you, but I'm also in love with Mason."

Vincent chuckled.

"I know you're in love with him, and I honestly hope things work out between you two but, in the meantime, I still need to know if I have a daughter."

Cherise sighed. "Look, I can't think right now. I'll talk to you later."

"Okay, good-bye."

As she leaned over to set her telephone on the nightstand, she noticed Mason standing in the doorway with a shocked look on his face. Cherise's heart jumped up in her throat. She had no idea what he'd heard.

"Mason, I didn't hear you come in."

As he walked toward her with a strange look on his face, she scrambled out of the bed.

"That's obvious. Who the hell were you talking to?"

Cherise realized Mason had heard some of her conversation, and now her secret might be exposed.

"Just a friend."

Mason dropped his keys on the nightstand and calmly studied her.

"A friend that you love, but happen to be in love with me?"

She swallowed and stared at him. Mason was too calm. She didn't know what he was going to do, so she continued to play dumb.

"I don't know what you're talking about, Mason."

Mason looked up at the ceiling, then back at her.

"You really were having an affair, weren't you?"

She didn't know what to say because she didn't know how Mason was going to react if she told him the truth. He walked even closer.

"You can't deny it, Cherise. I heard you on the phone. Now tell me the truth!"

"It's been over for a long time, Mason," she answered nervously. "We're just friends now."

The reality of her words hit him hard, causing him to become light-headed. "Are you still seeing him?"

She hesitated because she couldn't afford for Mason to find out Vincent was the man she'd been sleeping with.

"No, I haven't seen him in a long time."

Mason folded his arms and demanded, "Who is he?"

The walls were closing in on her. Mason was so close she could feel his warm breath on her face. She tried to step around him so she could go to the bathroom.

"It doesn't matter now."

He grabbed her arm, stopping her. She could see his anger rising.

"It matters to me! Now tell me who he is!"

"Mason! You're hurting me!"

He released her and started pacing the floor.

"When did it start?"

She sat down on the side of the bed and tried to hold herself together.

"It started when you decided your job was more important than your family. Now, are you happy?"

"What do you think, Cherise?"

She walked over and stood in front of him, but he wouldn't look at her. Cupping his face, she made him look into her eyes.

"You were never here, Mason, and you were a different man back then. I never meant for it to happen," she whispered.

He pushed her away and walked over to the window.

"I don't believe you could do something like that, and then have the nerve to make me feel like I ruined your life by working undercover with this woman."

"It's still cheating, Mason."

Tears filled her eyes, so she walked over to the nightstand and retrieved some tissue. She wiped her eyes.

"Do you hate me now?" she asked.

He cleared his throat. "What happened to us?"

She shook her head. She'd asked herself the same question.

"The hardest image for a man to get out of his head is his woman screwing another man."

"It's no different for women, Mason," she proclaimed. "How do you think I feel knowing what I know about you and that woman? Remember, she's not the first, and what guarantees do I have that it won't happen again?"

He stared at her.

"It won't. That's why I never like to discuss my cases with you. You weren't supposed to find out about this woman."

"Is that supposed to make it easier for me to handle? You could've turned down the assignment if you thought it was going to jeopardize our marriage."

Mason was silent. He couldn't get it out of his head that Cherise had done the unthinkable. He'd been with Vada, but there were no emotions involved. Cherise had told the man on the phone that she loved him, and that was a totally different story.

"Where do we go from here?" she asked.

"I don't know, Cherise. Right now I feel like killing someone."

She looked up at him.

"Do you still love me?"

He frowned and his eyes became glazy.

"Don't ask me something like that right now. I can't even think straight."

She bit down on her lower lip, which was trembling. Mason was too calm, and it worried her. He looked away, deep in thought.

"I love you, Cherise, but right now I can't stand to look at you. My main concern is my children—period."

"Don't you mean our children?"

"No! My children," he yelled.

He walked toward the bedroom door and then stopped. Before walking out the door, he turned to her. Then, as if he had ice water in his veins, he made a spine-chilling announcement.

"Cherise, you're lucky that I love you too much to kill you, but if I find out who your boyfriend is, he's a dead man."

Cherise's eyes widened as Mason disappeared out into the hallway. She had to warn Vincent about what had happened. They both knew Mason was capable of pulling her telephone records, and then he would know exactly who she was talking to, which would be disastrous. Her head was spinning and she felt sick. Taking deep breaths, she knew she had to pull herself together in order to stop a tragedy waiting to happen. By the time she put on some clothes and got downstairs, Mason was nowhere to be found. She picked up the phone and frantically dialed Vincent's number.

"Hello?"

"Vincent, Mason knows about us! He heard me talking to you! He said if he found out who my boyfriend was he was going to kill him!"

"Calm down and tell me exactly what he said."

Cherise was breathless as she did her best to stay calm.

"He didn't put his hands on you, did he?" Vincent asked.

"No, but I thought he was going to at one point. He had me backed against the wall. He was too calm. Vincent, I'm scared."

"Where is he now?"

"I don't know. He left the house pissed, and I don't know what he's going to do next. I'm afraid he'll get his hands on the telephone records to see who I was talking to. If he does that, he'll know it was you."

Vincent sighed and ran his hands over his face. Maybe coming home had been a mistake.

"Don't worry, C. J. Everything will be okay. I'll see if I can find him. I'll call you back later. Just be cool."

"I'll try. Make sure you call me as soon as you find him."

Vincent hung up the telephone and pulled over onto the side of the road so he could dial without causing an accident. He tried not to appear worried, but he was. He looked at his watch as he waited for the person on the other end to pick up.

"Captain Reese," the gentleman answered.

"Yo, Domino, it's Vincent McKenzie. I need a favor." Vincent spoke hurriedly.

Domino leaned back in his chair and smiled.

"Vincent, I really enjoyed working with you the other night. It was just like old times."

"Yes, it was," Vincent responded.

"What can I do for you?"

"It's Mason. Is he there?"

Tapping his pencil on the desk, Domino responded. "No, he's not. Do you need me to have him get in touch with you?"

"No, and I don't have a lot of time to explain, but I need you to keep Mason from requesting phone records."

Domino sat up in his chair and frowned.

"Any records in particular?"

"Yes, the ones to his house. I'm not at liberty to go into any detail, but trust me on this one."

"I do trust you. Look, I'll make sure my people know to send any requests put in by Mason to me for approval. If this case is getting out of hand, I can do a fake arrest on Mason. I believe that's the only way T-bone will accept Mason being unavailable to be a part of his organization. I feel confident that we have enough evidence to move on T-bone and Pootie."

"Good. I appreciate it. Let me know if he shows up at the office."

"Will do. Take care, Vincent."

They hung up and Vincent immediately dialed Mason's cell phone.

"Yeah?" Mason answered solemnly.

"Hey, bro. Where are you? C. J. is looking for you. What's going on? She's worried about you."

It was obvious that Mason wasn't in a talking mood. "I don't know about Cherise anymore. She's not the woman I fell in love with."

"Where are you? Let me come pick you up so we can talk."

Mason was silent for a moment.

"Nah, little brother. I just need some time alone to think."

"What do you have to think about? You know C. J. loves you."

Vincent could hear what sounded like sniffing, and he became very concerned.

"Mason! Let me come get you. Where are you?"

"She slept with another man, Vincent," Mason said in a voice barely above a whisper. "How could she do that to me?"

A huge lump formed in Vincent's throat. The guilt was almost unbearable at this point.

He cleared his throat.

"Mason, I'm sure she just had a moment of weakness. We've all been there, bro."

"Not Cherise. I never would believe she was capable of doing something like this."

"Mason, if you're not going to meet me, then go home so you two can talk things out. You've thrown a lot of drama C. J.'s way. Don't you think she deserves the same support from you that she's given to you?"

"I don't know what to think right now, but what I do know is whoever that bastard is, he's dead when I find him."

"Come on, Mason, you're a cop. You can't go around saying stuff like that." Mason was silent on his end of the telephone.

"Mason, don't do anything crazy that'll get you locked up. You can't afford to do anything stupid."

"Why should I care about my career? It was my career that caused me to lose my wife," Mason said angrily.

"You haven't lost your wife. She's at home waiting on you like she always has been. Don't you realize that if she really loved that man, she would've left you by now?" Vincent asked. "C. J. is with you because that's where she wants to be, Mason. You're a family, and you'll always be a family if you find it in your heart to forgive her."

Mason sighed. "I hear you, Vincent, but I have to take some time to think about everything. I have a terrible migraine and my heart's not doing so well, either."

"Why don't you come over to my hotel and chill out for a little while?"

"I might just do that. I'll call you and let you know for sure."

"Well, I'm going to go by the house and check on C. J. She can't let the kids see her messed up like this. Please think about calling her to at least let her know you're okay."

"You do it. I don't feel like talking to her right now," he answered.

"She needs to hear from you, Mason."

"I'll think about it."

"Okay. I'll be heading back to the hotel after I leave your house, but whatever you do, call me back!"

"I will," Mason responded before hanging up his phone.

Vincent let out a deep breath. He knew this was only the beginning, and he was already exhausted. Now he had to go reassure C. J. and himself that every-thing would be okay. Pulling the car out into traffic, he hurried out to the McKenzie house.

"I'm sick of crying over you, Mason!!" Cherise screamed out in the empty house.

She blew her nose and stood to go take a shower at the exact same time there was a knock on her door. Startled, she quietly padded to the door to look out the peephole. She found Vincent standing outside her door looking distraught. She took a deep breath and swung open the door.

"Vincent, did you find Mason? Is he okay?" she asked frantically.

He walked through the door. "Not really, but I did talk to him over the phone." They walked into the family room and sat down.

"How is he? Is he still angry?"

"Of course he's still angry, C. J.! The man's heart has been ripped out! I did what I could to convince him to come home so you guys could talk."

She looked at him with teary eyes. "Is he coming?"

"I don't know. I mean, I don't think he's coming anytime soon. He's hurting and we're going to have to give him some space until he sorts everything out."

"That's what I'm worried about. I don't want him to sort everything out, because if he does, he'll put two and two together!"

"C. J., you're going to have to pull yourself together because I can't do this alone. Mason is a good cop, and if either one of us lets something slip, then we're busted!"

"What about the phone records?"

"I took care of that. He can't get access to them without going through his boss, and his boss knows not to approve the request," he assured her. "He is also in the process of trying to get Mason pulled from this case because one wrong move could be deadly for him."

She started crying again. "I wouldn't be able to live with myself if anything happened to him because of me."

He hugged her shoulders.

"Nothing's going to happen to Mason. He's going to come home and you guys are going to work this thing out."

"Thank you, Vincent," she replied as she wiped her eyes.

"Maybe we should just tell him the truth, C. J."

"No! We can't!" she begged.

"You know how he is. He's not going to stop until he finds out who it is."

"Vincent, what are we going to do?"

"I don't know, C. J. I'm going to head back over to the hotel. Mason might swing by."

"Okay, but keep me posted," she said with a whisper.

He kissed her on the cheek.

"Will do."

She walked him to the door and tried to smile. He turned to her and touched her chin.

"Try to act as normal as possible around the children. If they see you upset, they'll know something's wrong. Can you do that?"

"I'll try. Janelle has a ball game and I can't miss it. Mason is so upset he might've forgotten all about her game. Janelle loves it when he's there."

He walked toward his car.

"I'm sure he'll remember, but if he comes by the hotel, I'll remind him. I'll check with you later, C. J. Try not to worry."

She nodded in agreement before closing the door.

Chapter Twenty-Five

Mason walked into his office, sat down at his desk, and started typing on the computer. Domino saw him and walked over.

"Hey, Mason. What brings you in today?"

"Just checking my e-mails and some other things," he responded without looking up.

Domino sipped his bottled water. "Do you have a lead on something?"

Mason looked up. "I might, but I have to check into some other things first."

"You look like hell, Mason. Why don't you go home and get some rest? T-bone's not going to make a move until they get all that dope cut. Oh, and we're pulling you off the case."

Mason's head swung around in disbelief. "What? Why?"

"It's getting too hot. We can't take a chance on your cover getting blown. It's much safer this way."

Mason leaned back in his chair. "Is there something you're not telling me?"

Domino stared at Mason and could see he wasn't himself.

"Not really. I just think it's best we do it now. My plan is to have you arrested and held on receiving and selling stolen merchandise. Once you call T-bone and let him know you've been busted, we can move in on his and Pootie's crews. We want to make sure we bust them before the dope and guns hit the street."

"How long will I have to stay in jail?"

"Not long. We'll leak information that you've been extradited overseas for international fraud."

Mason leaned back in his chair and frowned.

"Won't I have to testify against them in court?"

"No. I believe we can get by with the wiretaps and your written statement. This will protect your identity."

Mason looked across the room, deep in thought. Domino sat down next to him and whispered. "Are you okay? You seem like you're a million miles away. I think this case has taken its toll on you. You need to take some time off to be with your family."

"I just might do that. Look, I'm out of here."

Domino stood, and so did Mason.

"Mason, just remember, I understand how hard this job is, and I know what it can do to your family life. If you ever need to talk, my door is always open."

"Thanks."

"Tell Cherise I said hello!"

Mason didn't respond. Instead, he walked out the door and down the stairs.

Cherise arrived at Janelle's ball game, but found it hard to concentrate. She kept searching the crowd for any sign of Mason. She cheered Janelle on and did her best to keep her spirits high, but it was difficult for her under the circumstances.

Janelle's team won. It wasn't until she was making her way down the bleachers that she saw Mason standing against the fence near Janelle's dugout with a lot of the other fathers. Her heart started pounding in her chest as she walked closer to them. As she approached, she could hear Janelle explaining the whole game to Mason.

"Momma! Did you see me hit that fly ball into center field?"

"Of course I did," Cherise responded as she kissed her daughter's dusty cheek. "Didn't you hear me screaming?"

Regis walked over and said, "Janelle, come on! Coach is getting ready to talk to the team."

"Daddy, I'll be right back!" she yelled with excitement.

"I'll wait for you right here, sweetheart," he answered as he tapped her on top of her baseball cap.

Janelle ran off with Regis. Mason turned and leaned against the fence without acknowledging Cherise's presence. She noticed how tired he looked, which made her feel worse.

"Mason, do you hate me so much that you can't even look at me?"

He stared down at the ground. "If I look at you, I'll only see a stranger, so why bother?"

His words hurt her, but she had to let him know he was wrong.

"I'm sorry I hurt you, Mason. I'm sorry I wasn't able to stay on the pedestal you've put me on. I do love you—I've always loved you. I made a mistake and I don't want our marriage to end over it."

Mason waved at Janelle and smiled as he listened to Cherise. He finally turned to her and saw the eyes he fell in love with.

"This is not the place to talk about our issues, Cherise."

"Then where, Mason?"

"I really don't know what to say to you right now, and I don't know when I'm going to be ready to talk. All I know is that I don't want my children affected by this, and I'll do whatever I have to do in order to protect them."

Cherise lowered her head in silence. Janelle ran back over and jumped into her father's arms.

"Daddy, Coach said we're probably going to the playoffs."

"That's great, sweetheart. Are you ready to go now?"

"Yeah!"

Cherise looked at them curiously. "Where are you guys headed?"

Mason took Janelle's hand and started walking off. "We're just going to eat pizza with the team to celebrate."

"Momma, are you coming?" Janelle asked.

Mason looked at Cherise with no expression on his face. She waved them off.

"No, you two go ahead and have fun. I'll see you later."

Janelle ran over and hugged and kissed her mother. "Okay, Momma. I'll bring you a slice of pizza!"

"Thank you, baby! Have fun!"

At the pizza parlor, Janelle was proud to have her daddy by her side. They spent about an hour or so hanging out with the team before heading home.

"Daddy! Can we get ice cream on the way home?" Janelle asked when they were on their way to the car.

"Janelle, you shouldn't be hungry. You're starting to eat just as much as your brother."

Janelle wanted to pout, but knew better. She looked up at him with familiar eyes—eyes like her mother's. He looked down at her and sighed. He'd never been able to tell either one of the women in his life "no," and tonight was no different.

"I'll tell you what, if you still want some ice cream by the time we pick up Mase, we'll get some. Okay?"

"Thank you, Daddy. I love you."

"I know you do, you little con artist. I love you, too."

Mason picked up Mase from a nearby arcade and they headed home, but not before Mason bought all of them ice cream.

As soon as they entered the house, Janelle headed up to her room. Mason frowned and looked at his watch. He wasn't ready to talk to Cherise, who he assumed was upstairs in their bedroom, so he walked into the family room and turned on the TV. He checked the programming and saw that a boxing match was coming on shortly, so he returned to the kitchen and found Mase searching for something to drink.

"Mase, I'm going out for a while. If you need me, call me on my cell."

Mase opened a bottle of juice and took a swallow.

"All right, Daddy. Do you want me to tell Momma?"

"If you want."

He picked up his keys and headed out the door. Watching the fight and drinking a few beers with Vincent would help take his mind off Cherise and the mystery man she'd been sleeping with.

Vincent was happy Mason had decided to come by the hotel. This would give him an opportunity to see where his brother's head was and how he was holding up. They got a table in the hotel bar and ordered a couple of beers. Mason sipped his beer and sighed.

"This is so good. It's been a minute since I drank one."

"There's nothing like a nice, cold beer and a heavyweight fight," Vincent acknowledged. "I'm going to order some appetizers, too. Do you want anything in particular?"

"Nah. You know I like everything."

Vincent waved the waitress over and ordered a platter with a variety of snacks. Across the room, they could hear patrons yelling as the bell rang and the boxers came out fighting.

"So, have you and C. J. had a chance to talk yet?"

Mason sat his glass down and shook his head. "No, and I'm not in a hurry to, either. I'm still trying to figure everything out. My mind is on rewind right now because I'm trying to figure out how I let her slip away from me."

Vincent looked at him curiously. "Have you seen her?"

"We were at Janelle's game earlier. She tried to get me to talk about things at the ballpark, but I wouldn't. When I dropped the kids off at home, I left right back out. She was upstairs in the bedroom, so I just told Mase to call me if he needed me."

Vincent picked up his mug and took a sip.

"I see."

Mason put his hands over his face in desperation.

"Do you think it could be a cop? She comes in contact with a lot of them. I'm going to try to get the logs from our telephone so I can see who she was talking to."

"How are you going to do that without raising suspicions?"

Mason smiled mischievously.

"I have a friend in the sheriff's office. He's going to get them for me. I didn't want anyone down at the office getting curious."

This bit of news blindsided Vincent. He didn't expect Mason to go outside his precinct to get his own telephone records.

"Do you really want to go through all that trouble, Mason? You said Cherise told you it's been over for a long time. Don't you believe she still loves you?"

Mason finished off his beer.

"She said she did."

"What about you? Do you still love her?"

Mason stared at the TV screen. "You know I do."

"Then let it go, Mason. You guys can get through this."

Mason picked up a potato skin and took a bite.

"You think so?"

"Yeah! You got through all that other mess, and you know if you hadn't heard C. J. on the phone, you would've never known."

Mason sat there in deep thought. Vincent looked at him seriously.

"Forget about the logs, Mason. Go home, hold your wife, and let her know she's number one on your list."

"She knows she's always been number one," Mason replied.

"Not really, bro. Telling her and showing her are two different things. You slept with three other women."

Mason quietly listened to his little brother as he continued to watch the boxing match on the TV screen. Vincent grabbed some food off the platter and waited for Mason to say something.

"When was the last time you took C. J. somewhere, just the two of you? When was the last time you surprised her with a romantic dinner, flowers, or just a foot rub, Mason?"

Mason stared at his younger brother.

"Vincent, you know it's hard to find time like that. Cherise's job is demanding, mine is demanding, and then the kids have their activities."

"Then you make time, Mason, because you have to. You know C. J. sees a lot of the same horrible images you see on the job. That can destroy a person emotionally, so do what you have to do to take her away from all of that. I'm not saying it has to be physical, either. You can take her away emotionally."

Mason laughed. "You're serious, aren't you?"

"Of course I am. When was the last time you guys used that huge hot tub out back?"

Mason scratched his head in frustration. "It's been a while."

"Exactly! All you have to do is have it hot and ready one evening with candles all around the patio, some wine, and soft music playing. Women love that kind of stuff, Mason, and I'm sure C. J. would damn near pass out if you did that for her."

It was at that point that the boxing match ended by a knockout, causing the patrons of the bar to scream loudly. Mason picked up a cheese stick.

"I guess you're right. I have to admit I haven't been there for her or the kids like I should've been, but it's still no excuse for what she did."

"How is it any different from what you did?" Mason stared at Vincent and then shook his head.

"It's not going to matter much longer because when I get those telephone logs I'll know exactly who he is, and then I'll take care of the rest. His ass is mine!"

Vincent stared at him, lowered his head, and sighed. "Mason, I need to tell you something and I want you to listen to me until I'm finished."

Mason took a sip of his beer and looked over at Vincent with curiosity. He had no idea what Vincent was about to tell him but he was in for a rude awakening.

"I can do that. What's up, bro?"

"It was me. I'm the one Cherise was having the affair with, but I want you to know it's been over for a long time."

"What did you say?" Mason asked with his glass halfway to his mouth.

"I said I'm the man C. J. was having an affair with but it's been over for a long time."

The patrons in the bar were very noisy and Mason still wasn't sure he heard Vincent correctly, so he laughed.

"You're full of shit, Vincent. How many beers have you had tonight?"

Vincent didn't respond. He just stared back at his brother. Mason set his glass down, looked Vincent in the eyes, and saw the truth.

"You're serious, aren't you?"

Vincent lowered his head with guilt.

"I wish I wasn't. Look, Mason, none of us are the same people we were back then, even you."

Mason almost fell out of his chair. He felt like someone had hit him in the stomach with a sledgehammer. He couldn't breathe and his heart was pounding hard in his chest. His first thought was to pull his gun out of its holster and shoot Vincent, but then he remembered loaded guns were not allowed in bars, and he had left his in the car. His face felt like it was on fire and his eyes began to water. Vincent could see the color in Mason's face changing, and he knew at any moment he was going to explode, so he held his hands up to stop him.

"Before you do or say anything, let me explain. First of all, it wasn't C. J.'s fault, and secondly, neither one of us meant for it to happen. Mason, you were never there and I put emphasis on never. C. J. was a young mother who felt like she was a single parent. She was an emotional wreck all of the time, and in the midst of me consoling her, things got out of control."

Vincent could see a vein pulsating in Mason's neck.

"You son of a bitch! I trusted you with my family, my wife!"

Mason started to stand, but Vincent stopped him.

"Wait, Mason! Please hear me out because I want you to know the whole truth."

"I think I've heard all I need to hear," Mason answered.

"No, you haven't," Vincent yelled in frustration. "Now sit down! Please!"

Mason was trembling as he eased back down in his seat. Vincent called the waitress over and ordered a stronger drink. If looks could kill, Mason had murdered Vincent right there at the table. The waitress brought Vincent's drink over and he swallowed the small glass of scotch quickly.

"I did what I could to stand in for you, Mason, but I swear I never planned to touch her. It was weird spending all that time alone with C. J. and Mase. It was like we were becoming a family when you were the one who should've been there for them. That woman loves you, and she always has."

"So I guess sleeping with you was the way she expressed her love for me?"

Vincent shook his head in disagreement.

"Mason, you're missing my point. She never, ever, not even once gave me any indication that she wanted more than a physical relationship with me. C. J. and I were nothing but friends. I just happened to be there. Had I not been, it would've been someone else."

Mason looked around at the room full of people and cleared his throat.

"Is that supposed to make me feel better? Why the hell are you telling me? Why now?" Mason asked. Vincent noticed that Mason's leg was shaking.

"I'm telling you because you're my brother, and whether you believe me or not, I love you. I want you to understand the circumstances of how and why it happened. C. J. wanted to hurt you back then, but she's trying to protect you now. That's why she never wanted you to know. She'd kill me if she knew I told you."

Mason glared at him with fiery eyes.

"What makes you think I'm not going to kill you?"

"I know you want to kill me, and if it would make you feel better, go ahead. You're the only family I have, and if I lose you, what's the use in living anyway?"

"Bullshit!" Mason yelled.

Vincent closed his eyes briefly.

"There's something else you should know before you start judging people, bro."

"What?" Mason asked with hesitation.

Vincent took a sip of his drink and leaned back in his chair.

"C. J. knows about your affair with that lawyer."

Mason froze. He hadn't thought about that woman in years. She'd worked in the district attorney's office and had worked on cases with Mason on more than one occasion. He'd slept with her a couple of times before she took a better job in Washington. Mason took a deep breath.

"Is that why she slept with you? To get back at me?"

Vincent ordered another scotch and took a sip.

"I don't know what was in her head at the time. All I know is she was feeling lonely and abandoned, and thought that you didn't love her. She couldn't understand what you saw in those other women that you didn't see in her. I didn't know she knew about that lawyer until recently."

Mason just sat there, stone-faced, curious as to why Cherise never confronted him about the lawyer.

"Did she ask you if you knew about it?" Mason asked.

"Of course she did!"

"That woman didn't mean anything to me," Mason mumbled.

"She meant everything to C. J. She wasn't the same after that."

Mason sat there in deep thought after listening to Vincent.

"Look, Mason, C. J. broke things off with me a long time ago."

Vincent knew he couldn't tell his brother about his more recent encounter with Cherise. That would only make things worse, and it was an incident unlikely to repeat itself in the future anyway.

Mason finished off the rest of his beer and stood up. Vincent also stood. He was worried about where Mason's head was.

"Where are you going?"

"That's none of your damn business!" Mason answered with a scowl on his face.

"Let me go with you."

"No! You stay the hell away from me! You're lucky we're in a room full of people, because if we weren't I would probably do something that would put me on the eleven o'clock news. Don't you realize what you've done? Goddamn it! You're my brother!"

"I'm sorry, Mason. I wish C. J. loved me as much as she loves you, but I'm not that lucky. We're human, and for some reason, she found comfort in me when you weren't there. We made a mistake and I want you to understand that while you're persecuting us, what you did with that lawyer and that police officer and Vada is no different."

"Now that's where you're wrong, little brother," Mason said angrily. "You're family, and you committed the ultimate betrayal."

Mason walked toward the door, but stopped once he got there. He turned around, came back, and hit Vincent in the face. Vincent fell, knocking over a table. Mason pulled his brother up by the collar and started punching him in the face. Vincent didn't even try to defend himself because in his heart he knew he deserved every punch Mason gave him. When management ran over to intervene, Mason flashed his badge so they backed off. He released Vincent, who was now bloody and bruised.

"Stay away from me, and stay away from my family! If I see you anywhere near my house again, I will kill you!"

Before Vincent could pick himself up off the floor, Mason was gone. Vincent looked around and noticed all the patrons staring at him. A waitress walked over and attended to him.

"Are you okay? Do you want me to call the police?"

Vincent showed her his badge.

"I am the police."

The waitress helped Vincent up off the floor and to his seat. A bartender walked over and gave Vincent some ice for his jaw.

"Sir, if you need anything, just let me know."

He pulled out his cell phone and dialed Cherise so he could warn her that Mason knew about their affair and was on the rampage.

"Hello," a sleepy voice answered.

"Hey, C. J., it's me," Vincent said sadly.

She could tell something was wrong by the tone of his voice.

"What's wrong?"

"Mason knows about us. I had to tell him the truth."

She sat up in bed and went into a panic.

"Why did you do that? Are you trying to get me killed?"

"Mason would never hurt you. He beat the hell out of me, but he let me live."

Nervousness swept over her body as she threw back the covers, climbed out of bed, and paced the floor. "What makes you think he's not going to do the same to me? Why would you do something so stupid, Vincent?" she asked frantically.

"It was only a matter of time before he found out. He found another way to get your phone records, and I couldn't stop him. He would've known before the night was over that it was me so I had to tell him. You know Mason. He's a cop, and he wasn't going to stop until he knew who you were talking to on the phone."

Cherise tried her best to pull herself together. "What did you tell him?"

"I told him it wasn't your fault and that the reason it happened was because he was never there for you and Mase. I let him know we never meant for it to happen and that you never wanted more from me than what it was. I made sure he knew that you always loved him and felt guilty about the whole thing."

Tears fell from her eyes.

"I can't believe you took it upon yourself to tell him about us without discussing it with me first."

Vincent was doing the best he could to make Cherise see why he had to tell Mason the truth. He got onto the elevator and made his way up to his room.

"Mason would've been suspicious of every man around you. I was afraid he would hurt the wrong person. He was a ticking time bomb."

She was almost hyperventilating at this point as she sank down on the floor.

"Does he know about Florida?"

"No, but he wanted to know when it ended. I told him you broke it off a long time ago."

"I'm scared, Vincent. I don't know what to say to him."

"Just tell him how you feel. Tell him the truth and explain to him how you felt during those years."

"What if he asks me about the last time we slept together? Then what?"

Vincent stepped off the elevator and walked down the hallway to his room.

"You can't tell him the truth about that. I think it'll be too much for him to handle."

At that moment, she heard the garage door go up.

"Oh, my God! He's here! I don't know what to do."

"Calm down, C. J.," Vincent said as he walked into his hotel room. "If he asks you if I called, tell him the truth. Okay? He would never hurt you after all the cheating he's done."

"I think I'm going to be sick, Vincent."

"No, you're not. Be strong and stand your ground. If Mason gets out of hand, call me."

Vincent hung up the telephone and turned on the TV. His jaw was throbbing and his lip was bleeding so he went into the bathroom and grabbed the ice bucket. He wrapped some ice up in a towel and put it up to his face. He sat down across from the TV and started watching the news. He was confident Mason wouldn't hurt Cherise, but he would definitely give her hell.

A news report came on regarding the homicide in Piedmont Park and the status of the investigation. They showed footage of the murder scene and interviews with the detectives and Cherise. Vincent listened as Cherise commented briefly on the case. After her statement, the reporter went on to reveal who the detective and Cherise were, and their affiliations with the case. Vincent felt terrible that things had fallen apart between him, Mason, and Cherise. He prayed tomorrow morning would bring a better day for all of them.

After Cherise hung up the telephone, she sat down in the chair and prayed. She figured if Mason was going to kill her, she wanted to look him in the eyes before he did. She hoped that he would recognize the part he had played in their marriage's demise.

Mason walked into their bedroom and acted as if she wasn't even there. He went straight into the bathroom and turned on the shower. When he returned, he had on some sweat pants and a T-shirt. He walked over to the bed, grabbed his pillow and a blanket that was laying across the foot of the bed, and walked out the door. Cherise reluctantly followed him into the guest room across the hall.

"Mason, can we please sit down and talk?"

He gave her a look that could kill, and before she could say another word, he had her by the throat against the wall. Cherise's eyes widened as she tried to get his hands away from her neck.

"Do you have any idea how much I hate you right now? Why Vincent? Was I that terrible of a husband to you, Cherise?"

She couldn't respond because he was tightening his grip, making it difficult for her to breathe. He released her and walked over to the window. She slid down on the floor, gasping for air.

"You and Vincent have made a damn fool out of me. It makes me sick to look at you."

Cherise was still coughing and trying to catch her breath as Mason stared down at her.

"You'd better be glad my children are here, or I'd kill you where you stand."

Cherise couldn't believe Mason wanted her dead after he'd violated their marriage on more than one occasion. She pulled herself off the floor and pushed him against the wall in anger, stunning Mason.

"You bastard! Mason, you have a lot of goddamn nerve to stand here and act like you're not guilty in this mess! I did everything I could to make you happy but it was never good enough for you. No! I didn't plan on having an affair with Vincent, but he made me feel loved when you acted like you didn't give a damn! You constantly put your job before your family and now you want to stand there and blame me for sleeping with your brother? Hell to the no! At least now you know what it feels like to be hurt by someone you love. I know it was wrong, but I want you to know that what happened between me and Vincent wasn't planned. I tried over and over to talk to you and reach out to you. Every time I did, you would push me farther and farther away. Why, Mason? Why couldn't you just love me like you promised me you would?"

Mason stared back at her with so much hate. His hands were shaking as he walked around her, sat down on the side of the bed, and covered his face.

"Goddamn it, Cherise! Leave me the hell alone before you make me hurt you!"

"If that would make you feel better, go ahead, but I want you to know I'm not going to sit here and let you hurt me when you're the reason we're in this mess in the first place."

Mason had a deranged look in his eyes—a look she never thought she would see on him.

"I'm so sorry I hurt you, Mason, but there's nothing I can do to change the past."

Mason jumped up off the bed and punched a huge hole into the wall inches away from her head. He then leaned into her and burst into tears. Cherise held onto him and cried along with him.

"How could you do something like this to me?" he asked between sobs.

She laid her head against his chest.

"I guess I was looking for the same thing you were looking for in those women. It just so happens that I found what I was missing with Vincent. You were never there, Mason."

Mason wiped away his tears and stared at her. His knuckles were bruised and bleeding from where he'd punched the wall.

"I didn't care about those women."

"You cared enough to sleep with them, Mason. If you want to hate me for the rest of my life, then go ahead. I've apologized to you and to God for what I've done. I believe he's forgiven me, and I hope you can find it in your heart to forgive me, too."

He shook his head in disbelief. He sat back down on the bed and hung his head. Cherise looked down at his hand.

"Let me go get something for your hand, Mason. You're bleeding."

"My hand is the least of my worries, Cherise."

She lowered her head and wiped the tears off her cheeks.

"Where do we go from here? You are my life. All I ever wanted was for us to be together as a family."

"Go to bed, Cherise. I'm done talking tonight."

Without responding to her, he walked out the door and down to the kitchen to get an ice pack for his hand. Cherise went back across the hallway into their bedroom and climbed into bed. When Mason came back upstairs he went back into the guest room and closed the door. Cherise turned over in the bed and sobbed. She felt like her world was crashing down on her. If she lost Mason, she would never be able to forgive herself.

Across the hallway, Mason lay in bed, staring at the ceiling. He thought about everything Cherise said to him about their life back then and realized she'd made some valid points. He knew one thing for a fact. He would never see her in the same way ever again.

He thought back to those days in question when he was never there for her, and he tried to figure out what went wrong. He needed to understand why the only woman he'd ever loved would look for love in the arms of his brother. He remembered that Cherise was working just as hard as he was, but she still found time to be a good mother to Mase and Janelle. He always knew she was a good woman, and she had been a good wife in order to put up with him and the job he had. It was still no excuse for her to sleep with Vincent, of all people. The two people he loved the most in the world, outside of his children, had done the unthinkable, and he just didn't know if he could ever forgive them.

Mason climbed out of bed, walked down the hallway, and opened Mase's door. He walked over to his bed and looked down on his sleeping son, who looked just like he had at that age. It was at that moment that he realized that Cherise had done an excellent job of raising him basically alone. Mase was becoming a strong, black man and it was his wife who in large part had made that happen. He leaned down and kissed Mase on the forehead and eased out of his room. His next stop was Janelle's room. She was his angel and he saw all the makings of a young woman developing right before his eyes. He owed all the credit to Cherise. Mason sat down on the side of Janelle's bed and tenderly stroked her hair. Before leaving her room, he gave her a kiss on the cheek. Mason loved his children, and he didn't want them to grow up in a broken home. As he made his way down the hallway he heard Cherise crying, causing his heart to thump in his chest. He stood outside their bedroom door for a few seconds listening to her before walking across the hall to the guest room. After closing the door behind him he prayed for strength and guidance to get through this madness.

Chapter Twenty-Six

It was late and Vada was getting frustrated because Mirage wasn't returning her calls. She'd been trying all day with no success, and she was beginning to worry about him. Her body was missing him the most, and she was yearning.

"Damn it, where are you, Mirage?"

She hung up the telephone and turned on the TV. She was sipping on a Corona and eating some hot wings. Bored, she flipped through several channels until she got to a special report on recent murders in Atlanta. As she sat there watching the program, they showed footage of police press conferences and crime scenes. At one particular crime scene she noticed a face that looked somewhat familiar. She sat up and looked closer at the black woman on the TV screen. It was the same woman she had run into in the mall parking lot, who happened to be driving a car just like Mirage's. She listened as the woman spoke into the microphone regarding the murder. The reporter identified the woman as Cherise McKenzie, the lead crime scene investigator in Atlanta who was in charge of all the evidence from various homicides.

Vada sat there thinking. Then a light bulb went off in her head.

"Oh shit!"

She grabbed the telephone and dialed frantically.

"Talk to me," T-bone answered.

"Hey, I think we have a problem. A big problem," Vada said.

"What's up?" he asked.

"I don't want to talk about it over the phone. Get over here quick. It's about Mirage."

Mason woke up at the crack of dawn the next morning. He didn't know what time he finally dozed off, or when Cherise had stopped crying. What he did know was he had to figure out what he was going to do with what was left of his marriage. The house was quiet when he stepped out into the hallway. He walked into their bedroom and found it empty. After showering he got dressed and went downstairs to make coffee. Pulling his cell phone out of his pocket, he checked his voice mail. Vincent had left him two apologetic messages. He poured a cup of coffee and opened the door to the garage. That was when he noticed that Cherise's truck was missing. He didn't remember hearing her leave for work, but he figured she wanted to get out of the house so she didn't have to face him. The kids would be up in less than an hour, so he started making breakfast for them. Moments later, the telephone rang.

"Hello?" he answered.

"Mason, don't hang up," Vincent pleaded. "I'm worried about C. J."

"Why doesn't that surprise me?" Mason asked sarcastically.

"Look, I'm beyond how you feel about me right now. I'm concerned about C. J., and you should be, too."

"Why?" Mason asked as he sipped his coffee.

"We had plans this morning to meet for coffee at her office but she's not here. I called her cell, but I didn't get an answer."

"Maybe she changed her mind."

Mason could hear the panic in Vincent's voice.

"No! She's missing, Mason."

"What do you mean, she's missing?"

"Her truck is in the parking garage, but Cherise is nowhere in the building."

Mason's heart almost stopped beating at that moment.

"Has the building been searched?"

"We searched the building before I called you," Vincent said frantically.

Mason tried to keep himself calm and think logically.

"Maybe she changed her mind about meeting you this morning."

Vincent paced the floor in Cherise's office.

"I'm not feeling that, Mason, but you need to get down here as soon as possible. C. J. wouldn't leave without letting somebody know where she was."

Mason cleared his throat and realized Vincent was right.

"The kids are here. I can't leave them. Let me check with her parents to see if they've heard from her first."

"You're right! Look, call me right back. I'm getting ready to go through the building again with the security guard."

"I'll be there as soon as I get the kids out to school."

"All right, but hurry up," Vincent said before quickly hanging up.

Vincent tried to call Cherise several times, but he still only got her voice message. He left yet another message for her to call and let him know where she was. He had a bad feeling about this and his gut feelings were never wrong.

Mason didn't have time to take the kids to school and so he wouldn't worry them, he told them they had to catch the bus because he had to rush to work. The kids were used to their spontaneous lives so they didn't think anything about the change in plans. Once they were on the bus, Mason jumped in the car and headed to Cherise's office to meet Vincent. Mason prayed that Cherise was okay, and he tried his best not to think the worst. Mason pulled into the garage and found Vincent waiting on him. Mason parked next to Cherise's truck and climbed out.

"Have you heard from C. J. yet?" Vincent asked as Mason approached Cherise's truck.

"Not yet," Mason replied as he inspected the outside of Cherise's truck.

Just as Vincent reached for Cherise's car door, Mason stopped him.

"Wait!" He opened the trunk of his car and pulled out two pairs of latex gloves. "Here, put these on."

Vincent was so distraught he'd almost forgot the first rule of being a detective: Don't contaminate potential evidence. The two put the gloves on and opened the door of her truck. Almost immediately, they knew something was wrong. Her purse was gone but her cell phone was in the caddy next to two cups of coffee. Mason felt the cups; they were cold.

"Look at this, Mason."

Mason came around and inspected a stain on the edge of the door that looked like blood. Vincent could see the anxious look in Mason's eyes.

"That's it! I'm putting a call in for missing persons. Call Cherise's team down here to go over this truck. I want to keep this as quiet as possible. I don't want the media getting ahold of this. I need to let Cherise's parents in on what we've found so far and to be on standby to get the kids out of school if it's necessary."

Mason was dying a slow death inside. Vincent pulled out his cell and called Cherise's office to get her team downstairs immediately. Mason climbed back into his car and dialed Cherise's parents' house. He tried his best to explain things to them without alarming them, but he was unsuccessful. He could feel a migraine coming on as soon as he hung up. He remembered telling Jonathan that he would always love and protect Cherise. Now it seemed like he'd let him down in more ways than one. As he sat there he tried to think of a place to start looking for her, but he was interrupted by his ringing cell phone.

"Cherise?" he answered frantically.

"No, this is not Cherise, but I might let you talk to her…detective."

Mason nearly passed out. It was T-bone-somehow he'd found out he was a police officer.

"What have you done?" Mason asked.

"I must say, you have excellent taste in women, Detective," T-bone taunted.

Vincent noticed Mason's expression and the way he was gripping the phone. He walked over to him.

"What's wrong?" he asked.

"Where is my wife, you son of a bitch?"

"Oh, she's cool. Me and the boys are keeping your loving wife very happy. I must say you almost got me, Mirage, or whoever you are." T-bone laughed. "After Vada told me she saw your wife on the news and realized she was the same woman she ran into at the mall driving your car, I knew something was wrong. Luckily I have a friend on the force, who was happy to provide me with all the information I wanted to know about your wife and how she was connected to you. I paid him a lot of money for the information and it was worth every goddamn dime."

Tears fell from Mason's eyes and Vincent knew whatever it was, it was bad.

"If you touch one hair on her head I will bury you myself. Do you hear me? Let me talk to her!"

T-bone laughed devilishly. "I guess I can do that, Detective, but I don't know if you'll want her back once we're done with her."

Mason could hear T-bone laughing as he put the phone up to Cherise so she could speak.

"Mason! I'm so sorry! I should've been more careful. I love you!"

He closed his eyes and let out a breath because he was relieved that Cherise was still alive and seemed to be okay.

"I love you, too, baby, and don't worry, I'm coming to get you. Have they hurt you in any way?"

"No, but I'm scared," she said on a sob.

"I know you are, baby. Just try to stay calm. I'm coming for you."

T-bone pulled the telephone away.

"The clock is ticking, Detective. Come and get her if you want, but you know I'm not going to make it easy for you."

"Oh, I'm definitely coming. You just keep the porch light on for me."

Mason's arrogance angered T-bone. He yelled obscenities into the telephone.

"You're the one who violated my business, my trust, and lastly, my sister. It's payback time, Detective, and if you want your lovely wife back, then bring it on before I send her back to you, piece by piece!"

The line went dead and Mason started shivering. Everything that had happened between him and Cherise prior to this was irrelevant. Cherise's life was in danger and he wasn't about to let anything happen to her. Vincent frowned and questioned Mason.

"Who was that, bro? What's going on?"

Mason tried to clear the lump out of his throat. His voice was hoarse as he spoke. "It was T-bone. He's got Cherise and he knows I'm a cop."

Vincent leaned against the car to steady himself. "What do you mean, T-bone's got her? How did he find out you're a cop?"

"He snatched Cherise when she came into work and he claims he paid off somebody in the force to get information on me," Mason revealed.

"Shit! Do you believe him?"

"I don't know!" Mason yelled back at him. "Cherise is all I care about right now."

Vincent let out a breath and pulled his gun out of its holster. He checked the ammunition and looked at Mason. The brothers looked at each other and realized this was a whole new ball game. Vincent put his gun back into his holster and opened the car door.

"What are we waiting on? Let's go get her."

It was at that time that Paul, one of Cherise's assistants, walked over, interrupting them.

"Detective McKenzie, we've dusted Dr. McKenzie's truck and gathered fibers from inside. We'll get them upstairs right away so we can start an analysis."

Mason handed her his card and instructed her to call if they got a hit on any of the fingerprints. Vincent climbed inside Mason's car and they peeled out of the garage. He sat there in deep thought as Mason drove them through the streets of Atlanta. Mason turned a sharp curve and pushed the gas pedal down, gunning the engine.

"Cherise was on the news last night. Maybe that had something to do with it," Vincent stated.

"What do you mean, she was on the news?"

Vincent turned to Mason and begin to summarize the news report for him.

"One of the TV stations aired a segment about the Piedmont Park murder. Cherise was at the crime scene and commented on the case."

"Goddamn it!!" Mason yelled.

"What is it?"

"Vada's behind this. I left my car at the house the other day and Cherise drove it to the mall. She told me a woman approached her and asked her if she knew someone named Mirage. I knew this thing was falling apart but I ignored it. It's my fault they grabbed Cherise," Mason confessed.

"They'll kill her if we don't go get her, Mason."

"I know, and I can't let that happen."

"Don't you think we need to call Domino and let him know what's up?"

"No. It's going to take too long. They crossed the line by grabbing Cherise. We're going to handle this by ourselves."

"Well, we're going to need more firepower than this. You saw what kind of weapons they were packing," Vincent reminded Mason.

"You're right. I know exactly who can help us."

Vincent closed his eyes and, as calmly as he could, made a startling observation.

"Mason, what about the kids? What if they know where you live?"

He gritted his teeth. "I'm going to call my in-laws and tell them to pull the kids out of school now. Those fools might try to grab them, too."

"What about protection? Don't you think we need to get somebody over there to look after them until they can get the kids?"

"Jonathan can handle it. I want them on a plane and out of here right away. I'll tell them to take them to Disney World or something so they won't have access to the news. I don't want my kids to know that their mother is in danger."

"Maybe you're right. Do you have any idea where T-bone's holding Cherise?" Vincent asked.

"I'm sure he'll be happy to tell me so he can try to take me out. Since he knows I'm a cop, he's probably expecting me to bring the whole force with me, but I have a trick for him. All I need is you, little brother," Mason replied.

"You're damn straight!"

T-bone walked back into the bedroom where he had Cherise tied up. He noticed Vada staring at Cherise in a crazed way while holding a gun on her. He walked over and put his hand on the gun.

"Chill, sis. I can't have you freaking out on me right now."

"I can't believe Mirage lied to me. I'm sitting here looking at his damn wife! That son of bitch played me!"

Cherise stared back at the woman. "You've made the biggest mistake of your life. He's not afraid of you."

Vada walked over to Cherise and pulled her hair hard. She put the gun up to Cherise's head.

"You better be afraid of me because by the time Mirage gets here, there'll be nothing left of you."

"Vada! Leave her alone and sit down!"

Vada turned Cherise's hair loose and laughed. "He might be your husband, but he wasn't acting married when he was getting down with me. We know each other very, very well. As a matter of fact, I had him screaming my name on more than one occasion."

"I guess cheap ass will do that to a man," Cherise said angrily.

Vada smacked Cherise hard across the cheek. She chambered a round.

"You bitch!" Vada yelled.

T-bone saw what Vada was about to do. He hit Vada's arm, causing her to shoot the ceiling instead of Cherise. T-bone wrestled her out of the room and closed the door.

"What the hell is wrong with you, Vada? She's our bargaining chip, and I won't let you mess this up just because you're sprung!" he yelled at her.

Vada sat down in the chair and started crying.

"Kilo, go in there and watch Mirage's lady."

Kilo grabbed a fish sandwich out of a nearby bag and walked into the bedroom. T-bone put his hand on Vada's shoulder to comfort her.

"You're going to have to calm down, sis. I know you're pissed right now, but you'll get a chance to speak your peace when Mirage gets here. In the meantime, eat a sandwich or something. Damn!"

T-bone walked over to the kitchen cabinet and poured out some white powder. He took a sniff and looked over at Tiny.

"Yo, Tiny! Go outside and check the perimeter. I'm sure Mirage is going to bring an army with him, but as long as we have his girl in there, we have nothing to worry about."

Tiny nodded at T-bone, grabbed his Uzi off the table, and eased out the back door.

Mason had called the gun store on their way over so they wouldn't waste any unnecessary time. The pair entered the store and an elderly gentleman who appeared well into his seventies motioned for them to follow him into a back room. Once out of sight, the gentleman greeted Mason with a friendly handshake.

"Mason, it's so good to see you again."

"Same to you, Mr. Andrews."

"Now, son, how many times do I have to tell you it's Vernon?"

Vernon Andrews was a former police officer who had served forty years on the police force before eventually retiring so he could open his business. He was well respected by their fellow police officers and people in the community. Mr. Andrews did his best to keep guns out of the wrong hands and he also mentored to young people in the area.

Mason smiled and nodded toward Vincent. "I'm sorry. Do you remember my brother, Vincent?"

Shaking Vincent's hand, Mr. Andrews smiled at Vincent.

"Of course I do. It's good to see you, Vincent."

"Same here, sir."

Mason nervously looked at his watch. "Well, we're in kind of a hurry, Vernon, so I hope you're able to help us out."

Mr. Andrews locked the door to his office and opened up a huge safe he had hidden in the wall behind a refrigerator in the corner of the room.

"Mason, these came to me hot off the street, so remember, you didn't get them from me."

He handed them a couple of Tec-9s and several clips to go with them. Mason and Vincent inspected the weapons carefully.

"They work, Mason. I've tested them myself."

"I trust you, Mr. Andrews."

As Mr. Andrews closed the safe, he turned and smiled. "Don't forget, you were never here."

Mason smiled back at him. "I won't forget, and don't forget if you need anything, just call me. I owe you."

Mr. Andrews waved him off. "Don't worry about it. Consider it my contribution to the cause."

Mason hugged him lovingly. "Thank you."

"If you insist," Vernon said and laughed.

Mason looked at his watch and then at Vincent.

"We need to get going. Are you ready?"

"I've been ready," Vincent said as he put the new gun under his jacket.

They exited the store and as soon as they got on the interstate, Mason accelerated to nearly one hundred miles an hour.

Kilo sat in the room watching TV with Cherise. He took a bite of his second fish sandwich and looked over at Cherise.

"Yo, Slim, are you hungry?"

"No, but I have to go to the bathroom."

He sighed and walked over to her. He pulled out a switchblade to cut the duct tape on her wrists. Before cutting it, he looked at her seriously.

"Slim, if you try anything stupid, you're not going to like what I do to you. Do you understand?"

Cherise believed him and nodded in agreement. She held out her hands so Kilo could cut the tape, and she allowed him to help her off the bed. He walked her over to the bathroom and opened the door. Her blouse was torn, her head was throbbing, and the cut on her head had dried blood on it. Cherise turned to close the door behind her, but he put his hand up and blocked it.

"Sorry, Slim, you're going to have to do your business with the door open. Don't worry, you don't have anything I haven't seen before," he said with a wicked grin.

Cherise lowered her head and proceeded to unzip her pants. Kilo stood there watching her as she lowered her clothing and sat on the toilet. She felt so degraded, but she knew she couldn't protest. She tried to empty her bladder as quickly as possible, since he was making her feel so uncomfortable. Once she finished, she quickly flushed and pulled up her pants. She quietly walked over to the sink and washed her hands. As she walked back into the bedroom, Kilo blocked her path.

"I can see why you're Mirage's old lady. You're fine as hell. Maybe I can help you pass the time away until he gets here."

He leaned down and tried to kiss her, but she pushed him away.

"I'd rather die than let you touch me."

Kilo grabbed her by the neck and pushed her hard against the wall just as T-bone walked into the room.

"Kilo, what the hell is going on in here? Why isn't she tied up?"

Kilo released his grip on her and stepped back. "She said she had to use the bathroom."

"Then why are you trying to break her damn neck?"

Kilo just shook his head in frustration and grabbed Cherise by the arm. He pushed her down on the bed, grabbed the roll of duct tape off the dresser, and tied Cherise's wrists back together.

"Slim has a big mouth, man. I was just reminding her who was in charge," Kilo explained.

T-bone shook his head in disbelief.

"First Vada, now you. Why are ya'll letting her get in your head?"

T-bone walked over to Cherise and leaned down in her face.

"Sweetheart, if you don't chill, your husband is going to find your lifeless body when he gets here. Do you understand what I'm saying?"

Tears fell from Cherise's eyes as she nodded in agreement. He looked over at Kilo. "Now, are we going to have any more problems here tonight?"

"Nah, man, I'm cool."

"Good!" T-bone yelled as he went back into the front room.

Vincent and Mason were exiting the city limits and were amazed that they didn't get pulled over by law enforcement. On the ride there, they went over their strategy for rescuing Cherise.

"Look, bro, I want you to know that I'm trying to squash all that drama that happened between us. I wasn't the man I should've been back then, and I'm not surprised Cherise stepped out on me."

Vincent lowered his head. "She found comfort with me and that's all."

Mason sat silent for a moment as Vincent's comment sunk in.

"Look, Vincent, if anything happens to me, I want you to take care of Cherise and the kids."

"Don't even talk like that, bro. We're going to get C. J., and we're going home. We're family and we take care of each other no matter what," Vincent informed him.

Mason smiled.

"You're right, lil' brother. Let's do this!"

Mason gave Vincent a high-five before racing the engine toward T-bone's house.

Mason parked the car around the corner from T-bone's house and turned off the engine. He also noticed it was a busy street and a considerable amount of people were outside.

"Vincent, right now is not a good time to hit them. Look, there are too many people around."

Vincent pulled his baseball cap down on his head and sighed. "You're right. We can't afford to get a lot of innocent people hurt."

Mason looked at his watch. "It's about eleven o'clock now. We're going to have to wait until dark before we move in. I just pray they haven't done anything stupid. I'll kill them dead if any of them have put their hands on her."

"Don't worry, Mason. T-bone's not that crazy."

"I don't know, Vincent. He might take pleasure in letting me know he's done something to Cherise. He'll hurt me any way he can."

"Okay, what do we do to pass the time away?"

Mason looked over at a nearby deli.

"I have an idea. Come on."

The pair walked across the street to the store, past a group of men shooting dice. The older gentleman behind the counter greeted them when they walked in.

"What can I get you young men today?"

Mason looked up at the menu and studied it

"I'll have a Reuben on wheat and a Pepsi."

He turned to Vincent, who was watching T-bone's house through the window. He told Mason to order him the same.

Mason paid the clerk fifteen dollars and told him to keep the change. Vincent sat down at a nearby table and waited for Mason to come over with the sandwiches.

"This store has a perfect view of the house. I'm going to have a chat with the owner about us holding up in here until dark. Once things settle down, we can make our move. T-bone knows I'm coming, but what we have to our advantage is that he doesn't know when."

Vincent agreed and bit into his sandwich. They watched as customer after customer came in and out of the store. As time passed, Mason motioned for the owner to come over and sit down with them.

"What can I do for you gentlemen?" he asked.

Mason and Vincent discreetly pulled out their badges and showed them to the owner.

He leaned back in his seat and folded his arms.

"I don't know why you're here, but I can assure you I run a reputable business. It's those knuckleheads out there playing dice that you should be worried about."

Mason leaned forward and whispered to him. "Sir, we have no doubt that you're an honest businessman, and we're not here to cause you any trouble, but we do need your help."

"How so?" he asked curiously.

"We would like your permission to use your store to stake out a house in the area. We might need to be here past your closing time. Would that be a problem?"

The gentleman shook his head reluctantly. "I don't want any trouble around here. I've been in business for over thirty years."

Vincent interrupted. "Sir, we can assure you, we'll treat your place like it's our own."

The man scratched his cheek and hesitated again. "I'll consider it on one condition."

"What's that?" Mason asked.

He pointed outside.

"Get those knuckleheads to move their dice game somewhere else, and you have yourself a deal."

Vincent quickly stood. "Consider it done."

Mason grinned and watched as he brother walked outside and joined the group that was shooting dice. When he walked up to them, they looked up at him suspiciously. Vincent put forty dollars down on the pavement and picked up the dice.

"Hey fellows, can I roll?"

One of the young men with gold teeth frowned at him.

"You got more where that came from, Pops?"

Vincent laughed. "That's for me to know and for you to try and find out."

"Okay, Pops, show me what you got," he said.

Before it was over, Vincent had taken practically all of their money. As expected, the men didn't like it that a stranger had invaded their space and taken all their money. The young man with gold teeth started to reach inside his pocket, but before he could pull anything out, Vincent already had his nine-millimeter in his face.

"Don't even think about it," Vincent said. "If you can't handle losing, don't play the game."

The guy held his hands up in the air.

"Hold up, Pops! You just can't walk up in our space and roll out with our money."

Vincent gave them the meanest look he could.

"I don't want your money. What I do want is for you to take your game somewhere else permanently."

Another young man stepped forward defiantly. "Who are you to tell us where we can hang out?"

Vincent looked over at Mason standing in the doorway of the deli, revealing his gun for the young man to see.

"Trust me, you don't want to know."

The other guys seemed to be too afraid to confront Vincent, so they remained silent.

He reached inside his pocket, pulled out a wad of money, and tossed it on the sidewalk.

"Here's your money. Now, do I have your word that you'll take your game somewhere else?"

The guy with the gold teeth picked up the money.

"Yeah, Pops, you don't have to get all hostile. Come on, ya'll."

The young man and his crew slowly walked down the sidewalk toward a nearby park. Vincent holstered the gun and walked inside the deli. Mason looked over at him and laughed.

"You're crazy."

Vincent also laughed. "Until the day I die," he said.

Cherise was becoming weary sitting in the dusty room with the likes of Tiny and Kilo. She didn't want Vada anywhere near her, and she was glad T-bone had pushed her out of the room earlier. She'd lost track of time, but she could tell daylight had turned to darkness. She just wished Mason would hurry up and rescue her. She had a feeling he was close by, but he was waiting until the right time to make a move. She just prayed he didn't get hurt and they could go back to their life, free from drama. Sleep was bearing down on her, and she didn't know how much longer she could stay awake. Her stomach was also growling, but she didn't want to eat any of their food. Kilo had brought her some bottled water earlier, but she didn't want to drink too much after the bathroom incident between them earlier. Her wrists had become numb from being taped together for so long, and as she lay there, she felt herself dozing off to sleep. She didn't know if her children were safe, and it saddened her to think she might not ever see them again. She didn't want to cry, but she couldn't help the few tears that rolled out of her eyes. As sleep overtook her, she was unaware that two dark figures walked slowly down the street toward the house.

It was nearly two a.m. and T-bone's turn to keep an eye out for Mason. The rest of the crew had succumbed to sleep. T-bone wasn't sure when Mason was coming. He thought he would've been there by now. Since he wasn't, he figured it wouldn't hurt to catch a quick nap. Before settling down, he looked in on Cherise, who was sound asleep. He returned to the living room and made himself comfortable in the recliner. He held his Uzi across his chest and closed his eyes.

Vincent ducked down behind the shrubbery in the neighbor's yard and inspected the perimeter. Mason moved in closer to the house and eased up to a window to look in. What he saw was exactly what he'd hoped for. Everyone was asleep, but Cherise was nowhere in sight. He eased back down and motioned for Vincent to join him.

"Keep an eye on them. If anyone wakes up, give me some type of signal."

"What are you going to do?" Vincent asked.

"I'm going to check the back of the house to see if I can find Cherise. I'll be right back."

Mason quietly disappeared around the corner and came upon a window, which appeared to look into a bedroom. He slowly stood up and peeked through the dirty glass. He rubbed the dirt off a portion of the window and saw Cherise lying on the bed. His heart sank at seeing her so close, but yet so far away. He tried to raise the window, but it wouldn't budge. There was no way he was getting in the house this way, so he had to come up with another plan. He took a coin out of his pocket and tapped on the window as quietly as possible. Cherise stirred in her sleep, so Mason kept tapping. Seconds later, she slowly sat up and tried to get a sip of water out of the bottle. Mason tapped again, drawing her attention over to the window. As soon as she saw him, he put his finger up to his lips for her to be quiet. Cherise slowly climbed out of the bed and walked over to the window. She started crying almost immediately. Mason had to use hand motions to talk to her, but Cherise was able to read his lips as well. He pointed to the latch on the window, but she whispered that it was nailed shut. He asked her if she was okay and she nodded, but he could see the fear in her eyes. He told her he was going to get her out of there and that he loved her. She told him she loved him as well. Lastly, he told her to go back over to the bed and he would be back for her as soon as possible. He snuck back around to the front of the house where Vincent was waiting.

"I found her. She's in the back bedroom."

"You couldn't get her out through the window?" Vincent asked.

"No, it's nailed shut. They also have her wrists duct-taped together."

"What now? We could go in there shooting, but I'm afraid Cherise could get hit accidentally."

"We need a diversion to get her out of there. T-bone's not going to just let us walk out the door with her."

"Do you have any ideas?" Vincent asked.

Mason thought for a moment.

"You know, we might not have to use our guns after all."

"What do you mean?" Vincent asked, confused.

Mason smiled.

"Have you talked to any firemen lately?"

Understanding what Mason was thinking, Vincent laughed. "No, but I'm sure we can find a few."

About thirty minutes later, Vada woke up and walked into the bedroom, finding Cherise sitting on the side of the bed.

"What's wrong? You can't sleep?"

Cherise didn't answer or look at Vada, so Vada walked closer to her.

"Don't look like Mirage is coming for you, sweetie. Maybe he'd rather see you and Kilo hooked up."

Cherise stared down at the floor and prayed Mason would hurry.

"What's wrong? You don't have anything to say?"

"Just leave me alone," Cherise whispered.

Vada wanted Cherise to look at her. She walked over and stood in front of her. Just as she reached out to touch her, T-bone opened the door.

"What the hell are you doing back in here? Get away from her!" he yelled.

"Why do you care about her so much? Mirage ain't coming for her, so why don't we just get rid of her and get out of here before the cops come?" Vada asked.

Pointing to the living room, T-bone said, "If the cops were coming, they would've been here by now. And for the last time, stay the hell away from her. I don't trust you around her."

Walking toward the door, Vada frowned. "You act like you want her for yourself or something."

T-bone smiled and looked at Cherise with a wicked grin. "Maybe I do. Maybe I want to sample her for myself. Mirage wouldn't like that, would he?"

Cherise widened her eyes and felt sick to her stomach after hearing T-bone's insinuation.

"Knock yourself out, bro. Have fun," Vada said with a smile as she closed the door.

Cherise bit down on her lip and stood as T-bone approached her. She could hear sirens in the distance and prayed it was Mason coming back with the police. He set his gun down on the dresser and walked toward her.

"How do you think Mirage is going to feel once he finds out I've had a piece of you?"

She backed away from him, but found herself in a corner of the room. T-bone palmed her breasts and kissed her neck. She was about to pass out just from the smell of him. She didn't know how she would ever go on living if he violated her. T-bone continued to explore her body with his hands. She could feel the hardness of his body against hers and began to cry.

"Shut up!" he yelled as he pushed her down on the bed. He straddled her body and ripped open the front of her blouse.

"Please don't do this!" Cherise begged.

Cherise tried to push him off of her, but was unsuccessful. He pulled out a knife and started cutting away her clothes. Cherise was sobbing hysterically.

"Damn! This is going to be fun!"

Cherise let out a scream and T-bone smacked her hard across the cheek.

"Shut up or I'll let Tiny and Kilo in here so they can have a turn with you," he snarled.

Kilo and Tiny jumped after hearing Cherise scream. They jumped up and Tiny pointed toward the window.

"Look at that."

Vada and Kilo looked over at the window and noticed red lights flashing outside. They quickly grabbed their guns as Vada peeked out the window.

"Chill out! It's only the fire department. Somebody's house must be on fire."

Tiny and Kilo looked out the window and noticed two firemen walking toward the front door.

"Hide those guns and the coke!" Vada yelled.

The firemen knocked on the door. When Vada opened it, she was hit square in the chest with a stream of water. It knocked Vada on the floor and up against the wall. Tiny and Kilo tried to pull out the guns they had just put under the sofa cushions, but the stream of water was too powerful for them; they were nearly drowning in the water. As Vincent continued to hose down the pair, Mason turned his attention to the back bedroom where Cherise was being held. It was then he noticed T-bone was missing from the room. As he walked down the hallway, he prayed that Cherise wasn't injured or worse.

Cherise was still trying to push T-bone off her body, but he was too strong for her. He pried her thighs apart as she continued to plead with him.

"Oh, God! No!"

Mason burst through the door with the fire hose. Seeing T-bone on top of Cherise caused him to lose it.

"You son of a bitch! Get off of my wife!"

Before T-bone could react, Mason opened the hose full blast, knocking him away from Cherise. As soon as he was well away from Cherise, Mason turned off the hose and ran over to T-bone. His fist connected over and over with T-bone's face. T-bone's face was a bloody mess, but Mason continued to beat him senseless. Vincent walked into the room after leaving the others in the custody of local police officers outside. He found Cherise half-naked and in shock, with Mason still pounding on T-bone. Vincent took off his fireman's coat and wrapped it around Cherise's body. He cut away the tape on her wrists and hugged her.

"Are you hurt, C. J.?"

Her lip was cut, but otherwise, she appeared to be fine. "I don't know," she responded.

"Hold on a second," Vincent requested as he watched Mason continue to pummel T-bone. "I think he's had enough, Mason."

Mason was in a deranged state of mind and ignored Vincent's remarks. Vincent had to pull Mason off of T-bone before he killed him.

"Mason! Cherise needs you! Forget about him!" Vincent yelled.

Releasing his collar, Mason pushed T-bone down on the floor before walking over to Cherise. He pulled her up into his arms and watched as Vincent gave T-bone one last kick to the ribs before walking away.

"Did he hurt you?" Mason asked softly.

Cherise couldn't answer. Mason looked down at her torn clothing and asked again, "Cherise, baby, did he touch you?"

"No. I just want to go home, Mason. I just want this to be over."

Mason and Vincent helped Cherise up off the bed. As they walked toward the door,

T-bone pulled out a gun hidden in an ankle holster and aimed it at them. Vincent turned to take one last look at T-bone, and ended up looking down the barrel of a gun. Things seemed to move in slow motion after that.

"Gun!" Vincent yelled.

He knocked Mason and Cherise to the floor and pulled his weapon just as T-bone pulled the trigger. The room was quiet and smelled of gunpowder. Cherise screamed as T-bone raised the gun again and aimed it. Mason pulled his gun and fired at T-bone, striking him twice in the chest. Cherise looked over at Vincent, who lay bleeding on the floor, and let out a blood-curdling scream.

Chapter Twenty-Seven

At the hospital, Vincent was rushed immediately into surgery. He'd been hit once in the abdomen and had lost a lot of blood. Cherise was taken into an examining room with Mason close behind. The hospital was swarming with officers who were questioning Mason and Cherise regarding the shooting. Mason didn't have a lot of answers for them, and he was more concerned about his brother than their questions. Domino arrived not long after receiving a call from Mason. He was able to give answers to most of the local officers' questions for their investigation.

Upstairs Vincent was fighting for his life. As he lay on the operating table, he felt weightless. Looking down at himself, he realized he was slipping away. He watched as the surgeons frantically worked on his body, but there was nothing he could do to help them. Seconds later, he heard the sobs of Cherise coming from another room. He walked out into the hallway and found Cherise and Mason locked in a tight embrace, praying for him. He could see them, but they couldn't see him, which wasn't a good sign at all. Vincent watched their loving exchange and listened to their prayers. It bruised his heart. Maybe it would be best if he were out of their lives forever. It was obvious they had a true love connection, and if he stayed around, he would always be a distraction. He still loved Cherise dearly, but he had done an injustice to his own blood by violating his brother's trust.

Vincent stood there and listened to Mason's prayer. It was a sincere prayer. He knew he could never make up for the hurt he had caused Mason. Vincent couldn't stand seeing the people he loved hurting any longer. He watched as a nurse gave a distraught Cherise some type of medicine to calm her. Having seen enough, he turned and walked back toward the operating room and disappeared through the door.

Domino and other members of the Anti-Crime Task Force joined Mason and Cherise in the waiting room. Mason's heart ached, knowing his brother had risked his own life to save him and Cherise, regardless of the drama they'd recently had between them. To lose him now would be a terrible loss. He looked down and saw that Cherise was now asleep in his arms. She looked so fragile, and he knew he would have to be a different kind of man in her life from now on.

While waiting for Vincent to come out of surgery, Mason took the time to telephone Cherise's parents to let them know she was safe. Unfortunately he had to break the bad news to them regarding Vincent. After briefly speaking to Jonathan and the kids, he was able to direct all his thoughts and prayers toward Vincent.

Hours had passed, and Mason and Cherise, along with everyone else, were still waiting for word on Vincent's condition. Mason looked up and noticed the surgeon coming his way. The expression on his face was unreadable, and it worried him. He woke Cherise up and stood to receive the news.

"Mr. McKenzie, your brother is out of surgery, but he lost a lot of blood. We had to remove his spleen and one of his kidneys. He's in recovery, but he's not out of the woods yet. We're going to monitor him closely, but the next twenty-four hours are going to be the determining factor for him."

Mason cleared his throat. "When can we see him?"

"We're moving him into recovery now. You can see him, but only for a few minutes."

"What are his chances, Doctor?" Mason asked.

"I don't like to give odds, Mr. McKenzie, but I will say your brother needs a lot of prayer. The next forty-eight hours are going to be crucial."

Mason nodded and shook the doctor's hand. Cherise hugged his neck.

"We can't lose him, Mason."

"I know, baby. I know."

After receiving the status of Vincent's condition, Mason and Cherise took turns sitting with him the whole time he was in intensive care. Mason tried his best to get Cherise to go home and rest, but she was determined to stay by his side. Since the children were in good hands with her parents, she felt her place was by Mason's side until Vincent's condition improved.

Several days had passed since Vincent was moved to the ICU. He was still in critical condition, but stable. Mason was overwhelmed with guilt, knowing Vincent had risked his own life to save the life of his brother. Cherise was at the hotel resting, leaving Mason alone with his thoughts. As he sat there, he thought about all the awful things he'd said to Vincent after finding out about their affair. Sitting in the hospital gave him time to do a lot of thinking and it quickly humbled him.

Domino walked into the ICU waiting room to try to lift Mason's spirits. He informed him that Vada and the rest of T-bone's crew, along with Pootie and his gang, were going to be spending a lot of years behind bars. Mason pulled his badge out of his pocket and handed it to Domino.

"What's this?"

"Do me a favor, Domino."

"Anything, Mason," he replied.

"Turn this in for me. I won't need it any longer."

Shocked, Domino looked at him. "I thought you were going to transfer to another department?"

"No, I'm done."

"Are you sure about this, Mason?"

He smiled. "I've never been clearer about anything in my life. My family needs me, and I'm going to be there for them."

"Why don't I just hold on to it for you until Vincent gets better? Give yourself a chance to let all of this drama subside before making a final decision," Domino offered.

Mason waved him off. "No, I'm not going to be changing my mind, Domino."

Domino patted Mason on the shoulder. "I'll just hold on to it, anyway. There's no reason to rush things. You and Vincent were born to be cops, and you're good ones. It would be an injustice for you to leave so early in your career."

Mason looked up at Domino with tearful eyes. "The way I feel right now, I'd rather be a crossing guard at my daughter's school than a cop."

"Mason, you did a great job bringing down T-bone."

"Yeah, and look what it cost me. My marriage is on the rocks, and my brother was nearly killed."

Domino tucked Mason's badge into his pocket and sighed. "I'm sure Vincent will pull through just fine, and as far as Cherise, she's a cop's wife, and she loves you. She might not understand your sacrifices right now, but she will. Give me a call if you change your mind."

"I will," he replied.

"How's your back? I know you strained it when Vincent pushed you guys down on the floor."

"The doctor gave me some pain pills to help with the pain, and I'm going to see a chiropractor as soon as I know Vincent is going to be all right."

"Make sure you take care of that as soon as possible."

Mason yawned and stretched. "I will."

"Okay, I'll holler at you later. Call me if you need anything."

Mason shook Domino's hand and sat back down in his chair. Domino walked down the hallway just as Cherise was returning from their hotel. Domino greeted her and they talked briefly before he left the hospital. She joined Mason on the sofa and handed him a cup of coffee.

"Thanks, sweetheart. Were you able to get any sleep?"

"Just a little. How's Vincent doing?"

"He's still resting. No change, which I guess is good."

She caressed his neck and looked into his tired eyes.

"Why don't you go back to the hotel so you can get some rest? I'll call you if anything changes. You don't need to aggravate your back any worse than it already is."

Mason stood up and stretched. He kissed her forehead and tucked his cell phone in his pocket.

"You're right. I could use a nap, but I'll be right back."

"No rush, Mason. Drive carefully."

Cherise watched as Mason walked out of the waiting room. She pulled a Kleenex out of a nearby box and dabbed her eyes before she headed to look in on Vincent. The sounds of the IVs and monitors were beeping in a harmonious tone. She walked over to his bed, leaned down, and kissed him on the cheek. She sat down in a nearby chair and stroked his hand lovingly as a nurse entered to change his IV bag.

"How's he doing today?" Cherise whispered.

The nurse smiled at Cherise as she moved around the room.

"Vincent had a good night, and he's holding his own under the circumstances. Dr. Powell should be in shortly so you can ask about his progress."

"Thank you, I will," she responded.

Cherise looked over at Vincent, who looked so weak. Once he woke up from the coma the only thing left hanging over their head was whether Janelle was his daughter. After what he'd done to save their lives, she realized he needed to know the truth once and for all. He deserved that much after all he'd done for them. Her relationship with Mason had a long way to go, but at least it looked like they were on the road to recovery in more ways than one. Having a DNA test done would be the best thing to do to settle the mystery once and for all; if the test came back the way she hoped, Mason would never have to know. Cherise pulled the sterile swabs she got from Vincent out of her purse. She also pulled out a small tube of Vaseline for Vincent's chapped lips, so if she was interrupted she could use that as her alibi for hovering over him. She quickly swabbed the inside of Vincent's mouth and put the sample in a container to avoid contamination. Now all she had to do was get a sample from Janelle, which wouldn't be difficult, and then have the test sent off for analysis.

Seconds later the doctor and nurse walked in and greeted Cherise. The doctor quietly examined Vincent while Cherise looked on attentively. The nurse charted the information that Dr. Powell dictated to her as he examined Vincent. The news the doctor gave Cherise was encouraging, and all that was left was for Vincent to wake up so they could give him a complete exam.

Cherise walked back over to his bed and spoke softly to him as she pulled the blanket over his body.

"Vincent, wake up, babe. You've slept long enough. We have some barbeque waiting on you, and I know how much you love your barbeque." As Vincent lay there, he could hear Cherise's faint voice echoing in his head. She stared down at him, hoping for any reaction to her voice or her touch. She could feel the lump in her throat again, as well as the tears welling up in her eyes. She laid her head against his chest and listened to the rhythm of his heartbeat. She remembered lying against his chest like this on many occasions in the past, but that was what it was—the past. She had no idea whether he and Mason had somewhat settled their differences before her rescue, but she'd been praying for a peaceful solution ever since Mason found out about their affair.

Cherise closed her eyes and hummed a song that Vincent loved to hear her sing. As she continued to hum, she noticed a change in his breathing and his eyes began to flutter. She stared at him.

"That's it, Vincent. Wake up."

She gently stroked his face and continued to whisper into his ear. Vincent's eyes fluttered even more and his body slowly began to twitch. Cherise reached over and pushed the button for the nurse.

"May I help you?" a voice said over the intercom.

"I think Vincent might be waking up. Could you please get Dr. Powell in here?"

"I sure will," the nurse responded.

She leaned down in Vincent's ear and whispered. "You're doing great, Vincent. I'm right here. Open your eyes."

Moments later, Dr. Powell and the nurse walked in and looked at Vincent. They noticed the same things Cherise had seen. As the doctor examined Vincent, he responded just like the doctor hoped. After about five minutes, Vincent's eyes slowly fluttered open and tears flowed down Cherise's face.

"Welcome back," she softly whispered.

She could tell that Vincent was trying to speak, but was unable to. The doctor looked over at her and asked her to step out for a moment so they could examine Vincent further. Overjoyed, she grabbed her purse and walked out into the hallway to get some air. As she dialed Mason's number, she was unable to hold back her tears. Mason answered the telephone in a sleepy voice. He could hear Cherise crying on the other end, which caused his heart to leap up into his throat.

"Cherise! What's wrong?" he yelled frantically into the phone.

"Mason! He's awake. Vincent's awake!"

"I'll be right there!" Mason yelled before hanging up the telephone.

It only took Mason about fifteen minutes to reach the hospital. Cherise met him in the hallway and they gave each other a huge hug. Mason practically ran through the door of the ICU so he could see Vincent and thank him for saving their lives. He walked over to the bed and looked down into Vincent's eyes.

"Hey, bro. I've been waiting on you to wake up so I can tell you if you ever try a stunt like this again, there's going to be hell to pay."

Vincent was weak, but he was able to smile up at his brother. Tears rolled out of Mason's eyes.

"Thank you, bro," Mason said softly.

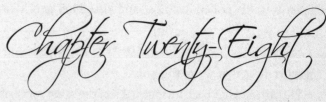

Chapter Twenty-Eight

A week later, Mason and Cherise were finally able to bring Vincent home. Janelle and Mase were overjoyed at having their mom and dad back home. Janelle was so attentive to Vincent that she would not leave his side. She loved playing his nurse and waited on him hand and foot.

On their first night home, Cherise lay in bed next to Mason, staring at him. It was after midnight and she couldn't sleep.

"Mason," she whispered.

He turned to her. "Yes?"

"Are we okay?"

He rubbed his eyes and turned to her. "Cherise, I believe that God has given us a second chance. In spite of everything that's happened, I still need to repair my relationship with my brother."

"Mason, all I've ever wanted was you," she whispered.

"You slept with my brother, Cherise."

"I know," she admitted painfully. "Would it have made a difference if it had been someone else?"

"You're my wife, Cherise, so it would hurt regardless, but because you slept with Vincent it makes the whole situation foul," he admitted. "I married you for better or worse and I know I'm not without guilt here. I do want to go on the record by saying I didn't love those women I had affairs with. But I know that you love Vincent."

"Not the way that you think," she whispered. "I want my family, my whole family, back together and at peace with each other. Is that asking too much?"

"You've always had my heart, Cherise."

She wiped her eyes. "If I did, you wouldn't have been with those women and I wouldn't have been with Vincent."

He stared at her and it finally hit him. He had done the same thing to her, but he was trying to maximize his pain over her betrayal because of who her lover was. He pulled her close and kissed her gently on the lips.

"I'm sorry I let you down."

She laid her head on his chest. "I'm sorry I let you down, too, but what's important is that we're together."

He caressed her back lovingly. "I feel the same way, babe. Let's get some rest."

Cherise threw the covers back and stood. "Okay, but I want to check in on the kids first."

"Hurry back."

"I will. Good night, Mason."

"Good night, sweetheart."

Cherise stepped out into the hallway and looked in on Mase first. He was sound asleep. She exited his room and pulled a small purse out of the linen closet before quietly entering Janelle's room. She sat on the side of her bed. Janelle was a hard sleeper so knew she wouldn't have any trouble getting a sample from her. She stroked her soft hair lovingly as she slid the stick into her mouth and swabbed her cheek. Janelle stirred slightly as Cherise put the swab inside a sterile sleeve and then back inside the small purse. She eased out of Janelle's room and quietly put the purse back inside the linen closet. Now all she had to do was send the sample off and pray for a miracle.

Two weeks later, Vincent was finally well enough to go home to Texas. Janelle made her way into the guest room to talk to Vincent as she watched him pack his belongings.

"Uncle Vincent, when are you coming back?"

"Why? Do you miss me already?"

She giggled and her smile warmed his heart. She was so much like Cherise, and if she were his daughter it would make him the happiest man on earth.

"Yeah, Uncle Vincent, you're fun just like my daddy. Are you still sore?"

Vincent laughed out loud.

"A little, but I won't be sore much longer, so I can play ball with you like your daddy does."

He zipped up his suitcase and sat it in the corner. He walked over to the dresser and put on his watch. Janelle walked over and saw Vincent's loose change on the dresser. She started counting it out loud.

"Janelle, you take care of your daddy while I'm gone. Okay? You know his back is bothering him."

"I will, Uncle Vincent."

She continued to count the money without losing count.

"Why don't you take that change and put it in your piggy bank?"

Janelle didn't hesitate before scooping the money into her hand.

"Thank you, Uncle Vincent."

He leaned down and gave her a hug and a kiss. "You're welcome. Where's your mother?"

"She's in the kitchen with Mase."

Vincent set her down on the floor.

"Well, I guess I'd better get to the airport. Give me another hug before I go."

Janelle jumped up on the bed so she could give Vincent a very tight hug. She was careful not to hurt him, though. He kissed her on the cheek.

"Janelle, call me if you need anything, and I'll see you again real soon."

"I will, Uncle Vincent."

He picked up his bags, and walked out into the hallway.

"I'd better get out of here. Go tell your mom I'm on my way down."

"Okay," she answered as she skipped down the hallway.

Vincent walked into Mason's room. Mason picked up his medicine bottle, popped a couple of pills into his mouth, and swallowed them down with some cranberry juice.

"Are you getting ready to leave?"

Vincent slid his hand inside his pockets. "Yeah, I need to turn in this rental car."

Mason walked around the bed toward Vincent and embraced him. "You're going to be missed around here."

Vincent patted Mason on the back. "Thanks, bro. I'm going to miss you guys, too."

They stepped back out of their embrace and stared at each other in silence.

"Are you sure we're cool, Mason? Will you ever be able to forgive me?"

Mason did love Vincent very much in spite of what had happened between them. After all, he did risk his own life to save him and Cherise.

"I'm still working on it, Vincent. I'm not going to be able to forget about everything overnight but I'm praying about it."

Vincent leaned against the door frame and let out a breath.

"That's understandable. I just hope that we can eventually get back to being brothers real soon."

"We'll always be brothers, Vincent. Now get out of here before you miss your plane, and make sure you call when you get home."

Vincent picked up his luggage.

"I will and take care of that back of yours."

Mason walked him to the door.

"I will. The doctor told me just to take it easy. These pain pills are helping me cope."

Walking out into the hallway, Vincent turned one last time before disappearing down the stairs.

"Be careful with those pain pills, Mason."

"I will."

Vincent started down the stairs and Mason softly called out to him.

"Vincent?"

"Yeah?"

"I love you, little brother."

Vincent smiled back at him.

"I love you, too."

A lump formed in Vincent's throat as he descended the stairs.

In the kitchen he found Mase eating a sandwich and Cherise putting away dishes in the cabinet.

"Hey, Unc, are you getting ready to leave?"

"Yeah, it's about that time," Vincent acknowledged as he put his luggage down. Mase stood up and gave Vincent a warm hug.

"I'm going to miss you, Uncle Vincent. When are you coming back?"

He looked over at Cherise and smiled. "I'm not sure, but I'm hoping no more than a couple of weeks. I'll be in touch."

Cherise walked over to him, wrapped her arms around his neck, and kissed his cheek.

"You'd better. Where's Mason?"

Vincent opened the refrigerator and pulled out a bottle of water.

"He just took some pain pills so he's getting ready to lie down."

The kids never knew their mother had been kidnapped, and the adults wanted to keep it that way. All they knew was that Vincent had been shot in the line of duty. Cherise held onto him and whispered into his ear.

"I could never repay you for what you've done for us. You saved our lives and I'll always love you for that."

He kissed her cheek and caressed her back.

"You're welcome, and I'm going to miss your cooking."

She wiped away a tear and smiled.

"Speaking of cooking, I invited the family and a few of Mason's friends over for a cookout tomorrow. Are you sure you can't stay any longer?"

"Sounds yummy, but I really need to get back. As soon as I can get everything taken care of, I can move back here for good."

"Are you sure that's what you want to do?"

"I'm sure."

"In that case, we'll be here," she replied as she wiped her hands on a dish towel. "Oh! Guess what? I heard on the radio where they arrested a suspect in that Piedmont murder."

"That's great!"

Janelle danced into the room and hugged Vincent's leg. He looked down at her and stroked her head with affection. He was staring into her angelic face when Cherise interrupted his thoughts.

"Vincent, are you sure you don't want us to go to the airport with you?"

"I'll be okay. There's no reason for you guys to go out in all that traffic."

"Okay, well drive safely and give us a call before you get on the plane, and once you get home."

Before walking out the door, he gave her a quick peck on the lips.

"Love you! Good-bye, guys!"

Cherise, Mase, and Janelle walked Vincent outside and waved as he drove away.

Hours later, Mason woke up worried that he hadn't heard from Vincent. He started calling his cell phone and his home phone, but Vincent didn't answer or return any of his calls. Mason placed a call to the Houston Police Department, and after identifying himself, he was delivered some devastating news. Vincent had been murdered.

Apparently Vincent had stopped at a store on his way home and walked in on a robbery in progress. Vincent, being the cop that he was, had tried to overpower the robber, but received a stab wound to the chest and died before the paramedics arrived. Mason knew the news would overwhelm his family as well. Before telling them the horrible news, he called for Jonathan and Patricia to come over. Cherise knew something was wrong because Mason wouldn't look her in the eyes. Once Cherise's parents arrived, Mason broke the news. Cherise and Janelle screamed out in horror and Mase burst into tears. Cherise's parents did their best to console them, but they were overcome with grief as well. Mason was unable to contain his own emotions as he tried to comfort Cherise, who at this point was hysterical. Patricia's voice was distressed.

"Mason, what are we going to do? We have to go out there and see about Vincent."

Mason wiped away his tears and stood. His hands were trembling and he seemed confused.

"Call the airlines. I'm going upstairs to pack," he replied.

Mase jumped up. "I'm going, too!" he yelled.

Cherise and Janelle were still screaming as Jonathan held them tightly in his arms.

"No, son, I need you to stay here with your mother and sister."

"No, Daddy! I want to go! He's my uncle!"

Mason looked over at Jonathan and he nodded.

"Okay, son. Go pack so we can get to the airport," Mason said as he hugged him.

Patricia stood and looked at Jonathan frantically.

"Honey, you have to go with them. I'll stay here with Cherise and Janelle."

"I wouldn't have it any other way, sweetheart, but I need to call the airlines first. I'm going to hurry home and pack. I'll pack a bag for you, too. This is horrible."

Patricia closed her eyes and started praying out loud.

A few days later, Mason, Jonathan, and Mase returned with Vincent's body, which was transported directly to the church for the funeral. Cherise had the horrible task of making all the funeral arrangements, which included remarks by several dignitaries in the greater Atlanta area. Government officials from Houston, including the mayor, were also in attendance since Vincent had worked in a high-profile position. It was a beautiful service with a packed audience and an abundance of flowers surrounding Vincent's coffin.

The ceremony was beautiful until they got to the most dreaded part of the day. Family members filed slowly past the coffin to say good-bye one last time. Mason, Cherise, Mase, and Janelle all went up at the same time. Janelle and Mase both kissed Vincent, who looked like he was sleeping. He was dressed in his police chief's uniform and he looked as handsome as always. Mason walked Mase and Janelle back to their seats as Cherise said her private good-bye to Vincent. She caressed his cheek, leaned down, and gave him one last kiss. Mason rejoined her at Vincent's coffin.

"Do you want me to stay?"

"Yes," he said as he kissed her forehead.

It was obvious he was overcome with emotion. Cherise held onto him as best she could.

"Good-bye, little brother," Mason leaned down and whispered. "I love you."

Before Mason walked away, he kissed Vincent on the forehead. Turning away, he hugged Cherise and sobbed. They made their way back over to their seats and sat down. They watched as the funeral directors slowly closed the lid of Vincent's coffin. It was then that Cherise let out a loud scream, which caused nearly everyone in the church to become emotional. The scene became somber as Vincent was rolled out of the church, surrounded by a sea of police uniforms, and placed inside the waiting hearse.

After the services, the family returned to Mason's house for dinner. Mason immediately retired to his bedroom. It had been an emotional day and his back was throbbing. Cherise followed him up to their bedroom so she could change into more comfortable clothes.

"Mason, can I get you anything before I go back downstairs?"

He unbuttoned his uniform and quietly sat on the side of the bed.

"No, I'm just going to bed."

"You need to eat, Mason. Can I at least bring you a plate?"

"Not right now, honey," he said as he crawled into bed. "I'm just tired."

She leaned down and gave him a tender kiss.

"Okay, I'll check on you later. Get some rest."

"I'll try. Apologize to the family for me."

"Everyone understands you're not feeling well, Mason. I'll send Mase up with some food later."

"Thank you."

She closed the door and rejoined the rest of the family.

Mason continued to toss and turn in bed. He slowly woke up out of his restless slumber and stared at the ceiling. He felt cold and then he realized his T-shirt was soaked with his perspiration. He sat up on the side of the bed to gather his thoughts and realized he was still a little woozy, but it was nothing a hot shower couldn't cure. Mason slowly walked across the floor to the bathroom and closed the door. He removed the wet shirt from his body, as well as the rest of his garments, and stepped into the hot, steamy shower. He closed his eyes and allowed the water to run over his head and body. He applied the suds and cleansed his body. As he did, he thought about Vincent and immediately began to cry. Since he had let his pride get in the way, now he was devastated that he would never get the chance to tell Vincent he was forgiven. After composing himself, he turned off the water and stepped out of the shower. He pulled a towel from the rack and dried off. After applying his lotion, he slid into his terrycloth robe and re-entered the bedroom.

When Mason stepped into the bedroom he dropped the bottle of lotion on the floor. He shivered and realized he had finally lost his mind, because at that very moment he was having a vision. It was a heavenly vision that chilled him down to his bones. Standing right in front of him was none other than Vincent. Mason was speechless. He'd heard of ghosts, but he'd never thought he'd ever see one. When their parents passed away, they never came back, so why was Vincent haunting him? Mason tried his best to say something, but he couldn't. Vincent started laughing.

"What's up, bro? Why are you looking at me like that?"

Mason slowly walked toward him without responding.

"Mason, are you okay?"

Mason tried to clear his throat so he could speak. He reached up and touched Vincent's face. Vincent didn't know what to think of Mason's weird behavior, and it worried him. Vincent took Mason by the arm and led him over to a nearby chair so he could sit down.

Cherise walked in with an arm full of clean towels. She noticed the looks on Vincent's and Mason's faces.

"What's wrong?"

"I don't know. He looks like he's seen a ghost. I hope he's not having a heart attack or a stroke. He's having trouble talking."

Cherise walked over to Mason and kneeled down in front of him, feeling his head and checking his pulse.

"Sweetheart, what's wrong?" she asked Mason. Mason said nothing.

"I don't know, C. J.," Vincent said. "We might need to get him to the hospital. Something's wrong."

Cherise grabbed Mason's face. "Mason! Say something!"

Tears fell from Mason's eyes as he looked up into Vincent's face.

"You're alive?" he finally whispered.

Vincent laughed out loud. "I'd better be."

"Why are you here, Vincent?"

Vincent sat down on the side of the bed and frowned. "Well damn! I thought you would be a little happy to see me. My plane was delayed so I decided to postpone my trip home for a few more days so I could get some of that delicious barbecue C. J.'s been promising me."

Confused, Mason looked at him in disbelief. Mason put his hands over his face in confusion.

"What are you talking about? We buried you today."

Cherise stood and looked over at Vincent with concern.

"Maybe we do need to get him to the hospital, Vincent. He's not making any sense."

"What the hell is going on here?" Mason finally yelled. "You're not supposed to be here!"

"Mason, you've been asleep all afternoon. Vincent didn't make it back to Houston because his plane had a mechanical problem. What are you talking about?"

Mason jumped up out of his chair and wiped the tears from his face. He walked over to Vincent and embraced him tightly. Vincent smiled and returned the hug.

"I'm happy to see you again, too, bro."

Mason sat down on the bed and trembled.

"I had a horrible dream, Vincent. I dreamed you were murdered when you went back to Texas. I can't believe I imagined the whole thing."

Vincent laughed out loud. "I'm not dead, bro. I'm right here."

"Everything about it was so real," Mason explained. "I've never experienced anything like this in my life."

"It was just a bad dream, Mason. I'm standing here as living proof. Do you want to touch me again?" Vincent joked.

Mason looked up at him and yelled. "It's not a joking matter, Vincent! I thought I had lost you. Do you have any idea how that made me feel?"

Cherise and Vincent could see the seriousness on Mason's face as he spoke. Vincent sat down beside him and put his arm around Mason's neck.

"I'm sorry, Mason. I had no idea you'd experienced something like that, and I would feel the same way if I had lost you. You're my blood and I have brotherly love for you, man."

Cherise picked up a medicine bottle off the nightstand.

"Maybe it's these strong pain pills you're taking, Mason. How many did you take?"

"Three," he softly answered.

"Three! You're supposed to take only two, Mason! No wonder you had that crazy dream!" she scolded him.

"I'm sorry. Two wasn't dulling the pain enough. The last thing I remember is saying good-bye to you."

"Damn, bro. That's pretty deep."

"I'm just glad you're okay, Vincent, and I want you to know that I forgive you."

"Thank you, Mason. That means everything to me."

"That dream really spooked me, so if you don't mind, please postpone your trip until I can go back to Houston with you," Mason requested.

"Are you serious?" Vincent asked.

"You're damn right, I'm serious," Mason replied. "That dream screwed up my head, so I'm not about to let you out of my sight for a while."

Vincent clapped his hands together

"Whatever you say, Mason. Now let's eat, and after we eat. Afterward, I'm taking you to the doctor so they can find out why your back is hurting you so badly, because these pills are not good for you."

"Whatever you say, Vincent. Whatever you say."

Minutes later they all met downstairs for some mouthwatering barbecue.

Chapter Twenty-Nine

A few days later, after the kids had left for school, Cherise drove down to her office to gather her mail. Her heart leapt into her throat when she saw the return address label on the express envelope lying on her desk. She reluctantly picked it up and closed her eyes because she knew the envelope contained the results of the DNA test. She frantically put it in her purse and hurried home.

Once back in the confines of her home, she made her way into the family room. Minutes later, Vincent made his way downstairs with his luggage. He sat it in the hallway and walked into the family room where he found Cherise sitting alone clutching her purse. He walked over and sat down next to her.

"Are you getting ready to go somewhere?"

She looked over at him without responding. Mason walked downstairs and set his luggage in the hallway next to Vincent's. He walked into the family room where he found Vincent and Cherise sitting quietly together.

"Hey guys, I'm getting ready to run to the bank. Cherise, do you need anything while I'm out?"

She smiled. "No, babe. I'm fine."

"Vincent, do you want to ride?"

"No, but if you don't mind, pick me up one of those real estate books so I can start house hunting. I'm going to run by a friend's house and say good-bye before I leave."

Mason looked at his watch. "All right. I'll meet you back here in about forty-five minutes."

"Alright, Mason."

Mason walked out the door and pulled out of the garage. Vincent turned back to Cherise and studied her expression.

"Okay, now that Mason's gone, what's going on?"

Cherise reached inside her purse and pulled out the envelope. He took it out of her hand and looked at the return address. He sank down in a nearby chair.

"Wow! When did you do this?"

"While you were in the hospital," Cherise admitted.

Vincent stared at the envelope. "I can't believe it's really here. Do you want me to open it?"

Cherise shrugged her shoulders. Vincent hesitated a moment before ripping the envelope open. He pulled out another legal-sized envelope and opened it as well. He removed the folded-up piece of paper and unfolded it. Cherise put her hands together in prayer as Vincent read the results. After scanning it, he looked up at Cherise with tears in his eyes. He held the document out to her so she could read the results.

"What does it say?"

Tears ran down her cheeks as she slowly took the piece of paper out of his hand and saw the words.

Sample (A) has 60.0 % inclusion to Sample (B).

She folded the piece of paper back up and wiped away her tears.

"I'm sorry, Vincent."

"So am I. My day will come."

She nodded and kissed him gently on the lips.

"Well, I'd better get out of here before Mason gets back."

He stood and walked out into the foyer. Cherise followed him to the door.

"I'm so sorry, Vincent. I know how badly you wanted Janelle to be your daughter."

He pulled her into his arms and hugged her tightly.

"Life goes on, C. J. Thanks. I'll see you later."

They released each other and Vincent walked out to his car and drove off. An hour later, Vincent and Mason caught their plane and were on their way to Houston.

Cherise was happy to have her family back and her life finally back on track.

With all the drama her family had been through, she was looking forward to some peace and quiet. To make that happen, she decided to use some vacation time from her job and spend some quality time with Mason and the children. She vowed they would take the children on a much-needed vacation to Florida just as soon as Mason returned from Texas.

Epilogue

A week later, Cherise was cleaning the house. She wanted everything to look nice for Mason when he returned home later that evening. She was just pulling out the vacuum cleaner when the doorbell rang. The kids were at school and her mom and dad always called before coming over, so she had no idea who it could be. She peeped out the window and saw an express delivery driver on her porch. She opened the door and smiled.

"Good afternoon, Mrs. McKenzie. I have a package for C. McKenzie," he said as he handed it to her.

"Thank you," Cherise replied as she signed for the package and noticed it was mail forwarded to her from her office.

The young man took the clipboard out of her hand.

"Have a nice day, Ms. McKenzie."

Cherise closed the door and walked into the kitchen to get some water. She sat down at the kitchen table and opened the package. Inside she noticed an envelope with a familiar return address. As soon as she saw it, her hands started trembling uncontrollably. Curious to what it could be, she opened the envelope and started reading.

Attached you will find the correct results of your recent submission. Due to a computer error, you were sent an incorrect genetic report. We apologize for any inconvenience, and if you would like to submit a new sample for testing, feel free to contact us at your earliest convenience; however, these test results are from the samples you originally submitted.

Sincerely,

Victoria Thomas

Prime Diagnostics

Cherise closed her eyes and let out the breath she was holding. She slid the second page out of the envelope and read the results.

Sample (A) has 99.9 % inclusion to Sample (B).

Cherise screamed at the top of her lungs as a flood of tears ran out of her eyes. She clutched the paperwork to her chest in disbelief. Without hesitating another moment, she ran over to the fireplace and picked up the lighter. She held the pieces of paper in her hand and lit the corners. She held it in her hand and watched as it burned. When it was almost completely engulfed in fire, she threw the paperwork into the fireplace and watched as the truth disintegrated right before her eyes.

"No one can ever know the truth, not even Vincent," Cherise whispered as she watched the papers turned to burnt ashes.

About the Author

Darrien Lee is originally from Columbia, Tennessee, but now resides in LaVergne, Tennessee, with her husband of fifteen years and two young daughters.

Darrien admits that she picked up her love for writing while attending college at Tennessee State University and it was those experiences, which inspired her debut novel, *All That and A Bag of Chips*, in 2001. She is a two-time *Essence* magazine best-selling author, with four published works by Strebor Books International.

The sequel, *Been There, Done That*, followed up in 2003 and Darrien's third novel, *What Goes Around Comes Around*, was released in July 2004. Part four of Darrien's series titled *When Hell Freezes Over* was released in October 2005.

Darrien is also in the process of completing some new and exciting projects for future releases, which include a teen novel and a children's book.

Darrien can be reached at her email address, DarrienLeeAuthor@aol.com. You can also visit Darrien's website at www.DarrienLee.com.

EXCERPT FROM

WHEN HELL FREEZES OVER

BY DARRIEN LEE

PUBLISHED BY STREBOR BOOKS INTERNATIONAL

CHAPTER 1

T he room was dark and Keaton had listened to Dejá giggle for over an hour. He'd met her at the gym where she worked as an aerobics instructor. She possessed a pair of long, shapely legs, beige skin, and seductive green eyes. She was physically fit with a derriere so firm, you could bounce quarters off it.

"Keaton, why don't you come over here and give me that massage you promised me?" she beckoned him.

She'd been coming on to him for weeks now and had become extremely hard for him to resist; not that he really wanted to. Dejá was very sexy and wasn't the least bit shy about telling him exactly what she wanted.

"I had no idea you was so uninhibited, Dejá," he replied.

She scooted over to him and kissed her way down his body until she made him quiver in ecstasy.

He hissed seductively and moaned, "Damn, girl," while his eyes rolled back in his head.

It had been way too long since he'd been intimate with anyone and Dejá was working him like a magician.

After a few minutes, she giggled childlike. "My turn!"

He grinned as he watched her scoot backwards on the bed. He stood and said, "No problem, but first let me get the ice cream."

"Ice cream? Keaton, you're such an animal."

He left the room and quickly returned with a half-pint of strawberry swirl. Dejá's eyes widened as she watched him dip his finger into the cool mixture. He turned to her, growled, and said, "This may be a little cold."

Dejá took a breath to prepare herself. Keaton smiled, disappeared under the sheets, and happily returned the pleasure.

Keaton's doctor had put him on mandatory medical leave, keeping him from working at his beloved San Antonio restaurant, Lorraine's. It was named in memory of his grandmother, who'd spoiled him to no end as he was growing up. Because of that, it meant everything to him. Now, he wasn't even allowed on the premises, just because his blood pressure had been registering a little high. Everyone in his family had become worried that a stroke was inevitable and vowed to help him regain control of his health before allowing him to return.

Locked out from his restaurant by his parents, he didn't know what he was going to do with himself until his sister, Arnelle, had invited him to come to Philadelphia for some rest and relaxation. He'd be sharing a home with his sister, who was a sports medical doctor at her friend's clinic. Winston, Arnelle's husband and a prominent lawyer, would be spending most of his days in court. Following close behind were their two small children, MaLeah, age four and a half, and Fredrick, age one.

Keaton's parents assured him they'd keep a watchful eye on his restaurant while he was away. He tried to remain positive, knowing he had a dependable staff running the restaurant in his absence.

Leaving Lorraine's in the hands of his trusted assistant manager, Trenton, wasn't something he wanted to do. However, Trenton had done an excellent job running things during a brief absence once before. He'd never been away this long and he couldn't wait until his medical leave was up so he could return.

His father, Judge Herbert Lapahie, was in the process of gearing down his campaign to be San Antonio's next mayor. He was patiently awaiting elections, which would take place within three months. Almost daily, his parents had stressed the importance of following the doctor's orders before he left for Philly. He only hoped his visit to Philly would be a short one.

CHAPTER 2

Keaton was awakened by his energetic niece, MaLeah. She found it amusing to sit on his back and bounce up and down like she was riding a horse. He'd had a long night with Dejá and had returned home a few hours earlier.

MaLeah tugged on his T-shirt and yelled, "Uncie Key, wake up!"

Keaton thought he was dreaming at first.

"Uncie Key, I'm hungry! Wake up!"

Keaton turned over, causing MaLeah to roll off his back. She giggled as she tried to pry his eyes open with her fingers. Keaton suddenly grabbed her and started tickling her. MaLeah screamed with laughter as her uncle playfully wrestled with her. Her long pigtails swung wildly as she kicked and screamed for mercy. He finally stopped allowing her to catch her breath. She looked adorable, dressed in her Philadelphia Eagles football jersey.

"Shorty, what are you doing in here waking me up so early? Where are your mom and dad?"

"Mommie's feeding Freddie," she announced as she poked his dimples.

Freddie was MaLeah's one-year-old brother, Winston Fredrick Carter IV. Keaton threw the covers back and climbed out of bed. MaLeah stood and started jumping up and down on the bed, turning it into her personal trampoline.

He turned and said, "Stop before you fall and break your neck."

"K!"

He sat her on the side of the bed. "Sit right there until I come out of the bathroom. Then we'll go make breakfast."

MaLeah giggled and clapped. Her uncle couldn't do anything but laugh as he entered the bathroom.

Dressed in sweatpants and a T-shirt, Keaton returned to the room, slid into his slippers and took MaLeah by the hand. Walking out, he noticed the time: seven-fifteen. He sighed and figured this was the first of many rituals he'd have to perform while visiting his sister and her family.

Downstairs, Keaton and MaLeah found Arnelle finishing up breakfast with Fredrick.

Arnelle looked up and smiled. "You had a late night last night, Keaton. Why are you up so early this morning?"

He nodded toward MaLeah as he raised his coffee cup up to his mouth.

She laughed. "You know she can't help herself. You created that monster. That's why she stays up late with you, and she's your alarm clock in the morning."

"I'm going to start locking my door," he proclaimed.

"You know that won't stop her. She'll sit outside the door, calling for you until you open it. Accept the fact, dear brother, that MaLeah Carter is going to continue to be your little shadow. At least until her daddy comes home. Only then will you get a temporary break."

They laughed together.

Keaton added more cream to his coffee, then asked, "Where's Perry Mason?"

Arnelle threw Fredrick's toy at him. "Winston had to go into the office early this morning, and stop calling him Perry Mason."

Keaton grinned. "He'll always be Perry Mason to me."

She smiled and walked over and poured herself a cup of coffee. "Whatever, Keaton. You and Winston are always teasing each other about one thing or another."

He defended himself. "He starts it most of the time."

Leaning closer, she whispered, "Look, Keaton, I hope you're being careful with those women you've been going out with."

"Of course I am," he answered with a frown. "Do you think I'm crazy?"

"You'd better be," she argued. "You know your history with women."

Without responding to her last comment, he walked over and kissed Fredrick on the cheek before adding pancakes to MaLeah's plate. He didn't need Arnelle playing momma to him. If that was going to be the case, he'd find somewhere else to chill until he could return to Texas.

MaLeah tried to follow in her uncle's footsteps by walking over to her brother. She glanced up at Fredrick as he sung and made other baby noises. She leaned in and planted a kiss on his tiny hand. As she turned to walk away, he grabbed one of her pigtails with a kung fu grip. It took only seconds for her to let out a bloodcurdling scream. Both Arnelle and Keaton turned at the same time to find Fredrick trying to put MaLeah's hair into his mouth. Arnelle quickly went to them and popped Fredrick's hand so he'd release his grip. Startled, he closed his eyes briefly, but continued to hold on to her hair.

"Fredrick! Turn your sister's hair loose!"

Fredrick was big for his age and he wasn't easing up on his grip at all. She popped his hand again as MaLeah continued to scream. Arnelle couldn't believe that she'd popped his tiny hand twice and he'd neither cried nor turned MaLeah's hair loose. Keaton watched this go on for a few more seconds. He shook his head, then walked over with his plate in his hand.

He stood in front of Fredrick and yelled, "Fredrick! Let go!"

Fredrick's eyes quickly filled with tears as he looked up at his uncle who was frowning at him. He slowly released MaLeah's pigtail as he looked at his momma and burst out crying. Keaton turned around and casually sat down at the table to eat his breakfast.

Arnelle hugged MaLeah. "Don't even try it, Fredrick! You hurt your sister!"

MaLeah clung to her momma's neck for comfort. Looking over Arnelle's shoulder at her uncle, she saw him wink at her and smile. A few sobs later, she kissed Arnelle on the cheek and walked over to Keaton.

He smiled and asked, "Are you okay, Shorty?"

"Freddie hurt my head," she said as she pointed to her hair.

"I know, but he's sorry. Aren't you, Fredrick?"

Fredrick was still crying as Arnelle hurriedly cleaned up the kitchen. She had no sympathy for her crying toddler.

Keaton picked up MaLeah and took her back over to her brother. He knelt down. "Fredrick, stop crying and give your sister a kiss so she'll know you still love her."

He poked out his bottom lip and looked at his uncle. He was only one but seemed to understand.

Keaton said again, "Kiss, Fredrick!"

Fredrick leaned over and kissed MaLeah on the cheek.

"Now, MaLeah, you kiss your brother," he instructed her.

MaLeah reluctantly kissed her brother, then quickly jumped back into Keaton's arms. When all was finished, he sat her in her chair with her plate of pancakes in front of her. Arnelle watched him be the peacemaker with her children. She thought to herself, realizing he'd make a great father one day.

"Why did Winston have to go in so early this morning?" Keaton inquired.

Giving the kitchen another look, she replied, "I don't know, but I need to hurry up and get out of here myself."

Keaton laughed. "Are you guys ready for tonight?"

He was talking about the Professional African-American Awards banquet. Winston was up for Man-of-the-Year.

Arnelle turned on the dishwasher. "As ready as we're going to be. Winston's so excited, but if he doesn't get it, he's okay. He enjoys working with those young boys over at the youth center. Since he's taken over, the attendance has risen."

"Dang, Sis, those kids must really like old Winston."

She smiled with pride. "They love him and so do I."

Keaton watched his sister's eyes brighten when she spoke of her husband. They'd had a rocky start, but neither of them could fight off the inevitable. With what they'd shared, they were destined to be together. He couldn't imagine having that kind of love and connection with one woman for the rest of his life. Besides, marriage wasn't for everyone.

Looking around the kitchen once more, Arnelle said, "Okay, I'm out of here. We should be home by four so we can get ready for the banquet. Are you sure you're going to be all right with these two rugrats tonight? Camille said she'd watch them for us."

Keaton frowned at his sister. "You act like I'm the babysitter from hell or something. I told you, I got it. We'll be fine!"

Arnelle threw up her hands in surrender. "Okay, okay. I didn't mean for you to get all bent out of shape."

"I'm cool. I have a lot of fun and games planned for these two."

MaLeah was smiling at her uncle as she sat eating her pancakes. She'd heard the words "fun" and "games" in the same sentence. When her uncle said "fun" he meant *fun*.

On that statement, Arnelle grabbed her jacket and said, "Well, it seems you have everything under control so let me get out of your way."

Before walking out the door, she kissed Fredrick, MaLeah, and lastly Keaton.

"See you guys later," she said as she pulled on Keaton's ear playfully like he was a little boy. Even though he was her younger brother, he looked older than his thirty-two years.

"Bye, Mommie!" MaLeah loudly shouted.

CHAPTER 3

Later that evening, Keaton helped MaLeah with her bath while Arnelle and Winston dressed for the banquet. As MaLeah splashed and tossed her duck at Keaton, he sat on the toilet seat and tried to read his *Sports Illustrated* in peace.

"Uncie Key!"

Without looking up, he answered, "Yes, Shorty?"

"Look! My ducky can fly!"

Keaton glanced over and watched her throw the duck against the wall and giggle loudly.

He shook his head. "Are you almost done?"

"Nope!"

About that time, Winston walked in looking debonair in his suit.

"Daddy!"

Keaton eyed him up and down. "Dang, Bro, you look like you stepped off the cover of *GQ*."

"Thanks. So how did it go with Dejá last night?" Keaton smiled mischievously. Winston laughed. "Say no more. Are you sure about being the nanny tonight? I mean, you don't have another date or something?"

Keaton chuckled. "Get the hell out of here. I have everything under control and no, I don't have a date. You just make sure you win tonight."

"Oooo! Uncie Key said a bad word!" MaLeah screamed.

Keaton rolled his eyes while Winston laughed.

Winston folded his arms. "You do know she watches and listens to everything you say and do?"

"Yeah, I know. I hope I don't leave any bad habits with her when I leave."

Winston looked over at his daughter. "MaLeah, you make sure you behave tonight and help take care of your brother with your uncle. Now blow me a kiss 'cause you're not about to get me wet."

Keaton stood up. "Hold up, Bro. That'll never work with her, and you know it."

Keaton grabbed the towel and pulled MaLeah's naked, slippery body out of the suds. He wrapped the towel around her body, pinning her arms to her side so she couldn't move.

"Now, give your daddy a kiss."

She smiled and gave her dad a welcomed kiss.

Afterwards, Winston yelled, "Arnelle, you'd better get in here so you can give your daughter a goodnight kiss while she's retrained!"

MaLeah saw this entire scene as a game. She giggled as she looked up at her daddy. "Daddy, kiss, kiss!"

"You're greedy, just like your momma," he said with a smile.

Arnelle walked in looking stunning in her ivory beaded gown. "I heard that, counselor," she warned him. He turned to kiss Arnelle on the cheek. "Hurry up, woman, so we won't be late." She looked at her brother, standing there holding her daughter imprisoned in the towel.

"What have you done to my baby?"

Keaton laughed. "I'm attempting to keep you and Winston dry. Hurry up before she figures out this towel is a restraint and not a game."

Arnelle kissed her daughter. "MaLeah, we'll be back later, so make sure you don't drive your Uncle Keaton crazy tonight. Okay?"

"K!"

Keaton looked at his sister. "You clean up real good, Sis. You look beautiful."

"Thanks. Now make sure you call if you need us, and all the important numbers are by the telephone in the kitchen. Fredrick is sleeping right now, but he'll probably wake up in a few hours for some milk and a diaper change."

Keaton dried MaLeah's body. "Arnelle, I got this! Go! Get out of here with your Man-of-the-Year."

Kissing him on the cheek, she smiled. "Okay. We're out of here."

MaLeah yelled, "Bye, Mommie!"

CHAPTER 4

Keaton and MaLeah had been watching TV for almost two hours. Dejá had called his cell phone three times, but he'd let his voicemail catch her calls. He'd been out with her several times, and it seemed like she was starting to get too attached to him, demanding more of his time.

MaLeah sat next to him, sharing popcorn and Pepsi. Fredrick's monitor had been silent for a while, so Keaton said, "Come on, Shorty. Let's go check on your brother. He should've been up by now."

"K!"

"You're supposed to say 'okay,' Shorty; not just 'K.'"

She giggled as Keaton took her hand and led her up the stairs. When they reached the landing, he knelt down. "Now you have to be quiet so you won't wake your brother."

"K! Uncie Key."

Hearing her say "K" again made him shake his head and laugh. It would be a while before she got it right.

They pushed open Fredrick's door and walked over to his bed. Keaton looked down on him and ran his hand across his back. It felt unusually warm. Frowning, he picked him up and cradled his head against his neck.

"Whoa! MaLeah, your brother feels kind of warm. We'd better take his temperature."

Keaton moved Fredrick over to the changing table, with MaLeah following closely behind. When he laid him down, he woke up crying.

"Hold on, little man. I'm getting ready to take care of you."

He removed the footie pajamas from his chubby body. Fredrick screamed louder as MaLeah looked on.

She watched her uncle fumble with the pajamas, then yelled, "Be quiet, Freddie!!"

Keaton softly said, "MaLeah, your brother doesn't feel well so be nice."

"K!!"

After removing the soaked diaper from Fredrick's bottom, he immediately released a stream of urine directly in Keaton's face.

"Oh shit!!"

He tried to duck, but it was too late.

MaLeah giggled out loud. "Ooooo! You said another bad word, Uncie Key!"

"I know, Shorty. I'm sorry and I better not hear you say it either," he explained as he wiped the urine from his face with a baby wipe.

She nodded in agreement, then said, "Freddie tee-teed in your face, Uncie Key!"

He placed a cloth diaper over Fredrick's naked body and continued to wipe his face.

"Yeah, he got me, Shorty. Man! I don't see how people do this every day!"

When he finished cleaning his face, he cautiously removed the cloth diaper and cleaned Fredrick's body. MaLeah watched with curiosity as she handed him the powder and fresh diaper. Fredrick had calmed down a little, until Keaton put the thermometer in his ear. While waiting for the results, he rubbed his round tummy in a soothing manner.

"Hold on, little man. I'm just taking your temperature," Keaton said as he tried to remain calm.

About that time a beep sounded and Keaton looked at the digital reading.

"Damn…103 degrees! Not good, Fredrick!"

Keaton now took on a serious tone. "MaLeah! Go get the telephone," he instructed, trying not to panic. He hardly ever called her MaLeah so she looked at him as if he was talking to someone else.

He raised his voice slightly this time. "Shorty! Go get the phone!"

MaLeah sprinted out of the room and brought back the cordless phone. Fredrick continued to cry as Keaton put a fresh diaper on him. He gently put his pajamas on him and picked him up.

"Let's go get your brother some milk. I have to get his temperature down. Shh, Fredrick! I'm going to take care of you."

When they walked into the kitchen, he removed a bottle from the refrigerator.

"MaLeah, hand me that piece of paper on the table."

"K!"

MaLeah handed the piece of paper to him as she watched him balance Fredrick and the telephone on his shoulder. Keaton dialed Arnelle's cell phone, but got an out-of-area message.

"Damn it!!"

MaLeah covered her mouth. "Oooo! You said another bad word, Uncie K!"

"Not now, MaLeah, and stop being the bad word police. Okay?"

She smiled. "K!"

Keaton tried to dial the number again and once more, got the out-of-area message.

Fredrick's bottle was almost empty and Keaton sat there trying to figure out what to do next. He knew Craig and Venice were also at the awards banquet so he couldn't call them for help. As Fredrick continued to suck on his bottle, it soothed him temporarily.

"MaLeah, I can't get your parents on the phone."

She patted him on the leg. "I'm sowwy, Uncie Key."

"I know. Oh! I can call your Ms. Camille," he remembered.

Keaton dialed Camille's number, trying to stay calm. Within seconds, a female voice answered.

"Hello?"

"Ms. Camille. This is Arnelle's brother, Keaton."

"Oh yes! How are you?"

"Fine, but Fredrick's not doing so well. Arnelle and Winston are out for the evening and I can't get either of them on their cell phones."

Ms. Camille asked, with worry in her voice, "What's wrong?"

"Fredrick's crying and has a fever of 103 degrees. He's drinking his milk right now, but I don't know what to do."

"The best thing is to get him to the hospital right away. I'm sure he'll be fine. If I didn't have the Bennett children, I could meet you there. Look, I'll keep trying to get in touch with Arnelle and Winston. Call me from the hospital and let me know what's going on. Do you have MaLeah with you?"

"Yes, Ma'am."

"Well, wrap her up good. It's cool outside. I'm sure it's nothing, but we're better off safe than sorry."

Keaton stood. "Thank you. I'll call you back later." He hung up the phone. "Let's go get some clothes on, Shorty. We have to take Fredrick to the doctor."

"K!"

Available from
Strebor Books International

Baptiste, Michael
Cracked Dreams 1-59309-035-8
Godchild 1-59309-044-7

Bernard, D.V.
The Last Dream Before Dawn
0-9711953-2-3
God in the Image of Woman
1-59309-019-6
How to Kill Your Boyfriend (in 10 Easy Steps)
1-59309-066-8

Billingsley, ReShonda Tate
Help! I've Turned Into My Mother
1-59309-050-1

Brown, Laurinda D.
Fire & Brimstone 1-59309-015-3
UnderCover 1-59309-030-7
The Highest Price for Passion
1-59309-053-6

Cheekes, Shonda
Another Man's Wife 1-59309-008-0
Blackgentlemen.com 0-9711953-8-2
In the Midst of it All 1-59309-038-2

Cooper, William Fredrick
Six Days in January 1-59309-017-X
Sistergirls.com 1-59309-004-8

Crockett, Mark
Turkeystuffer 0-9711953-3-1

Daniels, J and Bacon, Shonell
Luvalwayz: The Opposite Sex and Relationships 0-9711953-1-5
Draw Me With Your Love
1-59309-000-5

Darden, J. Marie
Enemy Fields 1-59309-023-4
Finding Dignity 1-59309-051-X

De Leon, Michelle
Missed Conceptions 1-59309-010-2
Love to the Third 1-59309-016-1
Once Upon a Family Tree
1-59309-028-5

Faye, Cheryl
Be Careful What You Wish For
1-59309-034-X

Halima, Shelley
Azucar Moreno 1-59309-032-3
Los Morenos 1-59309-049-8

Handfield, Laurel
My Diet Starts Tomorrow 1-59309-005-6
Mirror Mirror 1-59309-014-5

Hayes, Lee
Passion Marks 1-59309-006-4
A Deeper Blue: Passion Marks II
1-59309-047-1

Hobbs, Allison
Pandora's Box 1-59309-011-0
Insatiable 1-59309-031-5
Dangerously in Love 1-59309-048-X
Double Dippin' 1-59309-065-X

Hurd, Jimmy
Turnaround 1-59309-045-5
Ice Dancer 1-59309-062-5

Jenkins, Nikki
Playing with the Hand I Was Dealt
1-59309-046-3

Johnson, Keith Lee
Sugar & Spice 1-59309-013-7
Pretenses 1-59309-018-8
Fate's Redemption 1-59309-039-0

Johnson, Rique
Love & Justice 1-59309-002-1
Whispers from a Troubled Heart
1-59309-020-X
Every Woman's Man 1-59309-036-6
Sistergirls.com 1-59309-004-8
A Dangerous Return 1-59309-043-9
Another Time, Another Place
1-59309-058-7

Kai, Naleighna
Every Woman Needs a Wife
1-59309-060-9

Kinyua, Kimani
The Brotherhood of Man 1-59309-064-1

Lee, Darrien
All That and a Bag of Chips
0-9711953-0-7
Been There, Done That 1-59309-001-3
What Goes Around Comes Around
1-59309-024-2
When Hell Freezes Over 1-59309-042-0
Brotherly Love 1-59309-061-7

Luckett, Jonathan
Jasminium 1-59309-007-2
How Ya Livin' 1-59309-025-0
Dissolve 1-59309-041-2
Another Time, Another Place
1-59309-058-7

McKinney, Tina Brooks
All That Drama 1-59309-033-1
Lawd, Mo' Drama 1-59309-052-8

Perkins, Suzetta L.
Behind the Veil 1-59309-063-3

Pinnock, Janice
The Last Good Kiss 1-59309-055-2

Quartay, Nane
Feenin 0-9711953-7-4
The Badness 1-59309-037-4

Rivera, Jr., David
Harlem's Dragon 1-59309-056-0

Rivers, V. Anthony
Daughter by Spirit 0-9674601-4-X
Everybody Got Issues 1-59309-003-X
Sistergirls.com 1-59309-004-8
My Life is All I Have 1-59309-057-9

Roberts, J. Deotis
Roots of a Black Future 0-9674601-6-6
Christian Beliefs 0-9674601-5-8

Stephens, Sylvester
Our Time Has Come 1-59309-026-9

Turley II, Harold L.
Love's Game 1-59309-029-3
Confessions of a Lonely Soul
1-59309-054-4

Valentine, Michelle
Nyagra's Falls 0-9711953-4-X

White, A.J.
Ballad of a Ghetto Poet 1-59309-009-9

White, Franklin
Money for Good 1-59309-012-9
1-59309-040-4 (trade)
Potentially Yours 1-59309-027-7

Woodson, J.L.
Superwoman's Child 1-59309-059-5

Zane (Editor)
Breaking the Cycle 1-59309-021-8
Another Time, Another Place
1-59309-058-7